NOTHING SHORT OF WONDROUS

AMERICAN WONDERS COLLECTION,
BOOK 2

NOTHING SHORT OF WONDROUS

REGINA SCOTT

THORNDIKE PRESS
A part of Gale, a Cengage Company

Copyright © 2020 by Regina Lundgren.
Thorndike Press, a part of Gale, a Cengage Company.

LIBRARY OF CONGRESS CIP DATA ON FILE.
CATALOGUING IN PUBLICATION FOR THIS BOOK
IS AVAILABLE FROM THE LIBRARY OF CONGRESS.

ISBN-13: 978-1-4328-9744-4 (hardcover alk. paper)

Published in 2022 by arrangement with Revell Books, a division of Baker Publishing Group

Printed in Mexico
Print Number: 01   Print Year: 2022

To those we call family,
especially Meryl, Kris,
Marissa, Kathy, and Kelli,
and to the Lord,
who leads us to those
who will love us for who we are.

1

Yellowstone National Park, September 1886

What was it about men and danger? Did they all want to die?

Kate Tremaine leveled her rifle at the back of the stranger standing beside the rainbow-colored mud pots, a long, twisted branch in his hand. "Stop right there, mister. Drop the stick."

Broad shoulders stiffened in his navy cavalry coat. Normally she had the utmost respect for the military, especially after seeing how Captain Harris had worked to protect Yellowstone since arriving last month. But she'd caught more than one of the horse soldiers a mite too close to the boiling geysers and heated paint pots. It wouldn't do them or the park's reputation any good if they were burned by the scalding water.

He tossed the stick off the geyser field and turned slowly, lemon-yellow stripe on his light-blue trousers flashing in the sunlight. Rather determined face — strong cheekbones, straight nose pointing to the firm line of his lips, square jaw. The only thing soft about him was the beginnings of a warm brown beard and mustache, a shade darker than the hair at his temples. That was about all she could see of his hair under his floppy, wide-brimmed dun hat with its crossed sabers in gold on the crown.

The cavalrymen riding by her hotel every day were all looking scruffier. It couldn't be easy living out of nothing better than a white canvas tent. It wasn't easy keeping things clean and tidy in the hotel either. She and her staff were run ragged, and she still couldn't find time to fix all the things that seemed to go wrong at the least provocation. Occasionally she was tempted to hack off her thick black tresses rather than to keep taming them back in a braided bun behind her head. Perhaps dress in a buckskin coat and trousers instead of poplin and wool bodices and skirts that bespoke a prosperous hotel owner. Even those small changes might help give her more time.

The man in front of her nodded toward her Winchester. "Do you know how to use that?"

Why was it that a hint of a Boston twang

8

was enough to set memories beckoning? She'd left that life behind. She was a different woman. The daughter of a cobbler and a milliner hadn't needed to know how to shoot a rifle, outlast a Yellowstone winter, or manage one of the busiest hotels in the park.

She aimed the rifle at his chest. "I sure do. Now, move away from those paint pots — straight forward. Right or left, and you'll boil those fancy boots right off your feet."

He glanced down at the ground. The knobby crust covered decades of mud that had bubbled up from the depths of the earth. Around them, spikes striped in lime, buttercup, rust, and rose smoked contentedly, the cough and murmur here and there telling of more mud spilling over. Her guests at the hotel found the paint pots fascinating. She did too, but she had to be constantly on guard that no one strayed onto the softer ground. She gave everyone a welcome speech, insisted on accompanying some of the oldest and youngest visitors, and did a sweep every morning and afternoon, just to be safe.

He picked his way forward, and she edged back until they both stood on the well-worn path to the hotel. The Geyser Gateway Inn sat with its back to a stand of pine, clapboard sides a cheery yellow she had to

9

repaint after every good storm. Toby had fallen in love with the place at first sight, and she hadn't been far behind. If her late husband hadn't gone out that night a year ago, he might have been waiting on the veranda even now.

But he would never have confronted people with a rifle. For Toby, life had been about boundless enthusiasm. She'd always been the practical one.

Her quarry today relaxed his stance, watching her. Now that he was closer, she could see that his eyes were a clear greenish brown, like a reflection in a mountain lake. They narrowed at her.

"What are you planning on doing?" he asked. "Arresting me or shooting me for dinner?"

Toby would have accompanied the question with a good-natured grin. This man didn't look as if he knew how to grin. Why did she have the urge to test that theory?

Kate made a show of looking him up and down. "I doubt you'd make much of a meal for my guests. Too much grit. And I generally turn game your size back into the wild to grow up a bit."

He grimaced. "Should I thank you for that?"

Despite herself, Kate smiled. "No need.

10

All part of the service at the Geyser Gateway."

He nodded toward the hotel. "You must be Mrs. Tremaine."

Now, who would have told him about her? She'd had a single conversation with his superior, who had graciously allowed her to keep her concession, for now. She hadn't been sure about Captain Harris when he'd ridden into the park at the head of Troop M, but she'd applauded when he'd ousted D.W. Wear, the superintendent from Washington. Wear had all but washed his hands when it came to protecting the game of the park, claiming too few men and too little time. What did he know about time? Had he ever tried running a hotel?

She lowered her rifle. "I'm Kate Tremaine. Who are you?"

He took off his hat, showing short-cropped brown hair streaked with gold, and inclined his head. "Lieutenant Will Prescott. I've been ordered to patrol this part of the park with my men."

So that was how Harris was going to manage the vast acreage. Since his arrival, his men had been busy battling the wildfires raging over parts of the park. Wear claimed they had been set by his enemies. She knew better, and she'd been watchful lest the

11

same trouble start here. Having her own set of cavalrymen patrolling the natural wonders might be useful, so long as they didn't blunder in where they shouldn't.

"Glad to have you," Kate said. "Feel free to stop by for dinner. But mind your step in the future. Do you have any idea how hot that mud is?"

"More than one hundred and fifty degrees," he said with a glance at the nearest bubbling paint pot, which helpfully belched out another cloud of steam. "At least that's what the guidebook claimed."

Kate snorted. "Guidebook? Which one did they give you? Wylie isn't too bad, though you have to watch his directions or you could end up going over the falls. Don't get me started on Dabney. That man hasn't moved off his sofa in thirty years, much less toured Yellowstone."

He knocked mud off the heel of his black boots. Most of the cavalry officers wore spurs, the silver or brass winking and rowels chiming as they walked. His boots were bare.

"I've noticed," he said. "It's not easy to find your way around here."

So her guests claimed. She had no trouble, but she'd lived here for four years, ever since Toby had convinced her to use the money her parents had left her to invest in the inn.

"Think of the plateau as a big circle," she advised him. She nodded toward the inn, where a group of her most recent guests had come out onto the wide veranda to gaze at the grandeur. "We sit in the lower part of a basin filled with geysers, some twenty miles south of Mammoth Hot Springs and your commanding officer's tent city. South another five miles, and you'll reach Old Faithful, one of the biggest geysers in the park and the most reliable for timing. Directly east of us across the plateau is Yellowstone Lake and beyond that the Absaroka Range. To the north of it is the Grand Canyon of the Yellowstone. And all around you'll find crystal clear creeks, roaring rivers, and thundering falls."

"And grizzlies, buffalo, and scalding water," he added.

She wouldn't let him see the chill that went through her at the mention of the hump-backed bear. A stampeding herd of buffalo and the thermal dangers of the park could be avoided. No matter how carefully she moved, she was always aware a grizzly could be waiting around the bend. Danny might chafe under her restrictions, but she wasn't about to lose her son too.

"All that as well," she agreed. "And you

13

fellows better start building cabins, because those canvas tents you brought will never see you through a Yellowstone winter."

Before he could answer, she felt it, the faintest of rumblings under her leather boots. She grabbed his arm with her free hand. "Move."

He frowned at her, more than six feet of muscle holding him in place. "Why?"

The rumble shook her legs. Didn't he feel it too? Kate tightened her grip and yanked. "Now!"

He stumbled forward, catching her in his arms and forcing the rifle away from them both. For one moment, their gazes touched, held, and something whooshed through her, like the pressure building under the earth. His eyes widened as if he'd felt it more surely than the rumbling beneath them.

Then Morning Geyser let loose.

The spray shot into the air, double the height of her two-story hotel. Water pattered down a few feet beyond them, hard enough to splash fresh mud on his knee-high boots. She could hear the oohs and ahhs from her guests on the veranda.

The man holding her looked as awed. She thought she must too, but it wasn't the geyser's power that had shaken her. She'd been married for seven years, been a widow

14

for one. Any romantic feelings had been buried with Toby's mangled body. God understood she had work to do, a son to raise, a park to protect. Why did this man make her wonder if there should be more?

Will Prescott watched as the woman with midnight black hair pulled out of his embrace and tightened her grip on her gun. Wasn't there some myth about a goddess of the hunt, protecting the animals and forests? Even her practical fitted blue bodice and wide skirts couldn't quite erase the image from his mind. But more important was her ability to predict the geyser's eruption. It was well known Old Faithful was reliable. He doubted this one was.

"How did you know?" he asked.

Her misty gray eyes looked as heated as the spray that had just erupted feet away from them. "You live in a place long enough, you learn things about it. But if you don't stay away from the hot springs, you won't live long enough to learn."

He couldn't argue. He'd been part of the cavalry for more than ten years, most of them out in Indian Territory. Yellowstone was like nothing he'd ever seen, marvel after marvel. Small wonder the first trappers and explorers to tell of encountering the place

15

hadn't been believed.

Much like Captain Harris hadn't been believed when he'd asked for scouts.

"We must protect millions of acres," he'd written to Washington. "I have three experienced guides ready to help. We can't cover so much territory quickly without them."

The answer had been swift. "Pay is authorized for one guide. Your men must learn the country."

Will had been here more than a fortnight, and he still got lost riding between the outposts. Captain Harris had stationed details at six locations, the most popular tourist stops like the Lower Geyser Basin. If Will was to protect his portion of the park, much less his men, he had to do better.

Of course, he'd been telling himself that for the last eight years, ever since he'd made the gravest error of his life.

He shook away the ugly memory. It had been a long, hard climb back to lieutenant from where he'd been justly demoted. He had a job to do now, and he intended to do it.

"I wasn't trying to steam myself into pudding," he told Mrs. Tremaine as they headed for her hotel. It was a welcoming place with green shutters on the windows and a covered porch wrapping around three sides.

With the nights growing colder, he envied her the building's warmth. "I was riding by and saw someone throwing sticks into the paint pots."

She pulled up short. "Who?"

He pitied the fellow if he met her and her rifle with that fiery look in her eyes. "I only caught a glimpse before he ran off. Tall man, top hat, black coat too fancy for out here."

"Ponsonby," she said. "He's staying at the hotel. Came with a group from New York yesterday. I'll speak to him."

He eyed the rifle cradled so casually against her. "Armed?"

She grinned. "If necessary."

His mouth felt odd, and it was a moment before he realized why. The muscles of his face were rusty. How long had it been since he'd smiled?

He forced his gaze away from her to the hotel. His horse was tied to the hitching post in front, the sorrel mare unaffected by the other horses around her. Bess was a good cavalry horse — the sound of gunfire didn't trouble her, those powerful legs could push her into a full run in a matter of seconds, and she could sustain that pace for nearly a half hour without tiring. Now her ears twitched as if she heard him coming.

Or maybe she was as intrigued by the

woman at his side as he was.

Once more, he pushed away his thoughts. He had much to atone for before he could be called a gentleman again. Sometimes he feared even God couldn't forgive what he'd done. He was fortunate the Army had been willing to let him start over.

Though it appeared as if Mrs. Tremaine might have to start over as well. Up close, he could see that the hotel needed work. A few of those jaunty shutters hung crookedly, as if bent by a strong wind, and the porch steps were sagging as three gentlemen and their ladies traipsed down them. It couldn't be easy managing a busy hotel, especially for a widow.

Bess raised her head as the front door banged open, and a towheaded youngster dashed out onto the porch.

"Ma!"

Correction: a widow with child. The hotel owner drew up as the boy clambered down the steps. A slender lad about seven with wide eyes and a stub of a nose, he hitched up his short trousers as he skidded to a stop in front of Will and Mrs. Tremaine. "Can I show Mr. Ponsonby our special spot?"

Mrs. Tremaine glanced at Will before gathering her skirts with her free hand and crouching before her son. "What did we agree on, Danny?"

The boy shuffled his feet, gaze on the dusty soil. "Our special spot is just for us." He spoke in a singsong voice as if repeating what he'd heard many times before. "But he likes buffalo."

"Lots of people like buffalo," his mother countered. "In stew, with their heads mounted on walls, with their hides spread on floors."

Her son's eyes grew wider, his face paler, with each word. "Mr. Ponsonby isn't like that."

A man who threw sticks into mud pots, just to see what might happen, probably wasn't the sort to protect other parts of nature. Mrs. Tremaine must have thought the same, for she rose and patted her son's shoulder. "You leave Mr. Ponsonby to me. Have you finished your chores?"

His sigh was heavy. "Yes. I helped Pansy empty the chamber pots, scrubbed the kitchen floor, and cleaned out the salon hearth."

That was a lot of work for one morning, especially for a boy his size. His mother merely nodded. "Thank you. I expect Caleb could use some help chopping wood."

He made a face. "Caleb always needs help chopping wood."

19

The frustration in the boy's voice pulled at Will. His mother too, for she sighed. "I know, Danny. There's a lot of work to be done, but we have guests."

He glanced up at Will. "Another one?"

He could almost see the weight on the child's shoulders. He knew the feeling. He'd had to care for a mother grown weary from work after his father had died in the Civil War. How many times had he glanced out the window at other boys playing? He'd run off to join the military as soon as he was old enough. That wasn't the last time he'd think only of himself. But not anymore.

He saluted the boy. "Lieutenant Prescott, reporting for duty, sir."

The boy giggled. By the way Mrs. Tremaine smiled, she could do with hearing the sweet sound more often.

"I'm not a sir," Danny said. "Ma is."

He could well believe Mrs. Tremaine warranted a salute as well as she turned his way, face coloring. "I think your business here is done, Lieutenant."

He ought to agree. He'd been riding by when he'd spotted Ponsonby out among the paint pots. The rest of his men were setting up their tents to the north, near the Fire Hole Hotel. He never liked it when he couldn't see them, though this batch was handpicked and ought to be trustworthy. But an audacious idea had presented itself. He shouldn't trust it either, but it might help him, his men, Mrs. Tremaine, and her son.

"I heard a rumor about the huckleberry pie at this establishment," he said. "I'd be neglecting my duty if I didn't try a slice."

"Our cook Alberta makes good pie," Danny agreed. He tugged on his mother's arm. "We should give him a piece. He's sort of a guest."

Mrs. Tremaine readjusted the rifle under her arm. He'd have given a lot to know what was going on in her mind as she glanced from him to her son and back again.

"Go tell Alberta to cut a slice," she finally told the boy.

His eyes lit. "A big slice?"

Her mouth turned up. "A big slice."

"For me too?"

She laughed. "For you too. But you must save me a bite."

"Deal." He turned and ran for the hotel.

Kate Tremaine leveled her gaze on Will again, deadlier than the rifle she'd pointed at him earlier. "All right, Lieutenant. What do you want?"

He'd never been known for charm, but he had to try.

21

"You obviously care about this park," he told her, "or you wouldn't have come after me. If I'm to protect this part of Yellowstone, I need a guide."

"Plenty of men will hire on for that," she allowed. "I could recommend some."

"I'm not authorized to hire anyone," Will explained. "I need a volunteer."

She shook her head. "With winter coming soon? No one has time to work for free."

"What about pay in kind?" he pressed. "I do a favor for them, they do a favor for me."

She wiggled her lips a moment. "Most men out here don't much approve of favors. That's why they came West — for the independence."

Most men, but maybe not one woman. "But you have a hotel that must need work," he replied. "As you said, winter's coming."

She bristled. He held her gaze, willing her to realize the truth of his statement. If she let him help, her son could be a boy again, and Will might find a little peace. The good Lord knew he needed that.

He stuck out his hand. "Deal?"

She stared at it, mouth once more working. He could almost feel the pride, distrust, and need colliding inside her. Finally, she took his hand, and her touch ricocheted up his arm to his heart.

"Deal," she said.

And Will could only wonder what he'd just gotten himself into.

2

What had she gotten herself into?

Kate glanced at Lieutenant Prescott as they followed Danny into the hotel. His hat was tucked under one arm, his head slightly bowed, but he still walked across the plank floor with the command of a military officer. Would he take her direction about what needed to be fixed at the hotel? Since Toby's passing, she had been in charge of the Geyser Gateway. She'd managed most of the work even when Toby had been alive, truth be told. But to enlist the aid of a stranger?

She shook herself. He was a means to an end. She, Alberta, the three maids, and young Caleb, who kept the animals and grounds, were worn enough as it was. And she wasn't making enough of a profit to hire the work done, if she could find someone willing to come into the park this late in the year to work. She could only hope those shoulders were as strong as they looked.

And his offer was as honest as it sounded.

She caught him glancing around, slight frown gathering. What did he see to cause concern? The Geyser Gateway salon had high ceilings with massive wood beams holding an oil lamp chandelier. She'd recently lowered, cleaned, and refilled the lamps herself, so they glowed with a golden light. The fireplace was of stones gathered from the Firehole River, the grays, rusts, and tans complementing the wood of the walls. The burgundy upholstery on the two curved-back sofas flanking the hearth had been brushed, the blue-and-burgundy-patterned rug on the floor beaten. Through a wide archway directly ahead, the six tables — four big enough to seat eight guests apiece — were draped in smooth white linen Pansy had ironed only yesterday, and most of the ladderback chairs stood ready to receive their guests for dinner.

Alberta Guthrie had Danny at one of the smaller dining tables with a generous slice of pie in front of him. The cook had been working at the Geyser Gateway when Kate and Toby had taken over management of the property, and Kate had never regretted keeping her on. There was something warm and welcoming about Alberta, from her ample figure swathed in calico and a voluminous apron to her flyaway silver hair. She aimed a broad smile at the cavalryman, deepening the wrinkles around her mouth and bronze-colored eyes, as he and Kate approached.

"Why, Danny, you never said how handsome the lieutenant was," she said, fluttering her lashes.

Danny looked up from his pie, fork in the golden crust. "Is he?"

Alberta's gaze darted to Kate's as if the cook was urging her to confirm the fact.

"Lieutenant Prescott has offered us help around the inn," Kate said instead.

Alberta yanked out one of the chairs. "Well, that's an answer to a prayer. You just sit right here, Lieutenant, and I'll bring you the best pie you ever ate."

Lips quirking as if he wasn't sure how to respond to her welcome, he sat. Alberta bustled for the kitchen.

"Interior looks good," he ventured as Danny dug into his pie.

Only because of the work she, Alberta, and the inn's maids — Pansy, Sarah, and Ida — put in each day. There were always beds to air, linens to launder, dishes to wash, and floors to sweep. The white chalky dust from the geysers got into everything.

26

"We try," Kate allowed, "but there are loose boards upstairs, and some of the mortar around the hearths needs replacing."

"Make me a list," he said.

He had no idea what he was offering.

Alberta returned and slipped a red-rimmed china plate down in front of him with one hand, extending a silver-plated fork with the other. "You take a bite and tell me if I'm a liar."

He took the fork so cautiously it might have been a rattler. Alberta puffed out her chest as if she was holding her breath as he inserted the utensil into the flaky crust and brought the piece to his mouth, huckleberry juice dribbling a purple path across the plate.

He chewed a moment, then cocked his head. "You're no liar."

Alberta beamed at him.

Kate cleared her throat.

Alberta collected herself. "And one for you, Mrs. Tremaine. Right away." The kitchen door swung shut behind her.

"No wonder your hotel is so busy," Lieutenant Prescott said before forking up another mouthful.

Danny was halfway through his slice. "Really busy."

27

"And aren't we thankful for that?" Kate reminded him.

"Yes," he said dutifully, but the word held considerable doubt.

"How long have you had the concession?" the lieutenant asked.

"This is our fourth season," Kate confessed. "But we invested in the property before it was built. Captain Harris let us keep our lease until spring."

Her annoyance at the decision must have sounded in her voice, for his fork paused as he hurried to assure her. "He's reassessing every lease. He'll decide come spring which to renew for ten years."

"Ten years!" Oh, what stability. Kate leaned closer. "What's his criteria?"

He shrugged, fork digging into the pie again. "Lack of complaints, compliance with the rules."

Kate straightened. "We have always complied with the rules and more. And no superintendent ever heard a complaint about the service or quality of the Geyser Gateway. I mean to keep it that way."

The cavalryman regarded her. "Did you approve of the previous superintendents?"

"Some," Kate admitted. "Times have changed. Poachers, hunters, and vandals all moved in on the last two superintendents' watch."

"They'll move out on ours," he predicted.

She wanted to believe him, but she'd heard too many idealists claim what they'd do to help Yellowstone. Many left frustrated they couldn't manage so vast a wilderness.

"We should agree on this deal," she said as Alberta returned with her pie. Not quite as large as what she'd given to Danny or the cavalryman, Kate noticed as she sat.

As if Alberta had read her look, she tugged at one strap on the apron covering her broad chest. "We need to conserve if there's to be enough for supper. We have thirty guests tonight, according to the book."

The guest book on the front table listed everyone who had ever stayed at the Geyser Gateway. It held names of famous statesmen, artists, and natural philosophers. Kate's favorites were the scrawled names of the children who came, eyes wide with wonder.

"Thirty guests plus the staff," Kate confirmed.

With a nod, Alberta headed back to her domain. Lieutenant Prescott finished another bite of pie.

"I'll make your list as soon as I can," Kate told him. "What kind of help do you need from me?"

"I need to confirm the main places of interest in this area and the trails used to access them."

It could take her days to ride around and show him all that. "I'll draw you a map," Kate said. "How many hours can you give me a day to work on the inn?"

His gaze went to Danny, who was scraping the last crumbs off the thick white china. "When I'm not on patrol, two or three."

When was a cavalryman not on patrol? Was he trying to back out already? "How often will you be on patrol?"

"Four days out of every week, until the tourist season ends."

"Early October, then." Kate calculated in her head. "So, at least two dozen hours."

"He could chop wood," Danny said, glancing up at her, eyes bright.

How he tugged at her heart. And how easy it would be to let him do as he liked each day. But his future depended on him learning this business. And surviving.

"With you helping Caleb by stacking, I think we have a sufficient number of people working in that area at present," she told him. "But six more cords should arrive in the next few weeks."

Danny made a face and leaned closer to the cavalry officer. "And then we have to bring it in."

A bit at a time to burn in the big stone fireplace. But that wood would stave off the chill of a Yellowstone winter, just as the coal in the coal shed fed Alberta's big stove.

"So what do you have in mind for me?" Lieutenant Prescott asked her.

Was that a challenge she heard in his gravelly voice? That air of power might work on the privates under his command. She couldn't be bothered. Already a dozen jobs cried out for her attention. She could set him to repairing the steps, straightening the shutters, replacing the cracked shakes on the roof. The kitchen chimney was smoking overly much, two of the guest room doors were sticking, and the barn could use a good cleaning before the last hay arrived to keep the horses and cows fed for the winter.

That was enough to fill a sizeable portion of the hours he'd offered, and she hadn't even completed her list. Best to prioritize. Who knew how long he would be here or when he would decide he'd had enough of the work? The Army's control of the park was only temporary, until the Department of the Interior and Congress decided on the next superintendent. She should take advantage of Lieutenant Prescott's goodwill while she had it.

"I'll let you know tomorrow," Kate said, "when you return for your map."

A map, she said. Will shook his head as he descended the veranda steps. Could any map possibly do justice to this wild place? The ones in the guidebook he'd been given were woefully inadequate. He could only hope Mrs. Tremaine's would be better.

Bess nickered a welcome as he slipped his hat onto his head and came to untie her. Some of the high-ranking officers had horses with commanding names like Admiral and Emperor. He wouldn't have traded his Bess for them. She was too reliable, too patient. She waited now as he swung up into the saddle. Then he set her at a trot toward the circuit road beyond the hotel.

When his commanding officer, Captain Harris, had assigned him to this portion of the park, he'd suggested finding a campsite closer to the Fire Hole Hotel. Now that Will had seen the Geyser Gateway, he could understand why. Mrs. Tremaine's establishment was compact and tidy, and it likely appealed to the more genteel travelers. He didn't foresee much trouble there.

The two-story Fire Hole Hotel and its

flanking cottages, on the other hand, were part of a sprawling complex with a blacksmith shop and multiple stables and corrals. Between the stagecoaches coming and going and the camping companies and their parties moving through, the place had plenty of people who might cause trouble.

He could only hope his men wouldn't be part of the problem.

The five privates assigned to him had the four tents set up at the edge of a meadow just south of the complex and hidden from it by a stand of pine. Captain Harris had divided his fifty men into seven roughly even groups, keeping one for himself at Mammoth Hot Springs, where Troop M of the First Cavalry was headquartered in the park. He'd sent the others out with a noncommissioned officer to patrol the most popular areas.

Will was the only commissioned officer who had been given the rough duty. He was the most junior officer after all, not counting his previous rank and years of service. Still, being out in the field gave him more opportunities to advance after his previous lapse in judgment.

At least Captain Harris had allowed him his pick of the men. Cavalrymen were, by and large, a motley crew. Frontier work was difficult, deadly. Those who joined as privates generally had something to prove or something to hide.

His men scrambled to attention as he reined in, then Waxworth broke rank to come hold Bess. The oldest of his men, the sharp-nosed private with dirty blond hair seemed to think the more he toadied up to Will, the greater his chances of making corporal at last. He'd volunteered to serve as cook, though Will doubted he could do much with the supplies the Army had sent with them.

"Everything as you ordered, sir," Waxworth said as Will swung down.

"Jah, ve have a camp," Lercher added from his place at the end of the line. The big, square-jawed German still mixed his *v*'s and *w*'s on occasion. At Lercher's heavy-browed scowl, Waxworth hurried to the picket line with Bess.

Will glanced around the camp. Sitting at the north end of a meadow, the A-framed white canvas tents stood straight and true around a firepit recently dug, edged with rocks, and already heating a massive iron pot. A pile of dirt to the south spoke of a privy in progress. So did the muddy spades lying not far from Franklin, his most engineering-minded private, and O'Reilly,

34

his most vocal. The horses were lined up along the picket, heads already in feed sacks as if lulled by the splash of the Firehole River just beyond. The saturnine Smith, the last of his privates, was watching them as if wondering how far he could ride before Will assigned him another task.

"Very good, Privates," Will said. "When is dinner?"

"Half past five, sir," Waxworth supplied, dashing back to the fire.

O'Reilly narrowed his green eyes. "And it's sure to be pork and beans." The Irishman spit on the ground as if not looking forward to the meal.

After that huckleberry pie, Will wasn't much looking forward to it either. "Detachment dismissed until then, but remain in camp."

They relaxed and went about their business. Waxworth bent over the fire and stirred the pot while O'Reilly and Franklin stowed their shovels. Lercher roamed the edge of the camp, picking up downed limbs for firewood. And Smith . . .

Heavier-than-regulation dark brown beard and mustache bristling, the lean cavalryman was pacing along the pines, rifle at the ready. Will hadn't ordered a guard, but he didn't call the man in. Smith tended to keep to himself at the best of times, and there were those in the park who resented the Army's presence. It didn't hurt to be watchful.

He'd been given a folding campaign table and canvas-backed chair, which someone had erected in front of his tent. He ignored both to sit with his men on the ground around the fire. The Army considered distance between officers and enlisted men important, a way to keep order. He wasn't about to abandon his men, even by a few feet, not for long.

Dinner was hot and salty, and the memory of that huckleberry pie intruded again. Maybe he'd have a chance to eat more of the cook's excellent handiwork when he was helping the Widow Tremaine. Nothing better than to eat good food with a beautiful, intelligent woman.

He sucked in a breath so hard Waxworth paused in his eating and sniffed the food as if certain Will had found fault. Will couldn't tell him it wasn't the meal but his thoughts that concerned him. He hadn't volunteered to help at the inn because of Mrs. Tremaine's lustrous black locks or shining gray eyes. Everything must take second place to his duty. He had vowed never to forget that again. Mrs. Tremaine was a means to an end. Unless he and his men knew where they were going and how to get back, they were useless.

When he'd finished his share of the meal, he glanced around at his men, waving to prevent them from standing at attention.

"Lights out at nine," he ordered, watching the flicker of the fire turn their tanned faces red. "Franklin, Smith, and O'Reilly, you're on guard duty tonight, change every three hours. Lercher, Waxworth, and I will share guard duty tomorrow night. We'll start patrolling tomorrow at eight, from the fork of the Firehole River to the pools past the Geyser Gateway Inn, hitting all the points of interest we know so far."

"Are we knowing the points of interest, then, sir?" O'Reilly asked.

Franklin, Lercher, and Waxworth watched Will expectantly. Smith looked bored.

"Mrs. Tremaine at the Geyser Gateway will supply us with a map," Will told them. "I'll have Franklin make copies for each of you."

Someone blew out a breath in obvious relief.

"And what will we be doing if we catch someone misbehaving?" O'Reilly pressed. "Sure'n but we have nowhere to hold them."

Not until they were allowed to build more

sturdy accommodations.

"We'll escort them to Mammoth Hot Springs," Will said. "Captain Harris will likely expel the miscreant from the park."

His men nodded.

"Like Jessup," O'Reilly said and spit into the fire, setting it to sizzling.

This time the implied disdain was warranted. Roy Jessup had been the first poacher Captain Harris had evicted after Troop M had arrived in the park. When they'd all been at Mammoth Hot Springs, Will, Waxworth, and O'Reilly had been riding out along the Virginia Canyon Road toward the Grand Canyon of the Yellowstone when they'd spotted a grizzled-haired mountain man ahead of them. Buckskins worn and dirty, he was towing a string of pack mules behind him.

"God bless America," he said with a crooked-tooth grin as they caught up with him. "Glad to see you boys in the park. Can't be too careful."

Waxworth preened, but O'Reilly nodded to the pack on the first mule. "Something's dripping."

Will saw it too, a dusky crimson staining the bottom of the leather, drops even now sprinkling the dust of the rough road.

He pulled Bess in front of the mountain

man. "Halt right there. What's in those packs?"

"Now, then, Captain," he wheedled, "there's no need for concern. I'm just delivering meat to the hotel camp near the canyon. Has to be fresh to please our guests." He winked.

"Then you won't mind if we take a look." Will nodded to O'Reilly, who swung down and approached the mules.

"The Yellowstone Park Association won't thank you if I'm late," the mountain man warned, shifting on the saddle. His hand strayed toward the rifle in its sheath at the side. Will drew his pistol, and the man stilled.

O'Reilly threw back the top on the heavy pack, took one look inside, and reared back, paling.

"What is it, Private?" Will called.

O'Reilly swallowed. "Buffalo head, sir. Fresh kill. Sure'n but those eyes can look right through a man."

Will leveled his gun on the poacher. "Your name."

Face hard, the man glared at him. "Roy Jessup. And you better remember it, because I'm the man who's going to run the Army out of Yellowstone."

"Roy Jessup," Will barked, "you are under

39

arrest for poaching. Your animals and belongings are forfeit. Surrender your weapons, and come with me to Mammoth Hot Springs."

Jessup chuckled, and the sound held no humor. "What are you going to do if I refuse?"

In truth, he had no option, but Jessup didn't need to know that. "The Army is in charge of this park. There are penalties for disobeying the rules. Private Waxworth, relieve Mr. Jessup of his weapons. Private O'Reilly, take charge of the animals."

Hemmed in on all sides, outgunned, Jessup had had no choice but to surrender. Captain Harris had given Will the honor of escorting him from the park.

"This isn't the last you've seen of me," the poacher had threatened as they'd reached the northern boundary. "This land belongs to everyone. You've no right to keep me from it."

"And you've no right to despoil it," Will had countered. He'd only wished he'd been able to do more than force Jessup to dismount and watch him walk toward the town of Gardiner with only his buckskins to his name.

How many more people like Jessup would they find hiding in the park? Would they have any idea where to look without a competent guide?

Mrs. Tremaine's map couldn't come too soon. He only hoped it would be enough.

3

With everything to be done around the hotel, Kate didn't have time to start on Lieutenant Prescott's map after all. Her first chore before dinner was to chat with Mr. Ponsonby. She located the dandy lounging on the porch swing that faced the trees and the circuit road, pipe in one hand. He hastily put it out as she approached and stood to meet her.

"I forgot," he said. "You asked us not to smoke on the premises."

At least he hadn't lit up in his room or out among the trees. Fire was a constant danger in the park. "Apparently, you also forgot another of the rules here. Nothing is to go into any geyser or mud pot opening."

He waved a hand before settling back on the swing as if assuming she'd join him. "A ridiculous precaution. Have you seen how high those geysers shoot? Surely a stick or two wouldn't interfere with the process."

42

"You might be surprised," Kate said, remaining standing.

He pushed the swing lazily with one foot. "I am not easily surprised. And that soldier interrupted a scientific experiment."

Is that what he called vandalism? "Nevertheless, sir," she said, "if you cannot respect the rules, I will have to ask you to leave."

He stared up at her, paling. "Leave? But there isn't another suitable hotel for miles."

"Very likely not," Kate agreed sweetly. "But there's always the Fire Hole to the north. I understand they've nearly managed the bedbug infestation."

He cringed a moment, then rose, chin up. "Very well. I will abide by these childish rules. I'm leaving tomorrow, in any event. And you can be sure I will mention to the park superintendent that your hospitality was distinctly lacking."

"If you feel you must," Kate said. "I will, of course, be required to inform Captain Harris about the distressing incident with the stick and the mud pots. I don't believe he's settled on consequences, yet, but I doubt they will involve much jail time."

He pushed past her for the hotel.

Kate shuddered. Unpleasant fellow. Most of her guests were far more understanding. And if they weren't, they, like Mr. Ponsonby, would be shortly gone. Few stayed more than a day or two as they toured the park.

And the ones currently at the inn deserved her attention.

She returned inside to help her maids set the tables, then served beside them to keep the food and lemonade flowing while Danny ate his dinner in the kitchen with Alberta and Caleb. While the maids washed up, she managed a few bites of the beef stew before chipping in to dry and store the china and silver in the white-painted cupboards that ran the extent of one wall in the long kitchen.

"Another fork gone," the tallest of the maids, Ida, said as she laid the last utensil in the wide drawer near the door to the dining room. She shoved her light-brown hair off her forehead, face sagging. "What, do they eat them?"

Sarah, the youngest at sixteen, giggled, blonde ringlets bouncing. "No. They collect them, like the rocks."

"And why them either?" Ida asked, clearly perplexed. "Like that lady last week who wanted Caleb to break her off a piece from Morning Geyser."

Pansy, who had been with Kate the longest, shook her head, blonde hair glinting. "They shouldn't be taking anything from

Yellowstone but memories."

"And those pictures Mr. Haynes sells," Sarah reminded her. "I'm going to bring one home to Ma when the season's over."

"Not long now," Ida said with a grateful sigh.

Not long at all. With the exception of Alberta, all her staff would be leaving by the end of September, and work wouldn't start again until late April at the earliest, when the roads cleared.

"I haven't had a chance to talk to you about next season," Kate said, going to hold the door open for them to leave the kitchen. "I hope you'll all consider returning."

Ida smiled at her as she passed. "I'd like that, Mrs. Tremaine. Thank you."

Pansy went so far as to drop a curtsey. "Me too, Mrs. Tremaine. The guests are ever so kind about leaving considerations."

Sarah gave her a bright smile. "I'll have to let you know. I hear the big hotel at Mammoth will be hiring. All the best people stay there."

Ida and Pansy frowned at her as she flounced past.

Kate bit back a sigh as she watched them head up the stairs to the staff quarters. Keeping staff was never easy. Like Alberta, Pansy had worked here since Kate and Toby had arrived. Elijah had started a year later; she still remembered when he'd ridden out to meet Toby and convinced him to take a chance on a new tour company. Caleb was coming on two years now. But everyone else changed, found other work, better work. And now she had to contend with the fancier hotels the Yellowstone Park Association was building. She would have to advertise for help farther out, hope someone suitable would answer. After all, Alberta had originally answered an advertisement in Ohio.

She had planned to start the map right after breakfast the next day, but she had no sooner swept the plank floor around the tables when the rattle of tack and drum of horses' hooves heralded the arrival of a stagecoach. The Wakefield and Hoffman group had a corral, stables, and rooms for their drivers to the north of her, but their passengers often preferred to stay at the Geyser Gateway. The driver carried off eight of her guests for Mammoth Hot Springs. Another six had already left with their driver for Old Faithful. After seeing everyone off, she had to make her morning tour of the geyser field, where she discovered one of her guests attempting to boil a fish he'd caught in the Firehole River in one of the hot pools. She ordered him back to the hotel and spent the next little while trying to retrieve the bones from the pool with a wooden paddle while Danny offered advice from a safe distance.

It was noon before she sat down again, and then she was interrupted by the arrival of Elijah Freeman. Funny — she hadn't been expecting him today. She tucked her hair back into her bun and straightened her flower-printed fitted bodice before throwing open the wide front door.

"Welcome to the Geyser Gateway Inn!" she proclaimed as soon as Elijah drew his team to a stop.

Six pairs of eyes gazed back at her from faces displaying everything from delight to awe to concern. She understood. Some, like her, fell in love with the wondrous features of the park. Others found it all too wild.

Caleb hurried from the barn to take charge of the horses while the driver jumped down to land with a puff of chalk.

"Mrs. Tremaine, I bring you a distinguished group of visitors," Elijah declared, whipping his hat off his tightly curled black hair. "All the way from Berkshire, England. Lord and Lady Cavell; their daughter, Miss Cavell; Sir Winston Wallingford; and their servants."

Kate bobbed a curtsey and stepped aside as Elijah handed them down and they made their way into the inn. As the stage driver brought up the rear, Kate leaned closer. "Came all that way and didn't bother to reserve?"

Elijah's grin was conspiratorial in his dark face. "Oh, they reserved. The Bassett Brothers stage driver hadn't arrived yet when I stopped by the station at Cinnabar to see if anyone needed a tour. I convinced them to come here instead of the Fire Hole."

The Fire Hole Hotel to the north, like most of the hotels in the park, now belonged to the Yellowstone Park Association. It was also far more rustic than the Geyser Gateway.

"You keep poaching visitors, and someone will notice," Kate predicted.

He laughed. "Man's got to make a living. Why else drive in Yellowstone?"

With a smile, she hurried to check in her new guests even as Elijah went to bring in their luggage. By the time she had everyone settled, the day was advancing. Danny was helping Caleb with the horses, so she hurried upstairs to the small apartment at the end of the hotel, where she and Danny made their home. Sitting at the table in the center of the main room, she sketched a map. The hotels, the geysers and paint pots, the curves of the Firehole River and the footbridges across it, the bridle path to Fairy Falls, the Grand Prismatic Spring, and various lakes.

She hesitated on the area to the west of Fairy Creek, then purposely marked it "Off-Limits." It was an Army term she'd heard from Lieutenant Kingman, the Corps of Engineers officer in charge of improving Yellowstone's roads. She could only hope Lieutenant Prescott and his men were familiar with it too. If not, she'd have to take other measures to protect the area.

She had just come downstairs again when she saw Lieutenant Prescott hitching his horse outside. She patted her bun in place, bit her lips for color.

And froze.

What was she doing, primping? She was a widow, Toby gone barely a year. She wasn't courting, had no plans to marry again. She had too much to do as it was.

She straightened her shoulders, put on a smile that was no more than pleasant. The moment he walked in the door, she held out the rolled map. "Lieutenant Prescott. Here's my end of the deal."

His brows rose, but he accepted the map, then crossed to the desk that held the guest book and unrolled the map on top of it. Kate went to join him, careful to keep a respectable distance.

He nodded as his gaze swept over her drawing. "Nicely executed but inadequate."

Kate stiffened. "Inadequate? Why?"

"Distances, for one," he said. "Is this to scale?"

"No," Kate admitted. "I didn't think of that."

He pointed to the western meadows. "Who put this area off-limits?"

So, he did know the term. Kate lifted her chin. "I did. We don't take visitors there. It has no pools or waterfalls. No reason for strangers to intrude."

He straightened to eye her, and she was suddenly aware of his height, the width of his chest, the depth of his gaze. "This is Yellowstone, Mrs. Tremaine. We're all strangers."

Kate kept her head high. "It's part of my lease from the Department of Interior. And I choose to keep it off-limits."

He returned his attention to the map, and she felt an odd disquiet, as if someone had taken the last piece of huckleberry pie before she'd had a bite.

"I doubt Captain Harris realized your lease amounted to hundreds of acres," he said. "He intends to cut back all hotel lands to the immediate vicinity of the buildings themselves."

Then she had some convincing to do. "That's his prerogative, but, at the moment, my lease stands."

"I'm afraid this map doesn't." He let go of the paper, and it rolled up to rock on the book. "These aren't trackless prairies where a patrol can see for miles. We need to know the trails, the distances between stations, the location of fresh, cool water for us and our mounts, the hazards of scalding fountains and pools. I have a responsibility to keep my men safe."

"I thought your bigger responsibility was to safeguard Yellowstone," Kate countered. "But I see your point. I'm not sure I could draw you a map that would detail all those points. Even the men who hire on as guides would be hard-pressed to draw such a map."

He sighed. "So much for our deal."

She was not about to let him off so easily. The list of things needing fixing was growing in her head to epic proportions. And they only had until the snow started flying six weeks from now.

Or sooner.

She could think of only one alternative, one that would take her away from her hotel and into the company of this man who made her think of things long buried. But if Captain Harris was to renew her lease, all of her lease, she needed him to know she supported the Army.

"The deal stands," she insisted. "I'll simply have to show you around myself."

Will stared at her. Those misty eyes looked hard as stone. Her chin jutted out, and her rosy lips were compressed.

"I thought you had a business to run," he protested.

Her eyes narrowed. "I do, but I won't if I don't have help. Since I'll be doing a favor for the entire detachment, I imagine I'll find uses for all your men."

It was one thing to offer her his time off, another to put a detachment at the disposal of a civilian. "I can't promise that."

She cocked her head. "One day a week, all meals provided?"

Her staff's cooking? Waxworth would be drooling. Perhaps Will could convince Captain Harris it was in the best interest of the Army. Better food generally meant better prepared soldiers.

"I'll consider it," he said. "In the meantime, I have four hours at my disposal now. What would you like me to do first?"

Her eyes lit, like moonlight through mist. "Fix the front steps. We need to make a good impression on new arrivals."

One look at her would do that. Will cleared his throat, though he hadn't said the words aloud. "Do you have the tools?"

"In the barn around back. If Caleb or Elijah is there, tell him I approved of you."

She seemed to expect him to set right to work, for she strode off toward the back of the hotel. Something begged him to follow. He made himself head for the barn behind the hotel instead.

The clapboard building listed slightly to the west, or perhaps that was because it had been constructed on uneven ground. He rather hoped it wasn't on her list for him to fix. It would take more than him and all his men combined. He stepped through the wide, open door into the shadows, the scent of hay and manure heavy in the air. A voice called overhead, and he glanced up into the hayloft to find Danny staring down at him, straw sticking out like a piece of his pale hair. He ducked back out of sight.

"Can I help you?"

He dropped his gaze to meet that of a slender man with skin as dark as the shadows of the barn. His coat was off, sleeves of his gingham shirt rolled up. The cock of his head was friendly, but the look in his brown eyes was assessing.

"Lieutenant Prescott," Will said. "Mrs. Tremaine sent me for tools to fix the steps."

His black brows shot upward. "That a fact? Well, I don't mind seeing the Army work. How about you, Caleb?"

A lanky youth stepped out of one of the stalls, brown hair partially covered by a battered cap. He stared at Will a moment before shaking his head even as he pulled up his dun-colored britches.

The other man, likely the Elijah Mrs. Tremaine had mentioned, stepped aside and waved to the wall of the barn, where a bench held any manner of tool. "Help yourself."

Will moved past the stalls for horses and cows and selected a hammer and a keg of nails. But as he turned, Danny slid down from the loft.

"What are you doing, Lieutenant Prescott?" he asked, eying the tools in his hands.

"Lieutenant Prescott is going to fix the front steps," Caleb told him.

"Are you going to help?" Danny asked.

Caleb shook his head again, this time so sharply his cap slid off to cover his dark eyes.

Elijah chuckled. "Looks like you're on your own, Lieutenant."

Danny skipped over to Will. "I'll help you."

Will took a step back. "You should play." He started for the door.

Danny scrambled to keep up with him. "Can I at least watch?"

"Why?" Will asked, making for the inn.

"So I'll know how to do it next time."

A logical response, but one of the reasons he was doing this was so he could give the boy an opportunity to enjoy himself. He ought to order him to leave be, but he had no authority over Danny. And he had no heart to turn him away.

They reached the steps, and Danny climbed to the top and sat. Will reached the second step from the bottom and bounced experimentally.

Danny winced. "It sure squeaks."

"I'm more concerned about the way it moves," Will said. "Steps should be hard as rocks."

"Why?" Danny asked.

Will dropped back to the ground. "Think how many people climb these every day. Would you want the steps to crack on them?"

Danny shook his head. "No."

"Then they need to be fixed." Will bent to look through the open backs of the stairs.

He hadn't much experience with carpentry, his father having worked in a livery stable before enlisting in the Army, but even he thought there ought to be a middle brace on so wide a set of steps.

He glanced up to find Danny still watching him. "Isn't there something else you'd rather be doing?"

His thin shoulders rose and fell in a shrug. "I should stay close to the inn. Ma might need me, like she needs Alberta and Pansy and Elijah and Caleb."

The boy had more of a sense of duty than Will had had at that age. He resigned himself to be the diversion of the moment. "What does Elijah do here?" he asked, reaching for the hammer.

"He drives the stage and brings us visitors. He brought six more today. One's a real lord. He's met the Queen of England. I wish I'd met a queen."

Will glanced back at the steaming geysers. "You live someplace even lords come thousands of miles to visit. I'd say that's pretty good."

Danny nodded. "That *is* pretty good."

Just then the door opened, and the fellow Will had seen yesterday by the paint pots came out. Ponsonby, Mrs. Tremaine had called him. He started down the stairs with a nod to Danny.

"Fetch me a horse," he ordered Will. "That stage won't be returning until tomorrow, and I have decided to leave now."

The fellow didn't notice Will was wearing a military uniform? "You'll have to fetch your own horse," Will said. "I don't work here."

Ponsonby raised one brow as he glanced from the hammer in Will's hand to his face. "Do tell. Very well, I'll make do with that one."

Will put his free hand on the fellow's shoulder before he could start for Bess. "She's taken."

Ponsonby shook him off. "Really, sirrah. Do you know to whom you are speaking?"

"That's Mr. Ponsonby," Danny put in helpfully.

"Don't much care," Will said. He jerked his head toward the inn. "There are horses in the barn, but I suggest you talk to their owner before making off with one. Horse stealing is theft, inside the park and out."

With a huff, the fellow stomped back into the inn.

Mrs. Tremaine passed him on her way out onto the porch, flowered skirts swinging. If she'd noticed the scowl on Ponsonby's face, she ignored it.

"How's it coming?" she asked Will.

"Slowly," he admitted. "We may need to add braces. I'll have my men cut the timber."

She clucked her tongue. "Think again. There's no cutting of timber in Yellowstone. Your captain even agreed."

She was right. Any lumber needed, even to repair a set of stairs, had to be freighted in, unless special permission was granted by the Army Corps of Engineers, which operated a small sawmill at Mammoth Hot Springs. And it was doubtful he could get permission to fix a civilian building. Will blew out a breath.

"Do you know to whom you're speaking?" Danny demanded of his mother.

Mrs. Tremaine's gaze dropped to the boy on the step. "I know to whom I'm speaking now, and he had better reconsider his attitude."

Danny wilted. "Yes, ma'am. Sorry."

"Alberta says two of the pumpkins you planted are ready. Would you like to see if she needs help cleaning them?"

He nodded as he rose. "I sure would." He ran for the door and into the hotel.

"Maybe I should follow him," Will said. "I might be more use cleaning pumpkins."

Her smile warmed him. "I wouldn't waste

my lieutenant on pumpkins."

Her lieutenant. Why did that make him smile?

She pressed both hands to her lips, and Will spun to see what had so amazed her. None of the geysers was going off. Steam drifted across the basin, giving him glimpses of the trees beyond.

He returned his gaze to her. "What are you looking at?"

She lowered her hands. "You. You should smile more often."

Maybe I would, if I stay here long enough.

He inclined his head. "Ma'am. I should get back to work. My employer is a demanding sort."

"But she offers considerations, like huckleberry pie," she reminded him. "If Danny finishes the pumpkins before you leave, I'll send him back out. He'll have to take over the hotel one day. He could use a good example."

Will couldn't respond with anything that would allow her to keep her admiration of him. Still smiling, she turned for the hotel.

The sooner he finished his part of the deal, the better. He didn't want to be around when she discovered he was no sort of man to serve as an example, to anyone.

4

At least *he* was willing to work.

Kate grimaced as she checked the dining area for issues before dinner. Why was she comparing Lieutenant Prescott to Toby? They had little in common. The lieutenant was controlled, cautious, in command of every situation. Sometimes she thought Toby had been nothing but an overgrown boy. He would set out to prune the apple trees planted by the hotel's original manager, and she'd find him with Danny watching the paint pots bubble. He'd ride for supplies and return with an armload of wildflowers and stories of how he'd followed the bison herd. He'd brought chaos and wonder, uncertainty and delight into her life. And he'd given her Danny.

Gray dots appeared on the white linen of the dining table. Kate wiped her cheeks with her fingers before more tears could fall. Toby's curiosity, kindness, and eagerness to explore had been some of his charms. They had also led to his death. She was not about to let Danny follow in his stead. Better that he copy Lieutenant Prescott than his father.

She was helping Pansy set the tables for dinner when Danny came out of the kitchen a few minutes later.

"I'm all done with the pumpkins," he said as he passed. "I want to see what Lieutenant Prescott is doing."

So did she. Funny that the pull was so strong. Kate followed her son to the door and onto the veranda, the scent of Alberta's savory soup drifting out with her.

Lord and Lady Cavell and their party were sitting on the benches, watching the geysers. At least, the older couple was watching the geysers. Sir Winston was watching Miss Cavell, as if entranced by her shiny blonde curls. Miss Cavell was watching Lieutenant Prescott.

He was a sight. He'd removed his cavalry coat and rolled up the sleeves on his cream-colored cotton shirt to reveal muscular arms. They, like the rest of him, glistened with sweat that molded the shirt to his form. He wiped perspiration from his brow with a handkerchief, spiking his short-cropped hair, and glanced up at Kate as Danny ran down the stairs to his side.

"Take a turn and see what you think," he suggested.

She couldn't notice any difference by looking at the steps, but she lifted her skirts and descended cautiously. Nothing gave.

"It stopped squeaking," Danny marveled, peering at the steps.

Kate reached Lieutenant Prescott's side and glanced back at the steps, surprised. "What did you do?"

He bent at the waist and pointed under the steps. "I couldn't fix the boards themselves, so I shored them up from below."

Danny dropped to his hands and knees, and Kate bent as well. In the recess under the steps, she sighted the pale shape of rocks, arranged so that they supported the steps at either side and the middle. Danny scuttled forward as if to touch them.

"Where did you get those?" she asked, straightening.

Lieutenant Prescott straightened as well. "Found them in a pile near your necessaries. I figured it would only help nature to remove some of the debris."

The pile of rock had been left when the privies had been dug, before she and Toby had come to manage the hotel. She'd never had time to scatter the ugly things. Yet he'd used them to fix the steps without taking from Yellowstone.

"There may be hope for you yet," Kate teased.

His stern lips hinted of the smile she'd seen earlier. "Enough for a chance at that meal I smell?"

"Enough," Kate agreed. "But you should probably eat in the kitchen with Danny."

Danny popped to his feet. "Yes, please!"

That smile blossomed, warmer than the rays of the sun through the pines. "I'd be delighted."

"You might want to wash up first," Kate warned Danny before he could pelt up the steps. "You too, Lieutenant Prescott. I'm not sure my guests would appreciate the other aroma."

He glanced down at his damp shirt. "I'll put my head under the pump before joining you."

There was a pump in the kitchen, but she didn't want to think how Alberta and the maids might react to seeing him like this. She nodded toward the side of the hotel. "Danny, show Lieutenant Prescott the pump near the barn."

"This way, Lieutenant," Danny sang out, already on the run.

"Meet you in the kitchen shortly." He headed after Danny.

Someone, most likely Miss Cavell, puffed out a sigh.

Kate climbed the steps and smiled at her guests. "Enjoy the scenery while you can. Dinner will be ready in a few minutes." She sailed into the hotel.

The maids had the tables set and were adding steaming tureens of beef and barley soup and baskets of plump, crusty rolls.

"But no more than eight pats of butter per table," Pansy was reminding them. "Mrs. Guthrie says we must economize, as the cows stop producing for the winter."

That was true enough. Good thing Captain Harris had been persuaded to be reasonable when he had declared there would be no grazing of domestic livestock in the park. If the Yellowstone Park Association could keep sheep on the mountain meadows to feed their guests, she was surely allowed her two cows and four horses.

Still, she put four of the little squares Alberta cut from the creamy butter in front of Danny and Lieutenant Prescott when they sat at the big worktable in the middle of the kitchen to eat.

He must have done what he'd promised, for now all of his head was wet and the collar of his military jacket looked damp, as if the water had dripped on it. He shoveled down Alberta's soup so quickly he might have thought Kate intended to steal it from him.

Of course, Danny copied him.

"Easy," Kate said, ruffling her son's hair, so unlike hers in color and texture. "You can have more, you know."

Danny nodded, soup running down his chin. "And apple pie for dessert. We'll have pumpkin tomorrow. Alberta said so."

"Now, there's a feast," Lieutenant Prescott said, spoon pausing.

"I helped," Danny bragged. "I scooped out all that stringy stuff. The pumpkin seeds too. Alberta salted and toasted them. She's going to put them in the oatmeal tomorrow for breakfast."

"Makes me sad I won't be here for breakfast," Lieutenant Prescott said.

"You could be," Kate offered. "I'll have Alberta make extra. My guests should be done by eight. Bring your men at half past, and they can eat right before I show you around the geysers."

Now, that was an offer too good to refuse. So, at a quarter past eight the next morning, his men mounted up.

All except Smith. Someone had to stay behind to guard the camp from scavengers, four-footed and two. To Will's surprise, the cavalryman had volunteered.

"I have never been overly fond of oatmeal," he'd said by way of an excuse.

Will couldn't imagine anyone liking hardtack better, but they'd left the fellow making coffee and headed out.

The weather had been fine since they'd ridden into Yellowstone in mid-August. Today was no different. Sunlight seemed to want to linger like any other tourist. The sky was an endless blue over the spikes of pine as they rode into the yard of the hotel, steam from the geysers and pools rising to form their own clouds.

"All clear?" Will asked as Mrs. Tremaine and Danny came out onto the porch to greet them. The boy was as eager as always, a cowlick sticking up in his pale hair like a flag as if he'd already been out running. His mother looked more like she'd joined the Army — navy jacket over a navy skirt so long on one side she'd had to button it up on her hip.

"All my guests have breakfasted," she reported. "Elijah will be taking the Cavell party north shortly. And the Wakefield and Hoffman stage came through for their group and carried away my other guests. The hotel is yours." She spread her hand toward the door and stepped aside.

His men didn't need another invitation. They hitched their mounts to the post and hurried up the stairs into the hotel. He caught Lercher gazing up at the beams in the salon and Franklin studying the layout with an appreciative eye. Waxworth and O'Reilly beat them to the tables, where the cook had bowls and spoons waiting.

"My, what fine gentlemen we have visiting today," she said, lashes fluttering as she started ladling thick oatmeal into the bowls.

Someone giggled. Will glanced toward the door to the kitchen, where two young ladies and an older woman were peeking out at them. Waxworth and Franklin sat a little taller.

"Will you say the grace, Lieutenant?" Kate asked.

Hand on the silver spoon, he paused. His men were all watching him, spoons anywhere from stuck in the oatmeal to steaming in front of their open mouths. He looked to Waxworth.

"Private Waxworth, do the honors."

The spoon plunked back into the bowl as Waxworth clasped his boney fingers together and aimed his pointed nose and gaze skyward.

"Heavenly Lord," he said so loudly he

might have thought God needed an ear trumpet, "thank you for this glorious meal, for the kind hands that prepared it, and the good soil that grew it. May it be a blessing to our bodies. Amen."

An answering amen rumbled around the table, and spoons commenced flying.

Like everything else he'd consumed at the Geyser Gateway, the oatmeal was filling and tasty. Besides pumpkin seeds, the cook, who insisted they all call her Alberta, had thrown in walnuts and raisins and served it with heaping bowls of sugar. Lercher piled on eight spoonfuls alone. And he'd never seen his men drink so much coffee.

"I could make it this good," Waxworth said, eying the china cup, "if I had a stove at my disposal."

Somehow, Will doubted that.

Still, even with the number of bowls of oatmeal put away, he and his men were out front by nine with Mrs. Tremaine.

She had led a horse from the barn to join theirs, sidesaddle conspicuous on its back. "May I trouble one of you gentlemen for help?" she asked as she reached the porch.

Waxworth leapt into action, barely edging out O'Reilly to her side. He took the reins with one hand and swept her a bow with the other. Smirking at his comrade, the

Irishman cupped his hands and bent.

"If you'd be putting your foot here, milady, I'll boost you up."

Waxworth glowered at him.

One hand on the saddle, Mrs. Tremaine slipped her foot into O'Reilly's keeping, and he pushed her up and into place. She anchored her leg about the pommel and unhooked her long skirt to drape it over the side.

"Thank you both." She looked to Will. "Lieutenant Prescott, perhaps you should introduce your men. It doesn't seem right to shout 'Ho, Private!' every time I want their attention."

"You can call us anything you like," Waxworth assured her as she gathered her reins. "We'll always come a-running." That grin would have melted butter.

"Mount up, Soldier," Will ordered, and his private collected himself and hurried to his horse.

"Incline your head when I call your name," he told his men. "Lercher."

The German bobbed his blond head, nearly knocking off his fatigue cap.

"Waxworth."

The toady smiled fatuously at her, then apparently remembered Will's command and bobbed like a bird on a wire.

69

"O'Reilly."

The strawberry-blond-haired private bent over his horse's mane in a bow. "At your service, milady."

"Franklin."

His private's lean face turned red as he inclined his head. "Mrs. Tremaine. Thank you for your help."

"Private Smith is in camp," Will finished. "I'll explain the terrain to him when we return."

"Very good." She directed her horse away from theirs and turned the mare to face them.

"Gentlemen," she said, voice as clear as a bugle call. "Welcome to the Lower Geyser Basin. This part of the park has more fountains and hot pools than any other. It has some of the prettiest waterfalls and sweeping vistas too. I understand you have the honor of protecting it all from despoiling."

Franklin and Lercher sat taller in their saddles. O'Reilly bunched up his cheeks, leaned over his horse, and caught Mrs. Tremaine's eye. Swallowing the spit, he straightened.

"Allow me the honor of protecting you," she continued. "The water in many of these pools is hot enough to scald. So is that mud.

It's also thick with the minerals that give it those lovely colors. Don't splash it on you or in you. If you see one of my guests or anyone else getting too close, I'd appreciate it if you'd warn them away."

His men glanced over at the colored mud pots as if reconsidering them.

"Today," she said, "I'll take you on a tour of the area nearest the hotel so you can familiarize yourself with the beauties and the dangers of the areas you're going to patrol."

Lercher was nodding, but Waxworth and Franklin were beginning to frown.

"Didn't realize she was such a school-marm," his cook muttered to his engineer.

He'd have to have words with them later. They were all in Yellowstone's school now, and Mrs. Tremaine was their best hope for a teacher.

"Column behind me and Mrs. Tremaine," Will ordered when it became clear she had finished speaking for now. She turned her horse and waited as he drew Bess alongside. His men fell into place, two abreast, behind them.

The same two older hotel guests who had watched him repair the stairs yesterday ventured out onto the porch. They must be the Cavell party Mrs. Tremaine had mentioned. As before, their clothing would have graced the finest parlors back in Boston.

"Oh, are we having a parade?" the woman asked in a British accent.

"Cheers to the men in uniform," the gentleman, most likely her husband, called. "Subdue those red savages."

Will's stomach clenched at the crude term. "Column, move out," he ordered, and Mrs. Tremaine clucked to her horse. The lady guest waved her handkerchief as they rode past.

"You probably won't see an Indian in the park," Mrs. Tremaine said, voice hinting of sadness. "They've all been sent to reservations."

He knew. The First Cavalry had had a hand in that, and he still wasn't sure it had been the right thing to do. Warlike tribes no longer preyed on peaceful tribes or settlers, yet both warlike and peaceful groups had been misplaced from the lands on which they had been accustomed to hunt and raise their families for generations. And there had been so many casualties.

"The Bannocks still come through sometimes," she added, oblivious to the memories that stalked closer to him. "They hunt and fish and gather berries. I suppose Captain Harris won't like that."

Will roused himself. "No hunting on park lands. No exceptions."

She nodded as they circled the paint pots. Even the well-trained cavalry horses drew back from the sulfurous smells, the belching plops.

"That's probably wise," she said. "The bison herd, in particular, is having difficulties. They deserve our protection."

He had only heard of the great beasts. The herds had been gone from the plains when he'd ridden through as a young private, and there had been none in Oregon and Washington Territory, where he'd seen much of his service. Still, it was hard to imagine anything as strong and sturdy as a buffalo herd needing his protection.

She nodded to an area where orange streaked across the chalky ground, steam rising. "That's the Silex Spring. Trust me, you do not want to drink that water."

"No, ma'am," Waxworth agreed with a shudder.

"And keep your horses well away," she advised, causing O'Reilly to swerve back into line. "What looks like solid ground may well be only a crust, with boiling water just below."

All his men were more careful after that.

A little farther along, she reined in beside

a pool as blue as the sky overhead. His men stopped around her, and O'Reilly craned his neck to peer over his horse's head into the depths.

"As you can see by the steam, every pool around here is hot. This one is Celestine Spring, but most of the others are geysers. Unlike Old Faithful, they're not predictable. If you're riding, listen for a hiss and watch for an increase in steam. If you're on foot, you'll feel the rumble in the ground before they start."

So, that was how she'd predicted the eruption yesterday. He caught her eye and nodded. Her smile brightened the day even further.

She led them past a group of lodgepole pines struggling to stay alive in the minerals and heat and through an area where the ground looked as if it was covered with bubbles that had hardened into rock. She nodded toward a pool as blue as blueberry preserves.

"That's Jelly Geyser. It's a frequent squirter, so watch for it. Farther out, that pale white hole with the crusty sides is Jet Geyser. It will shoot almost as high as my hotel. Over there is Spasm Geyser. It's more of a bubbler. That one with the yellow center and the green front is Clepsydra. She should go off . . . now."

As if the geyser obeyed her least command, water shot up from multiple vents, sending steam into the air. Except for Bess and Mrs. Tremaine's horse, the other horses shifted, balked, and it took a moment for his men to get them under control.

"Every three minutes," she explained. "You'll get used to it. But the biggest show around here is Fountain Geyser."

She nodded to the large, still, blue pool they were approaching.

"Doesn't look so bad," Waxworth said.

"You wait," Kate said. "It will shoot twice the height of my hotel and last for more than a quarter hour. The only one bigger in this area is Morning Geyser beyond it and closest to the hotel. But it's rarer."

"Who named such things?"

That bewildered tone was Lercher's. Mrs. Tremaine must have realized it, for she turned her head to give him a look. "Some were named by explorers, but many were named by the US Geological Survey. This way, gentlemen, and try to keep up."

Will bit back a smile as they rode past the hotel again. His men were looking more concerned by the moment, picking their way along and giving every colored patch of earth wide berth. Danny waved from the porch. Franklin waved back.

She pointed out Twig Geyser, a creamy pool that could shoot water up a few feet for as long as an hour; the Leather Pool, which was as brown and rough as its name; and a patch of gray ground that hissed like a pot on the boil. Suddenly, she reined in. His men followed suit, jerking on their reins and glancing around as if expecting a geyser to go off on either side.

Instead, she pointed across the geyser field to the circuit road beyond.

On the other side of the dusty road, a small clearing was nestled among the pines, sage dotting the pale soil, its gray-green leaves holding the golden yellow of the fall bloom. Among them, shoulders dark and humps tawny, a dozen elk browsed. Will caught his breath.

"Oh, for one shot," Waxworth said with a groan.

She swiveled in the sidesaddle to glare at him. "For shame, Private. Look at that power, that majesty, and your first thought is to kill it?"

Waxworth flamed. "No, ma'am, my first thought is how many hungry cavalrymen one of those would feed."

"I'll keep you fed, Private," she promised. "You just make sure those beauties go on living to inspire others."

"Remember the rules, Private," Will added. "No hunting on park lands."

Waxworth deflated with a sigh.

But his other men were nodding. How extraordinary. They were surrounded by animals and geology meant to inspire, and the greatest source of inspiration, for him and his men, was Kate Tremaine.

5

Once again, the men seemed all too eager to rush toward danger. A bull elk could weigh as much as seven hundred pounds. Those horns could puncture a lung or spleen, and one kick could break bones. When a herd made an appearance near the hotel, she had to be constantly on guard with her guests to prevent close encounters.

She glanced over at Lieutenant Prescott. His rugged face held a look of awe, the sort of respect these great creatures warranted. The only problem was that he wasn't looking at the elk.

He was looking at her.

She hastily gathered her reins and turned her horse to face theirs again. She was here for a purpose, not to gaze at the scenery.

"Lieutenant Prescott, how far south are you patrolling along the circuit road?" she asked.

"We haven't set a boundary," he admitted, shifting on his saddle. "There's another detachment at Old Faithful. They'll patrol partway up the road to the north. I'll have to check with them at some point to confirm we're covering everything."

She nodded. "If you're coming up the road from the south, it might look easy to cross straight through the geyser field for the inn. Resist that urge. The terrain is deceptive. We had a grown man and a young boy die by falling into the paint pots two years ago."

"It's no wonder you're being so cautious then, ma'am," O'Reilly ventured.

Kate glanced his way, and his round cheeks turned a shade darker than his strawberry-blond hair. "They were not guests at my hotel, Private O'Reilly. They came from Marshall's, the hotel now called the Fire Hole, not far from your camp, I understand. Unfortunately, I cannot watch over every visitor who wanders by. But you can."

Lieutenant Prescott's mouth quirked, but he said nothing. Could he hear the determination in her voice? She had always tried to protect her guests while showing them the wonders of Yellowstone. Toby's death had only steeled her resolve.

She led them back toward the hotel, pointing out other hazards along the way.

"Don't pick mushrooms," she advised when she saw Waxworth eying a clump near the base of the pines. "Several species in the park are deadly. And watch out for water hemlock — it can look like wild parsnips or carrots, but you won't survive until morning if you eat a sizeable amount."

"There goes Waxworth's stew," someone muttered.

"If you find a warm pool, don't go bathing," Kate continued. "It might be warm now, but heated water can push up from the bottom and boil you alive. Don't use the pools for laundry — you'll clog the geyser and end up shooting your clothing all over creation, and I can promise you it will be in no shape to wear again. And, whatever you do, don't feed the bears."

"Is there nothing in this park that von't kill you?" Lercher asked, heavy voice incredulous.

"Nothing, Private," she called back. "Best you remember that."

As they reined in in front of the hotel, she turned to Lieutenant Prescott again. If anything, he looked slightly bemused, brows down and mouth in a firm line.

"Have you planned what route you'll take on your patrol yet?" she asked.

He raised his head. "My hope was to cover all the locations of most interest to tourists as well as areas frequented by poachers in the past. At the moment, we're following the circuit road from the forks of the Firehole River to the Geyser Gateway."

"A sensible route," Kate allowed. "You'll be able to keep the peace with the tourists. You may miss the poachers, though. They don't generally stay at the hotels." She gripped the smooth leather pommel with one hand and twisted as much as she could in the sidesaddle to point with her other hand toward the north.

"Start at the forks as you intended. I'll show you other areas to patrol near there another day. As you head south, you'll pass through some meadows — detour through them and watch for recent kills. That will alert you to poachers. They tend to leave a mess."

"No hot pools or boiling geysers there?" Franklin asked.

"Not in that area, but the closer you get to the Geyser Gateway, the more you'll find," Kate explained. She swiveled again so she could point west. "Beyond the geyser field, you'll reach Tangled Creek. It takes the runoff from the geysers, so it can be warm. I wouldn't drink from it. Follow it up and around that hill, and you'll find a footbridge over the Firehole. You might want to check that area as well."

Now came the tricky part. She couldn't trust any of them, not even Lieutenant Prescott, with the secret. Word might get out.

"Don't go more than a few yards beyond the river unless I am with you," she said, making sure to meet each gaze in turn. "That area has a number of hidden dangers. I wouldn't want you to lose your horse or your life."

They were all staring at her. Private Lercher's blue eyes were wide, his big jaw hanging slack. Private O'Reilly leaned from the saddle and spit, but whether to emphasize her warning or disagree with it, she wasn't sure. Well, her admonitions were for their own good. She hardly wanted another death on her hands.

She turned to Lieutenant Prescott. "That ought to be sufficient guidance to know your way around the immediate area. Was there anything else you needed right now?"

"No, ma'am, much obliged." His voice held a note of relief. Had he thought her too authoritative? Well, how else was she to protect him and his men? Toby hadn't listened to her, but the cavalry surely knew how to obey orders.

He nodded to his men. "Lercher, O'Reilly, you're on patrol. Escort the others back to camp, start at the Fire Hole Hotel, and work your way south as Mrs. Tremaine advised. Waxworth and Smith will spell you this afternoon. Franklin and I will make a final sweep this evening. Dismissed."

His men turned their mounts and headed out of the yard, studiously avoiding the geysers and mud pots.

"At least they're following the path I suggested," Kate said, watching them.

"For now," he said. "Do you need help getting down?"

She buttoned up her skirt, lifted her leg over the pommel, and slid from the sidesaddle to land on the chalky ground. "No, but thank you for offering."

He shook his head. "You're an independent woman, Mrs. Tremaine."

"That's the best kind," Kate told him with a grin.

"Can't argue there."

Well, that was a first. She'd met quite a few gentlemen in the last year who thought a woman couldn't manage a hotel in the wilderness. His response was warm enough that she thought he'd smile, but he looked toward the road, where his men were disappearing around the bend.

"I hope they heed your warnings," he said. "A few of them have been recruited in the last couple of years, but most are veterans of the Indian Wars. They don't scare easily."

"That's a shame," Kate said, gathering the reins. "Tell me, Lieutenant, can you reason with a native?"

He frowned, gaze coming back to her. "Depends on the native, but then I would say that about most people."

"You can't reason with nature. Scalding water is scalding, whether you meant to touch it or not. And grizzlies don't wait for an explanation before attacking."

Her hands were starting to shake. She gripped the reins tighter, and Aster, one of her riding horses, stamped her feet, head bobbing. She reached up to stroke the mare's neck. At least she could calm her horse even if she couldn't calm her thoughts.

"I recognize the dangers," he told her. "I just wonder how many of my men will take your lessons to heart."

"That's their choice," Kate acknowledged. "All I can do is warn them."

"You can lead a horse away from scalding water," he said, one side of his mouth turning up, "but you can't stop him from return-ing."

"You most certainly can," Kate insisted. "You can lock him in the barn."

He shook his head. "I can't lock a cavalry horse in the barn or confine my men to camp. They have work to do."

"Work I want them to do," she assured him, just as Elijah drove the coach up in front of the hotel. "I just don't want to see anyone hurt while doing it."

He nodded toward the paint pots. "Even him?"

She followed his gaze and puffed out a sigh. Sir Winston had evidently decided to take one last look around before leaving, for he was bending entirely too close to the pot in easiest reach. She wrapped the reins about the hitching post. "Excuse me."

She navigated the safest path out onto the field. In places on either side, the fragile amber-colored crusts were dented by recent footsteps. The fool! He could have fallen in a dozen times. Then she spotted the pen-knife in his hand, and her blood boiled nearly as hot as the geysers.

"Stop," she said, and he jerked upright. "Back away from the formation."

He looked over at her, nose so high she wondered the sulfurous fumes didn't flow up it into his brain, however small his brain might be.

"I am not accustomed to taking orders from the female help," he informed her.

"Then it's surprising you've survived this long," Kate countered. "It's not safe for you out here, and I fear the geologic features aren't safe from you. Come back to the hotel."

"When I'm finished," he snapped. He turned for the formation, where the first three letters of his last name had been etched in the hard-baked mud.

Could her temper climb any higher? "Do you know how many years it will take to cover that?"

"Decades, one would hope," he replied, intent on chiseling the next letter.

Oh, for her rifle! But then, perhaps she shouldn't have a gun in her grip when she was already tempted to strangle him with her bare hands!

"That's enough, mister."

The gravelly voice behind him made her guest turn. Lieutenant Prescott stepped up beside her, but his gaze was on the vandal.

"I am not under your command, sir," Sir Winston said with a curl of his lip.

"No," Lieutenant Prescott allowed, "but an Act of Congress gives the Army jurisdiction over this park. I hereby arrest you for defacing government property."

Kate wanted to shout, to cheer, to wrap her arms around him and hug him close.

Well, maybe not that.

She allowed herself only a grin as he collared the still-protesting Sir Winston and forcibly marched him off the field.

"This is an outrage," her guest sputtered. "I am a British citizen. Your laws hold no power over me."

"I don't think your queen would see it that way," Lieutenant Prescott told him as they approached the hotel. Elijah, loading trunks onto the stagecoach, raised a brow as they passed, and Caleb, holding the horses, stared outright.

"Are you going to lock him up, Lieutenant Prescott?" Danny asked from the porch.

Sir Winston shrugged out of his grip. "He is not. I refuse to be manhandled."

"Too late," Kate said, unable to stifle her glee. "I'll send your regrets to England." She turned to the lieutenant. "I know you haven't had time to build a jail yet, but you can use the laundry or the root cellar to hold him if you like."

Sir Winston took a step back. "Root cellar?"

Lieutenant Prescott inclined his head, face

firm but the faintest light brightening his moss-colored eyes. "You are too kind, Mrs. Tremaine, but I wouldn't want to inconvenience you or your staff. It will have to be one of our tents, though the accommodations are sadly lacking compared to your fine establishment. I'm not sure we can spare a bed, but since Sir Winston is so fond of the formations, he likely won't mind sleeping on the ground."

"Oh, I say," Sir Winston protested.

Lord and Lady Cavell and their daughter must have heard something of the ruckus, for they came out onto the veranda, their servants right behind. Her ladyship and her daughter gasped, hands pressed to the fine muslin over their chests.

His lordship stepped forward. "See here. What is this all about?"

Lieutenant Prescott kept his gaze on his quarry. "This fellow decided to carve his name into government property. There's a penalty for that."

Sir Winston threw his hands in the air. "It was only a mud pot!"

Lord Cavell snorted. "What can it possibly matter if he carves his name on that?"

Kate glared up at him. "The park is set to claim more than four thousand visitors this season. How do you think those formations would look with four thousand names carved on them?"

"Well, I . . ." He glanced from Kate to the lieutenant, then squared his shoulders. "I see your point. Be a good chap, Winston, and apologize."

Sir Winston looked to the man he obviously hoped might be his father-in-law one day and swallowed. "Yes, of course. A terrible mistake. It won't happen again."

Kate wasn't sure she believed him, but she looked to Lieutenant Prescott. His impassive face gave away none of his thoughts.

"As housing you would inconvenience my men," he said, "I'm inclined to let you off with a warning. But if I hear one more complaint about your behavior — from Mrs. Tremaine, her staff, or any other occupant of the park — I will see that a formal reprimand is sent to your queen. Understand?"

Sir Winston nodded so quickly he might have dizzied himself. "Certainly. I'll just get on the coach now." He hurried to suit word to action.

Danny applauded. So did Miss Cavell and her mother.

Lieutenant Prescott's brows rose in obvious surprise, but Kate didn't have a chance to see the rest of his face before she wrapped her arms around him and hugged.

Heat rushed up Will, and not just because of the applause from the hotel guests and Danny. Kate Tremaine was hugging him as if he'd done something tremendous, as if he was worthy of her admiration.

Gently, he pulled back. "Thank you, ma'am. But I was only doing my duty."

The glow in her gray eyes said otherwise. "And nicely done at that. Yellowstone has its own knight in shining armor."

She wouldn't say that if she knew the truth about him.

Miss Cavell and her mother came down the steps, Lord Cavell right behind and the servants trailing after. The ladies simpered at him as if he was a great hero. The man-servant offered him a nod of approval.

"Valiantly done, sir," Miss Cavell said, going so far as to lay a hand on his arm.

"Don't be late for your coach, dear," Mrs. Tremaine said.

Miss Cavell's smile faded, but she suffered herself to continue with her mother.

"Lieutenant," her father said as he passed.

Will watched as Elijah helped them all into the stagecoach. The things were designed so that the windows held no glass or shutters. They could seat six to eight tightly packed inside, while others could ride on the roof. He'd seen as many as ten crowded together. That wouldn't be the case with the Cavell party, of course. They had sufficient funds to tour in style. Miss Cavell took out her handkerchief and waved it at him as Elijah drove them out of the yard. Caleb sent him a shy smile before heading back to the barn.

Will turned his attention to Mrs. Tremaine, whose eyes were narrowed on the coach as if she could will it out of the park.

"Let me know if you have any further trouble," he told her.

Face clearing, she looked up at him. "Oh, I will. And please remember my invitation. You are welcome to dine with us anytime."

"I appreciate the offer." But perhaps it would be best if he refused from now on. He excused himself and went to see to Bess. The mare eyed him as if she understood full well he was running away.

"At least you know me," he muttered to his mount.

And whose fault was it that his closest confidante was his horse?

Will sighed as he rode back toward his camp. Even now, the vast lands of the park seemed to settle around him. The elk had gone; the dusty road was empty to the north. No hawk called overhead. It was all too easy to feel alone.

But being alone was a decision in the Army. Despite Captain Harris's admonitions, Will chose to spend more time among his men than the typical cavalry officer would. He'd learned a number of things about them. Lercher had a fondness for cinnamon. Franklin still wasn't easy in the saddle. O'Reilly had a sweetheart who wrote to him at least once a week. They each had reasons for being in the Army. Lercher and Waxworth wanted promotion, O'Reilly a way to distinguish himself, Franklin the opportunity to move into the engineering corps, and Smith, if Will was right, the chance to begin a new life. As their superior, he could help them reach those goals.

Unfortunately, he knew more about them than any of them knew about him. Becoming close, to anyone, held challenges. Captain Harris had reviewed his service record, but Will's men were in ignorance, as far as he could tell. At least no one had asked why a second lieutenant had made rank without earning his spurs, something even new recruits strived to do in their first few months. He could not confess how he'd earned them and lost them. His men had joined the regiment since that fateful day eight years ago, and most of the remaining parties involved had moved on. No one was left to tell the ignoble tale, unless he opened his mouth. So he didn't open it any more than necessary.

A shame that didn't stop him from remembering.

6

Will Prescott did not come to dinner. Kate wasn't the only one who noticed.

"I thought Lieutenant Prescott was joining us," Alberta said as she ladled some stew in a bowl for Danny.

"He has work to do, same as us," Kate said, filling a cloth-lined basket with more of Alberta's buttermilk biscuits for the guests in the dining room beyond.

"I saw him ride by," Danny offered, perched on the chair at the worktable and foot swinging. "He didn't stop."

His disappointment echoed inside Kate. "He probably noticed there were no visitors on the geyser field. No reason to stop."

Alberta humphed. "A man needs to eat. My Joe always remembered that. Mr. Tremaine as well, God rest their souls."

Kate offered her a smile. Alberta had lost husband and son to the War Between the States. She'd been serving as a cook at a

94

boardinghouse in her native Ohio when she'd seen an ad about a position in Yellowstone. Kate had asked her once why she'd taken such a chance, moved so far from everything she'd ever known.

"Too much darkness in my life back then," she'd said. "I wanted to spend the rest of my days surrounded by beauty."

She couldn't have chosen a better place, to Kate's mind.

Her latest visitors seemed to agree. Elijah had driven the Cavells and Sir Winston out of the park and would likely stay at least a day or so with his wife and son near Cinnabar. But the Wakefield and Hoffman stage driver had brought another eight visitors. They'd hurried out of the coach, chatting eagerly. From what they'd written in the guest book, they intended to stay only a night.

That was the way of the tourist trade in Yellowstone. Visitors came by rail to either Monida or Cinnabar, then traveled by coach, wagon, or pack train through the park for a week to ten days. Some camped. Most stayed in hotels. The stage companies escorted their groups from the rail station, through the park, and back. Some visitors who came on their own wrote ahead to secure a room. Others simply showed up at her door, expecting hospitality. Toward the end of the season, like now, she could more likely accommodate them.

As well as the circuit rider, Mr. Yates, who rode in just as the sun was setting that evening.

Mr. Yates was one of several ministers who traveled through the park each season. Kate was a little surprised someone hadn't built a permanent chapel yet. Most of the circuit riders stopped at Mammoth Hot Springs and Old Faithful, but Mr. Yates had shown up at her door in June, and she'd given him permission to use the salon for services. He took his place before the stone hearth that morning, dark frock coat at odds with the natural colors of the stones. Her guests settled on the dining chairs, which Pansy and the other maids had lined up in front of him. Alberta and the rest of her staff slipped into the back row with Danny.

Kate stood in the doorway to the kitchen, drying dishes and only half listening as the minister opened in prayer and his makeshift congregation all bowed their heads. Beyond them, Will Prescott was coming in the front door. She thought he might join them, but he pulled up short, then gingerly backed out as if determined not to disturb the service.

A few moments later, the back door creaked as it opened, and she turned to find him edging inside.

"Didn't want to bother your guests," he said quietly.

She nodded, but she drew a deep breath, as if the warm kitchen was filled with the heady scent of roses rather than the familiar smell of Alberta's oatmeal. Odd that having him here made her feel more comfortable in her own kitchen.

He moved cautiously toward her around the big worktable, and she closed the door as Mr. Yates began reading from the Psalms. *The Lord is my shepherd, I shall not want.*

She smiled against the tug of the words. She and Danny did not want for shelter or food, and she was grateful. But both were predicated on keeping the inn running smoothly.

"I can finish drying if you'd like to be out there," Lieutenant Prescott said.

Kate chuckled. "I'm not about to waste your help on something Danny and I can manage on our own. That's why you're here, isn't it? To offer your time?"

Something crossed behind his eyes. "Of course."

Now, why did that disappoint her? What other reason could he have for appearing in her kitchen?

Kate focused on her list. "Next is the chimney here in the kitchen. Alberta says it's not drawing properly. Can you fix it? Unless you want to attend services yourself."

"No, thank you." He began unbuttoning his coat. "But excuse me while I shuck this off. I need to keep my uniform clean of soot. Not much opportunity for laundry."

"Have one of your men come use ours," Kate offered, trying not to notice the play of muscle as he pulled the coat off his shoulders. "Saturdays and Tuesdays we generally have less."

"Thanks. I guess that means we'll owe you more hours."

Kate grinned. "I guess it does."

As he draped his coat on a chair, she put the dish away and picked up another from the towels in the center of the table. Mr. Yates's sermon was no more than a buzz beyond the door.

Lieutenant Prescott approached the massive stone hearth on the outside wall and twisted to put his head inside and look up. The low fire below him lit his profile and reflected pink on his cotton shirt.

"Something's partially blocking it higher up," he said, voice echoing. "Hand me a broom."

Kate went to the corner cupboard, where the brooms and mops were stored, and brought him back a long-handled broom. Clutching the corn at the base, he shoved the stick up into the flue — once, twice.

The buzzing grew louder, and it was a moment before she realized Mr. Yates wasn't shouting at her guests. Like black smoke, wasps poured from the opening.

Kate grabbed Will's arm and tugged him back, then ran to the rear door of the kitchen and threw it open. "Get out!" she shouted at the swarm. "Go on!"

The wasps circled the kitchen, an angry cloud of frustration, and she seized one of the other brooms to defend herself. But they arrowed for the door and disappeared into a cloudy sky.

Kate lowered the broom and drew in a breath. Will was eying the fallen remains of a wasps' nest, the papery shell flaming in the fire. A few stragglers crawled out to take off up the chimney.

"I didn't mean to kill them."

His tone was stricken, raising an answering ache inside her. Setting the broom aside, she closed the distance. "Were you stung?"

His face was pale, his eyes unfocused. Alarmed, she touched his arm. "Lieutenant

Prescott? Will? Are you all right?"

His Adam's apple bobbed as he swallowed. "Fine."

Gently, Kate turned him to face her. He looked past her, as if he couldn't meet her gaze.

"It's all right," she said. "I know I scolded your men for even thinking about harming the wildlife, but this was an accident."

"They're still dead." So was his voice, his aspect.

"No, they aren't," she protested. "Most went out the door. They'll make another nest before winter. No harm done."

His breath came in a gulp. "No harm done," he repeated, as if desperate to believe the statement. "If that will be all, Mrs. Tremaine, I should go."

He turned away from her before she could protest that he'd given her less than a quarter hour. Then she caught sight of the swelling red welt on his neck.

"Hold on there, Soldier," she ordered. "You've been injured."

He frowned, and she pointed to his neck. "One of your foes left a mark. Sit over there. I have baking soda."

For a moment, she thought he might refuse, but he went to perch on the chair that held his coat, and she was pleased to

100

see color returning to his cheeks.

She went to grab the container. After shaking a bit in a bowl, she added enough water to make a paste and returned to him. As she pulled away the neck of his shirt, he tilted his head to one side. The column of his neck was so smooth, so strong. A flutter faster than wasp wings started in her chest.

Silly. She'd tended Danny's scrapes and stings, Toby's bruises, the minor injuries of her guests. The work had never left her feeling warm and slightly dizzy. Perhaps the baking soda had gone bad. She sniffed the bowl and shook her head.

"Something wrong?" he asked as if he'd noticed her reaction.

"No," she assured him, dipping up some of the paste to dab it on the welt. "Just feeling thankful. Considering how many there were and their agitation, it's a miracle we weren't stung more."

"Well, it is Sunday," he said. "Good day for miracles, if you believe in that sort of thing."

She eyed him as she wiped her fingers off on the edge of the bowl. "You don't believe in miracles?"

His gaze met hers at last, deep, dark, troubled. "Do you?"

She went to take the bowl to the big

porcelain sink. "Maybe. This whole place is a miracle if you ask me — the colors, the geysers, the bison."

"So why not attend services?" he asked.

Why not?

The question poked at her, demanded an answer. She turned, putting her hands behind her on the cool rim of the sink. He was watching her, head still cocked, shoulders slumped as if he'd ridden long and hard.

"I don't know," Kate admitted. "Toby, my husband, always went whenever a preacher came within riding distance. Now there's one on the other side of that door, and I can't seem to walk through."

He straightened and dropped his gaze toward his black boots. "Easy to think you don't belong."

That wasn't it. This was her home, her place. If she belonged anywhere, it was here. She knew some wondered whether she blamed God for Toby's death. She didn't. Toby had brought his death on himself. She still wished he'd listened to her that night, but Toby had always done what Toby wanted to do.

"We belong," she told Will. "We just put other duty first. I don't think God minds."

■ ■ ■ ■

We, she said, as if her conscience could possibly be as stained as his. He had a long way to go before he felt comfortable bringing his thoughts or his presence before God, even in a church as informal as the salon of the Geyser Gateway.

His reaction to the wasps proved as much. For one moment, as flames licked up the nest and its inhabitants struggled to escape, he'd remembered other bodies lying on the soil, belongings scattered as if they'd tried to run. And that time, none had lived.

"I gave up trying to think like God," he said, rising. "But I agree we have a duty. I should get to mine."

Her brows went up. "After less than a half hour?"

A half hour and eight years, but he couldn't bring himself to tell her that. "Sorry. Best I can do at the moment. And at least you crossed something off your list."

She smiled. "There is that."

"I'll be busy the next few days," he said, edging for the door and feeling like a coward again, "but I'll check in when I have time to offer."

She nodded, and he left, her curious gaze

following him from the hotel.

He tried to push back the thoughts of his past as he worked that day and into the next week. They weathered a storm that sent lightning and thunder across the basin, the bright jagged forks plunging into the surrounding hills. He followed his men on patrol, made sure they were heeding her advice on where to ride and what to consider, especially Smith, who had remained in camp during her instruction. He ordered his standoffish private to introduce himself to Kate and her staff.

"I took the liberty," Smith had assured him. "Interesting woman. I can see why she fascinates you."

The others had glanced up from their dinner at his comment.

"My only fascination," Will had told them all, "is the Geyser Gateway and its ability to comfortably house those who come to Yellowstone."

They had seemed to accept that, though Smith continued to eye him, brow raised.

The only trouble came from a party at the Fire Hole Hotel on Monday. The six men were determined that they had a right to hunt. Only drawn weapons had convinced them otherwise, thankfully before any elk, deer, or antelope were killed.

"Not like when Roy Jessup roamed these parts," one of them complained as Lercher confiscated their guns and ammunition.

"Mr. Jessup has been escorted from Yellowstone," Will told him. "He will not be returning."

The big-boned man had sneered at him. "That's what you think."

"If you have information about a poacher in the park, you better start talking," Waxworth had threatened.

The hunter had shaken his head. "Doesn't matter. You won't catch him this time. He's too savvy. But you better watch your backs."

"That's enough from you," Waxworth had said. "Or we'll be watching *your* backs, all the way out of the park."

They'd left the hunters, and the management of the Fire Hole Hotel, with a warning. He could only hope they would heed it.

Tuesday morning, as Will was overseeing the collection of laundry to be taken to the Geyser Gateway, a teamster drove into camp with supplies from Camp Sheridan at Mammoth Hot Springs, including a load of lumber to begin building a more permanent structure for their station.

"Enough lumber and nails for about ten-foot by ten-foot square," Franklin reported to Will after the other supplies had been stowed and the building materials inventoried. The private had worked with a contractor before joining the military.

"Sure'n that will be making for close quarters," O'Reilly said, studying the pile.

"Vill they send vindows too?" Lercher asked with a frown.

"Glass panes are too difficult to transport," Will told him. "Private Franklin, you are in charge of the building. Smith will take your place on patrol. As for windows, leave holes on each side and cover them with internal shutters."

None of his men looked thrilled by the prospect. Will was just glad to know they'd have a roof over their heads before winter, even if that roof would have to be made of sod.

Then again, sod was a lot easier to deal with than Kate's cedar shakes.

That was her next task for him when he reported for duty on Wednesday — repairing the inn's roof where a windstorm had displaced some of the cedar.

"I have a box of shakes from the lumber mill at Bozeman," she said, pointing him toward the barn, "a mallet, and a ladder. Tap any loose shingles back into line, and replace any that have been cracked or lost."

He studied the sharply slanted roof two

stories above him. "You don't have a mountain goat you could ask?"

"Alas, they're busy with the laundry," she said.

"Eagle?" he tried.

"At a ball at Mammoth Hot Springs. It will have to be the cavalry."

He saluted her. "Ma'am."

With an encouraging smile, she returned to the inn.

Her son came out onto the veranda as Will was positioning the ladder. His blue eyes brightened. "Can I come up too?"

"Officers only," Will said, trying to think how to carry the shakes and a mallet up the wooden ladder.

"But I could help," Danny protested. "I'm really good at climbing, and I could show you the places that need to be fixed."

No way was he allowing the boy on that precarious slope.

"You know what would help the most?" Will asked.

Danny shook his head.

Will pointed to the box of shakes and then the roof. "Figure how to get those up there."

Danny came down the steps and turned to look up at the roof. Then he shot Will a grin that looked suspiciously like his mother's. "That's easy."

An hour later, Will heard Kate's voice below. "What are you doing!"

He shifted carefully and glanced down. She had her hands on the hips of her tailored blue dress and her head was bent as she looked down at her son. Sunlight sparkled in the black tresses.

"Helping Lieutenant Prescott," Danny said. "Watch." He picked up a shake from the box, heaved back his arm, and let it fly. The cedar clattered down within a foot of Will. He reached out to keep it from sliding farther.

"You could have hit him," Kate scolded. "Or worse, broke a window."

"No, ma'am," Will called down. "He has a real talent for it. He hasn't missed yet."

Danny puffed himself up.

Kate shifted on her feet, setting her skirts to swinging. He could see the struggle in her. Pride in her son warred with concern for his safety.

"What if one slides off, hits you on the head?" she asked the boy.

Danny rolled his eyes. "I would see it coming, Ma. Besides, Lieutenant Prescott is good too. He only let one slide off."

Kate aimed her glare his way.

Will held up his hands and nearly lost his balance. "What can I say?" he called down when he'd righted himself. "The eagles are still at the ball."

"What ball?" Danny asked, brows lifting.

"He means a dance," Kate explained.

"Eagles go dancing?"

Her face softened. "You might think so the way they ride the wind."

"So can I keep helping?" Danny asked. "Please?" Will sent down.

"Please?" Danny repeated with considerably more of a wheedle in his voice.

She laid a hand on her son's shoulder. "Yes, Danny. It sounds like you and Lieutenant Prescott have worked things out so both of you are safe."

She glanced up at him again, and he nodded. "Yes, ma'am. Thank you."

She released her son. "You're welcome, Lieutenant. It's nice having two men about the house again."

"Like Pa," Danny said.

The mallet nearly slipped from his grip. It had been a long time since anyone, especially himself, had considered him a candidate for a husband or a father. He wasn't sure how long Kate had been a widow, but surely she'd correct her son.

Instead, her smile was sweeter than her usual grin, as if she wasn't opposed to the idea.

He stared at her, stunned.

She gazed back, assessing, challenging, but her cheeks were turning redder than O'Reilly's hair. He couldn't speak as she dropped her gaze at last and hurried for the inn.

Which was for the best. Very likely neither of them was ready to think about Will taking a more formal role in the life of the Geyser Gateway Inn, or the heart of its pretty owner.

7

Kate swept into the hotel, feeling as if her face were on fire. What was she doing staring so boldly at Will Prescott?

Danny had compared him to Toby. Toby had been friend, comforter, husband, yet he'd rarely made her feel as if she was the most precious being in the world. But sometimes, the look on Will's face and the tone of his voice combined to make her feel positively beautiful. And his hard work was only to be praised. That must be why she admired him so much.

Still, she and Danny weren't the only ones who admired Will's presence at the inn. Having the cavalry around certainly affected Kate's visitors. Lady travelers were more likely to venture out when they saw a man in blue riding by. Gentlemen stopped bringing back souvenirs of the pieces they'd broken off the geysers. She hadn't had to pull out her rifle in days, and she hadn't spotted any newly carved marks on the formations or the trees when she did her morning and afternoon sweeps of the area. And Ida reported no more forks missing.

"An excellent improvement," Elijah agreed when he brought her the next group of guests on Wednesday. "I hear Captain Harris has Mammoth Hot Springs nearly licked into shape as well. A shame the season's almost over."

Kate felt it too. Temperatures were slowly dropping. The late wildflowers had appeared in the meadows beyond the circuit road, yellows and blues and whites poking up sleepy heads. She and her maids had been to pick the last of the huckleberries. The basin would see its first frost soon. She had a lot to do to be ready to ride out the winter.

Will finished the roof on Thursday afternoon. He climbed down the ladder and jumped the last three rungs to land on the chalky soil with a puff of dust that coated his boots.

"Mission accomplished, General," he told her as she came in from her afternoon sweep.

She smiled. "Well done, Lieutenant. You can start on the shutters next. I want them straight and oiled before the next windstorm."

He saluted. "Ma'am."

Danny, who had been waiting on the ground, saluted as well. "Ma'am."

"Ah, no, Private Tremaine," Kate said. "I have another mission for you."

Danny's face fell. "Don't we have enough wood?"

It might not be the most glamorous job, but neither were many of the routines around the inn.

"Stack one more row," Kate compromised. "Then you can come help me."

Danny's eyes narrowed. "What will you be doing?"

Kate wiggled her brows. "Painting. Just down the wall from Lieutenant Prescott."

"Yes, ma'am!" Danny ran for the back of the inn.

"Never knew painting was such a treat," Will said, watching him round the corner.

"I have a feeling the treat isn't the painting," Kate said. "It's you."

"Best I get the hammer and the oil can." He turned away and headed for the barn.

Kate shook her head. He was so different from Toby. From most of the men she'd known, truth be told. Both her father and Toby had preened for any praise given. Toby had gone so far as to encourage it.

"Excellent piece of work, if I say so

myself," he had declared after putting up signs displaying the names of the various geysers. Then he'd looked to her.

"Very helpful," Kate had said, taking her cue.

"Attractive too," he'd pointed out. "Black lettering on white. The new superintendent should be pleased. Do you think the guests will like them?"

Before he was satisfied, she'd had to assure him that the superintendent at the time, his assistants, and the hotel guests would admire them as much as she did. He'd nodded along, but she'd heard him pointing out his handiwork to visitors for weeks afterward.

Will never sought approval. In fact, praise and appreciation seemed to make him uncomfortable. He appeared to be confident he'd accomplished what he set out to do, and that was enough. Rather commendable.

Not that he'd accept praise for those traits either.

A short time later, she was on the veranda, swathed in an apron and armed with a paintbrush, touching up spots along the front of the hotel. The southwest wall on her left bore most of the brunt of the wind, but her guests' first impression of the hotel was the more important. She still remembered her first impression when Toby had brought her here after learning that their investment might be in jeopardy.

Toby had invested in many things, sometimes only a little and often with as little return. It was part of his visionary nature, the same nature that had become obsessed with taking over the lease from the original owner. Mr. Carter, an entrepreneur originally from the Boston area, had built the Geyser Gateway and convinced old acquaintances, like Toby and his father, to invest.

"Think of all the people who will flock to a national park," Toby had said, eyes gleaming. "And we can visit there every year if we like."

Then Mr. Carter had been injured. He'd written that unless one of his investors could arrange for a new innkeeper, they'd all lose their money. Toby had insisted that he and Kate come out to see the place. One night at the inn, two days in this glorious country, and she'd offered him the money her parents had left her to buy out the other investors. They had never returned to Boston. She never planned to leave. Toby would certainly never leave. His body was buried in the cemetery at Mammoth Hot Springs with a simple stone cross she'd commissioned in Bozeman.

But she and Danny might be forced to leave if she couldn't prove to Captain Harris that the Geyser Gateway had as good a service or better than any other park hotel. And the hope of that ten-year lease beckoned. She could rest secure that she and Danny had a home. Captain Harris just had to see the glory of the Geyser Gateway.

So, she kept working. With a wire brush, she scraped off the loose paint, then covered the raw wood with yellow. Butter yellow, Toby had claimed when he'd brought home the gallons of paint the first time. She couldn't deny it was cheerful.

Just down the way, Will pushed up on a shutter and held it in place while he tightened the hinges. Then he squeezed out a few drips from the oil can.

"That looks much better," Kate told him.

He swung the shutter back and forth as if testing it. "It should do. When do you and Danny leave for the winter?"

Kate chuckled as she rasped the wire brush over the next piece of wood. "Hoping to get out of our deal sooner rather than later?"

He stepped back to eye the shutter as if confirming its alignment. "No. Just trying to determine the amount of time my men and I have to prepare. Captain Harris sent lumber for a permanent building."

"You'd better get to work then," Kate said, slathering on paint. "I figure four weeks, maybe six if we're lucky, before the snow starts flying."

He grabbed the shutter on the other side of the window and nudged it up and out. "Might be enough time for what we have. Franklin figures we can construct a ten-by-ten shanty."

She paused. "For six men?"

He tightened the hinge. "Six men, six months. We'll either be a band of brothers or mortal enemies by the end."

Kate shuddered as she returned to her work. "You won't make it. The supplies alone will take up most of the space. I know how much we have to put up for Alberta, Danny, and me."

Now he paused. "You overwinter?"

"We're one of the few," she acknowledged. "We move our beds to the salon and only heat it and the kitchen. We stock the cellar under the kitchen to the rim. We do get an occasional guest — usually a visiting professor or an avid gamesman. And the presence of the geysers means this area keeps a little less snow on the ground than in the higher elevations of the park."

He shook his head. "Two women and a

boy alone for months. Is that safe?"

She grinned at him. "You wait, Lieutenant. There's nothing like a Yellowstone winter. Few venture in. Many of the animals hibernate. It's probably the safest time to be out here."

"Done!" Danny shouted as he ran around the side of the hotel. "Where should I paint, General?"

Much as she approved of him copying Will, she couldn't quite accustom herself to being called by a military rank.

"Where should I paint, Mother?" she suggested.

"Yes, where?" He scampered up the steps and to her side.

Will moved to the shutter closest to her. Kate handed Danny the wire brush. "Why don't you buff off the old paint, and I'll follow with the new?"

"Deal." Danny set to work.

Kate painted on the yellow and stepped back to check for other bare patches. That's when she noticed Will hadn't moved. Indeed, her cheeks warmed in his regard.

"You missed a spot," he said.

Kate frowned, glancing at the wall. "Where?"

He closed the distance between them. "Just there." His thumb caressed her cheek.

She couldn't seem to breathe, to move. She was tumbling, into his gaze, toward his embrace.

No, no, no. Such feelings were not in her plan. She had so much to do. He wouldn't be here long. She had to take care of Danny. She knew the dangers of falling in love again.

Would those excuses be enough to convince her heart?

No, no, no. Where had these feelings come from? He wanted to hold her, to protect her as fiercely as she protected her son and these lands. But he had a job to do, men to lead. Lercher, Waxworth, Franklin, and the others were his family now. He was still atoning for his actions eight years ago. He had enough on his hands without the added responsibility of Kate and Danny.

He pulled away. "There. No harm done."

"None at all," she said, but her eyes narrowed as if she didn't believe that. She turned away from him to inspect her son's work.

Will blew out a breath. What had he been thinking to touch her that way? Sure, there'd been a drop of yellow paint on the golden tan of her skin, but he could have just let her know or offered her his handkerchief. There was no reason to let his thumb linger on the soft, smooth skin, so warm, so vibrant.

He marched himself down to the next shutter and gave it a shove. The hinges creaked in protest.

He had just finished tightening them when he heard the drum of a horse approaching. Kate and Danny also turned at the sound. Will had become accustomed to the movements of her guests. Most set out and returned at a leisurely pace. This rider galloped down the road, and Will caught sight of the cavalry coat and yellow-striped trousers a moment before he recognized O'Reilly. The Irishman careened into the yard and pulled up his horse so sharply it reared.

"Message from Captain Harris," he barked as he settled to earth. "Forest fire raging to the southwest of Mammoth Hot Springs. He's asking for our help to fight it."

Will set the oil can on the porch rail and nodded to Kate. "I must go." He started for the steps.

"Will, wait."

The sound of his first name rather than the command pulled him up short. She moved to his side. Her misty eyes were

120

wide, her lips trembled.

"Ma'am?" he asked.

She laid a hand on his arm. "Just . . . be careful."

He smiled. "You've taught us well. We'll be on the watch for any danger."

She released him and stepped back, and he went to fetch Bess from where he'd left her in the corral beside the barn.

He and O'Reilly cantered back to camp together. "Who brought the news, Private?" he asked as they rounded the bend from the Geyser Gateway. Something tugged at him, like a hand on his shoulder, urging him back to the inn, but he shrugged it off.

"It was brought by the telephone," O'Reilly said, awe creeping into his voice. The Yellowstone Park Association had put in telephones at all its hotels, allowing the Army free use. The messages ran down telegraph wires strung in discreet locations to prevent distracting from the wonders.

"Fellow from the hotel took down the words and carried the message over to us," the Irishman continued. "Private Lercher was all for waiting until you returned, but Mr. Smith insisted we open it right then."

"Smith was right," Will said. "A message from headquarters should brook no delay. Did it mention whether the fire started from a lightning strike or some other cause?"

"Captain Harris wasn't saying," O'Reilly allowed. "But the clerk from the Fire Hole had his own opinion, he did. The story going about is that Jessup is back in the park and looking to take his revenge." He spit over the side of his horse.

But the note held a bit more explanation when Will received it at camp. Captain Harris had ordered him to send three of his men north, while the rest remained on duty at the Lower Geyser Basin.

Three of his men. Not him. Harris was excluding him from any chance of valor or promotion. It seemed Will wasn't the only one who thought he needed to do penance. Still, he knew who would most benefit from the opportunity.

"Smith and Franklin, with me," he told his men. "Waxworth, Lercher, and O'Reilly, gather your kit. Report to Captain Harris at Mammoth Hot Springs. And gentlemen," he added as they started for their tents, "do us proud. Mr. Jessup doesn't get away with this."

O'Reilly paused to salute. "Sir."

Will's stomach tightened as he watched his men ride north a short time later. What he'd told Kate was right — they knew the dangers. And they knew his and Captain

Harris's expectations of them. That had to be enough for them to reach Camp Sheridan with no repercussions, to them or to Yellowstone.

"We'll need to adjust the routine," he told Smith and Franklin as they finished a dinner of salt pork and beans Waxworth had started earlier. "We'll each take a watch at night. Private Smith, I expect you to pick up the cooking."

Smith raised a dark brow. "You're a braver man than I took you for, Lieutenant."

Franklin hastily added a second helping to his plate, as if concerned it might be their last decent meal.

Will chose not to respond to Smith directly. "We'll alternate patrols during the day. I'll take mornings with Smith and afternoons with Franklin. That way Smith can be in camp to cook dinner, and Franklin can work mornings on the cabin."

Franklin shook his head. "I appreciate your faith in me, Lieutenant, and this opportunity to prove I'm more than a horse soldier, but I can't make much progress on my own."

"And I imagine the Widow Tremaine will miss your company if you must patrol all day," Smith put in, sliding a sliver of wood into his mouth like a cigar.

"I've done enough to repay Mrs. Tremaine for her kindness to us thus far," Will said, reminding his private of the purpose of his visits. "We still need her help to learn the wider area, but we'll hold off on that until we're fully staffed again. Any questions?"

"Only about the cabin, sir," Franklin said. "As far as I can tell, there isn't enough lumber to build bunks, and not enough room to sleep six to a floor and still have room for supplies."

Just as Kate had warned.

"I'll alert Captain Harris to send more lumber," Will promised. "After they've dealt with this fire."

"If he doesn't, we'll be drawing lots as to who keeps a tent," Smith predicted.

"Leave the provisioning to me, Private," Will said. "None of us would survive sleeping out this winter."

"And what of the horses?" Smith challenged. "If there's not enough wood for bunks, there won't be enough for a barn."

He was right. Will was so used to living in a well-provisioned fort, or terrain that didn't require shelter from snow, that he hadn't considered what they'd do with the horses. Besides the barn, they'd need hay, oats for the winter. There'd be nowhere to graze. Surely Captain Harris had considered that.

Yet Kate had said there was only a month or six weeks left before they'd need those supplies and shelters. When did Harris think they'd have an opportunity to build?

As if he was having the same concerns, Franklin edged closer in the firelight. "Any chance of us requisitioning space from one of the property owners, sir?"

"Not from the Fire Hole," Smith told him. "I've spoken to the manager a few times as I rode through. They plan to close up for the winter by the middle of October."

They both looked to him, and he knew what they were thinking. The only buildings left in the area that might have space to house them and their horses were the ones at the Geyser Gateway. Kate had plenty of room for them in the hotel, and she had plans to overwinter. With Elijah's six horses out of the park, there would be space for their horses in the barn. But adding another six people to the inn would tax her supplies to the breaking point. Even with the supplies Captain Harris would surely send for the cavalrymen and their mounts, there was the additional wood for heating more rooms, the laundry, the strain of having guests for months.

He would have to make some tough choices soon. And he didn't relish having to explain the situation to Kate if he was forced to choose the well-being of his family over hers.

8

Kate couldn't deny the surge of relief as Will and Private Smith rode into the yard the next morning.

"False alarm?" she asked as they reined in beside the hitching post. "No, ma'am," Will said, touching the brim of his dun hat. "Three of my men are up north, helping Captain Harris fight a fire."

Kate frowned. "Careless campers?"

Will nodded to Private Smith, who set his horse on a circuit around the perimeter of the geyser field. Most of Kate's guests had moved on, but a couple from Minnesota was out among the wonders. Their gasp floated back to her just as Fountain Geyser shot steam and spray dozens of feet into the cloudy sky.

Will swung down from the saddle. "No campers, as far as I know. This fire was most likely arson, set by a vengeful poacher." He tied his horse to the hitching post. "I wouldn't worry. The flames shouldn't head in this direction."

"You're right about the direction," Kate said, watching Private Smith make a wide berth around the paint pots. "But you may be wrong about why it was started. Superintendent Wear seemed to think the fires earlier this summer were set by men out to damage his reputation. There's another reason why a poacher would set such a fire."

Will eyed her. "Oh?"

Kate nodded toward the north. "Think of the location — southwest of Mammoth Hot Springs this time. The northeast corner of the park earlier. In both cases, the prevailing winds would push the flames to the northeast, right out of the park. And the animals will flee before it."

He reared back, brows shooting up like a geyser. "Someone's trying to drive the animals beyond the park boundary."

"Where hunters can ply their trade all they like," Kate confirmed. "I never could get Superintendent Wear to listen."

"I'm listening," he promised, settling on his feet. "I'll telephone Mammoth Hot Springs as soon as we finish the morning patrol. A shame I didn't talk to you sooner."

Kate wagged a finger at him. "Well, then, learn your lesson, Lieutenant. You should always discuss your orders with me first."

He snapped a salute. "Yes, General Tremaine."

She could get used to that smile. "I shouldn't keep you from your appointed rounds."

He nodded toward Private Smith, who was coming around the back of the Celestine Pool, the brown of his mount reflected in the blue waters. "We have it in hand. It's quiet this morning. Are you low on visitors at the moment?"

"I'm expecting a party of six for the night."

"And you've had no further trouble like you had with Sir Winston?"

She smiled, remembering. "None. Your patrols are very effective. Must be something about a man in uniform."

He snorted. "Just don't tell them we have little legal recourse. I know there were constables in the park for a time, before the laws of Wyoming no longer held sway. The best we can do is seize their belongings and escort them to the park boundary."

Kate sighed. "That may work for the sightseers, but the poachers will just re-equip and return."

He shrugged. "Our hands are tied unless Congress acts." He nodded beyond the geyser field, where Private Smith was just approaching Jelly Geyser. "What's to the southwest of us, the area you marked as off-limits on the map? Perhaps we ought to patrol there too, make sure no one is setting fires."

She wasn't ready to show him what lay in that direction. Treasure, Toby had called it with shining eyes. Danny called it their special spot. As far as she knew, none of her guests and no poacher had discovered it yet, and she intended to keep it that way for as long as possible.

"We have bigger fish to fry," she told him. "Do you know your way around the vicinity of the Fire Hole Hotel yet?"

His mouth quirked. "I'm sorry to say the manager there has been far less helpful than another innkeeper I could mention."

She should not feel so pleased about that. "A shame. But I've been in this park longer than he has, and I can show you what to watch for."

"I hadn't planned on studying the terrain now, and I can't repay you with work," he warned. "Until my other men return, I won't have time off to help around the inn."

"Disappointing, but understandable," Kate allowed. "Still, when you finish at the geyser field, we should take a little ride north."

He inclined his head. "Happy to oblige, ma'am. May I saddle you a horse?"

"That would be very helpful, Soldier. My sidesaddle should be hanging over the first stall."

She watched as he sauntered toward the barn. She could get used to that sight too.

She hastily directed her gaze out over the geyser field. Private Smith was circling Morning Geyser. He reached her just as Danny came running around the side of the hotel.

"Good morning, Mrs. Tremaine," the private said, tipping his cavalry cap to Kate.

"Private Smith." Kate put out a hand to catch her son before he darted past. "I'll be joining you and the lieutenant on the way north."

"Our pleasure," he said. "Are you headed out of the park?"

"Only to the Fire Hole," Kate assured him. "I promised Lieutenant Prescott I would show you some areas you need to consider in your patrols."

Danny squirmed in her grip. "I finished my chores. Can I come too?"

The word no pressed against her lips. Habit. She truly had no reason to deny him this time. Surely with two cavalrymen and her on the ride, he'd be safe.

"All right," she said. "Saddle Buttercup, and you can join us. If you'll excuse us, Private, I need to change into my riding habit."

A short time later, they all rode out of the yard. Danny sat as tall and proud as a cavalryman on the pony she kept for smaller guests. He'd had to shorten the stirrup strip for his legs, but it seemed to Kate that the leather was a little longer than the last time they'd gone riding. She would have to make him new trousers for winter. Would he still be able to wear them come spring?

Yet that round face was all boy. She reached out to ruffle his silky hair.

He ducked away with a protest, causing the pony to shy. "Ma!"

His ears were red, but Will and Private Smith didn't comment.

"Captain Tremaine," Will said with a nod to Danny. "Allow me to introduce you to Private Smith."

The private's busy beard parted as he smiled and saluted Danny. "Your servant, sir."

Danny giggled. "I'm not really a captain."

The private nodded wisely. "I thought as much. Clearly a major."

Danny shook his head, but he was all smiles now.

"Oh," Smith said. "Major General. My mistake, sir. It won't happen again."

"Keep protesting," Will said to Danny, "and you might find yourself president." He turned to Kate. "I yield to you, ma'am. Guide us where you wish."

For a moment, held in his gaze, she nearly forgot where she had intended to take them. She shook herself and turned her horse north.

When she'd first come to Yellowstone, the road toward the Norris Geyser Basin and Mammoth Hot Springs had been little more than a rutted trail through the pines and across the basin floor, stumps still evident. Now it was in good shape, thanks to the work of the Corps of Engineers. Lieutenant Kingman and his road crews had mounded the dirt so that water ran off both sides. They'd also added drainage ditches along the edges to carry the runoff away from the road. It was wide enough that stagecoaches could pass each other if needed.

The road wound through a wide prairie where white soil showed through sparse grass. A hawk circled overhead, then dove for prey. Antelope bounded away at their approach.

"Good spot for game," Will observed.

"That's why I suggested you check it once

in a while," Kate said. She nodded to the cream-colored cloth flapping against the bark of the lone pine they were passing. "I see your Captain Harris has been busy."

One corner of his mouth tilted up. "My men were told to post those hunting warnings at regular intervals along the road and at major attractions. We ran out before we reached the Geyser Gateway, but I figured you had that covered."

She smiled. "I do my best." Glancing back, she saw that Danny was moving along, gaze darting from tree to prairie to Private Smith riding beside him. He met her look and waved, then hastily clutched his reins again.

"Are there other children in the park?" Will asked as if he had noticed the direction of her smile.

"Elijah sometimes brings his son, Markus," Kate replied as they reached the pine forest on the other side of the prairie. "They live outside the park, near the Cinnabar Rail Station. Mammoth Hot Springs has a few children. We have a teacher and school there during the winter months. I send Danny when I can."

His gaze was out over the road ahead. "Must get lonely for him."

She glanced back again. Danny was chatting with Private Smith, asking him about his horse, his gun, how many outlaws he'd tracked down, all in the course of the moments she watched. The private began to look as if he faced a firing squad.

She turned to the front. "I don't think Danny knows how to be lonely. He's like his father that way. He never met a person who wasn't his friend within the first few minutes."

"Nice way to live," he said, and she thought he sounded envious.

Ahead, the pines opened up again to a meadow on either side of the road, leading to the Little Firehole River. To the left, a dirt track ran toward the hotel. The two-story block squatted among scattered pines, windows staring at the road as if awaiting the next guests.

"Including the two cabins," Kate said, "the Fire Hole can house two dozen guests, give or take. You'll need to keep an eye on them. The Hendersons run the place now, but before they arrived, George Marshall wasn't too serious about enforcing the rules where hunting and alcohol were concerned. This way."

She moved out in front of Will, then turned away from the ford of the stream and followed the sparkling waters into the meadows beyond. Pines ringed the space, perfuming the area with their clean scent. The air held the hint of fall, sharp, crisp. Not long now.

Will drew level with her again. "What brings tourists out this way?" he asked.

"Some for the fish," she acknowledged. "That stream carries brown trout. Others come to remember. Your General Howard chased Chief Joseph and the Nez Perce up this way in 1877."

"Troop M was ordered to remain at Fort Colville." His gaze continued up the creek as if he could spy the column of Indians seeking freedom. "Or we might have been part of the campaign."

He didn't sound sad to have missed the opportunity to harass the tribe. She appreciated that. "They came within a mile of the Geyser Gateway, according to Mr. Carter, the original owner."

"He was fortunate. I heard there were a few casualties in Yellowstone."

"Fewer than what the Nez Perce sustained before or after." Kate nodded to the meadow. "This is another good spot for elk and bison. I generally refuse to let my guests head this way with guns, but I suspect the folks at the Fire Hole might feel differently.

And they don't always serve beef in their stew."

"Good to know."

"Ma! Look!"

Kate turned to see what Danny had found, and her heart nearly flew from her chest. She couldn't breathe as the bear ambled out of the woods.

Will had seldom been this close to a bear, but he knew how to respond should he encounter one. Bess noticed before the other horses. Her step stuttered, and she pulled at the reins as if trying to escape. Upwind of them and across the creek, the black bear's tan muzzle twitched as its head swung in their direction.

He glanced at Kate, expecting a lecture. Her eyes were wide and wild, her face white. Before he could speak, she wheeled her mount and rode for her son. "Danny! With me. Now."

The other horses started balking, tossing their heads. The bear took a few steps into the meadow.

"Mrs. Tremaine," he said, keeping his voice calm. "Slow your mount."

She'd already pulled her son off his pony and cradled him against her, but she reined in. Her chest rose and fell with her rapid breaths.

"Smith, take the pony's reins and settle your mount. I'll deal with Mrs. Tremaine and Danny. Turn slowly and move away. No more than a walk, Private."

"Are you quite certain we should put that thing at our backs?" Smith's baritone voice sounded higher than it should.

"I want to give it no reason to engage," Will said, turning Bess. When Kate didn't move, he reached out to shake her reins. "Mrs. Tremaine, an orderly retreat. Now."

"Ma?" Danny asked, voice trembling.

That seemed to wake her. She turned her horse and rode beside Will. Smith took the lead, pulling the pony. They edged along the creek toward the circuit road. Though Will glanced back, the bear did not follow. He thought everyone breathed easier when they reached the ford again.

"Apparently we should expect to encounter bears in this area," Smith said, then he paused, as if waiting for Kate to confirm it.

She said nothing.

"Black bears, to be precise," Will supplied for her. "A grizzly has a hump on its back. Correct, Mrs. Tremaine?"

She hugged her son tight. "Yes."

"My pa met a grizzly," Danny said in a

whimper. "He never came back."

"My condolences, General Tremaine," Smith said softly.

Kate didn't respond.

Will wanted to gather her close, hold her as she held Danny. Had she been with her husband when the bear had attacked or only found the body later? Either way, it was no wonder the sight of any bear had shaken her.

The best he could do was give her time to recover her usual composure.

"May I help Danny remount?" he asked gently.

She blinked, then drew in a deep breath. "Yes, thank you."

Will dismounted, came around, and held up his arms. Danny slid into them. His face was still peaked, and he clung to Will as he carried him to the pony.

"A fine animal, General Tremaine," he said, giving the pony a pat as Danny settled himself into place. "She must have a fine name."

"Buttercup," Danny admitted, accepting the reins from Smith. "But I think she'd be better named Lightning."

Will refused to smile at the appellation for the placid pony. "Good name for any mount."

Smith raised his brows as Will moved back to Bess. Before mounting, he put a hand on Kate's skirt. "All right, Mrs. Tremaine?"

She drew another breath, as if she couldn't get enough of the cool air. "Yes, Lieutenant Prescott. Thank you."

With a nod, he swung up into the saddle and turned Bess south.

Kate rode beside him, gaze on the distance. A rabbit bounded across the road and paused on the verge, ears sticking up from the tufts of grass. Kate didn't comment. To the southwest, steam rose among the pines. She didn't name the pool or offer to show it to them.

"Private Smith," he said as they cleared the meadow, "General Tremaine has a skill for reconnaissance. Ask him about the pie at his establishment."

"A true delicacy, I take it?" Smith asked behind them.

"The best in Yellowstone," Danny bragged. "I bet Alberta would give you a piece. If you help me with Lightning when we get back, I'll ask."

"Thanks." He called up to Will. "Permission to confirm the claim, sir?"

"Granted," Will said. "Save some for me."

The two rode around him and Kate and headed for the inn.

She remained silent as they approached the hotel. When they reached the hitching post, Will dismounted and came around to her side. She'd proven she didn't need help dismounting, but he offered it anyway, and she slid down into his arms. For a moment, he held her, carefully, gently. He knew he should release her, but he couldn't manage to let go.

"I'm sorry to hear about Danny's father," he murmured. "That's a hard way to lose a man."

Her head came up to brush his chin. "Is there an easy way?"

At least she was showing some of her usual spirit.

"I suppose not," he said. "But he'd be proud of how you're raising Danny, managing this hotel."

She remained in his embrace, as if his presence brought her comfort, and he marveled at the possibility.

"I've done the best I can," she said. "But I can't be everywhere, every moment. I don't know what I'd do if something happened to Danny."

"Nothing happened," he reminded her. "No one was hurt. You taught us all well."

"I didn't teach Toby," she said, voice hinting of tears. "He ran after every wonder, no matter whether it could scald him, poison him, or break all his bones." She shuddered. "I can't let that happen to Danny."

"You protect your son well," Will assured her. "I see that. All anyone can do is their utmost. No one can ask for more."

She laid her head against his chest, as if listening to the sound of his heart. And his heart, the heart he'd buried eight years ago in Oregon, beat harder.

For her.

9

How long had it been since she'd been held? Toby had never been much of a hugger. Too busy doing. For a moment, she closed her eyes, breathed in the scent of warm wool and leather, allowed herself to feel cherished, protected.

But the feeling was only temporary. She had no claim on this man. He could be called elsewhere at any time. His work could lead him into danger. She wouldn't survive losing someone else she loved.

Her heart protested as she pulled away from him, but she ignored the cry. She had responsibilities, to her son, to her inn. That's what mattered.

"You better talk to Alberta about that pie before Danny and Private Smith eat it all," she said, gaze on her horse.

He didn't move. "I have a feeling you could use some pie yourself."

She might at that, but work sounded a

better tonic. "I'll be fine. We're expecting that group shortly. I should make sure the rooms are ready." She gathered the reins and led Aster toward the barn, feeling a bit as if she was running away from her own inn.

Which was ridiculous.

She loved her inn, she loved her world. This morning had shaken her, but she couldn't forget how fortunate she was. She'd never expected to live in such an amazing place. Instead of the skies dark with soot and hemmed in by buildings, she looked up into a heaven so blue it went on forever. Instead of the rattle of lorries and the din of industry, she woke to the song of the yellowthroat and meadowlarks and the rumble and splash of a geyser. Where she had grown up in Boston, the only wildlife visible had been the squirrels in the park. Danny was growing up with elk and bison.

And bears.

She shivered. That was the first bear she'd encountered since Toby had died. It had been a year. She'd thought she could handle herself. It hadn't even been a grizzly. And still, she'd panicked, trapped inside her terror. If Will hadn't taken command . . .

She shook off the fear that threatened and headed for the hotel. Will had been there.

Danny was safe. And she had work to do.

So, she kept busy the rest of the day and Saturday. Wakefield and Hoffman brought her six more guests on their way out of the park, and Bassett Brothers deposited three more heading for Old Faithful in the morning.

She spotted Will and either Private Smith or Private Franklin making the rounds, but she did her best to avoid contact. Bad enough that the lieutenant intruded on her thoughts all too often.

"Ma?" Danny asked when they were helping Caleb by feeding the chickens Friday. She looked from him to the hens flocking at her feet and hastily shoved her hand in the basket of corn before she and Danny were overcome. Will rode past quietly, head up and gaze over the geysers.

"He's a fine man, that lieutenant," Alberta went so far as to point out Friday night as Kate leaned against the worktable after serving dinner and watched Danny dig into the chili and corn bread.

"Is he?" Danny asked, mouth half full.

"Chew and swallow, please," Kate advised him.

"He is," Ida answered him, elbows on the table and gaze dreamy. "And Private Smith isn't half bad either."

Sarah, moving past with an empty crystal pitcher, wrinkled her nose. "Too bushy. Makes you wonder what he's hiding under all that hair."

Ida tossed her head as she straightened. "Well, Private Franklin is too scrawny. Give me beef to chicken any day."

Kate cleared her throat and nodded to Danny, and her maids quickly found other ways to occupy themselves.

But Danny wasn't about to let the matter go. "Do you like beef or chicken better, Ma?" he asked her after they'd said their evening prayers that night.

She wasn't about to explain what Ida had meant by her comment. "I like whatever Alberta cooks," she temporized as she sat at the side of his bed to tuck him in.

He snuggled deeper under the wool blanket. "Me too."

She was congratulating herself on escaping the worst of his questions when he added, "But do you think Lieutenant Prescott is handsome?"

"It's not for me to say," she replied, tucking the blanket around his slender frame. Already the nights were cooling, and the heat from the big hearth only reached so far.

"Why not?" Danny asked with a frown.

"I have better things to do than gaze about at cavalrymen," she told him.

"Do you think *I'm* handsome?" he asked.

Kate smiled. "Very handsome. And someday you'll make a fine husband." She leaned over and kissed his forehead.

"Like Pa," he said. "He was a good husband, wasn't he?"

Kate kept her smile in place. "I never complained. Now, get some sleep."

"Yes, Ma." He dutifully closed his eyes. Kate rose and left.

How she hated not telling Danny everything, but he was so young. He couldn't understand what went on between a husband and a wife. He didn't understand his father's death either. He'd heard a bear had mauled his father. She hadn't been able to keep the guests or her staff from sharing that news. But she'd prevented him from seeing the mangled body. She still saw it in nightmares.

He remembered Toby's engaging side, the laughter, the games. He didn't understand the many ways Toby had failed her.

"It was just a card game," Toby had told her back in Boston when she'd realized they couldn't pay the grocer. "I'll win the money back next time."

She'd managed to convince him there

would be no next time, but she never knew what else would catch his fancy. He had spent rent money on a blind horse because he couldn't bear to see the animal put down. She had located a farmer willing to accept the poor beast. They'd gone without coal for a month one winter because he had wanted a sled large enough to take the neighbor children for a ride. He gave to every charity, helped anyone who asked, invested in every wild scheme proposed to him, with no thought of how it might affect her or Danny. He'd been throwing scraps to a grizzly he feared might be hungry when it had turned on him.

No, Toby had not been the best husband, but she missed his smile, his ability to see the silver lining in every cloud.

Will didn't seem to be a silver lining sort of fellow. At times, she thought something troubled him. That handsome — well, she could admit it to herself! — face could look remarkably still when he wanted it to, giving away none of his secrets. But somehow she was sure he wouldn't have gone out in the middle of the night to feed a bear either.

The way he looked at her, the way he had held her, told her it would be all too easy for him to develop feelings for her. She was halfway to developing feelings for him.

A shame she could not feel comfortable taking a chance on love again.

Kate Tremaine didn't trust him.

Will shook his head as he rode his circuit with Smith late Saturday morning. He wasn't sure why he felt so certain of the fact. True, she seemed to be avoiding him. She had to wonder why he'd behaved as he had. He'd kept her at a respectable arm's length until he'd pulled her close the other day. And what had he offered in the face of her fears?

All anyone can do is their utmost. No one can ask for more.

Platitudes he surely hadn't lived. Platitudes he wasn't sure he believed.

But he wanted to.

So, what was he to do about Kate except honor the distance she seemed determined to put between them? She had helped him and his men so much, it felt wrong to ignore her, though she seemed intent on ignoring him. Danny, on the other hand, was always on the veranda, under the hitching post, or out on the geyser field every time Will rode by, as if he'd been listening for the sound of hoofbeats. And he always had a wave or a word for Will.

"The hotel people are here again," he

confided to Will that morning from the porch bench as Bess paused before the inn to eye the two strange horses tied there.

Will reined in and tried in vain to see through the open door. "Hotel people?"

"They own a lot of the hotels in Yellowstone," Danny supplied. "The fancy one at Mammoth Hot Springs, the big one going up at Old Faithful. They bought Mr. Marshall's hotel. I heard them tell Ma." He glanced toward the door. "I hope they don't buy ours."

The same hope surged up inside him. The Geyser Gateway without Kate? Impossible to imagine. But who could blame her if she'd had enough of the wilderness, especially after their recent encounter with a bear?

Just then, two men, one in a tailored black coat and trousers, the other in buckskins, came out of the hotel and started down the steps. The fancy fellow's face was red, his mouth set in a hard line. The guide's smile could only be called a smirk. He nodded respectfully to Will, but his client breezed past to untie his horse.

Kate followed them out onto the porch and watched them leave, hands on the hips of her plaid skirt.

"Did you say no?" Danny asked.

Her look dropped to her son. "I'm not selling the Geyser Gateway. This is our home."

Danny flattened himself onto the bench, as if his spine had turned to pudding. "Oh, good." He straightened. "Can I ride patrol with Lieutenant Prescott?"

"Wood?" she asked.

"Can't I stack it later?" he wheedled.

She jerked a thumb toward the back of the property. "You know the rules."

His sigh was heavy enough to down a few trees all on its own. "No fun before chores. Good thing *your* mother didn't come out to Yellowstone with you, Lieutenant Prescott. She probably wouldn't let you patrol until you washed the dishes."

"Daniel Tobias Tremaine," Kate said, "git!"

He got.

"Maybe it *is* a good thing my mother never followed me to a post," Will said, watching him trudge around the inn.

"Why?" Kate challenged him. "Was she a tyrant too?"

He returned his gaze to hers. Her eyes were a smoky gray in the shadow of the porch. "No, ma'am. I thought she was the hardest-working person I would ever meet, until I met you."

Her hands fell. "There's a lot to be done running a hotel."

"Then why not sell? Take the money and go somewhere safer for you and Danny."

She waved her hand after the disappearing businessman and his guide. "Because they offered me a pittance. They know how hard it is to overwinter. They thought I'd give in now."

"You could probably find someone to make you a better offer," Will said, though everything in him urged him to stop arguing and let her stay. "Lots of companies want a part of Yellowstone."

"Too many companies," she said primly. "I had three letters this season from the Virginia City Outfitters. The first offered a decent price. The second increased it. The third warned me I'd regret not agreeing to their terms."

Will shook his head. "They must never have met you, or they would have known not to threaten an independent woman."

"Very true. But I know what would happen if I sold the Geyser Gateway to opportunists like that. Cattle and sheep grazing in the meadows instead of elk. Trinkets tucked into geysers to be sold to tourists once the things crust up enough." She shuddered. "No, it's best for Danny and best for

Yellowstone if I stay."

"And what's best for Kate Tremaine?" Will asked.

She stepped out into the sunlight, gazed up into the sky. "Being here. This is home."

Once more, he wanted to reach for her, hold her, soak up some of the warmth that glowed about her. But this time, the comfort would be all his. Her presence, that sky, the whoosh of a geyser as it shot up, even the whiff of sulfur on the breeze — all tugged at him, pulled him closer than he'd ever been pulled before.

"Home." The word left his mouth before he could stop it.

She dropped her gaze to his. He couldn't speak. She didn't speak. It would take nothing to swing down from the saddle, climb those steps, gather her in his arms, and press his lips to hers.

"I completed the circuit, Lieutenant," Smith said as he reined in beside Will.

She blinked, as if suddenly finding the sun too bright, and lowered her gaze. "Hello, Private. Caleb and Danny picked apples yesterday. Alberta's been canning, but she has pies on to bake. You might be in time for a slice. Both of you," she added without looking at Will.

Smith didn't look to Will either, not even

for permission. "I'd be delighted to sample the wares, ma'am." He started for the back of the inn.

Will ought to reprimand his private, but he was more concerned about Kate. It seemed he'd made her uncomfortable again.

"I should finish the sweep south," he said. "Maybe this evening."

She nodded, but her smile looked brittle.

From the east came the most awful sound Will had ever heard. It started as a grunt and ended in a high-pitched scream. Bess shifted under him. He leaped from the saddle, vaulted the stairs, and put himself between Kate and the danger.

She laid a hand on his shoulder. "Will . . ."

"Get inside," he said. "Bar the door."

Her hand pressed against his shoulder, forcing him to turn and look at her. Something silvery danced in her eyes. "Will . . ."

The scream came again, urgent, demanding. He pulled away from her. "Tell Smith to follow me."

"No." She darted in front of him before he could jump off the steps. "Will, it's a bull elk. It's rutting season."

He stared at her. "That's an elk?"

She nodded, but a giggle escaped. "Really. It's nothing dangerous, unless you happen to be the other elk he's challenging."

He stared to the east, remembering the animals they'd startled the other day. "I've never heard them make that sound."

"They only make it this time of year," she told him, "and only for about a month. We're halfway through now. I'm surprised we haven't heard it before."

He never wanted to hear it again. "You're sure no one's being murdered on the other side of those trees?"

Her laughter washed the last of his tension away. "Fairly sure. None of my guests are out in that direction, and I doubt anyone from the Fire Hole Hotel came this far just to murder each other. But I thank you for wanting to protect us."

He did. All too much. That's why he excused himself and left.

He'd never considered himself a coward. His commendations in the past proved he knew how to react to challenges. Why was it the thought of more time with Kate both thrilled and terrified him?

He went a little way beyond the Geyser Gateway, far enough to spot the elk herd browsing calmly.

"Let's hope they stay that way," he told Bess, who seemed to nod in agreement as they turned and headed north.

He collected Smith and returned to camp,

then spent the next few hours helping Franklin with the cabin. By the time they'd finished, it had four walls, though they reached only six feet high and most of the lumber had been used. If he had to live six months in that, he'd be a hunchback by spring.

As Franklin went to saddle the horses for the afternoon sweep, Will looked around for Smith. The bushy-faced private was supposed to be inventorying supplies and making a plan for the next few meals, but he was nowhere in sight.

"Smith!" he shouted. "Report!"

"Coming!" The voice was faint, as if traveling a great distance.

Where was he? Will followed Franklin and saddled Bess. His man finally jogged out of the woods to the west of camp. His trousers below the knee were dark and damp, the proud yellow stripe sagging.

"You were supposed to be working on provisioning," Will reminded him.

"Sir," Smith acknowledged with his slow drawl as he came apace with Will. "I was working on provisioning, fishing to be exact."

Will eyed him. "And your trousers were bait?"

Smith shrugged. "I tumbled in."

Will wanted to believe him, but something felt off. "My condolences. Do you have a spare uniform?"

"I regret the Army didn't see fit to provide one except what they call a dress uniform, sir."

"Hey, Soldier!" Another man ducked out from under the pines. Short and burly, he was surely one of the tourists staying at the Fire Hole Hotel. Will had had to warn him about hunting only yesterday. He was so excited now he didn't appear to notice Will standing beside Smith or Franklin nearby.

"You were right," he said to Smith, round face breaking into a grin. "This was much better than a rod. Those fish are jumping clean through the opening into the net."

Smith didn't look the least abashed at being caught poaching. He straightened to attention. "Permission to retrieve dinner, sir."

"Denied," Will snapped. He raised his voice and stepped out around Bess so the tourist wouldn't be able to ignore him. "Park rules prohibit fishing by any means but line and hook. Release those fish, or I'm putting you both under arrest."

The tourist pointed at Smith. "But he said it would be all right."

Franklin shook his head in obvious disbelief that his comrade would be so brazen.

"Private Smith is mistaken," Will clipped out. "I suggest you'd be wise to follow my orders instead of his."

Smith sidled around Will. "I'll just release the fish, sir. Come on, Adams." He grabbed his crony's arm and tugged him toward the pines and the river beyond. Franklin swung up into the saddle and moved his horse away from the picket line.

Will gritted his teeth. How was he to protect Yellowstone as he'd promised Kate if he couldn't even control his own men?

As if Bess sensed his frustration, she puffed out a sigh.

Will climbed into the saddle and joined Franklin. Right now, the odds were against them successfully completing their mission over the winter. He already knew one alternative that promised greater success, though he'd have to convince Captain Harris of its wisdom.

But first he had to convince Kate.

10

Mr. Yates, the circuit rider, arrived Saturday evening and begged dinner. Will Prescott did not. Kate tried to tell herself it was all to the good. Will disturbed her, made her reconsider her choices. Besides, he wouldn't be in her life long. No need to give him any more of her time than necessary.

But her heart still bounded as happily as an antelope when he knocked at the kitchen door just after breakfast on Sunday.

She was finishing the dishes so Alberta and the others could attend services when he poked his head in. The cavalry sabers on his hat winked a welcome.

"Good morning, Lieutenant," she called. "Here for breakfast? I haven't turned out the oatmeal yet."

He removed his hat as he came fully into the kitchen. "Thank you, ma'am, but I've had breakfast. I came to talk to you."

She set the dish she'd been rinsing on the

towels to dry, but her pulse sped as if she'd run to Old Faithful and back. "Oh? About what?"

"Supplies and provisions," he said, and she nearly sighed.

What was wrong with her? Did she want him to say he was here to court her?

Yes.

No!

"Having trouble in that regard?" she asked aloud.

"Too much." He came to join her by the table. "Park rules forbid hunting, as you know. We weren't issued fishing gear. A man can only take so much salt pork. Yesterday I caught one of my privates fishing, with an improvised net."

Kate winced. "I thought better of Private Franklin."

"It wasn't Franklin," he said. "But it might as well have been. If I'm having this kind of trouble already, I don't like to think about overwintering in the field. Six men in a ten-by-ten cabin —"

"For six months," Kate reminded him.

He gazed at the ceiling as if begging heaven for help. "Six months of salt pork and hardtack with no windows you can open for light in a space smaller than this kitchen. Someone will break."

She could imagine. Toby had rarely survived a day or two before having to get out, sometimes on snowshoes. But he'd had a spacious, warm hotel and Alberta's cooking waiting on his return.

"So you'll need to leave," she said, wondering why her voice suddenly sounded so leaden.

"Actually, I'd like to propose to Captain Harris that we stay," he said, gaze meeting hers. "With you."

Kate stared at him. "What?"

He set his hat on the table and held up both hands. "Hear me out. We'll be given food for the winter."

"Salt pork and hardtack," she repeated, unable to keep the revulsion from her voice.

"I'm sure Alberta could make even that taste good. Better than anything we'd try. My point was that we might not be as much of a drain on your resources as you might think."

Kate put her hands on her hips. "You forget. I've seen how your men eat. You'd clean me out in a month."

"Then we'll help you put up more," he said, lowering his hands so cautiously she might have had her rifle trained on him. "The inn will be empty of guests — you

161

said so yourself. We could stay in the rooms."

"Which have no method of heating," she informed him.

"Two men to a room ought to heat it enough to get by," he said, and she knew he was right. They could keep the place warm enough just to bundle up for sleeping, then spend the days in the heated salon.

"We'd still patrol when we could to prevent hunters from taking advantage of the quiet times," he continued as if he could see her resolve weakening. "We'd help with food preparation, cleaning, wood chopping, any indoor maintenance, the care and feeding of the stock."

"The stock." Kate seized on the word. "You'd have to put your horses in the barn. I didn't plan on that much feed."

"The Army always feeds its horses, Kate," he said, "sometimes better than its men. With your permission, I'd also like to propose to Captain Harris that he pay you a stipend to house us and them. It wouldn't be much, perhaps three dollars a month per man and his mount. But we might survive the winter, and you might come out ahead."

Kate calculated quickly. Six men, a minimum of five months. Oh, what she could do with the extra ninety dollars. Add an extra horse for trail rides. Oh, or build a gazebo on the front yard for picnics. And all the things on her list of improvements and maintenance inside — six men for five months even a few hours a day would make such a difference!

She raised her chin. "Offer your proposal to Captain Harris, then. I'm willing if he is."

That smile. It lit his face. It lit the room. It lit a candle inside her.

"Thank you, Kate," he said. "I'll ride for Mammoth Hot Springs today. I'll report back as soon as I've returned."

Beyond the kitchen door, voices rose in song. He nodded in that direction. "You should go."

She should. When the dishes were done. She caught his hand. "Come with me."

The smile softened, brushed her like spring rain. "Maybe next week."

Kate nodded and forced herself to release him. Putting on his hat, he turned and left.

The room felt darker, colder. Melancholy slipped over her as easily as his hat had slipped onto his head. Enough of that! She had no intention of becoming one of those maudlin females who sat, day in and day out, face to the window, pining for a fellow. Will Prescott wasn't even her fellow!

He could be.

She snorted and went to finish the dishes.

But the voices on the other side of the door called to her, and she heard an echo inside. Maybe she should attend services for once, see what Mr. Yates was telling her guests. She was responsible for allowing him to preach. Her guests would associate him with the Geyser Gateway.

She set another dish on the towel and dried her hands on the apron around her waist. Maybe just a peek. She ventured to the door, but the voices had quieted until she heard only one: Mr. Yates, starting his sermon. Surely she shouldn't interrupt now.

Her hands disagreed with her, for they were already working at untying the apron and pulling it off her navy skirts. She stiffened her spine to keep from walking through the door.

You must be even busier than I am, Lord. You don't need my worship.

But she needed to worship. She could feel it.

She bowed her head. *Lord, I thought I was worshiping you every day, through my work, by keeping your creation safe. But I feel as if you're calling me to more. What more can I give?*

Something clinked behind her. She turned

to find one dish precariously close to the edge of the table. Maybe that was her answer. Work was her balm, her calm. Something she could control.

She went back to the dishes. Maybe she could work a little faster next week and be ready in time for services. The decision did not bring the peace she expected.

Still, she had everything washed by the time the others came through the door after Mr. Yates had finished preaching.

"We missed you," Alberta said, starting to help her put away the last of the dishes.

"Maybe next week," Kate said, remembering Will's promise. "So much to do."

Alberta glanced around the kitchen, and her broad shoulders slumped. "There is that. I best start on Sunday dinner."

Sarah tossed her head. "Not me. I'm packing. I'll be leaving Wednesday. Elijah said he'd have room for me on that run."

Ida sighed. "Me too."

Once again, sadness tugged at Kate, but this reason made more sense to her. The season was drawing to a close. Her guests would dwindle even further in the coming days. Caleb would leave at the end of the month, and she and Danny would have to add taking care of the animals to their tasks.

Unless Captain Harris agreed to Will's

proposal.

She made herself smile. "We've been pleased to have you both," she told Sarah and Ida. "I'll write when we're ready to start up in the spring." She turned to Alberta. "How much roast beef is left from yesterday's dinner?"

"A goodly amount," Alberta allowed. "I thought I'd start a stew." She moved slowly toward her apron hanging on a hook by the back door.

When had Alberta's hair lost its gleam, her step its vitality? Had Kate pushed even her cook beyond her abilities? She shook her head and went to intercept her, taking the apron from her grip.

Alberta looked at her askance.

"Roast beef sandwiches tonight," Kate told her. "The bread's already sliced, and it won't take much to slice the beef. We'll open some of the apple preserves. And there's still pie for dessert. That should allow you a few hours off."

"Oh, Mrs. Tremaine!" Alberta clasped her hands before her chest, eyes tearing. "What I wouldn't give for a walk in God's beauty. I hope this means you and Danny get time off too."

Kate glanced back to find Danny watching her. He fairly vibrated with hope.

"We will," Kate promised. "How about we visit our special spot, Danny?"

"Yes, ma'am," Danny said, and he saluted her.

That only reminded her of Will again. Maybe someday, before winter set in, she'd be comfortable sharing the secret with him. For now, she was merely glad for time with her son.

In the one place she had always found her heavenly Father there before her.

The sight of the Geyser Gateway never failed to raise Will's spirits, especially that Monday afternoon. Part of his reaction stemmed from his meeting with Captain Harris the previous day.

After a quick sweep of their area, he had taken Franklin and Smith north with him to Camp Sheridan at Mammoth Hot Springs. Captain Harris and the men he'd kept with him were making more progress than Will and his men. Already they'd constructed a T-shaped barracks and stable, both board and batten covered in a wash of lime and lamp blacking. Work had commenced on a storehouse, a guardhouse, a quartermaster's stable, and a hospital. But then again, they had a sawmill and twice the men he did.

Or at least twice the men on a typical day. As it was, only Captain Harris; his adjutant, First Lieutenant Herbert Tutherly; and two privates were left in the cantonment. The rest were still fighting the fire.

"Though we hear it is nearly contained," Will's commanding officer told him when he reported in. "And I appreciate your warning about the possibility of fire being used to drive animals beyond the park boundary. We'll be on the lookout for that."

For as long as Will had known the captain, Harris had kept his sandy hair short and mustache trimmed. Even now, he was better groomed than many of his men, his uniform clean and pressed, the brass buttons gleaming. His eyes gleamed nearly as bright as Will laid out his plan while standing on either side of the planks and sawhorses Harris was using as a desk.

"Excellent," the captain proclaimed when Will finished. "That will allow us to concentrate our lumber resources on the other detachments. I'll make sure to send the wintering supplies and hay to the Geyser Gateway. You're certain Mrs. Tremaine is amenable?"

"Mrs. Tremaine and her staff have done all they can to aid us, sir," Will assured him. "She wants Yellowstone protected as much as we do."

Captain Harris nodded. "Then, by all means, proceed."

Will saluted. As he lowered his arm, he met his commanding officer's gaze. "Permission for me and my privates to visit Gardiner, sir?"

Harris's eyes narrowed. "For what purpose?"

The closest town to the northern entrance, Gardiner had a reputation for wildness. The population stood at less than five hundred, but the town boasted more than a dozen saloons. Harris wasn't keen on his men visiting any of them.

"Mrs. Tremaine's son, Danny, has shown a potential aptitude for baseball," Will explained. "I was hoping one of the mercantiles might have a ball and bat for purchase."

Harris's face relaxed. "Permission granted. Just see that Private Smith stays away from the gaming tables. The miners and ranchers won't appreciate his style of play."

Will knew better than to question his superior. But that didn't mean he couldn't question Smith as soon as he left the blockhouse Harris was using as a command post. He found both his privates lounging in armchairs on the long porch of the big

National Hotel, feet out and heads back. Only Franklin jumped to attention as Will approached.

"We've been given permission to ride to Gardiner," he told them. "Franklin, see to the mounts. Smith, a word."

Franklin ducked his head and hurried past Will. Smith slowly climbed to his feet. "Lieutenant?"

"I have been advised to keep you away from the gaming tables," Will told him. "Why would that be?"

Smith spread his hands. "Other men have limited vision?"

"Or more vision than I do," Will allowed. "Is there something I should know, Private?"

"A great many things, I'm sure," Smith had drawled. "But you needn't worry about me. I have no interest in coming near a card table again." He had stretched like a cat awakening from a nap. "The Army is my life now."

Somehow, Will had doubted that.

But he couldn't doubt how eager he was to reach the inn now. He tried to tell himself he was looking forward to seeing how Danny liked his present, the leather-bound ball and ash bat he'd found in Gardiner. But he knew the real reason.

Kate.

Even the scream of the elk in the hills to the east didn't slow him.

"Do you expect trouble at the inn?" Smith asked beside him as if he noticed the swift pace.

"No," Will said. "Check the geysers. I need a word with Mrs. Tremaine."

"Of course you do."

Will refused to dignify the comment with a response.

Leaving Danny's present in his saddlebag, he hitched Bess and ventured into the Geyser Gateway. Kate's youngest maid, the one with the bouncy blonde curls, pointed him through the kitchen to the rear yard, where he found Kate, Danny, Alberta, and two older women gathered in a circle. Kate looked up, then grinned as he approached, and he hurried his steps.

"Just the man for the job," she declared. "Mrs. Pettijohn, Miss Pringle, this is Lieutenant Prescott, head of the cavalry detachment assigned to our area of the park. Lieutenant, meet my newest guests. They're sisters from West Virginia. They'll be staying with us for the next week or so."

Will removed his hat. "Ladies."

Two pairs of button brown eyes regarded him from wrinkled, powdered faces. Their hair was white and crimped into curls that

171

were fading in the warm, dry air.

"Are you mechanically inclined?" the taller lady inquired, both chins pointing in his direction as she stiffened in her tailored, violet-colored gown.

"Sufficiently muscled?" the shorter lady asked, gaze traveling from his boots to his face as her tiny hands smoothed the ruffles and ribbons on her lavender skirts.

Will looked to Kate. "Is there a problem?"

Her grin widened, and she stepped aside to wave at the contraption in the center of their circle. "We have all the ingredients for ice cream, but we can't get the crank to turn, even with Caleb's help."

"Ice cream is really nice on a warm day," Danny said wistfully.

"I'm your man," Will said. He dropped his hat onto Danny's head, where it tilted over the boy's eyes, then crouched beside the wooden bucket with its iron yoke across the top. The metal canister inside was surrounded by chunks of ice, salt sparkling on the flat edges.

"Where'd you get ice?" he asked, giving the bucket a shake to break any blockages.

"We brought it with us from Virginia City," the taller lady — Mrs. Pettijohn? — informed him.

"We brought many things with us," her

172

sister — Miss Pringle? — added.

Will settled the bucket between his knees and seized the handle. "Let's see what we can do."

He could feel their expectations as he cranked the handle to turn the canister. It stuck at first, and Mrs. Pettijohn tutted. Danny sighed, shoving the hat back on his head. Will glanced up to see Kate's smile. He tightened his grip and rocked the handle back and forth. He knew the moment the ice jam broke, for the chunks rattled against the wood. He started cranking to Danny's cheer.

Twenty minutes later, his arm was tiring, but he refused to let them see it. He switched arms as Alberta went to the kitchen. She returned with bowls and spoons as if sure of his success. Kate put her hand on his shoulder as if to offer to take over. The touch only encouraged him to keep going.

Danny leaned over the churn. "Maybe we should check it."

Will stopped, more grateful than he was willing to admit. "Good idea."

Danny's fingers trembled as Will tilted the yoke, but the boy opened the canister lid and looked inside. Then his head came up, and he beamed at Will. "Ice cream!"

"I'll take it from here," Alberta said, and she lifted the canister dripping from the ice and carried it to a wooden bench where her bowls waited. Danny and the older women followed.

Will climbed to his feet.

"Another fine rescue by the cavalry," Kate said.

Will inclined his head. "Just doing my duty, ma'am."

"I'm very grateful. Danny would have been so disappointed if we couldn't get it to work."

Will shook out his arms. "Glad to be of assistance. I was coming this way in any regard. I talked with Captain Harris. He accepted your kind offer."

She squeezed her shoulders up as if she were as excited as her son. "Oh, wonderful! Then you'll be with us all winter."

The prospect of overwintering in Yellowstone had never delighted him, until now. "I will. That is, we all will."

"I'm so glad." Her eyes glowed. That smile pulled him closer. He bent his head. She moved to meet him.

Pop. Pop. Pop.

Kate's head snapped up.

"Gunfire," Will said, gut dropping.

She met his gaze. "Poachers."

11

Alberta, Danny, and Kate's guests were so busy eating they didn't seem to notice, but the thought of a poacher so close made Kate's stomach bunch. Will started around the hotel, and she ran to pace him. "I'm coming with you."

He pulled up short. "Too dangerous."

"I've faced poachers before," she informed him. "The greater danger is you or your men riding into a hot pool. Let me guide you."

She thought he would refuse. His face was set and his eyes dark. But he snapped a nod. "You have ten minutes to change and mount. Can you do that?"

She whirled. "Danny — tell Caleb to saddle me a horse. Run!"

It was to her son's credit that he didn't argue. He shoved a dripping spoonful of ice cream into his mouth and sped for the barn. Kate ran for the inn, shouting instructions to Alberta as she went.

"I'm helping Lieutenant Prescott. Take care of Danny and the others while I'm gone."

She flashed past her startled cook and guests into the inn.

Nine and a half minutes later, according to the pocket watch Toby had seldom consulted, she was standing beside her horse in front of the hotel, Will on the ground beside her and Private Smith mounted. Mrs. Pettijohn and Miss Pringle were seated on the veranda benches, a second helping of ice cream in their bowls, watching avidly, as if they'd come to listen to a band play in the city park. Alberta and Danny stood in the doorway, her hands braced on his thin shoulders.

Will braced his hands on Kate's waist. "You sure about this?"

"Yes," she said. "If you'd be so kind."

He lifted her easily and set her on the sidesaddle. Kate adjusted her position and skirts, ordering her heart to slow as he stepped back.

"Have you heard any more shots?" she asked as he mounted.

"No," he admitted, gathering the reins. "And I can't even tell you which direction they came from."

176

"We have three good grazing areas for game animals near us," Kate said, turning Aster away from the hotel. "Across Tangled Creek and around that hill; to the northwest across the Firehole; and to the north, closer to your camp. I suggest we start with the nearest first."

He nodded, and she urged her mount forward to start around the geyser field.

"I took the liberty of asking Caleb to ride to the Fire Hole and tell Franklin the situation," Will said as they cantered across the dry, bleached soil. "He looked scared to death."

"He's just shy," Kate said, leading them west toward the banks of Tangled Creek. "He and his parents toured the park a couple years ago, and he loved the area so much they asked Toby if he'd consider taking him on as help. He's been a blessing with the animals."

Conversation dropped off as they splashed through the creek's warm waters and followed the curve of the pine-covered hill into the meadows beyond. Antelope raised their heads from the grass to stare a moment before bounding away.

"Not here," Kate said. "If there had been gunfire, those antelope wouldn't have waited until the second shot to bolt."

"Agreed," Will said, and he and Private Smith followed her up the banks of the creek to their next site.

Every moment felt too long, every yard too slow. True to its name, Tangled Creek trickled out in a wide fan to the Firehole River, creating a ford shallow enough for horses to cross. But the meadow on the other side was also empty of disturbance. The last of the season butterflies flitted over clumps of aster, their yellow wings bright against the blue.

"Not here either," Will said, turning his face and his horse away from the bucolic scene.

Private Smith sighed.

Kate's tension was too high to allow her a sigh. Perhaps they'd been mistaken. Perhaps the sound hadn't been gunfire. She wanted to hope as she led them back across the river and to the northeast. But she felt as if something rode on her shoulder, weighing her down. The tight line of Will's body told her he felt the same way.

They trotted out of a patch of chalk soil onto the meadows. Veined with tiny streams, the prairie stretched for acres until it reached the circuit road. She ought to have been able to spot a man standing, certainly a herd of any size.

She reined in. Will pulled up on one side, Private Smith on the other. The private's dark brown gaze roamed across the waving grass.

"Peaceful," he murmured, as if determined not to break the calm.

It was too calm. No birds sang. Nothing moved except the grass. Yellowstone seemed to be holding its breath. Kate held hers as well.

She craned her neck to see as far as she could, then let out her breath. There. That dark lump near the far side of the grassland. A lone bison, perhaps? Had it escaped the poacher?

"Careful," she said, relaxing back onto the saddle. "Head east, and watch for holes. One wrong step, and you'll lame your horse."

They picked their way across the grass, Kate's senses alert to any oddity. The lump didn't move as they approached. They were still a good twenty feet away when she realized why.

She reined in again, stomach roiling.

Private Smith frowned as he and Will joined her. "What is that?"

Kate swallowed her bile. "That's what's left after a poacher took the best parts of a bison. No head, no skin, no hooves, no tail."

Smith covered his nose with one hand and looked away.

Will's face hardened. "That means it's someone who knows what such things bring at market," he said, voice grim. "The flies are just beginning to swarm. We can't have missed him by much."

Kate looked away as well. "The easiest escape from the park from here would be the west entrance."

"Unless he wants more," Will said. He glanced around the meadow, then nodded to his man. "Check the ground around the kill. See if you can find any sign of a trail."

Smith eyed him. "You assume I have any skill in that area."

"Now, Private," Will barked.

Smith swung down and circled the kill.

Will put a hand on Kate's arm. "We'll catch who did this."

She nodded, but she didn't trust herself to speak. The loss of the bison pressed down on her, making breath difficult. So few left. Would they pass from this earth before Danny was grown?

"That way." Smith rose and pointed toward the north. "Even I can see the blood trail." At a look from Will, he remounted, and they headed in that direction.

Pines edged the prairie, and Kate wasn't

sure whether the needles littering the ground would mask the trail. But drops of blood on shrub and rock made it easy to follow the direction their poacher had gone, until they reached a bend in the Firehole River. The trail ended at the near bank. Here the river was narrower, rockier, the waters desperate to run.

Will's eyes narrowed, but not at the rushing waters white with foam, Kate thought.

"You know who it is," she guessed.

"I imagine all poachers leave a trail of blood from their prey," he said, but his gaze remained watchful. "Where do we go from here?"

"He won't be able to follow the river much longer," Kate advised. "The Firehole cuts through a canyon north of here. No place for a horse to travel. He'll have to risk the circuit road, at least until he reaches the Madison."

"Show us," he said, and she turned her horse away from the river.

But a short distance up the road, she realized her mistake. No trail of blood led them onward. No dust cloud on the horizon told of a horse ahead of them. They reached the bridge over the Madison River before Will reined in.

"Lost him." Kate heard the bitterness in

her voice. "He must have entered the Fire-hole. Who knows where he came out again?"

Will turned to Smith. "We need to notify the detachment at Riverside in case he's making for the entrance."

"We need to notify the detachment at Norris too," Smith replied. "He could just as easily be heading their direction. He'd find more opportunities to sell his ill-gotten goods to the north."

Will shook his head. "We can't go both directions. One of us must escort Mrs. Tremaine home."

Kate straightened in the saddle, shoulders protesting. "Nonsense. Norris is just as close as the inn from here. I won't let you lose this villain on my account."

Will leaned closer. "Riding in plain sight with the two of us might not raise comment, but coming alone with me to Norris might."

Kate waved a hand. "I'm a widowed woman, and well known in these parts. My reputation should be safe. Private Smith can go on to Riverside. All he has to do is follow the road. I'll show you the way to Norris, Will. I know a shortcut."

Sergeant Nadler had three men left at Norris, Will learned when they arrived a short while later. The others were fighting the fire. The tall blond seemed glad to know about the poacher but even gladder for the company when Will and Kate arrived at his station just as the sun was setting behind the mountains to the west.

The detachment at Norris had been housed in a rough frame house that had previously belonged to one of the civilian assistant superintendents. Nadler immediately ushered Kate into the main room, where a potbellied stove was smoking. His men scrambled to attention from where they'd been sitting on stumps they would probably end up burning for heat before spring came. Two of the rooms leading off likely served as bedchambers, the third for storage.

"Mrs. Tremaine," Nadler said after Will had introduced her and told him their mission. "Welcome to our humble abode." He held her hand far longer than Will thought appropriate. "Allow me to introduce my men. Privates Rizzo, Zabel, and Quincy."

The two black-haired young privates and the older blond stood at attention, gazes forward and chests thrust out, as if she were the head of the Army come for a surprise inspection. Their scruffy beards and dirty uniforms said they either hadn't been able to find laundry and bathing facilities or had decided against them.

"Gentlemen," she said as pleasantly as if she were meeting Lord Cavell and his party at a fine restaurant. "I appreciate all you're doing to keep the park safe."

Nadler released her to cuff Rizzo on the shoulder, then jerked his head toward the salt pork waiting in a frying pan by the stove.

"We were just fixing dinner," Nadler told her as his man rushed toward the stove. "I hope you'll join us."

"That's very kind of you," she said with a smile. "I'd be delighted."

Will could only assume the invitation included him as well.

As Rizzo set about frying the salt pork and pulling out slabs of hardtack, Quincy seized the only chair in the room, the slats missing from part of the back, and dragged it over to her. He whipped out his handkerchief and dusted off the battered seat. "Won't you sit down, ma'am?"

Kate spread her riding skirt and sat. Nadler drew up a stump and perched at her right. Will edged out Zabel to do the same on her left.

The pork sizzled as Rizzo turned it, and the pungent scent permeated the room. Besides the stove, stumps, and single chair, the space boasted only a set of shelves along one wall, where they'd piled their canteens, rifles, and ammunition. Wood for the stove was mounded too close to the heat for Will's comfort. He didn't want to see what the sleeping arrangements looked like.

Which meant Kate couldn't stay here.

He should have realized that. There would be no woman to play chaperone. He'd hoped the house might at least offer a private room with a locking door, but even that didn't appear likely. As Nadler asked Kate all kinds of questions, Will tried to think of alternatives.

Rizzo filled a tin plate with salt pork and hardtack and offered it to Kate with a flourish. Quincy followed with a tin cup of coffee so brimming Will was afraid he'd spill it on himself or her. Kate accepted their offerings with a ready smile and a word of thanks. Nadler and the others went to fill plates as well. Will and Zabel had to make do with bowls, as all the plates were taken. And he wasn't entirely sure that the crusty lump on the side of his bowl was from tonight's meal.

As the cavalrymen settled on their stumps and bent over the food, Nadler stiffened.

"Hey!" he shouted, and everyone except Will and Kate jumped. "Remember your manners."

Zabel and Quincy exchanged glances, clearly puzzled.

Nadler turned to Kate. "Mrs. Tremaine, would you say grace?"

She bowed her head, and the others followed suit. So did Will.

"Dear Lord," she said, voice clear over the crackle of the stove, "thank you for the food and company you've blessed us with. Please protect these brave cavalrymen as they protect your marvelous creation. Amen."

"Amen," they all rumbled. But Zabel and Quincy waited until Kate had taken a bite before eating again.

"I hear good things about your hotel," Nadler was saying, mouth half full.

Kate looked pointedly away and attempted to pierce the tough meat with her fork.

"The Geyser Gateway is one of the best hotels in the park," Will told him. "The best pie too."

She smiled at him, and he felt very clever. Quincy sighed gustily.

"Well, we have one of the best stations in the park," Nadler countered. "I hear you'll be overwintering in a cabin a quarter this size." He popped a piece of hardtack into his mouth and commenced chewing.

"Snug as a bug in a rug," Quincy jibed.

"Actually," Kate said, "Captain Harris has

agreed to allow Lieutenant Prescott and his men to overwinter at my inn."

Nadler's jaw tightened, and he stabbed his fork into the last of the salt pork so hard metal rang against metal. "Is that right? How nice."

"You need another man at the Lower Geyser Basin, Lieutenant?" Rizzo piped up, only to cringe as his fellow cavalrymen glared at him.

"I couldn't ask for better men than I already have," Will assured him.

Kate set her half-finished meal aside and rose. Nadler and Quincy shot to their feet, Rizzo and Zabel a heartbeat behind. Will felt a tug of annoyance at being last.

"Thank you for dinner, gentlemen," she said with a look all around. "Allow me to help clean up."

"Sure," Rizzo said, tossing his nearly empty plate aside and rushing toward the stove. "You can help me. I'll just start the water heating."

Nadler scowled at him before replacing the look with a smile as he turned to Kate. He picked up her plate and utensils. "Nonsense. You're our guest, ma'am. Zabel can help Rizzo."

"Sure," Zabel said, but his face darkened

as the sergeant shoved the plate and utensils at him.

"You just sit back and rest," Nadler continued to Kate with the fatuous smile Will was coming to hate. "That must have been quite a ride for you all the way from the hotel. I'm surprised Lieutenant Prescott asked you to endure it."

Oh, was he barking at the wrong tree.

Another lady might have fluttered her lashes, collapsed with a sigh, and lamented the rough life on the frontier. Kate merely gave him a look that would have made Danny sit straighter.

"The ride was far easier than my usual work at the hotel," she informed him. "Besides, Lieutenant Prescott didn't ask me to come along. I put him and Private Smith at a forced march after that poacher."

The news didn't change Nadler's approach. "Well, you don't have to worry about him bothering you ever again. We'll catch him and run him right out of the park."

"Until he reoutfits himself and returns," Kate said. "I do wish Congress would give you boys the right to arrest miscreants."

Nadler hitched up his trousers by the belt loops. "We're cavalrymen, Mrs. Tremaine, not constables."

"The Wyoming constables had more power," Kate argued.

Now Nadler's face was darkening. He might be slow, but he was starting to realize he was outclassed.

Will lifted his head. "Sergeant, Privates, see to your duties. Mrs. Tremaine, may I have a word?"

"Officers have all the luck," someone muttered.

"Certainly, Lieutenant," Kate said, but she followed him no farther than the door before stopping.

It was probably best they stayed within sight of the others. He wouldn't want to give anyone the wrong impression about his relationship with her.

"If you're going to advise me to treat Sergeant Nadler with more respect," she said, "save your breath. Respect is earned. And shared."

He was glad Nadler wasn't listening at the moment, though he was keeping an eye on them as he ordered his men to collect and clean the rest of the dishes. "That's not it. It's apparent to me you can't spend the night here."

She raised her brows. "If you start prosing on about my female sensibilities, I will ride back to the inn without you."

He chuckled. "I would never be so reck-less. I was just considering your reputation and the available accommodations."

She wrinkled her nose, making her look all at once less formidable, and he shifted his stance to block the view from Nadler and his men. They didn't need another excuse to be infatuated with her.

"I suppose you're right," she said. "Maybe I could beg a spot at the tent hotel."

"That might be best," Will agreed.

Her face relaxed. "At least I can do a little reconnaissance. It will be good to see how their accommodations stack up against the Geyser Gateway."

Now, why did he feel as if the smoky air had cleared? He turned to face the other cavalrymen.

Who hurried back to their work.

"Gentlemen," Will said. "I will escort Mrs. Tremaine to the hotel for the night, but I would appreciate accommodations."

Nadler saluted, face still stormy. "Yes, sir."

Rizzo elbowed Zabel. "At least allow us the honor of sending you off, ma'am."

"Certainly," Kate said, but Will could hear the surprise in her voice.

The three privates bunched together.

"Day is done," Rizzo started singing in a bright tenor.

"Gone the sun," Zabel and Quincy joined him in deeper tones.

"From the hills, from the lake, from the sky. All is well, safely rest. God is nigh."

He recognized the tune. It was the last bugle call of the night, the one to signal all lights to be extinguished. But he hadn't heard the words before, nor the verse that came next.

"Love, good night," Rizzo sang plaintively.

"Must thou go?" Zabel and Quincy harmonized with him.

"When the day and the night need thee so? All is well. Speedeth all to their rest."

Kate's cheeks were pink as they finished. "That was lovely, gentlemen. I don't think I've ever heard a finer serenade. Good night, and thank you for the hospitality. If you're ever down our way, I hope to return the favor."

Now they were all nodding eagerly. Will swept her out the door before they could abandon their post.

"You'll be seeing them again," he predicted as he escorted her out into the river meadow that housed the soldier station. Steam from the geysers drifted through the trees like will-o'-the-wisps. In the background, one of the fumaroles clanked as if it were a factory. Across the Gibbon River, torches burned here and there, lighting the way for staff moving among the hotel tents. The tents themselves glowed golden against the dark sky, a miniature mountain range with their sharp peaks.

"I don't mind if they come visit," Kate said, pacing him to the footbridge. "They've earned their slice of pie. You all have."

"Not until we catch this poacher."

They crossed the river and headed for the shanty that served as the hotel manager's lodging. There, Kate stopped short.

"About the poacher," she ventured. "You thought you knew him. Is he the same man who set the fire?"

She was too canny by half. "Why would you ask that?"

She shrugged. "It certainly drew your men away. Sergeant Nadler's too. With the Army engaged, your poacher would feel free to plunder."

"That's what I fear," Will confessed. "When we were still stationed at Mammoth Hot Springs, my men and I caught a poacher by the name of Roy Jessup. He had a buffalo head and pieces in a bag on the side of his saddle, dripping."

"Like our man today," she said, but he thought he saw a shiver run through her.

"Exactly. I'm sure he isn't the only one to

192

use that tactic. But Captain Harris suspects him of setting the fire as well. So, you're right. Jessup could be anywhere in the park, shooting whatever he wants."

"Then we must find him," she said.

The determination in her voice should have fired his spirit, but for once Will felt cold. How could he protect Kate if he had no idea where to look for their enemy?

12

Will had to knock on the door of the lodge keeper's hovel several times before a young man answered.

"Were you expected?" he asked, glancing from Kate to Will and back again.

"Lieutenant Prescott is lodging at the soldier station," Kate informed him. "I require a bed for the night."

"Bedding's extra," he said.

If he could not be bothered to introduce himself, she felt no need to offer her name. "How much extra?"

Will put a hand on her arm. "The Army will pay the cost. We inconvenienced Mrs. Tremaine."

The lodge keeper blinked. "Mrs. Tremaine? Of the Geyser Gateway?"

Kate managed a smile. "The same."

"Well, we're glad to have you, ma'am," he said, ducking back inside to reappear with a bundle of sheets and blankets in his lean arms. "You're going to enjoy this. I hear your place is pretty rough."

"Who told you that?" Kate demanded, but Will squeezed her arm in obvious warning.

"Oh, you know," the fellow said, starting for the nearest dun canvas tent. "You hear things from the guests."

Kate's teeth clenched as she followed him. Will released her, but he continued at her side as if to make sure the accommodations suited her. She was fairly certain they wouldn't.

In fact, they were barely civilized. The tent was held up by a tall pole in the center and a shorter pole at each of the four corners. The floor was of rough wood with gaps between the boards. Each room was furnished with a crude wooden bedstead, a simple chair, and a small table holding an oil lamp. She could see the lumps in the tick from here and could only hope they were caused by uneven packing and not burrowing vermin. The familiar sulfur scent of the hot pools was muted by a more musty, dusty smell that could have been the canvas.

The lodge keeper nodded toward the partition. "The Kingston family is sleeping on the other side — husband, wife, and three youngsters, so you'll have a chaperone." He jerked his head in the opposite direction. "We had another unexpected arrival this evening, a Mr. Jones. He's in the tent next door."

Will frowned. "What do you know of him?"

The clerk bristled. "I don't gossip about our guests."

No, only about her hotel. Kate nodded to Will. "It's fine, Lieutenant." She turned to the lodge keeper. "How much?"

"Two dollars," he said, dropping his load on the bed and sticking out his hand.

The Army was giving her three a month for Will's men and their horses! "That's robbery!" Kate cried.

Will slipped some coins into the fellow's palm. "Half now. The remainder when Mrs. Tremaine assures me she had a good night's rest."

The man opened his mouth to protest, met Will's gaze, and closed his mouth to snap a nod.

"Lights out in a half hour," he informed Kate. "Necessaries are behind the tent. You can get breakfast at the lunch station tent nearest the geyser field." He didn't wait for any questions before stalking off.

Will glanced around the tent again. "You're sure you'll be all right here?"

196

Kate bent to press on the tick. Her hand barely made a dent, but something squeaked. She shuddered as she straightened. "It's one night. I'll survive."

Still, he hesitated. "Maybe I should introduce myself to Mr. Jones."

As if to gainsay him, a hearty snore rumbled from that direction.

"I'll be fine," Kate insisted. "Mrs. Kingston and her husband would no doubt come to my aid if anything should happen." She shook her head. "Who would ever consider the Geyser Gateway rough accommodations compared to this?"

She had a better idea in the morning when she climbed stiffly from the bed. She didn't appear to have any bites or welts, but she'd slept in her clothes for added protection from the cool night air and whatever was sharing the bed with her. The riding habit was wrinkled, but Kate shook out the skirt before buttoning up the long hem so she could walk.

The oldest Kingston girl offered her the use of a comb.

"Mama says this is the frontier, and we need to be kind to each other," the twelve-year-old said as Kate winced her way through the snarls in her hair.

"You must stay at the Geyser Gateway,"

Kate told her. "It's in the Lower Geyser Basin. Beautiful geysers within an easy walk."

She smiled. "That sounds nice, but the man who brought us here from Virginia City said we shouldn't stay at the Geyser Gateway." She leaned closer and lowered her voice. "It has bugs." She straightened with a shudder.

"It most certainly does not," Kate informed her. "And the beds are softer than this, with bedding supplied, and the food is excellent. And we charge eight dollars a week."

She'd handed Miss Kingston back her comb, and the girl had hurried to return to her mother. By the narrow-eyed glance Mrs. Kingston sent her way through the gap in the partition, she appeared to have changed her mind about kindness. Well, who would take advice about lodging from a woman who slept in her clothes and had to borrow a comb?

And who would doubt the advice of a well-meaning stage driver as to accommodations elsewhere?

"They are slandering me," she complained to Will after a meager breakfast of a cold baked potato and a slice of bread for the exorbitant price of a dollar at the lunch station tent. "They're making up stories to keep the guests away from my hotel. It's that group in Virginia City that keeps writing to me. I know it."

"Your guests will have something to say about that," Will predicted as they went to fetch their horses from the soldier station stables. "I'm sure you receive nothing but praise."

"Not always," she admitted. "As far as I know, no one ever took a complaint to the superintendent, but there's no pleasing some people. Why I had a woman tell me I should arrange the geysers and paint pots in a more pleasing order, from shortest to tallest."

He laughed. There — how could she not smile at so warm a sound?

"Captain Harris has already been asked why he doesn't round up all the animals and put them in an enclosure so everyone has a chance to see them," he said as he saddled her mount for her.

Kate stared at him. "He wouldn't!"

"He wouldn't," Will assured her, cinching the saddle in place. "He has the utmost respect for the denizens of Yellowstone."

She sighed. "Even those who run uncomfortable, shoddy tent hotels."

"Oh, he's none too pleased with some of

the hotels," Will told her, coming around to her side. "He was the one who put George Marshall on notice to clean up his hotel or forfeit his lease."

"I think that's one of the reasons Marshall and his wife sold out to the Yellowstone Park Association," Kate said.

He took her by the waist, and, even though she knew the only reason was to put her up on the sidesaddle, her stomach fluttered as he lifted her.

"The Association is a force to be reckoned with," he allowed, stepping back as she adjusted her skirt. "The big hotel at Mammoth is impressive."

She tried not to take umbrage. "I haven't had the pleasure. But even if it's the shining jewel of the park, it's miles from the other landmarks. The Geyser Gateway is more centrally located. I don't know why Captain Harris would only renew my lease until spring."

"From what I've seen, you have nothing to fear." He went to mount his horse.

She wished she believed him. She and Toby had put all they had into the Geyser Gateway. If Captain Harris recommended to the Department of the Interior that she lose her lease, would the government compensate her for her improvements? Some people who had had claims in the area before it had been declared a park had received little. A few had been evicted as squatters. If she was forced out, where would she and Danny go? How would they live?

For if she had to leave Yellowstone, she would be leaving her heart as well, and not just because of the inn. She'd miss the sun rising through plumes of steam, the roar of a geyser shooting into a cerulean sky. She'd miss their special spot and the wonders it held.

And she'd miss a cavalryman with eyes the color of a forest pool and a chuckle that never failed to make her smile.

Danny flew off the porch as Will and Kate rode into the yard of the Geyser Gateway later that day.

"Where have you been?" he challenged his mother as Will helped her down from the saddle. "Did you catch the poacher? Did he catch you?"

Kate hugged him tight. "We lost him near the Madison, but we needed to alert the cavalry detachment at Norris. It was too late to return to the inn. Were you worried?"

"No," he said, disengaging, and Will wasn't entirely sure of the truth of that answer. "Private Franklin checked on us last night, and Private Smith came home this morning. And he brought me a baseball and bat."

Will glanced up. In the shadow of the porch, seated on the bench, Smith offered him a lazy smile. Will had left the baseball and bat in the barn, intending to give them to Danny when he returned. Apparently, Smith had decided to do the honors for him and taken all the credit.

"Good afternoon, Lieutenant," he drawled, not bothering to rise.

Before Will could comment, the door opened for Alberta, who held out a plate. "Apple pie, Private? I can bring you cream if you'd like."

"You are an angel of mercy, my dear Alberta," he said, accepting the plate with an incline of his bushy head. "Perhaps we should offer some to the lieutenant and Mrs. Tremaine as well."

Alberta swung to face the yard, as if noticing them for the first time. "Mrs. Tremaine, Lieutenant Prescott, how good to have you back! Are you hungry?"

"I'm hungry," Danny put in hopefully.

"I appreciate you feeding my men, Alberta," Will said, jaw tight, "but we have work to do. Smith!"

202

Smith shoved in a mouthful of the pie and handed the plate and fork to Alberta. "Duty calls."

"You're welcome to stay," Kate told Will as his private ambled down the steps.

"Thank you," he said, "for everything. But we have a patrol to ride. We still don't know whether the poacher remains in the area."

Her face tightened. "I'll keep watch here too."

Danny glanced between them. "Will you come back and show me how to play baseball, Lieutenant?"

The pleading tone, the wide eyes, pulled at his heart. "As soon as I can, Danny. I promise."

Kate slipped her arm about her son's shoulders and turned for the porch.

Will looked to Smith. "Where's your horse?"

"In the barn. I found the veranda a marvelous vantage point for viewing the entire geyser field. You should try it, Lieutenant."

"Perhaps after I've confirmed the rest of the area is safe," Will gritted out. "At least tell me what you learned at Riverside, assuming you actually reached Riverside."

"I did," he said, shifting on his feet as if standing for so short a time fatigued him or Will's conversation bored him. "They saw no sign of the poacher. I take it you and the Norris fellows had no better luck."

"None," Will admitted. "But with three detachments keeping an eye out for him, we're sure to locate him. Now, get your horse, and we'll finish the patrol."

"Sir." He pivoted toward where Danny was about to enter the inn. "Ho, General Tremaine. Would you be so good as to fetch me my horse?"

"Sure," Danny said, and he broke away from Kate to dart down the porch before Will could stop him.

"What are you doing?" he demanded of the private. "He has enough chores of his own."

Smith sighed. "Don't we all?"

Will shook his head as Kate stepped back from the door.

"Your duties are lighter than most," he told Smith. "Rizzo in Nadler's detachment is looking for a change. Perhaps I should trade you."

"You could," Smith allowed, lower lip sticking out over his beard as if he was pondering the matter. "But I'd put Nadler in his place on the first day. I assume the reason you chose me was because you thought you could keep up with me."

"I thought," Will said, "you might have

something you were trying to make up for, especially after Harris's comment about card games."

Those dark eyes glittered. "Ah, you would know something about making up for past mistakes, wouldn't you?"

Cold trickled down his back for all the day was warm. "Go fetch your horse, Soldier."

Smith strolled after Danny.

Kate moved back into the sunlight. "Everything all right, Will?"

When she looked at him that way, face soft and eyes wistful, everything should be all right. But he couldn't tell her the shame that threatened, the revulsion of who he'd been, what he'd done.

"Just thinking about the poacher," he said.

Her smile was sad, as if she commiserated. "You'll catch him. I have faith in you."

And that made him all the more determined to live up to her expectations.

As Kate went inside at last, he mounted Bess and gave her a pat.

"Just a little farther," he said softly in her upright ear.

Smith came riding around the hotel, and Will led him from the yard. He set them toward the north.

His private rode along, as easy in the

saddle as he'd been on the veranda. As they cleared the pines and started across the grassland, he heaved an audible sigh.

"Such a shame about Mrs. Tremaine."

Will had to fight to keep from tightening his grip on the reins. "What do you mean?"

Smith glanced his way with a half-smile. "More concerned about the lady's reputation than your own? How commendable."

"My reputation speaks for itself," Will told him. "So should Mrs. Tremaine's."

"I daresay the lady's will take some effort to dim. More so than a man who's served in Indian Territory."

The fellow's words were like slugs slipping down Will's back, cold and slimy. "If you have something to say, Private, say it."

Smith turned his attention to the road, but that self-satisfied smile remained. "Perhaps at a more opportune time."

Was that a hint of blackmail to come? Will wouldn't stand for it. He'd sooner have everyone in the detachment know what he'd done than to live under the constant fear of discovery.

"There is no more opportune time, Smith," he told him. "Whenever you choose to say what you think you know, I'll be there to refute it."

"Or confirm it," Smith agreed. "After all,

206

I can't be the only one to notice you wear no spurs. But you needn't be concerned. I'm impressed with your ability to rise above your circumstances. Sir."

"Adding sir doesn't help your insolence, Private," Will said. "You know I can order you on nothing but hardtack."

Smith pressed a hand to his chest like a dowager shocked by the latest fashion. "The horror. I'd only appeal to Alberta to rescue me. Such a dear. Too bad her livelihood is also at stake."

He ought to punish the cavalryman for his behavior. Captain Harris didn't stand for anyone dishonoring rank. But he had to agree with Kate that respect was earned. He had to be the man whom his men respected.

"Tell me what you heard about the Geyser Gateway, Private," he ordered.

Smith raised a brow but answered readily enough. "One of the Wakefield and Hoffman drivers spoke to me earlier at the Fire Hole. He's been told to favor that hotel over the Geyser Gateway."

Will frowned at him. "That's ridiculous. Captain Harris called the Fire Hole an unsatisfactory shanty."

"Better a shanty run by a respectable gentleman and his wife than a fancy hotel run by a harlot."

Will reined in. "Watch your words, Soldier."

Smith stopped as well. "Not *my* words, sir. I'm just repeating what the driver said. It seems others have heard that Mrs. Tremaine extended her hospitality to us over the winter. I believe the exact phrase used to describe the Geyser Gateway was 'fit only to be barracks.' And there appeared to be a question as to why a widow would want to spend so much time alone with soldiers."

"She won't be alone," Will protested. "Alberta and Danny will be with us. I wouldn't have proposed the scheme if I thought her reputation would be damaged."

Smith raised one hand. "Far be it from me to disagree with your plan, Lieutenant. I'd rather spend the winter at the hotel with Alberta's fine cooking than shivering in a cabin with you. You asked me what was being said about Mrs. Tremaine, and I told you."

Kate had expressed outrage that the Virginia City Outfitters would denigrate the Geyser Gateway. The rumors were spreading, but Captain Harris would surely find the place exceptional when he made his next inspection come spring. Will would personally recommend a ten-year lease for

Kate, however much good his word was with the captain and the Department of the Interior.

But the quality of the hotel was easily verified by its cleanliness, comfort, and cooking. A reputation was far harder to verify. Once lost, it might never be regained. He knew from experience.

"You may have to shiver, Private," he said. "Because if associating with us could damage Kate Tremaine's reputation, we will cease associating with her, no matter the cost to us."

13

Kate walked into the main salon of the inn, feeling oddly out of place. Why? Not a speck of dust showed on the furnishings; the hearth was swept clean. Sarah and Ida passed the arch on the other side, readying the tables for dinner. Alberta had a stew on — Kate could smell the rich scent. The inn was exactly as it should be. Was she the one who had changed?

Danny must have come through the kitchen, for he popped out of the dining room, biscuit in one hand. Kate caught him as he started past and hugged him a moment. His soft hair brushed her cheek. He smelled like the cinnamon and nutmeg Alberta used in her pies. She hadn't thought about him while she was away, comfortable in her staff's care of him. But she couldn't seem to get enough of him now.

He wiggled in her arms, and she reluctantly released him. Shoving the last of the biscuit in his mouth, he skipped around the nearest sofa. Oh, for an ounce of that energy.

"What did you do while I was gone?" she asked, watching him.

"We finished the ice cream," he informed her, making for the opposite sofa in a figure eight. "Miss Pringle and Mrs. Pettijohn played cards with me. Beggar-my-neighbor. Miss Pringle won. Mrs. Pettijohn didn't like that. I didn't mind."

She'd almost forgotten about her guests too! "Where are Miss Pringle and Mrs. Pettijohn?"

Danny skidded to a stop and cocked his head as if thinking about the answer. "They made Caleb take them to Old Faithful in the pony cart. They're coming back for dinner. You could talk to them on the telephone. Elijah said there's one at the tent hotel there and one at the Fire Hole Hotel. Telephones can talk to anyone."

"Not anyone," Kate said. "But we can reach many locations in the park now." She glanced around at the empty room. "And where are the other guests who were to arrive?"

"They went to the Fire Hole," Danny said, returning to his loop about the sofas. "They didn't want to stay here."

Kate blocked him as he rounded the sofa. "Why?"

Danny shrugged. "I don't know. Maybe they wanted to be closer to the telephone. Could we get one?"

"Maybe the Army will put one in for the winter," Kate told him. "It would be a lot easier than sending people between detachments." She turned him to face her. "Did we get any more guests?"

"One," Danny admitted, meeting her gaze. "Mr. Jones rode in from up north. He came to take the waters. I heard him tell Alberta."

That was odd. While many people believed the hot springs had healing properties, most invalids stayed near the bathhouses at Mammoth Hot Springs. Even the Fire Hole Hotel boasted a hot spring bath. Then again, the Geyser Gateway was less expensive than Mammoth Hot Springs and more comfortable than the Fire Hole. At least she had some advantages.

"Well, he's very welcome," Kate said. "We'll find a way to meet his needs."

"Or we could ask Lieutenant Prescott," Danny said, darting away again. "He helps everyone. I knew he'd take care of you last night."

Kate nodded, mind already working. "He

did. And we should take care of our duties too. You should probably go see if we need . . ."

"More wood brought in," Danny finished, shoulders slumping.

Kate pulled him close once more. "I was going to say more help tasting those biscuits."

He glanced up and back, eyes lighting. "Yes, ma'am."

As she released him, he skipped toward the kitchen.

Kate straightened with a sigh. A shame she couldn't be satisfied with biscuits. But the rumors were spreading. She had to fight them! Will was right that her guests knew the truth about the Geyser Gateway, but she wouldn't have guests if the Virginia City Outfitters scared off all her customers before they even walked in the door. She'd hoped that hosting Will and his men through the winter would give her money for improvements. That money would have to go toward paying Alberta's salary if Kate couldn't keep the trade she'd predicted through September.

Though a Mr. Jones had not been on the list.

She checked the big guest book to be sure. There was Miss Pringle's reservation and her precise handwriting noting her arrival. Mrs. Pettijohn's writing was more sprawling as she claimed her room. Nothing for a Mr. Jones. Had no one even signed him in? Perhaps she should introduce herself, see how much assistance he required, after she changed into more suitable clothing.

A quarter hour later, gowned in a blue-and-white striped bodice and blue skirts, Kate went in search of her newest guest. But Alberta had no idea where Mr. Jones had gone, and most of the rooms Kate poked her nose in were empty. She finally located Pansy cleaning out the last room on the south side of the hotel. Kate had always felt the rooms comfortable, but the polished mahogany headboard, thick quilt with its green-and-brown-patterned blocks, and feather pillows looked downright luxurious after her stay in the tent camp. How could anyone complain?

"Where's Mr. Jones?" she asked Pansy.

"He left his two horses in the barn and a saddlebag in room eleven across the way and went out again," Pansy said, snapping the clean sheet up and out so that it floated down on the tick. "I thought he was going to view the geysers."

Kate helped her tuck in the corners. "I'll find him and then come back and help you with the rooms. I'm expecting a group of six from Monida later this week."

Pansy nodded, and Kate went to walk the geysers.

Fountain was living up to its name, the spray obscuring most of the west side of the field. She stood and watched the falling water a moment, the cool breeze bringing her stray drops that left dark patches on her skirts. Sulfur clung to the air. There was no sign of a cavalryman, but Will and Private Smith would have reached their camp by now. Still, Danny was right. Will was a handy fellow to have around. He'd been right at her side until she'd gone to sleep at the tent camp. And he'd only left her alone there for practical reasons.

She sighed as she started around the field. Toby had been one to take chances, never considering the consequences. Will tended to think things through, look for possible problems, and resolve them before they grew. He appeared to be a man one could count on. The urge to do so was surprisingly strong.

She paused to watch the paint pots bubble, thick and gloppy so late in the season. She'd managed this hotel alone for a year, survived last winter as well. Why was she so willing to entertain the idea of letting

215

someone else come alongside her, give him part of her work, her life? Wasn't she just opening herself up to trouble?

Besides, what would happen next spring? As soon as the Department of the Interior appointed a new superintendent, the Army would leave. And Will would go with it. Did she truly want to give her heart to a man who, like Toby, would leave her behind or expect her to arrange her life to suit his?

She rounded Silex Spring and spotted another man out by Jelly Geyser. He wore stained buckskins and a coonskin cap, but he must not have any idea where the geysers were, for he was coming in from the southwest, where none existed. Kate cut across the area to try to reach him.

"Mr. Jones?" she called.

He didn't react. Was he hard of hearing? He might wander into a paint pot if he couldn't listen for the plop-plop. She hurried forward.

He turned then and smiled at her, stopping as if to allow her to catch up. A short, stocky, craggy-faced fellow with a rough grizzled beard and crooked teeth, he stuck out a hand. "You must be Mrs. Tremaine. I understand I just missed you yesterday at Norris. I slept in the tent camp last night with you."

Kate accepted his hand and gave it a shake, surprised by the strong grip. "We're glad to have you. Tell me, what do you think of the Geyser Gateway?"

He glanced past her toward the hotel. "A fine establishment. Best I've seen in the park."

He sounded as if the observation came from long experience. "Have you traveled through before?" she asked, watching him.

"Once or twice." He returned his gaze to hers, his blue eyes cool and assessing. "Maybe you could answer a question for me. What do you all do for excitement around here?"

She pointed to the east of the field. "Watch the paint pots bubble over."

He laughed. "I never could understand the attraction. A man of my years has seen enough that he needs more to stimulate his interest."

He waited. What did he want her to say? She knew what excited some men. Liquor was forbidden in the park, except in the dining room of the National Hotel and the Fire Hole, and she wouldn't have served it anyway. Nor could she condone gambling. And she wasn't about to suggest he go hunting.

"I was told you'd come to take the waters,

Mr. Jones," she said. "We don't have a bath-house here, but we have on occasion brought in warm water for bathing. We have two copper tubs. I'd be happy to have Pansy set one up in your room."

He waved a hand. "If I want to soak, I know where to go. I didn't come here for the bathing. I've run across a rough patch of luck, and it suits me just fine to recuperate at your excellent establishment." He glanced back at the hotel again, then pulled his cap lower, until it nearly covered his eyes. "In fact, I think I'll avail myself of the pie your cook offered me before I came out here. Excuse me."

He started for the inn just as Will rode into the yard.

It wasn't time for his afternoon patrol. Was something wrong?

Had he come to see her?

Kate shook herself and hurried back. By the time she reached him, he was reining in and the door was banging shut behind Mr. Jones.

Will nodded to her in greeting before dismounting. "New guest? I just caught his back in passing. He seemed in a big hurry."

"Apparently he likes pie," she said. "But he was behaving himself on the geyser field. I don't think he'll be any trouble."

"Unlike me and my men."

She glanced at him in surprise. "Why? What have you done?"

"Damaged the reputation of the Geyser Gateway," he said, eyes dipping at the corners. "And for that I apologize. Now I just need to figure out what to do about it."

She was frowning so fiercely, head tilted as if she just couldn't believe what he'd told her.

"What have you heard?" she fumed.

He grimaced as he pulled off his hat, then went to tie Bess to the hitching post. "More than you should hear. Suffice it to say, your honor and the quality of the hotel are in question because you agreed to let us stay this winter. I'll inform Captain Harris the arrangement is off."

Her eyes narrowed. "No. This is ridiculous! You can't tell me the other hotel owners wouldn't welcome the opportunity to have the Army protect their property through the winter."

"Most of the other hotel owners are men," he pointed out.

"So, I'm to be deprived of the protection because I'm a woman?" She threw up her hands. "I won't have it. We have an agreement, Lieutenant, and I expect the Army to honor it."

He knew only one way to respond to such bravery. He stood tall and saluted her. "Ma'am."

"At ease, Soldier," she said, familiar twinkle starting in her eyes.

Will shook his head as he lowered his arm. "I can't be at ease, Kate. I don't like the idea that our presence could damage your livelihood."

"It isn't your presence. This is the fault of the Virginia City Outfitters. Can't you see? They're spreading rumors to stop people from staying at the Geyser Gateway. You heard the lodge keeper last night. My place is rough. I lost guests this afternoon because someone convinced them to try the Fire Hole instead. As if the Geyser Gateway was in any way inferior."

"Smith overheard the guests claiming your inn was fit only to be barracks," Will admitted.

Her face darkened even as her lips tightened. "Oh, how scurrilous! The Army should be so fortunate as to have barracks this fine."

"No arguments there. Are you sure you want us here all winter?"

"Yes," she insisted. "And it won't be long now. Elijah and the other drivers are out of the park by October first. One or two private parties might come in by horseback or wagon in early October, but by Halloween, we'll be snowed in."

Hard to imagine those heated pools surrounded by white mounds. "Sounds like Yellowstone has three seasons — July, August, and winter."

She laughed. "See how well you know the place?"

"I'm learning," Will said. "And I wouldn't have half this knowledge without your help."

"Everyone needs help sometimes."

"Even you?"

She climbed to the porch and sat on a bench, and it struck him that this was one of the few times he'd ever seen her still on purpose. He came to join her, and they sat a moment, watching the play of water across the geyser field. Much as he hated to admit it, Smith was right. It was an excellent vantage point. He could see clear across to the pines beyond.

"I need help," she said, so quietly that her words were just audible over the plop of mud and hiss of steam. "You saw me the other day with the bear. If you hadn't been there, Danny or I might have been mauled."

"The bear didn't look all that interested in charging," Will demurred.

She knit her fingers together in the lap of her blue gown. "I thought I'd be fine, that I'd lived here long enough to know how to handle myself around animals. But look what happened. One glimpse, and I panicked." She nodded out onto the field, where the waters of one of the pools trembled a moment before shooting into the sky, crystal and bright. "Toby's death made me feel like that geyser, uncontrolled, unable to control. I don't know what I should have done differently, how I should have reacted." Her voice vibrated with confusion, pain.

"I suspect anyone could feel that way after someone they love dies," Will allowed.

She shook her head. "My parents died when Toby and I still lived in Boston. Influenza. I mourned them, missed them terribly. This is different."

He wanted to take her in his arms, but he settled on shifting closer to her on the bench. "What happened?"

She drew in a shaky breath. "We heard a noise out back one night, and we both went down to investigate. I could see it out the kitchen window — a huge grizzly rummaging around in the trash pit behind the hotel. We generally bury our waste, what the chickens don't eat, but it was toward the end of a busy summer, and the waste had gotten away from us."

Will nodded, letting the words flow out of her like steam from a geyser, hoping the very act of talking might relieve some of the pressure.

"Toby kept saying the poor bear was hungry. It probably was. Why else root through the garbage? I tried to tell him we didn't need to help it, but he insisted on taking out some of the brisket that was left from dinner." She paused to wipe at her cheeks. "Toby rarely listened to me. He did what he wanted, when he wanted. So he walked out to feed that bear. It went after the food, or maybe Toby — I don't know. I just remember screaming and screaming." She dropped her head, chest heaving.

Will put his arm about her back, and her head tipped onto his shoulder as if the memory had exhausted her. He could feel her trembling.

"There was nothing you could do," he told her. "You said yourself he wouldn't listen. If you had gone out after him, you might have been mauled too."

"I should have brought a rifle," she protested. "I should have thrown something from the kitchen. Elijah did. He heard my screams. So did Caleb. They both came running. They scared the bear away. But it was too late. Toby was gone. I couldn't save him."

She sucked in a breath, shuddering, and he just held her. What more could he say? He knew that feeling of helplessness, of wanting more than anything to change the past. But nothing would bring Danny's father back. And nothing would bring back those he had wronged.

She straightened away from him, raising her head to show tears gleaming on her cheeks. "Thank you."

He pulled back his arm, for all a part of him demanded he leave it right where it had been. "Just doing my duty, ma'am."

That won a chuckle from her. "Ah yes. I'm sure they cover that in cavalry training — caring for your horse, shooting a rifle while charging, comforting widows."

"Always was partial to the last," Will said.

She nudged him with her shoulder. "Well, don't become too enamored of it. I don't require comforting often."

No, she didn't. Already she was gathering her composure, tucking away the pain the same way she tucked up her riding skirt.

"I don't imagine you do," he said.

She rose from the bench. "I promised Pansy I'd help her finish making the beds. I should go. Was there anything else you needed?"

To stand at your side.

The words hovered on his lips, begged to be uttered. But he didn't have that right.

Could he earn it?

No denying the hope that surged up at the thought. He hadn't had a home, a family other than the Army, in more than a decade. Since Oregon, he'd never let himself dream of more. But he could see himself here, beside her, protecting the park, protecting her, teaching Danny to be a man.

A finer man than he'd ever been.

"No," he made himself say. "I'm glad you're still willing to allow us to stay the winter. I'll help, however I can."

Because maybe then he might be worthy of a place in her life.

225

14

Will was offering his usual help, but Kate found herself yearning for more, like a shoot craved the first drop of spring rain.

She forced herself to step back from him. "Are you going to patrol now?"

"Might as well, since I'm here." He slipped his hat back onto his head and tugged down at it. "Care to join me?"

Not feeling the way she did at the moment. She could imagine her hand slipping into his, their steps matching as they wandered the wonders, heads close together. Dangerous. Too dangerous.

"No, thank you," she said. "Elijah is due in soon. I want to see what he's heard about these rumors."

He nodded. She watched him as he descended the stairs and headed for the geysers, his walk purposeful, confident. If only she had similar confidence in her feelings. She turned for the hotel and went to help Pansy.

Making the beds, however, failed entirely to take her mind off the scene on the veranda. What was it about Will? Once more, she'd all but tumbled into his arms as she'd unburdened herself. Had those feelings festered since Toby's death? She hadn't realized she'd fallen into the trap.

If only, if only.

"If only wishes were horses, beggars would ride," she muttered to herself as she tucked in a sheet.

"Beg pardon?" Pansy asked, plumping a pillow.

"Just thinking out loud," Kate said.

Of course she'd wanted to help Toby that night. But the truth was, there had been nothing she could have done, much as she wished it otherwise. Will was right — if she had gone out after Toby, Danny could well have lost both parents. Terror had kept her rooted in the kitchen, watching the scene unfold before her. But that terror had saved her life and given her a chance to raise her son. She'd been carrying the guilt too long. Time to let it go.

She drew in a breath. "Where should I send word for you to return, Pansy?"

"I'll be staying with my sister in Virginia City," the older maid answered. "And I'd welcome hearing from you." She straightened her back and glanced around. "There's nothing like the Geyser Gateway."

No, there wasn't. If only Kate could help the park guests see that.

She and Pansy were putting sheets on the last bed when she heard the rumble of hooves that heralded the stage's arrival. Leaving Pansy to finish, she hurried out onto the veranda.

Only one couple exited the coach, the husband handing his wife down. As Caleb came to take charge of the horses, Elijah jumped to the ground to usher the two toward the hotel.

"What did I tell you?" he declared with a wave of his gauntleted hand. "Nicest inn in the park. And here's Mrs. Tremaine, the owner, to greet you."

Kate smoothed down her bodice and put on her best smile. "Welcome to the Geyser Gateway. We have a room ready just for you."

The woman, a buxom blonde who looked to be about Kate's age, gowned in a cream walking dress whose hem was dotted with the orange of a geyser field, glanced over to where Will was just finishing his sweep. "Do we have to share the sleeping room with soldiers?"

By the tone of the question, Kate couldn't tell whether she thought it a good idea or a poor one.

"No soldiers are staying at present," Kate assured her. "And every family is given its own room, a suite if there are children."

The husband, a tall man with raven hair waved back from his forehead, put a hand on his wife's elbow and narrowed his eyes. "How much?"

By the time Kate had finished explaining the costs, the meals, and the rules, she had them registered, and Pansy was standing by to escort them to their room. Elijah brought in their bags.

"Thank you," Kate said when he returned to the salon. "I understand they aren't the first ones expressing concerns about the Geyser Gateway."

Elijah shook his head. "Rumors are flying faster than my horses' hooves. Is it true? Are you going to house the Army?"

"Only this winter and only Lieutenant Prescott's detachment," Kate assured him. "No guests will be inconvenienced. And the Lower Geyser Basin will still have all its glories come spring."

He nodded. "I'll let my passengers know."

"Maybe put in a good word with the other drivers?" Kate suggested.

He chuckled. "Most of them like working with the Yellowstone Park Association too much to bring their riders to other hotels. And a few are hoping the Virginia City Outfitters will pay better. But don't you worry, Mrs. Tremaine. I'm not about to accept their offer."

Kate clutched his arm. "The Virginia City Outfitters made you an offer?"

"Second one this month."

She dropped her hand. "Oh, Elijah. Can I match it?"

His smile flashed. "Doubtful. But neither can they. They may like to pretend all is well, but they haven't managed to buy up a single lease. How are they going to pay with no beds to bring in income? You pay, and you pay reliably. And you treat me better than most. That counts with me."

The new couple, who Kate had learned were the Weatherbys, came down the corridor.

"How long do the geysers run?" Mrs. Weatherby asked.

"All day and into the night," Kate assured her. "Just stay on the path as I explained."

They ventured out onto the veranda.

"Thank you," she said to Elijah as the Weatherbys descended the steps. "I don't know what I'd do without you."

"Miss your mail and all the good stories," Elijah said with a laugh. "Nothing for you in the mail today, by the way, but I heard something else you might want to know. Lieutenant Kingman has been recalled. He leaves in about two weeks."

Kate stiffened. "Daniel Kingman has done more to build the roads in Yellowstone than most of the superintendents combined. Who's replacing him?"

"I expect we'll find out come spring," Elijah said. "I'm sorry to see him go too. Any road he built is built to last."

Kate cocked her head. "Do you expect to see him before he leaves?"

"He was up at Norris inspecting the changes there," he supplied. "You want to get word to him?"

"Yes. I'll write a formal note for you to take, but I'd like to invite him and his staff to dine before he goes. It's the least we can do to thank him for all he's given to the park."

"You write that note, I'll see it delivered," Elijah promised. His dark eyes sparkled. "You going to invite your lieutenant too?"

"Lieutenant Prescott is not mine," Kate informed him, but her cheeks were heating.

Elijah pursed his lips. "So, I should ignore the rumor that he's courting you."

231

"Absolutely," Kate said. "He's helping at the inn, and I'm helping guide him around the basin. That's all."

"If you say so," Elijah replied. "But he looks mighty intent for a man only interested in a guide." He nodded over Kate's shoulder. Turning, she saw Will coming into the hotel.

He removed his hat and nodded to Elijah before focusing on Kate. "Your new guests asked me about Fairy Falls. Have I seen that yet?"

No, because the route traveled perilously close to her and Danny's special spot. But Elijah was watching her, and she didn't dare mention her concerns.

"No," Kate said brightly. "It's a little ways from the hotel. You hadn't planned to stay more than one night, had you, Elijah?"

"No, ma'am," he said. "We are on a schedule. Norris tomorrow, then Mammoth Hot Springs and Cinnabar. And I'm taking Ida and Sarah with us."

That's right. She'd be down two staff shortly. "Then I guess the Weatherbys will have to miss seeing Fairy Falls."

"If the spot is well known," Will persisted, "I should see it."

"Maybe you should ask your guide," Elijah said with a look to Kate.

Will was watching her too.

Kate made herself smile. "Danny and I can take you there sometime. When Elijah hasn't brought me more guests."

Elijah laughed. "And that's my cue to go. I think I'll ask Alberta about dinner." He nodded to Will. "Lieutenant."

Will nodded back. "Mr. Freeman."

Elijah turned for the kitchen, and Will looked to Kate.

"Everything all right?"

Had he caught the interplay with Elijah? No way was she telling him about the rumor that she and Will were courting. But she should tell him about the other.

"Everything's fine," Kate assured him. "But Elijah had heard about the Army staying here too. I think Mrs. Weatherby also knew."

He winced. "Maybe we *should* call things off."

Not on her life. "No," she insisted. "You're staying with us this winter. But I have a lot to do before then, so perhaps we can take our trip to Fairy Falls in a week or two."

He frowned. "But I thought you said snow could be falling in a few weeks."

It could. But that would mean she didn't have to take a chance that he would find the meadow before spring. "Ah, well.

There's always next year."

The kitchen door banged as Danny ran out. He dashed through the dining room and to her side.

"Is it true?" he asked, glancing from Kate to Will and back. "We're going to Fairy Falls?"

She looked from one hopeful face to another.

Why not? something urged inside. *What do you have to lose?*

Kate sighed. "I guess so. We'll leave tomorrow, right after Lieutenant Prescott makes his morning sweep."

Will gave her the smile that warmed her heart, then turned to Danny. "In the meantime, let's break out that ball and bat and see if they're up to your arm."

Danny's eyes brightened.

The next morning dawned gray and thick. Despite her happy memory of Will and Danny behind the inn, tossing the ball and practicing with the bat, Kate felt a foreboding as heavy as the clouds. It didn't help that Sarah and Ida had left on Elijah's stage out of the park. Only Ida had looked tearful as she waved goodbye. Kate would have more work with them gone, and she had to keep Will away from the terrain she'd sworn to protect. Yet it seemed wrong, as if she shouldn't be hiding things from him.

Danny had no concerns. He chattered all the way through breakfast.

"Perhaps we should make the acquaintance of these Fairy Falls as well," Mrs. Pettijohn declared as she dug into a second helping of biscuits and gravy.

"It sounds lovely," her sister agreed, forking up a dainty mouthful. "But perhaps a bit too far of a jaunt. Besides, we wouldn't want to leave Mr. Jones without company." She fluttered her silver lashes at the frontiersman.

Mr. Jones shoved back his chair. "I'm more interested in seeing the famous animals of Yellowstone. Do you have any idea where to find antelope? Elk? Buffalo?"

"I do not," Mrs. Pettijohn informed him.

Kate wasn't about to answer.

He shrugged. "Then I'm going fishing." He stalked out of the room.

Mrs. Pettijohn turned to Kate. "We shall borrow your pony cart and young fellow Caleb, and go out the bridle path to see the geysers to the east of us."

Miss Pringle clapped her hands. "Excellent notion! The guidebook says one is pink."

Kate made sure to warn them and Caleb

of the potential dangers before sending them off. She and Danny were out on the porch, Danny jumping from one step to another, when Will rode in. As Kate set aside the broom she'd been using, her son froze on the middle stair.

"Where's Private Smith?" he asked as Will reined in. "I like him. He's funny."

"Private Smith will be patrolling both morning and afternoon," Will told him, dismounting. "I'm afraid you'll have to make do with me."

Danny glanced at Kate. "Can I ride with Lieutenant Prescott?"

"No one's riding," Kate said. "We're walking."

Will held out the reins. "But you could ride my horse to the barn for me."

Danny's eyes widened. "Can I, Ma?"

His legs would never reach the stirrup cups, but the cavalry horse seemed well trained, and it was only a little distance. "All right," Kate said. "We'll wait for you."

Will lifted him up into the saddle and watched as his horse walked toward the outbuilding. "When did he become so fond of Smith?"

When did I become so fond of you?

Kate made herself answer his question. "Ever since we spent the night at Norris,

236

apparently. Private Smith was kind to Danny."

"I wish I knew why." He turned to Kate. "Sorry. I didn't mean that the way it sounded. Anyone with any sense could grow fond of Danny. It's just that Smith tends to keep to himself. I'm not even sure Smith is his real name."

Kate frowned. "Doesn't the Army generally know who they recruit?"

"No," he admitted. "He showed up at Fort Colville one day. Only Captain Harris seems to know his particulars. Being in the cavalry in Indian Territory isn't the most sought-after position. We take debtors, criminals."

Kate stiffened. "You let a criminal near Danny?"

"Not willingly," he assured her. "And I don't know that Smith is one."

"Are there other cavalrymen I should worry about?" she asked.

He hesitated, and her heart sank. She could not imagine the clever Private Franklin or the big-boned Private Lercher as criminals. She couldn't imagine any of them as criminals!

Then he shook his head. "No. All my men are handpicked, even Smith. Most I'd trust with my life. I took Smith because I wanted to give him a chance to prove himself. Every man deserves that."

Normally, she would agree, but not when it came to influencing her son. Danny tended to mimic anyone he found interesting. She didn't like thinking what he might pick up from a criminal. But Danny was running back from the barn, and she didn't want to discuss the matter in front of him.

Still, she couldn't help thinking. She had welcomed these men to the park, to her kitchen. They'd be staying all winter. Did they pose a greater danger than to her reputation?

Will followed Kate onto a narrow trail directly west of the hotel.

"You can also reach the falls around the hillside to the south on the circuit road," she said as they walked through the field toward the Firehole River. "But this is the best route from the inn and the main geyser area."

It was a pretty place, low grass waving in tufts against a bone-white soil. A weathered footbridge with a handrail on one side allowed them to cross the rushing waters of the river. Once they reached the other side, Danny took the lead, humming to himself. He glanced back over his shoulder. "Can we show him the big spring too, Ma?"

"Bigger than what's by the hotel?" Will asked.

Danny turned to walk backward and spread his arms as wide as they could go. "Huge!"

"Pay attention," Kate ordered him, and he swung back around and loped forward.

"If you look in the guidebook you brought," Kate told Will as they skirted a hill covered in pine, "you'll likely find something called the Grand Prismatic Spring. I'm not sure whether it falls in your jurisdiction or in the area patrolled by the detachment at Old Faithful."

He wasn't either. "Popular stop for tourists?" he asked as they reached a bridle path leading south.

"Not as much as Old Faithful, and not all stages stop there, but it should be protected too."

"I'll work that out with the corporal in charge at Old Faithful."

Up ahead on the right, across the trickle she'd called Fairy Creek, the meadow lapped into a draw between two hills. "What's in there?" Will asked.

She turned her back on the space and nodded to their left. "It's what's over there that should concern you: a series of small lakes — Goose Lake, Feather Lake, and the

Goslings."

Will chuckled. "Someone liked geese."

She glanced at him with a smile. "I'm not sure why. But they are a popular destination for those who like a good stroll."

They followed the western edge of Goose Lake, the murky waters dark and brooding. Danny sped up as they continued south. Will thought Kate might order him back, but she didn't appear too concerned. Her gaze was bright, smile pleasant. Well, the grasslands did make it easy to keep an eye on the boy.

"This way!" he called, stepping off the path to start up a hill dotted by pines.

Will and Kate followed. The way was steep and slick with fallen needles. Will turned to help Kate. She passed him without comment.

"What, are you part mountain goat?" he asked her back.

Her laughter floated down to him. "Having trouble keeping up, Lieutenant?"

"I'm in the cavalry, not the infantry," he reminded her, but he managed to reach the top without slipping more than twice.

"Look," Danny said, pointing, as if Will could have missed the rainbow of colors below.

Will's first thought was that Danny was

right. The formation was huge. Its silver-gray deposits spread out over yards below him. The center of the massive pool was a blue so deep it was nearly purple, melding into rings of lighter blue, green, and yellow. At the edge, plumes of orange streaked out like the rays of the sun. Smaller pools huddled around it, dwarfed by its magnificence. And the entire area gave off a curtain of steam that fluttered on the breeze.

Will shook his head. "How does something like that come to be?"

"Men of science travel through now and again," Kate said, voice soft. "They talk about hot water and minerals and rocks reacting to each other. Doesn't make this one whit less amazing."

"I want to throw a rock in it," Danny said dreamily. "Right in the middle."

"Daniel Tobias Tremaine," Kate scolded. "We do not throw anything in the thermal features."

He hung his head. "Yes, ma'am."

Will nudged his shoulder. "Maybe we could see whether the Firehole River needs a few more rocks some evening."

Danny looked to his mother. "Could we, Ma?"

"The banks are lined with rocks that used to be in the river," Kate acknowledged.

"Putting them back in shouldn't hurt anything."

Danny grinned.

They descended the hill, all three of them sliding at times, and set off on the path once more.

"Is that something all men grow up wanting to do?" Kate asked as Danny ranged ahead once more. "Throw rocks and sticks?"

"Into things, over things, onto things," Will said. "I've never known a man or boy who didn't."

"No wonder we have to protect Yellowstone," she muttered.

"Now, you can't tell me you never had the urge," Will said, glancing her way. The walk had loosened her hair. The braid had come free of the bun and was hanging down her back, tendrils of black curling against her cheeks.

"Never," she said, nose in the air.

"And you never stuck your finger in Alberta's cooking either, I suppose."

Pink climbed in her cheeks. "Well, maybe once or twice."

"Thrown a snowball at someone?"

She grinned at him. "Guess you'll find out this winter."

All at once, he wished for snow.

"Up here!" Danny called, and Kate and

Will hastened their steps.

The trail came out at the foot of a rough gray cliff. Steep hills covered in pine narrowed in on the bowl at the cliff's base. Over the top tumbled a thin line of water, which plunged into a pool below. Behind the spray, the cliff had been eroded into a cave.

Danny ran to stand in the mist, the silvery drops all but obscuring him.

Kate stopped near the edge of the pool, and Will paused beside her, watching the water fall.

"You can see why they named it Fairy Falls," she said. "The water's so fine and misty, not like at the Falls of the Yellowstone. Those have power. You can hear the roar a mile away. This has its own quiet beauty."

"So do you." The words were out before he could think better of them, but he had no urge to call them back. Her eyes, as misty as the falls, widened as he bent his head toward hers.

15

Will was kissing her — softly, tenderly, as if she was impossibly precious. No one had ever kissed her that way before, full of wonder, awe. She wanted to bask in the moment, float in the feeling of bliss.

"Ew," Danny said. "You're kissing."

Will broke away from her, cheeks reddening. But his gaze remained on hers, searching. He'd taken a risk, and he wasn't sure how she'd react.

Neither was she. She hadn't invited his kiss, but she couldn't regret such a marvel any more than she would regret a rainbow over the Lower Geyser Basin.

Still, she had to say something, at least to Danny.

"Men and women kiss to show their regard for each other," she told her son where he stood beside the base of the waterfall. "I greatly admire Lieutenant

Prescott. And he admires me." She eyed Will.

He nodded, still looking a bit thunderstruck. "A great deal."

"Oh." Danny bent and hefted a rock at the edge of the pool. "Could I throw this in, Ma? Please?"

"Very well," Kate said.

The rock sailed over the pool and plunked down into the shallow waters. Then Danny ran to the cliff and set about trying to wiggle in behind the waterfall.

How quickly he forgot the kiss. A shame she couldn't forget so easily. But then, did she really want to? Her lips still tingled. Her heart still sang.

Will was rubbing the back of his neck with one hand, gaze now on the ground, as if as conflicted about what had just happened.

"Forgive me." His voice was barely audible over the splash of the waterfall. "I had no right."

"Do you want the right?" she asked.

He dropped his hand and met her gaze. "It's not that simple."

She could believe that. It wasn't simple for her either. Some would have said she owed it to Toby to mourn longer than a year. Others would have urged her to grab the opportunity that had fallen into her lap.

It wasn't a bad thing to marry a cavalry officer. Danny could do with a father.

A father who would stay by his side, not ride off to the next adventure.

She raised her chin. "Don't let it trouble you, Lieutenant. All this grandeur can go to anyone's head." She turned to eye the waterfall, then frowned. "Danny?"

No one responded.

Heart leaping into her throat, Kate rushed to the edge of the pool, looked left, right. "Danny! Danny, answer me!"

"He was right here," Will said, coming up beside her. He added his voice to hers. "Danny! Report!"

From somewhere not too distant, she thought she heard a giggle. She could not find it in her heart to laugh along.

"Daniel Tobias Tremaine!" she shouted. "Come out here right now!"

Danny darted out from the recess under the falls so quickly the water splashed his head and shoulders. Thoroughly damp, he waded to her side.

"You didn't know where I was," he said triumphantly. "That's a really good hiding place."

Too good for her nerves, that was for sure. For one moment, all she could think about was another mangled body.

"Yes, it was," she said, willing her speeding heartbeat to slow. "But you must always come when I call, Danny. I worry too much otherwise."

"You don't have to worry," Danny said, bending to pick up another rock from the shore. "I'm smart, and I'm strong."

She wanted to hug him tight, pick him up and carry him all the way back to the safety of the hotel. She managed a smile for his sake. "You are smart and strong, but bad things can happen even to smart, strong people."

"That's why you have a mother who watches over you," Will said.

Kate exhaled and inhaled slowly. "That's right. We must look to friends and family to help us when we need them."

Danny smiled up at Will. "Like Lieutenant Prescott."

"Yes," Kate said. "Like Lieutenant Prescott. Now, come along. It's time to start back."

He let go of the rock, just far enough away from his slender body that it plopped into the pool. Boys. Men! Would she ever understand them?

The walk back was even faster than the one out. Danny seemed as eager to reach the hotel as Kate, and Will strode along, glancing her way from time to time as if unsure what to say to her. At least she didn't have to direct his gaze away from their special spot. They passed the entrance to the meadow without a remark, and she told herself to breathe easier.

Impossible. Every time she looked at Will, she remembered the feel of those lips against hers, the warmth of his embrace, the tenderness in his eyes. She wanted to run toward him and away from him at the same time!

He could well have felt the same way, for he distanced himself from her the moment the three of them crossed onto the geyser field in front of the hotel.

Come on, Kate! You have to remember why you're here, why he's here. Do your duty.

As Danny ran ahead, Kate caught Will's arm. "Now that you know the way to Fairy Falls, you might check it and the Grand Prismatic Spring at least once a week."

"We will," he promised, face so still it might have been carved of stone, "as soon as the rest of my men return."

Kate released him. "Very well, then." She started past him, and now he moved to block her way.

"Kate, I . . . ." He stopped with a sigh. "I don't know what to say about that kiss."

248

"Not much to be said," Kate answered. "I understand. Neither of us is in a position to court. We both have responsibilities."

"Responsibilities, yes." He seemed to cling to the word like a lifeline. "I just want you to know I don't take such things lightly."

She cocked her head. "Do you mean responsibilities or the kiss?"

He visibly swallowed. "Both."

Kate straightened. "Good to know, Lieutenant. I wouldn't like to think you were trifling with my affections. You might find yourself near a geyser without a guide."

His smile inched into view. "I wouldn't want that."

With a nod, she passed him for the hotel even as he headed for the barn and his horse. Perhaps they could put that kiss behind them. Perhaps things would be calmer from here.

As if to disagree with her, Alberta came out onto the porch, door banging shut behind her.

"Is it true?" she begged Kate, big hands wrapping themselves inside her apron. "We're to host a fancy dinner for the Army?"

Who kept starting these rumors?

"I sent an invitation with Elijah to ask Lieutenant Kingman and his staff to dinner

249

with us before he leaves for the season," Kate told her. "This is his last summer in Yellowstone. But the dinner doesn't have to be anything fancy."

Alberta let go of her apron and drew herself up. "Of course it must be fancy! He deserves no less. I remember all the times he and Mr. Tremaine sat in this very hotel, talking and laughing." She sniffed, eyes filling. "It seems a long time since we heard such laughter."

Kate lifted her skirts and climbed to Alberta's side. "I know, Alberta. I miss Toby too."

Alberta sniffed again. "When my Joe and Tommy never came home, the world seemed so dark and cold. Coming here helped. Then you and Mr. Tremaine and little Danny arrived, and I felt like I had a family again."

Kate hugged her, breathing in the scent of cinnamon and fresh-baked bread. "Me too."

Alberta hugged her back, arms like firm pillows. Then she pulled away, and her round face became more determined.

"That's another reason we need this dinner to be perfect," she told Kate. "I want that ten-year lease as much as you do. We need everyone to understand the Geyser Gateway is the best."

Why hadn't she thought of that? Lieutenant Kingman would have to take his leave of Captain Harris before quitting the park. He could recommend her for a ten-year lease. She had always welcomed the lieutenant. The dedicated engineer had been as bemused as Kate by her mercurial husband. This was her chance to impress him with all the inn had to offer. He'd take word to Captain Harris and his superiors in the Army Corps of Engineers. Her lease would be assured.

"You're right, Alberta," Kate said, stepping back. "We must do our very utmost. If Lieutenant Kingman agrees to my invitation, we only have a short time to prepare. I suggested Friday."

Alberta pressed a hand to her chest. "Friday! That's only two days away."

Kate put a hand on her shoulder. "We'll gather everyone. We'll make a plan."

"But Sarah and Ida just left with Elijah," Alberta protested.

"I know," Kate commiserated. "But we can do this with Pansy's and Caleb's help. The table linens will need washing, ironing; the silver polishing."

"I'll bring out the best crystal," Alberta promised with a nod. "The pieces we save for wedding parties and anniversaries." She

251

raised her voice. "You'll stick up for us, won't you, Lieutenant?"

He was leading his saddled horse out into the yard. "I would defend the honor of the Geyser Gateway with my last breath, ma'am," he assured her. "Are we under attack?"

"Not if we manage this dinner," Alberta said.

He glanced from her to Kate. "Dinner?"

"I invited Lieutenant Kingman of the Corps of Engineers and his staff to dine," Kate explained, hand falling. "It must be the finest evening we can manage."

"It will be the making of the Geyser Gateway," Alberta predicted. "You'll come too, Lieutenant. You and your men, especially that Private Smith. He reminds me of my Tommy, so confident, so full of himself."

His gaze returned to Kate's, waiting. He was willing to accept whatever she offered, however small. And here she'd teased him about trifling with her affections. Will Prescott might look rough and tough with his dark gaze and his stoic face, but, she was certain, inside he was made of softer stuff. He wanted her good opinion as much as she wanted his. Perhaps even more.

She could still refuse, claim there wouldn't be enough room, enough food. But she found she liked the idea of him at her side as much as he seemed to like it.

Oh, but she was in trouble.

So, she'd invited him to dinner. Will glanced to the left at the waving grass of the meadow and the right at the wooded hill as he rode Bess back to camp, but he couldn't seem to focus on either. His thoughts veered back to that kiss. Kate had made light of it, put it down to the moment, the beauty of the falls. But the wonders of Yellowstone were nothing compared to the wonder that was Kate — strong, bright, determined, lovely.

Giving in to the moment was just an excuse. It wasn't the moment that had drawn him to her. He admired how she managed her hotel, how she dealt with difficulties, how she was raising Danny.

He admired Captain Harris too, and he certainly didn't think about kissing the man!

The mere thought of kissing Kate again set him to grinning.

"I probably look like a fool," he told Bess, and the mare bobbed her head as if agreeing.

Well, why shouldn't he take the kiss seriously? Kisses between an officer of the United States Cavalry and a respectable lady meant something. That kiss implied he was intent in his pursuit of Kate. That he was courting her with the idea of marriage.

That he thought himself worthy of being her husband.

And he didn't.

He clucked to Bess, who broke into a canter until they reached camp.

But camp was considerably more crowded than when he'd left. Franklin and Smith had returned from the first patrol, and Lercher, Waxworth, and O'Reilly had rejoined them at last. Good. Determining their next steps ought to take his mind off Kate.

Maybe.

His five privates were sitting around the fire, trading stories. All but Smith jumped to attention as he rode in.

"Fire up north contained, sir," Waxworth reported. He ducked his head before hurrying forward to take charge of Bess, as if he had never left.

"Captain Harris told us ve should report back to you," Lercher added as Will dismounted.

O'Reilly spit toward the edge of the fire circle. "And he was asking about the Geyser Gateway, sir. It seems rumor has it the place isn't fit for man nor beast."

They all looked to him. Waxworth's brows

were up as if waiting for Will to deny it. Smith's half-smile told his comrades he knew more about it than they did.

"Nothing has changed about the Geyser Gateway while you were gone," Will told them. "You'll have a chance to see for yourselves soon enough. Mrs. Tremaine is hosting a dinner for Lieutenant Kingman and his staff, and we're all invited to attend."

Most of his men brightened. As if satisfied, Waxworth headed for the picket line with Bess.

Smith gave Will a look. "All of us?"

Will still wasn't sure what the cavalryman wanted, but there'd be limited opportunity for him to make trouble at the dinner, not with Will at his side.

"All of us, Private," he said. "This Friday evening, if plans hold true." He glanced around at the rest of his men. "You might start brushing off those dress uniforms. I understand this is to be a fancy affair."

Lercher thrust out his broad chest. "Ve vill do honor to the troop and the Geyser Gateway, sir."

"Count on us, Lieutenant," Franklin agreed. "We'll show those engineers to respect the cavalry."

O'Reilly spit again.

As if he'd noticed, Waxworth scowled at the Irishman from the picket line. "None of that, now," he called. "We're gentlemen. We need to act the part."

"Act being the correct word," Smith drawled. He rose at last. "Do any of you know how to behave at a fancy dinner? Can you tell a water glass from a wine glass?"

Franklin stared at him. "They have two glasses?"

"Three if you count the cup for tea," Smith informed him. "Just be glad there won't be any difficult foods to eat. I doubt even the incomparable Alberta could find oysters on the half shell out here."

Lercher was white. "They have them at the big hotel at Mammoth Hot Springs. Brought them in by rail, then freighted them into the park. Ve heard the staff sergeant speaking of it."

Franklin gulped.

Will glanced around at his men. Waxworth was clinging to Bess's bridle as if ready to mount and ride as far and fast as he could. Lercher shifted on his feet as if he would join him. Franklin was chewing his lip, and O'Reilly had his gaze on the ground. Only Smith seemed relaxed, looking at them and shaking his head.

"I suppose you know how to eat oysters,"

Waxworth challenged him.

Smith offered him a little bow. "I spent some time on a Mississippi riverboat traveling from New Orleans. I know the difference between vichyssoise and bouillabaisse too."

"Vichy what?" O'Reilly asked, gaze coming up wide in obvious panic.

"New order of the day," Will announced, and everyone but Smith snapped to attention. "Two by two patrol, two hours on, two hours off. When not on patrol, report to Private Smith."

The others stared at Smith.

Smith frowned, gaze on Will. "Why?"

"Because," Will said, meeting his gaze, "you'll be teaching us how to behave like gentlemen. The reputation of the regiment and the Geyser Gateway is at stake. No man under my command is going to be ridiculed for not knowing how to eat oysters."

16

Any hopes they might delay the upcoming dinner were dashed when a Bassett Brothers stage driver brought back word on Thursday that Lieutenant Kingman and some of his men would be joining Kate for dinner the next day. While Will and his men continued their patrols, Kate and Alberta doubled their efforts to impress. Pansy moved from one task to another in a daze.

"It's not as if Lieutenant Kingman is a guest," she protested as she swept out the dining room. "I know he and his men are staying the night, but this isn't the first time."

Alberta brought out a mop and oil for the floor. "No, indeed. He's been a good friend to the Geyser Gateway, and to Mr. and Mrs. Tremaine."

Kate smiled as she accepted the mop from her. "Remember when he and Toby got into that argument as to what made a good road?

258

Toby wanted the most scenic route. Lieutenant Kingman advocated the most practical."

Alberta nodded, mouth turning up.

"Still," Pansy said, "he's just a first lieutenant. It isn't as if the president is visiting!"

"He's as important as the president," Kate assured her as Alberta poured some oil onto the floor. "He can recommend we get a ten-year lease."

Pansy gripped her broom and swept harder.

Alberta was even more vigilant in making sure everything was perfect. With no time to order supplies from outside the park, she sent Caleb to stop the meat wagon as it headed for the tent hotel at Old Faithful. The shy man-of-all-work returned triumphant with a dozen beef steaks. Alberta planned to serve them with mashed potatoes and gravy, green beans with bacon, and apple preserves, with pumpkin pie for dessert.

Kate juggled preparations with seeing to her other guests. Though most came and went as usual, two pitched in to assist, despite her protests.

"Nonsense," Mrs. Pettijohn said when Kate suggested she spend her time on Yellowstone's wonders instead of ironing the tablecloths. "It is our Christian duty to help those in need."

"Of course," her sister agreed, stitching up the hem on one of the tablecloths. "And it is ever-so-nice to feel a part of something important."

"Now, now," Mrs. Pettijohn said, iron moving briskly. "You were a great comfort to Mother and Father until they passed."

Miss Pringle held up the hem as if to inspect her work. "But you and Mr. Pettijohn were much more influential." She looked to Kate. "They were abolitionists."

Mrs. Pettijohn's heavy face turned pink, as if she was embarrassed by her sister's admiration. "We simply did what was right, as are you, Mrs. Tremaine."

Kate would never have compared her efforts to protect Yellowstone with ending slavery, but she thanked the ladies for their praise and their help.

Mr. Jones had no interest in helping. Each morning, he asked about any animal sightings, then declared his intent to fish. But he never brought back any trout, even though the Firehole was brimming.

"He isn't very good at the sport," Miss Pringle confided to Kate as they dusted the salon.

"He is likely exceptional," her sister argued. "He may be one of those who

260

catches fish for the challenge of it and promptly releases them again."

Miss Pringle's feather duster paused as she frowned. "But how would he know which he'd caught previously?"

"Maybe he recognizes them," Danny suggested as he brought in a load of wood and dropped it into the brass stand by the hearth. "I bet each fish is different, like people."

Danny was everywhere. He ran from one chore to another. He had generally been in bed when Toby and Lieutenant Kingman had talked, but he remembered the tall engineer. And he was filled with questions. How many were coming? Had any of them fought in battles? Did they have any children? Did they know how to play baseball? Could he have long pants to attend?

Only the last could Kate answer with any certainty.

"Your short pants will be fine for you to visit while we wait for dinner," she told her son, "but you will eat in the kitchen with Alberta and Pansy, as usual."

Danny, who had been assisting Pansy in polishing the dining chairs, stopped to look at her, rag in one hand. "Why?"

Enough of her guests had grumbled about the children of the families who visited that

261

she knew not everyone appreciated dining with a child.

"We may have to discuss serious matters during the meal," Kate said. "When you're older, you'll understand."

Danny made a face, but Pansy called for his help just then, and he returned to his work.

But his question about long pants made her think. Her son might be fine with his usual short pants and a clean shirt, but what should she wear to dinner? She intended the hotel to impress. Shouldn't its owner look impressive as well? Likely the officers and their men would come in dress uniform.

She hadn't sewn anything new for herself since she'd arrived in the park four years ago, except for her riding skirt, and that would hardly do. She did have one dress she used to wear to church in Boston. It hadn't seen much use in Yellowstone. Lace and ribbon didn't fare well in sulfur fumes and mineral-laden water. Would it still fit?

Pansy helped her try it on that evening after everyone else was in bed. The long blue bodice with the cream lace insert hugged her curves. And the bustle! Kate turned to glance behind her. She'd never be able to wear one of those for any other occasion. But just once, she'd look like a

Boston belle.

Three guests remained Friday evening: Mr. Jones, Miss Pringle, and Mrs. Pettijohn. Of course, she invited them to dinner as well. The two older ladies agreed with pleased smiles. Mr. Jones declined.

"I'm the solitary sort," he said, as if she could have thought otherwise. "I'll just take a tray in my room."

Those arrangements settled, Kate asked Pansy to help her dress for the evening and made sure she was in the front room when her guests began arriving.

Lieutenant Kingman and his men were first. His short-cropped light-brown hair looked much as she'd remembered, and his eyes still dipped down at the corners. She had never been certain whether the stiff set of his beard was because he held strong opinions or merely because of the shape of his chin.

"Welcome, gentlemen," Kate greeted them as they came in the door in their dress uniforms. Unlike the uniforms of the cavalrymen, the stripe down their trousers, the facings, and the collars of their coats were a vibrant red.

"Kate Tremaine," Lieutenant Kingman said, going on to introduce the sergeant and two corporals who had been sent to work with him that season. Pansy hurried to take their coats and kits back to their rooms.

Kate introduced her lady guests. Mrs. Pettijohn was in black taffeta, the high neck of the gown pressing against her double chin. Miss Pringle was in lavender, and she'd crimped her snowy curls into ringlets beside her round face. Both simpered over the engineers.

Danny scuttled to Kate's side, hair slicked back and collar crisp. "Sorry," he whispered. "Alberta said I had to wash again."

"You're just in time," Kate assured him, pride combining with affection. "You remember Lieutenant Kingman over there with our lady guests. Do you feel comfortable shaking his hand?"

Danny rolled his eyes. "Ma-a." He moved to join the engineers and the ladies.

Voices outside announced the arrival of Will and his men. Kate's throat felt dry as they climbed the steps to the door, and she smoothed her blue skirts over her hips.

Will walked through the door, muscular physique outlined in a navy coat faced in golden yellow. He whipped the yellow-plumed helmet off his head and bowed.

"Mrs. Tremaine."

That voice had never sounded more dear. "Lieutenant Prescott," she acknowledged as he straightened. "Privates. You are all welcome."

His men shuffled behind him, gazes darting around the room as if they expected to find it inhabited by hostiles. They wore dress coats too, brass buttons winking in the lamplight. Private Waxworth's hair looked nearly as wet and slick as Danny's, and Private Lercher's solid chin bore a cut where he must have nicked himself shaving. But the greatest change was in Private Smith. Gone was the thick beard, to be replaced by a pointed goatee and trim mustache. His dark eyes glittered as he came forward and bowed over Kate's hand.

"Mrs. Tremaine, a vision." He stepped aside and eyed his comrades.

Private Waxworth reacted first, moving forward to bend his lanky frame in a bow. "Thank you for inviting us, Mrs. Tremaine."

O'Reilly elbowed him aside, took her hand, and pressed it between his own. "Sure'n you're prettier than the heather on the hillside."

Smith cleared his throat, and the Irishman released her, grabbed Waxworth's arm, and pulled him away.

Franklin took his place, spine stiff and gaze off her left shoulder. "Mrs. Tremaine, thank you for the opportunity to meet with

265

the engineers." He snapped a nod as if satisfied by his performance and went to stand by O'Reilly and Waxworth.

Lercher ambled up to her, blue eyes wide. He clicked his boot heels together before bending to meet Kate's gaze.

"I have never attended so fine an affair," he assured her. "I vill do your hotel honor."

"I'm sure you will," Kate said, and he straightened to join the others.

With a nod to her, Smith followed him.

Kate gazed after them. "What's gotten into your men?"

"Respect for your hospitality," Will promised, offering her his arm. "And awe for their gracious hostess."

Kate accepted his arm, feeling as if bubbles from a geyser rose inside her. "Come, allow me to introduce you all."

As she accompanied them toward the group by the hearth, she noticed through the arch to the dining room that Alberta was pouring lemonade. She too wore her best dress, a navy taffeta with a high neck and flounces around the hem. The dark color made her white apron glow. Seeing she had Kate's attention, she held up one hand, fingers splayed. Right. Dinner in five minutes.

"Guess what, Lieutenant Prescott," Danny

266

said as soon as the introductions had been made. "Lieutenant Kingman knows how to play baseball."

"Played at the Academy," Kingman said with a smile. "Just for fun."

"We played at Fort Walla Walla on off hours," Will said. He put his hand on Danny's shoulder. "Danny here has quite an arm."

Danny beamed, and Kate couldn't help smiling with him.

"But we haven't been able to do more than go over the rules, hit a few balls, and toss the ball back and forth," Will continued. "Not enough players."

Kingman glanced around, as if counting heads. "Even if we were to join you in a game, we're still a few men short of two teams."

"A few men," Mrs. Pettijohn said, eyes narrowing, "but surely not a few women."

Now, there was an idea. How would the Army fellows react to ladies playing? Lercher and Waxworth exchanged glances as if wondering the same.

Lieutenant Kingman evidently found the thought amusing, for he smiled at Mrs. Pettijohn. "Very kind of you to offer, madam, but it can be a strenuous game with lots of running."

267

Miss Pringle blinked her eyes. "Why, Elmira, I do believe this young man just called us old."

Lieutenant Kingman colored.

"Nonsense," Mrs. Pettijohn averred. "He's just afraid we'll show him up in front of his men."

Lieutenant Kingman opened his mouth and wisely shut it again. Kate hid a smile.

"It's very considerate of you not to shame us, Mrs. Pettijohn," Will said solemnly. "It's hard enough trying to lead men of such talent and intelligence."

His men stood taller, and Kate let her smile out.

"Sure'n, we'd be honored to have you watch us play, milady," O'Reilly said gallantly.

"Thank you, Private," Mrs. Pettijohn said with a regal dip of her head.

Miss Pringle patted Will's arm. "And you won't mind if I root for Lieutenant Kingman, would you, dear? I like his beard."

Lieutenant Kingman pressed his lips together as if to keep from laughing.

"Ahem."

They all turned to find Alberta standing in the archway to the dining room. Beyond her, the white of the cloths and the silver gleamed in the lamplight. Alberta drew herself up.

"Dinner," she said, "is served."

Lieutenant Kingman looked to Kate. She knew what courtesy demanded. He was the guest of honor, the man she hoped to impress. She was his hostess. But there was only one man here whose arm she wanted to take.

She turned to Will. "Lieutenant Prescott, would you escort me to the table?"

Him? Kingman outranked him, being a first lieutenant to Will's second, and the dinner was in his honor, both reasons why he should be escorting the prettiest lady in the room. But Kate was waiting, smile bright, and Will humbly offered her his arm.

She glided along beside him to the head of one of the tables. He was used to her practical outfits, well suited to the wilds of Yellowstone. Tonight, she would have outshined the ladies of Boston. The deep blue of the dress reflected in her eyes, and the drape of the skirt was as graceful as her walk. She nodded to him to take the seat on her left, then smiled at Lieutenant Kingman as he escorted Mrs. Pettijohn to Kate's right. Kingman's sergeant led Miss Pringle to sit beside Will. As the other men sat farther down the table, Will spotted Alberta taking Danny's hand and tugging him for the kitchen. Very likely Caleb would have his dinner there as well.

Alberta and Pansy returned immediately bearing platters of steak, followed by a tureen heaping with fluffy mashed potatoes and a porcelain boat with thick, rich brown gravy. His mouth started watering.

His men must have felt the same, for they sat up and followed the movement of the platter with their gazes as it made its way from hand to hand. He could only hope they'd remember the instructions Smith had given them. There were no oysters in sight, but Kate wouldn't thank them for falling on the food like starving men.

Even if salt pork had long ago lost all interest.

"This is excellent, Kate," Lieutenant Kingman said as he cut another piece off the beef a short while later.

Will tried not to bristle at the use of Kate's first name, but something inside him tightened as the first lieutenant smiled in her direction.

"I'll have to tell Alberta how much I appreciate her cooking," Kingman continued, "and how much I'll miss it."

"I was very sorry to hear you were leaving," Kate told him. "You've done so much good around the park."

Will sliced through the beef and shoved it into his mouth. From farther down the table, Smith caught his eye and shook his head. Will made himself chew before swallowing.

"Yellowstone is an amazing place," Kingman agreed. "Sure to leave its mark on a man. But I don't have to tell you that. Your Toby loved this park."

She dropped her gaze. "Yes, he did."

Will seized his lemonade glass rather than take her hand in comfort.

"I don't know how many times we sat around this table, talking about the right way to manage such vast holdings."

She raised her head. "I remember. And I know you share my belief on the best approach."

He nodded. "We must leave the park as the hand of nature left it — a source of pleasure for all who visit. I can only hope you'll impress that on my successor."

Kate raised her glass to him in toast. "You can be sure I will."

And Will could only be glad Kingman would be leaving shortly.

Down the table came the screech of metal on china. Waxworth glared at O'Reilly, who scowled back.

"Would you pass the potatoes and gravy, Sergeant?" Smith put in smoothly. "I believe some of my colleagues would appreciate a second helping."

Kingman's sergeant passed the tureen of potatoes with a smirk. "You know what they say about Irishmen."

O'Reilly leaned away from the table, mouth working. Will fixed his eyes on him, warning him not to spit.

"That the Irish are a generous and kind-hearted people," Franklin put in loudly.

"Villing to overlook the faults in others," Lercher added with a smile to O'Reilly.

O'Reilly settled in his chair, but he accepted the tureen and served himself and Franklin a heaping pile.

"Sounds as if I won't have to worry about you overwintering this year," Kingman told Kate as Pansy began taking away the dishes. Most were empty, but Waxworth snatched the last bit of steak off the platter. Will was just glad he used his fork.

Kate smiled at Will. "No, indeed. This winter I'll have the assistance of the cavalry."

Will's men beamed at her.

She turned to the engineer, smile fading. "I'm a little concerned about next spring, though. Captain Harris only renewed my lease until then."

Kingman shook his head. "Shortsighted. I'm sure he'll see the wisdom of renewing."

"Perhaps you could put a word in his ear," Kate suggested.

He laughed. "A cavalry officer, listening to an engineer? That would be novel."

Will wasn't the only one to glower at him, but Alberta came through the door bearing a pumpkin pie, and all attention turned her way.

A short while later, Miss Pringle spoke up.

"At what time would you like us to be ready for the baseball game tomorrow, Lieutenant Prescott?"

All gazes swung his way, and only Kate's held sympathy.

"It wouldn't be fair to play against Lieutenant Prescott, Miss Pringle," Kingman answered for him. "My men have played for years. They're quite good. His are somewhat unschooled."

He didn't seem to notice the number of glares directed his way again.

"Oh, I don't know, Lieutenant," Kate told the engineer. "They might surprise you. I've found Lieutenant Prescott's men do well at anything they set their minds to."

Waxworth nodded approval.

Will looked to Kingman, determination

273

building. "So, what do you say, Lieutenant? Will you play an inning or two with me and my men?"

Kingman glanced down the table. O'Reilly grinned at him. Lercher cracked his knuckles.

"Six against four?" Kingman said, brows up. "Rather uneven."

His sergeant leaned forward. "For them."

O'Reilly snorted.

"Point taken," Will said before tempers could flare. "And it would be seven against four in any event. I know Danny will want to play."

A squeal from the kitchen told him the boy had been listening. Kate's smile confirmed it.

Kingman drummed his finger on the table. "That still makes eleven. The teams will be uneven no matter how we divide the men."

Mrs. Pettijohn opened her mouth, most likely to volunteer her services again, but Kate spoke first. "I'd like to play as well. If Lieutenant Prescott loans you two of his men, Lieutenant Kingman, the teams will be even, if not quite at the full complement of nine I understand is generally needed."

Will thought Kingman might protest, but he apparently knew Kate well enough not to argue. "Very well. Lieutenant Prescott may have you and Danny, and I'll take . . ." He glanced down the table. All Will's men but Smith leaned back as if avoiding his gaze.

"Lercher and Franklin," he finished.

Someone groaned.

"Done," Will said. "Does half past nine give your staff time to finish serving breakfast, Mrs. Tremaine?"

She nodded. "That should be fine, Lieutenant."

"Where exactly did you plan to play?" Smith put in. "I doubt Mrs. Tremaine would allow us to set up bases on the geyser field."

"There's a field across the road," Kate offered. "We graze the horses and cows there."

Kingman's nose twitched. "And the evidence of their occupation might make for a difficult game."

"Nonsense," Mrs. Pettijohn declared. "No cavalryman can possibly be concerned about a few horse droppings."

Miss Pringle covered her rosebud mouth with her hand, eyes widening.

"Sure'n no cavalryman," O'Reilly agreed with a look at Kingman's sergeant. "But it's probably above the high-and-mighty head of an engineer."

"Gentlemen," Kingman said as his sergeant looked daggers at O'Reilly. "No need for concern. There's a meadow to the southwest, across the Firehole River. I saw it when I was surveying for the road two years ago. It ought to be big enough, with fewer . . . obstacles."

Kate stiffened on her chair, but her voice came out calmly enough. "Not the best area for this sort of thing. I wouldn't be surprised if it wasn't rife with burrows. Someone could break an ankle."

"Oh!" Miss Pringle dropped her hand, eyes lighting. "And then we'd have to nurse him back to health."

"We'll check the ground before playing," Kingman assured them both. "The late Mr. Tremaine and I walked this area several times. It is the most likely space. Unless you've discovered another, Kate."

Her smile looked strained. "Perhaps you're right. I'll go out first thing in the morning to check it. It's the least I can do as your hostess."

The conversation moved on to other baseball games Kingman and his men had played, the positions they preferred to fill, how well they hit. He was trying to intimidate Will's men, but, by the looks flashing between them, they were having none of it. Will was more concerned about Kate. She kept sinking her fork into the pie, but she never took another bite.

She'd told him she'd put the area to the southwest off-limits. Now she'd tried to warn Kingman away. What was she worried about? If the area held some danger, why not name it?

He didn't have answers, but he knew one thing. She wouldn't be going out there alone come morning.

17

Dawn was a smudge of gold to the east when Kate tiptoed out of the Geyser Gateway the next morning, knapsack slung over one shoulder. Steam from the hot pools lay like sleeping sheep over the crusty soil, and the only sound was the faint plop of the paint pots. Hitching her knapsack higher, she struck out for the Firehole River. At the edge of the pines, she paused to glance back at the hotel. Nothing moved. No one followed. She headed for the footbridge.

Birds sang from the trees as she followed the river south. There was no trail into their special spot, but she knew the way. Hop the rocks to cross Fairy Creek, watch for the break in the hills, climb the slope between them, detour around the big cedar, and take a right at the lichen-capped boulder. A few more yards, and she broke free of the hills into a series of meadows that ran along a clear stream, just as the sun leaped above the Absarokas. Light spread across the grass, climbed the sides of the massive beasts cuddled together for warmth.

One, three, five, ten. Kate counted the shaggy heads of the bison. Only twenty individuals, all told, but the bulls were off on their own now.

"Hey!" she called. "Hey! Wake up and move! They're coming!"

The lead female, who Toby had named Big Bertha, heaved herself to her feet and chuffed at Kate, nostrils flaring as she sniffed the cool morning air. Kate's heart started pounding, but she held her ground. This wasn't a grizzly. These were old friends, even if they were big enough and wild enough to harm her. The bison could charge without warning, trample and gore her in seconds.

Bertha deigned to puff at her sister bison. One by one, the others rose too, rough hides dark in the pearly light. Kate thought it was more the day's advance than her encouragement that made them begin to amble up the grass for the farther meadow through the trees.

"Go on, go on," she urged them, daring to follow behind. "This is your home, but we don't have to let anyone else know."

Bertha looked back at her, eyes bright,

and Kate froze. Slowly, she bowed to the beast, arms spread. "I mean you no harm. I just want to keep you safe."

She glanced up to find Bertha had dismissed her, leading her group in a stately retreat until they disappeared beyond the pines.

Kate exhaled, sagging. Once Will and the others arrived, the bison would stay away for a while. That's what had happened every time Toby had grown boisterous in their presence. He'd gradually learned the great beasts didn't appreciate his enthusiasm for them. These meadows were the only place her irrepressible husband had been able to sit still and listen.

Now, to eliminate as much of their presence as possible.

She could do little about the fresh buffalo chips along the edge of the meadow, but she gathered the dry patties into her knapsack. There was a good-sized wallow on the southern edge, left by the bulls earlier in the season, the hollow dusty and raw. Maybe she could keep the game from including that area or claim the wallow was an old artifact. With a nod, she headed back toward the hotel. She was between the hills when she noticed movement among the trees ahead.

Kate straightened her spine and angled to meet him.

"Good morning, Will," she said as if they were greeting each other on the hotel veranda. "You must take this game seriously to be out so early."

He regarded her, the brim of his dun wool hat shadowing his eyes. "I might say the same for you."

Kate forced a shrug. "I was just out collecting fuel left from days past. See?" She opened the mouth of her sack and aimed it his way.

He recoiled. "Please tell me Alberta doesn't cook her pies with that."

"We only use it when wood or coal is scarce," Kate assured him, cinching the sack closed again. "And they don't smell nearly as much as you would think. But you'll be thankful for them when it's twenty below and snowing and you don't have to go out and chop wood."

His gaze went beyond her. "So, this is the area you put off-limits. Anything I should know?"

Nothing she was willing to tell him. "No. I glanced at the meadow Lieutenant Kingman wants to use. The grass isn't too high, and I didn't see any burrows. You should be able to play."

281

"Good." He nodded to her. "I wouldn't want to disappoint Danny."

He turned to walk with her as she set out for the hotel. "I heard you talk with Danny a little about this game. You hit a ball with a stick . . ."

"A bat," he corrected her.

She probably should use the correct terminology. "A bat, then. And you run around in a circle until someone throws the ball at you."

She glanced over in time to see him wince. "It's a little more precise than that. There's strategy involved as to where you hit the ball and how far. You don't run in a circle; there are three bases and home plate you must touch as you run. Every man has a position he must play, an area of the field he watches."

"Like a sweep of the geyser field," Kate allowed, making for the footbridge.

"Exactly. And the pitcher in the center of the field will be trying to throw the ball in such a way as to make sure you can't hit it."

That didn't seem very fair. "And you think Danny will enjoy the game?"

His smile was warmer than the sunrise. "I know Danny will love it."

But Danny wasn't the only one looking forward to the game, Kate saw when she and Will returned to the hotel. Miss Pringle and Mrs. Pettijohn were on the veranda, watching Lieutenant Kingman, his men, and Privates Franklin and Lercher huddle near the geyser field. Will's men were grouped on one end of the veranda, eyes narrowed and feet shifting as they eyed their opponents.

"Lieutenant Kingman is discussing strategy," Miss Pringle told Kate as she and Will joined the two ladies.

"And I should do the same," Will acknowledged with a tip of his hat to her guests. "Mrs. Tremaine, would you and Danny join us?"

"Give me a moment to stow this," she said, hand on her knapsack.

He nodded agreement and headed toward the end of the veranda and the rest of his men.

"Have you had breakfast?" Kate asked the two older ladies.

"Oh yes, dear," Miss Pringle told her.

"We refused to let anything slow the game," Mrs. Pettijohn agreed. "Now, hurry."

Bemused, Kate went to store the chips and search for Danny.

She found him in the kitchen, finishing his bowl of oatmeal. Mr. Jones was with him.

"He was a bit too excited to eat alone," her guest explained as if he'd seen the look of surprise on Kate's face.

Danny nodded, oatmeal dribbling down his chin. "Mr. Jones used to play baseball when he was a boy."

Kate had been under the impression the game was newer than when Mr. Jones had been young, but perhaps she was mistaken. "Then you are welcome to join in," she told the older man, going to the sink to wash her hands. "I'm sure either Lieutenant Kingman or Lieutenant Prescott would appreciate another experienced player on the team."

He patted his left knee through his buckskins. "Alas, an old war injury keeps me away from the game these days. You must tell me all about it when you return, Mr. Tremaine."

Danny giggled. "He calls me mister," he said to Kate.

"So I heard," Kate said with a smile. "Miss Pringle and Mrs. Pettijohn will be glad for your company, Mr. Jones, as they cheer."

He grimaced. "Miss Pringle and Mrs. Pettijohn seem mighty interested in single gentlemen. I'll head up to the Little Firehole and fish."

Danny scraped the last of the oatmeal from his bowl. "You'll miss all the fun."

"But I'll know my good friend Mr. Tremaine is having fun," he replied. "You and Mrs. Guthrie can tell me all about it when you get back."

Alberta looked up eagerly from the stove. "Can we all come, Mrs. Tremaine?"

Had the sun gone behind a cloud? Kate felt as if the light in the room had dimmed at the thought of leaving the hotel unattended. She hated making Alberta, Pansy, or Caleb stay behind, and she didn't want to miss Danny in his element.

Alberta must have seen something in Kate's face, for she took a step toward her. "We can lock all the doors. Surely everything would be fine for a couple hours."

Mr. Jones rose. "I'll just be on my way, then." He headed for the kitchen door.

Kate drew in a breath. "Very well. We'll all go. I'll tell Pansy."

Her maid was eager for the entertainment, so Kate sent her out to fetch Caleb as well. When Kate returned to the veranda, she found Danny already standing with the cavalrymen, wiggling as he listened to them discuss their plans. Will and his men all tipped their hats to her as she approached.

Will's smile made her shoulders feel less tight.

"Ready?" he asked.

She nodded. "I think so. It just doesn't feel right not to be working."

He took her hand. "You deserve to enjoy yourself, Kate."

Mrs. Pettijohn must have overhead the conversation, for she wagged her finger at Kate. "All work and no play makes Jack a dull boy."

Miss Pringle frowned. "I don't think any of them are named Jack, dear."

"And neither am I," Kate assured her. They were right. There was nothing wrong with enjoying herself. Head high, she released Will, took Danny's hand, and led the cavalcade for the meadow.

"Lieutenant Kingman is a good friend," Danny said as he walked beside her. "We should take him up to our special spot before he leaves."

"No," Kate said, glancing back to where Will and the others walked behind them. "And you must be very quiet about our spot at the game today, Danny. The particulars are for family only."

"Oh." Danny hopped over a rock. "Well, maybe we should tell Lieutenant Prescott.

He's almost family."

Almost, but not quite.

Will couldn't interpret the look Kate sent him over her shoulder, but the conversation was easy enough to understand. The special spot Danny talked about on occasion was obviously connected to the area Kate had put off-limits, the meadow they were approaching now. It was something shared only within their family.

And he wasn't family.

Not yet, something inside him whispered.

"Perfect," Kingman declared.

The way had opened into a meadow perhaps a hundred yards square. Will nodded, and Waxworth and O'Reilly went to lay out the scraps of lumber they'd brought to serve as bases. Miss Pringle and Mrs. Pettijohn wandered over to sit under the shade of the pines on the western flank, where Alberta and Pansy were laying out blankets, while Caleb clung to the shadows of the trees. Will had asked the shy fellow whether he wanted to play, but all he'd received in answer was the rapid shake of Caleb's head.

"What positions did you want us to play?" Kate asked, hand on Danny's as he vibrated like a string on a guitar, gaze darting every-where.

He and his men had worked out the strategy earlier. "I'll be pitching," he told her. "Waxworth and O'Reilly are playing first and third base. Smith is at home. Are you and Danny willing to take on second base and the outfield?" He pointed toward the base O'Reilly had just laid down.

Danny nodded eagerly, though Will suspected the boy would have accepted any position offered him. Kate led him out to the farthest point on the diamond.

Will's team had won the coin toss, so Kingman's team would bat first. Will accepted the ball and went to stand in the center of the diamond. Glancing around, he met each player's gaze. Waxworth nodded, Kate smiled, Danny waved, O'Reilly spit, and Smith squatted down behind Kingman, who was standing at bat.

Will studied the other lieutenant's stance, then wound up and threw the ball. It whizzed past the bat.

"Strike one," Smith called.

Kingman glared at him.

"Sorry," he drawled. "Strike one, sir."

"Yay!" Danny cheered.

Kate hushed him.

Will managed to get one more ball past

the lieutenant, but Kingman connected on the third, a hard drive to Will's right. By the time O'Reilly grabbed it from the ground and threw it to Waxworth, Kingman was safely on first.

"It's okay, Lieutenant Prescott," Danny called from behind second base. "You'll do better with this one for sure."

Will caught the ball from Waxworth, squared his shoulders, and struck out the first corporal.

"Hey!" he heard Danny complain. "That's not fair!"

Will turned to find Kingman on second.

"It's called stealing a base, young man," Kingman told Danny. He smiled at Will and bent low as if prepared to dash to third at the least provocation.

He got his chance with the second corporal, who sent a ball flying high over first base. Waxworth ran for it, but it fell down near the trees. By the time he returned to base, the corporal was on second, and Kingman was on third.

The sergeant came up next. He waved the bat around a moment, as if testing its strength, then settled it into position. "This is for the Irish," he called, and O'Reilly's eyes narrowed.

He hit the ball so hard it disappeared

among the trees over the heads of the watchers.

"Oh, very nice," Miss Pringle declared as O'Reilly ran in pursuit of it.

"You must do better, Lieutenant," Mrs. Pettijohn scolded, shaking a finger at Will as all three men reached home.

Yes, he must. Danny was counting on him. So was Kate. Her smile of encouragement buoyed him. He had the measure of Kingman's team now. He struck out Kingman and the first corporal.

"Three strikes, you're out!" Danny crowed as the teams traded places.

Kingman took up first base, his sergeant took second, and one of the corporals took third. That left him one corporal to range the outfield, while Lercher served as catcher.

Franklin tossed the ball in the air at the center of the diamond as Waxworth came up to bat. The first ball shot past, and Lercher went to find it among the grass and toss it back.

"Strike one!" he shouted as he resumed his place behind Waxworth.

Waxworth scowled at him, and he shrugged. The private wiggled his hips and settled the bat on one shoulder.

"Is that the best way to bat?" Kate murmured to Will.

"Perhaps not," Will acknowledged as the lanky cavalryman swung and missed.

"Strike two!" Lercher bellowed.

Waxworth's face darkened. His knuckles were white as he gripped the bat. Franklin threw. Waxworth swung. The ball snapped back toward the pitcher as if on a string. Waxworth dropped the bat and hurtled toward first, where he stopped, face flushed and chest heaving.

"Me! Me!" Danny begged.

Will bent to put his head on a level with the boy's. "I'm counting on you for later, Danny. I want to make sure we have at least one more person on base."

Danny nodded, trembling.

"Is that wise?" Kate whispered as Will straightened. "He's never played before."

Will bowed, sweeping his hand toward the plate. "Then show him how it's done."

She eyed him a moment before going to accept the bat from Lercher.

She positioned it a little higher off her shoulder than Waxworth had. Franklin carefully tossed the ball toward her. Kate didn't swing.

"Strike?" Lercher asked her.

"Nonsense," Kate said with a frown. "Private Franklin was clearly practicing." She looked toward the pitcher. "I'm ready,

Private. Give it another try."

Lercher threw the ball back even as Franklin reddened.

"You can do it, Private," Miss Pringle called. "We have faith in you."

"Knock it into next week, Mrs. Tremaine!" Mrs. Pettijohn ordered.

Franklin wound up and hurled the ball. Will had to stop himself from throwing his body between it and Kate.

She swung, and the ball arced up and over the field. Every man stood and watched it.

Except Will. "You did it!" he shouted.

She grinned at him.

"Run!" Alberta screamed.

Kate caught up her skirts and ran. Waxworth made it to third, and she made it to second, before the corporal returned with the ball and threw it to Franklin.

"Now?" Danny begged.

Will shook his head.

Smith was up next. He bunted toward third and reached first safely, but none of the others could reach home in time.

"Now?" Danny was hopping from foot to foot.

"Now," Will agreed.

He ran to the plate and grabbed the bat. It was nearly as long as he was. But he held it tight and didn't let it rest on his shoulder.

Once more, Franklin attempted a gentle toss. Danny connected with a thud, but the ball went up and came down behind Lercher.

"Strike one," Lercher called with an apologetic look to Danny. He returned the ball to Franklin.

"Whose side are you on?" Mrs. Pettijohn demanded.

"Why, Lieutenant Kingman's, dear," Miss Pringle reminded her.

"It's all right," Will called to Danny. "You can do it."

Danny's eyes were wide as he lifted the bat again. This time it wobbled in his grip. All Kingman's men moved into the infield.

"Don't coddle him!" Kate called from second base. "He can hit it."

The bat stopped wobbling.

Franklin threw, straight and true. Danny swung so hard his whole body arced. Crack! The ball sailed into the woods, and the corporal went running.

So did Danny. As Will cheered, he hit first and stopped. As the ball veered toward Franklin, Waxworth cleared home.

"Stay there!" Kate called from third as Danny started moving toward second. He leaped back onto the base. Kingman smiled at him.

Will moved into place and picked up the bat.

"You can do it, Lieutenant!" Danny called.

Maybe, but unlike Kingman's men, Franklin knew how Will played. He threw a ball just low enough that Will didn't swing.

"Strike," Lercher said. "Sorry, sir."

Not as sorry as Kingman, as Will connected with the second ball, and it flew for the trees. He followed Kate, Smith, and Danny around the bases.

"You did it, you did it!" Danny cried, jumping up and down.

Will hefted him into his arms. "We did it. Here's to our new top hitter."

Everyone cheered.

Will caught Kate's gaze, and the noise, the motions around him, Danny against him, seemed to fade until there was only her, smiling with pride, with affection. The very earth shook beneath him. It was a moment before he realized it wasn't just his emotions causing the sensation.

"Earthquake!" Kingman shouted.

18

Kate stumbled to Will's side and clung to his arm as he lowered Danny to the ground. She wasn't sure who looked the more rattled. All around them, the trees swayed with the movement of the earth, and she was certain the grass rippled along with it. In the distance, something rumbled, a rock-slide on higher terrain.

But the quake was gone as quickly as it had come.

"My word," Kate heard Miss Pringle say. "That was something."

She glanced over in time to see Mrs. Pettijohn draw herself up. "Does this happen often, Mrs. Tremaine?"

"Quite often," Kate assured her, taking Danny's hand in hers. "Though most are much less noticeable."

"The Geological Survey informed me that Yellowstone has at least one a day," Lieutenant Kingman said, joining them. "I can't say I'll miss them." He nodded to Will. "I concede your victory, Prescott. My men and I should get back."

"Now, Lieutenant," Kate teased him, "surely you're not put off by a little tremor."

He smiled at Danny. "No, ma'am. I'm more afraid of the drubbing your son would give us if we played much longer." He raised his head and glanced around. "Ah, Yellowstone. Nothing like it. I leave it in your good hands, Kate."

"A responsibility I cherish," she promised.

"A responsibility you carry better than anyone," Will said.

Warmth filled her. He held her gaze a moment, as if he held her in his arms. Then he turned to direct his men to secure the bases.

Kate gathered her composure and managed to herd everyone out of the meadow. She glanced back just before leaving, trying to make out any dark shape through the pines, but everything was still.

Unlike her son. Danny couldn't stop talking. He relived the moment he'd batted with Will and his men as they walked back to the hotel.

"He's a hero," Kate said to Will, watching her son reminisce with Miss Pringle and Mrs. Pettijohn after they'd bid Lieutenant Kingman and his men farewell. "He'll never

296

forget this."

"Bigger triumphs will likely overtake this one," Will said. "But I'm glad he had a chance to play. I don't know when we'll have enough players again."

Kate nodded. "Winter will be here very soon."

Will winked at her. "And then the real work begins. I have a feeling you've decided exactly how you'll keep us busy."

Kate laughed. "Oh, Will. You just wait."

Mrs. Pettijohn and her sister climbed to the veranda. Miss Pringle sighed. "So much excitement! What else shall we do today, dear?"

Mrs. Pettijohn pursed her lips as she sat on the bench. "Perhaps we should learn to fish."

As Kate and Will came up the steps after them, Miss Pringle brightened. "Perhaps Mr. Jones could teach us."

"I don't think I've laid eyes on him yet," Will told them. "And none of my men have mentioned him. You'd have thought the number of times we ride by each day, someone would have had the opportunity to talk."

She didn't see the mystery as so deep. "I grant you he isn't the usual visitor, but he does claim illness and injury. He may avoid conversation because his infirmities embarrass him, a once-strong man reduced to no more than fishing."

Miss Pringle stuck out her lower lip. "Poor fellow."

"I don't think he wants our pity," her sister informed her. "But I would appreciate a gentleman's perspective on the matter. You must meet him, Lieutenant."

"Perhaps when you come for church services tomorrow," Miss Pringle suggested.

He hesitated. "I'll stop by later today when we finish afternoon patrol." With a tip of his hat, he left them.

Kate excused herself from her guests and entered the hotel, thinking. So, Will still would not commit to attending services. She wasn't sure why that troubled her. She'd certainly avoided Mr. Yates's preaching. And perhaps the Army required that Will lead his own services in camp on Sunday mornings. She should ask him.

After the baseball game and the earthquake, the rest of the day seemed slow, for all she had plenty to do. The quake had shaken loose some of the dishes in the kitchen. Only a few had broken, but she helped Pansy sweep up and reposition the others. She also kept an eye out for Mr. Jones, but he didn't return to the hotel until the evening was well advanced, and Will and his men had already retired to their camp.

"I thought Mrs. Guthrie might appreciate these," he said, holding up a brace of trout, their speckled sides striped with crimson.

"She certainly will," Kate said, stepping aside for him to pass her for the kitchen. "I'm glad you had such luck today."

"I used to enjoy all the manly sports," he assured her before disappearing inside. Kate heard Alberta's exclamation all the way through the door.

It seemed Mr. Jones had finally met with success. She'd had guests who spent hours in a cool stream, casting and reeling. Nice of him to share his riches with the rest of the guests. The trout was excellent fried and surrounded by the last of the green beans. And Mr. Jones spent the evening on the sofa, listening to Danny tell him all about the baseball game. Hard to fault a man for that.

Mr. Yates must have preached at Mammoth Hot Springs or Norris first on Sunday, because he didn't arrive until early afternoon. Alberta, Pansy, Caleb, Miss Pringle, and Mrs. Pettijohn sat on chairs before the hearth. Kate marched herself away from her duties to join them. Mr. Jones once more made himself scarce, although he had spent part of the morning asking Danny about what other wonders he'd seen in the park. Danny had been only too happy to tell him about the ball game again.

Her son was still riding high from his victory. He wiggled where he sat in the back row, Kate beside him. She patted his shoulder and gave him a look, and he sat taller as Mr. Yates opened in prayer. Kate didn't know the hymn the minister started next, but Mrs. Pettijohn belted it out with a gusto that brought a smile to his face.

Across the room, the door to the kitchen cracked open, and Will glanced out. Kate slipped out of her seat to meet him.

"We're just starting," she whispered as Mrs. Pettijohn launched into the third verse. "You're welcome to join us."

"It's been a long time since I attended worship," he whispered back.

So, no services in the Army camp either. "It's easy to fall out of the habit," Kate assured him. "It won't take long. Mr. Yates doesn't preach for hours like some ministers."

"Maybe next Sunday," he said. "I just thought I'd see if I could meet your mysterious guest."

"He left," Kate offered. "Check the geyser field."

He nodded. Disappointment fell over her as the door swung shut. But Mrs. Pettijohn warbled to a stop, and Kate hurried back to her place beside Danny.

Standing before the hearth, Mr. Yates adjusted the spectacles on his broad-tipped nose.

"I take my text today from Luke. Caleb, you do not have my permission to sleep."

Caleb jerked upright in his seat as Pansy elbowed him.

Mr. Yates dropped his voice, tone conspiratorial. "Imagine this. President Cleveland has come to your town and decides to dine at your house. Oh, what a day!"

Pansy leaned closer to Alberta. "Almost as big a day as when Lieutenant Kingman visited."

Alberta put a finger to her lips.

"How much time will it take you to prepare?" Mr. Yates asked them. "A few hours? A few days?"

One house? Kate and Pansy could have the space spick-and-span in three hours, less time if they had Sarah and Ida to help. By the way Miss Pringle's head was cocking, she was making calculations of her own.

"And now our great president is before

301

you," Mr. Yates said, leaning toward them, "sitting in your parlor, telling about all the things he's done, the places he's gone. Dinner is moments away, your shining glory."

Alberta sat taller as if eager to hear what was on the menu.

"And your sister, the one person you could count on for help today of all days, abandons you to go sit in the parlor with the men and listen."

Alberta gasped, and Mrs. Pettijohn glared at Miss Pringle, who shrank in her seat.

"Such was the case of Martha and Mary," Mr. Yates said, hands braced on his waistcoat. "Martha worked her fingers to the bone preparing her home for a visit from our Lord. And her sister sat and listened." He glanced around at his makeshift congregation. "Poor Martha. Things like the state of her home and the quality of her meal had become the most important things in her life."

Kate nodded. And why shouldn't they be? Martha may not have been running a hotel, which would be judged by her guests, but her hospitality was going to be judged by all those who entered that day.

"And there was Mary, just sitting around, listening!"

"I'd be fired for sure," Pansy muttered to

Alberta, and the cook nodded before glancing back at Kate and reddening.

"So, Martha appealed to the one person her sister might obey — our Lord himself. Did he order Mary back to work? Show his displeasure that she thought to listen to the menfolk talk? No. He told Martha to leave her be, for she had chosen the most important thing."

He removed his glasses and stared at them all. "Those who come to visit Yellowstone plan and pack and travel far to reach its fabled lands. There are many things they could do. Only one is needful. Stop and listen to the words of the One who created all this for your pleasure. Remember your duty to him today, and every day. Let us pray."

Miss Pringle and Mrs. Pettijohn climbed to their feet and bowed their heads. So did Alberta and Pansy and Caleb. Kate's cheeks felt hot and wet. Was she crying? Why? She knew she served a mighty God. His wonders surrounded her.

But to stop her work, to simply listen?

To let him dictate the pace of her life?

She rose with the others, bowed her head. Mr. Yates intoned his prayer, but her heart spoke for her.

Lord, I feel as if you've been urging me to

303

listen. I'm just not sure what I'm supposed to hear. You know I have a hotel to run. I'm both father and mother to Danny now. I made time for this service.

Why did all that sound like an excuse? What did God want of her?

Your love, your trust.

Oh so difficult since Toby had died. Some of the light in her life had left with him.

Yet God had brought it back in Will. Will was calm, steady, but he still knew how to take time to enjoy things like ice cream and baseball. There was a lesson in that.

If she could just let go — of her fear, of her hurry.

My burden is easy, and my yoke is light.

An *amen* rumbled through the room, and she looked up in surprise. Miss Pringle and Mrs. Pettijohn were going forward to thank Mr. Yates and shake his hand. Alberta and Pansy were edging out of the row. Caleb was already halfway toward the door. Could her burden really be lightened? She certainly felt less encumbered than when she'd sat down for service.

Danny tugged on her hand. "Could we go somewhere and listen?"

Kate smiled. "That sounds perfect."

"I know where," Danny said. "Let's take Lieutenant Prescott to our special spot."

She'd fought the urge, told herself Will wouldn't be in her life long enough, feared for the protection of the great beasts. But taking him up to their spot seemed right, good. A step in trust.

Approved by someone higher than herself.

Kate nodded. "As soon as he finishes the morning sweep."

Will cantered up the road from the Grand Prismatic Spring. Mr. Jones had once more eluded him, and he'd sent Lercher back to camp while he checked the spring. No one had been in the vicinity. The number of visitors thinned more each day. There was no reason he couldn't have stayed for services as Kate asked.

Except he still wasn't sure of his welcome.

Oh, he realized she wanted him there. Miss Pringle and Mrs. Pettijohn would likely have greeted him happily. The minister wouldn't understand about his past. But Will knew. And so did God.

The thought made him flinch. He'd failed so many people that day, but most of all he'd failed his heavenly Father. Would there ever come a time he felt he'd atoned sufficiently to be accepted again?

He rode into the yard of the Geyser Gateway, and Danny hopped off the porch to meet him as he reined in. "Lieutenant Prescott! You have to come with me."

Caleb ran from the side of the hotel and offered to take charge of Bess. Will thanked him, patted the horse, and turned to Danny. "Something wrong?"

Danny's blue eyes sparkled. "No. Ma's going to show you our special spot."

He raised his head to eye the door of the hotel. "That so?"

Danny nodded. "And you're going to like it. I know you will."

The door opened, and Kate swept out onto the porch. "Will! Care to go for a walk?"

"Wherever you want to lead," Will assured her.

She raised her brows as she came down the steps. "That could be a dangerous offer."

"No, ma'am," Will said, meeting her. "I've never been in better hands. And I hear it has something to do with a secret."

Danny giggled.

"Go on then," Kate said with an arch look to her son. "You know the way."

Danny ran for the path to the Firehole footbridge.

"So," Will said as he walked beside Kate, "I finally get to see what's off-limits."

"You do," she said, lifting her blue skirts out of a muddy patch on the path.

"What changed your mind?" he asked.

She cast him a glance. "I was praying."

His mouth felt as dry as if he'd tasted some of the chalky dust of the trail. "About me?"

"And about me," she acknowledged. "I realized you've been nothing but a help, to Yellowstone, to the Geyser Gateway, to me. You deserve to see this."

And he could only feel humbled yet again.

She let Danny lead them until they reached the opening in the hills near where they had played baseball yesterday. Then she called the boy back to them. As soon as he reached her side, she put a hand on his shoulder and looked to Will.

"Will, what you are about to see only Danny and I know about," she said, gaze serious.

"And Pa," Danny put in. "He found it first."

Kate nodded. "And even though Danny's father was one of the most talkative men I've ever met, he never told another soul except me and Danny. Promise me you will take this secret to your grave."

She was so intent. He couldn't imagine what her late husband had found that would drive such devotion. But he had a duty too. "I can't promise you that without knowing how the secret will affect my position."

She scrunched up her lips a moment. "What if I promise this has nothing to do with the Army?"

Danny glanced back and forth between them as if he couldn't decide who would persuade the other.

"Can you make that promise?" Will challenged her.

She blew out a breath. "I suppose not. But the Army came to protect Yellowstone, *all* of Yellowstone. This comes under that mandate."

He could not deny his curiosity, or his responsibility. "Very well. I promise to protect Yellowstone with my dying breath."

She raised her head. "This way."

She started for the meadow, Danny darting ahead, as agile as a squirrel. Had Will missed something at the game yesterday? Surely there weren't geysers or hot springs in the area. He'd have noticed. And Kate herself had said there was nothing of interest to her guests.

She stepped out of the trees, then put out an arm to stop him from going any farther. Danny stopped too, gaze on the sunlit grass.

Sunlit grass covered in bison.

Some lay, contentedly chewing. Others moved slowly, calmly, heads lowered as they grazed, beards swinging. Tawny youngsters, most likely born that spring, bounded around each other, teasing, until a mother bumped one back into line.

They were massive, they were grand. They were the last of their kind.

Unthinking, Will took a step forward. The largest, with shoulders nearly as high as Will, raised her head and sniffed the air, black eyes glittering as she glanced Will's way. As if she'd taken his measure, she lowered her head and kept grazing.

"The wind is blowing our scent away," Kate said, voice as soft as her look. "Unless we shout or do something equally stupid, they won't take off or approach."

"Good." He certainly didn't want them stampeding. That mass would trample them if the horns didn't sever an artery or puncture a lung first.

"This is their favorite place in the park," Danny said, keeping stiller than any time Will had seen.

"One of them, anyway," Kate said. "There's another meadow beyond, through those trees, with a thermal spring that's just cool enough to be drinkable a few yards from the source. This location is the best-kept secret in Yellowstone — where the bison overwinter. Hunters have been searching for years. We can never let them know about it."

"That's why you didn't want me to patrol here," Will said. "Why you tried to dissuade Lieutenant Kingman from using the meadow. How did you make them invisible yesterday?"

"I suggested they move into the northern meadow," Kate said.

Will chuckled, shaking his head. Somehow, he could see even that lead female listening to her. Everyone else did.

That bison was moving now, one hoof placed precisely before the other. The rest rose, followed her toward the trees. Tribes had revered the shaggy beasts; hunters had coveted their hides, their heads. He knew the statistics. Where once millions had roamed the prairies, now fewer than six hundred were known throughout the nation, many in private herds. Most of the wild animals were in Yellowstone.

"You have my word," Will said, "I will tell no one about this place, these animals. I will do all I can to protect them."

Her smile blended faith and hope. It reached inside him, brightened the darkest places.

And he knew then that he would have to find a way to tell her the truth, about his past, and his growing feelings for her.

19

He understood. Kate could see it in Will's rapt expression, hear it in his gravelly voice as he vowed to protect the bison. And her heart soared like a bald eagle riding the wind.

They followed the bison to the upper meadow, took a seat under the pines, and watched for a while longer. Kate pointed out the younger members of the herd, their tiny horns and humps just popping into view. Danny told Will stories about past encounters.

"Sometimes the boys visit," he said, leaning against Will. "Pa called the biggest one Bill."

"Buffalo Bill," Kate whispered to Will.

He smiled. "I bet he even looks a little like Cody with one of those pointy beards. How often do the cows and calves come here?"

"Summer through winter," Kate explained. "The ground on the northern meadow is too soft in the spring."

The sun was heading for the west when they returned to the inn.

Will paused by the hitching post while Danny sped up the steps and into the inn.

"I'm riding to Old Faithful Tuesday," Will said. "I want to confirm who's responsible for watching the Grand Prismatic Spring." He glanced out across the geyser field and shuffled his feet. "I don't suppose you could break free to join me."

A dozen tasks called for her attention. She had guests arriving, the hotel to prepare for winter. Caleb would be leaving soon. She and Danny had to make sure they knew what needed to be done with the horses, cows, and chickens. And the road to Old Faithful was easy to follow. He didn't need a guide.

But nothing seemed more important than being with him.

Trust. Take time to listen, to enjoy, remember?

"I'd be delighted," Kate said. "And I can see the accommodations while I'm there too."

He chuckled as his gaze came back to hers. "You never stop working."

"Rarely," she admitted. "What time are

313

you starting?"

"After breakfast."

"I'll see you then."

He hesitated, feet once more shifting on the dry ground. Then he nodded and touched his hat. "Ma'am."

Kate watched him around the side of the hotel as he headed for the barn. His walk didn't look quite as confident as usual. Perhaps the sight of the bison had affected him even more than she'd thought. Pleased, she went into the hotel.

In the salon, Mr. Jones was seated on the closest sofa beside the hearth, Danny at his side. The man still wore his buckskins. She'd concluded he hadn't brought anything else with him. But his beard was neat, his hair freshly combed, if the precision of his part was any indication.

"That Lieutenant Prescott is one lucky feller," her guest said as she approached.

She put a hand on Danny's shoulder. "How so?"

"He got to spend the day with Danny and his pretty mama."

Was he attempting to flirt with her? Miss Pringle might have giggled. Mrs. Pettijohn would have demanded to know his intentions. But Kate had no interest in his attentions. She never dallied with guests.

"I forgot to check," she said, ignoring the remark. "How long will you be with us, Mr. Jones?"

He shifted closer to Danny and put his hand around her son's shoulders so that his fingers grazed hers. Kate pulled away.

"Oh, a few more days at the least," he said with a friendly smile. "I've grown accustomed to the gracious welcome of the Geyser Gateway. It feels like family."

"That's what we hope all our guests feel," Kate assured him, taking a step back. "Danny, we should see if Alberta needs any help with dinner."

"Yes, Ma." For once, his response sounded more relieved than resentful. He hopped down and walked with her toward the kitchen.

"Do you like Mr. Jones?" she asked as soon as they were out of earshot.

"He's nice," Danny allowed. "He's my friend. But sometimes he asks hard questions. He wanted to see the animals. I didn't like not telling him about our special spot."

"It's difficult to keep the secret," Kate said as they entered the kitchen. "But I'm proud of you."

He went to help Pansy with the dishes.

So, Danny wasn't too concerned about their odd guest. But she couldn't understand what Mr. Jones wanted. Certainly she would never encourage him as she'd encouraged Will.

Or think about him whatever she did, wherever she went the rest of the evening. She could hardly wait until Tuesday.

Wakefield and Hoffman brought three men traveling through on Monday afternoon, which kept Kate busier than she'd expected. The snowstorm didn't help. The temperature had been chilly all morning. Miss Pringle and Mrs. Pettijohn remained hunkered down by the hearth, sipping cups of tea. Mr. Jones hid in his room. The chickens clung to their roost. Caleb pulled shut the doors on the barn and kept the other animals inside.

The flakes began falling late afternoon from leaden skies. They sizzled and melted on the warm ground at first, winking out in the steam from the geysers like shooting stars. Will and his men patrolled in a swirl of white.

"I thought you said we had weeks until winter," he told Kate when he and Private Waxworth came inside to warm up while Caleb saw to their horses.

Kate spread her hands. "I have no control over the weather."

Miss Pringle looked shocked, and Mrs. Pettijohn humphed.

Danny could scarcely contain himself. "Can we build a snowman, Ma? Throw snowballs in the geysers? They'd melt."

"What's on the ground is more mud than snow," Kate protested.

Will pushed away from the hearth, where he'd been standing. "There's enough for a few snowballs. We have to keep that arm in shape. Come on, Danny."

"Coat first," Kate cautioned before her son could dash out the door. He ran for the stairs and their apartment.

Will crossed to her side. "You don't mind?"

"I don't mind," she said, but she couldn't help her grin. "Only you better watch where his snowballs hit. They'll likely have a few rocks mixed in."

Mrs. Pettijohn rose and shook out her skirts. "I would like to view the combat. Come, Serenity."

Her sister gazed up at her. "Must we? It's sure to be cold."

Mrs. Pettijohn eyed her. "Lieutenant Prescott and Private Waxworth valiantly hurling objects at each other — do you truly want to miss that?"

Miss Pringle turned pink and popped to

her feet. "Well, when you put it that way . . ."

"I thought so." She turned to Private Waxworth, who appeared to be trying to blend into the stone of the hearth. "Prepare yourself, Private. I expect you to acquit yourself well."

Waxworth shot Will a look of appeal.

Will chuckled. "You heard the lady, Waxworth. You've been conscripted."

As Danny came down the stairs, shrugging into his thick wool coat, the private stood at attention and saluted. "I will do my utmost, sir."

Kate narrowed her eyes. "That's two against one. Not fair."

Will's mouth quirked. "Care to join us?"

Perhaps she was learning the lesson God was teaching, for there was no question of her answer. "I wouldn't miss it."

Miss Pringle clapped her hands.

A few minutes later, they were all out on the yard, the sisters, Alberta, and Pansy bundled in coats and robes on the veranda; Kate, Danny, Will, and Waxworth in the snow. Pansy had alerted Caleb. He stood on the porch as well. Kate was just glad her three new guests were content to keep warm inside.

"Caleb, come help!" Danny urged.

In answer, Caleb ducked around the corner of the inn.

"Five minutes to gather ammunition," Will called. "Then the battle commences."

Kate made sure Danny was scraping off only the top layer of the snow before packing her own pile. Glancing over, she saw Will and Waxworth doing the same. Will caught her gaze, and his smile hitched up. Blushing, she returned to her task.

"Time!" Mrs. Pettijohn bellowed, and Miss Pringle gave a little squeal.

Will and Private Waxworth hefted a ball each.

Kate bent beside Danny. "One throw, then follow me."

Danny nodded.

Kate threw. The white flattened against Will's broad chest. Danny's snowball struck Waxworth in the knee.

"Now!" Kate cried, scooping up an armful of balls and running for the inn. Danny scurried after her.

"Is that all?" Miss Pringle asked as they rounded the corner.

"Not in the slightest," Mrs. Pettijohn declared. "After them!"

The next quarter hour was a mad scramble from the barn to the chicken yard to the front of the hotel. Kate hit Will twice more and Waxworth three times. Danny hit some-one every time he threw, though not always his opponents.

"Hey!" Alberta called as a ball sailed past to explode against Caleb's shoulder. "Watch out for the spectators."

In the end, Will surrendered, hands up, in front of the veranda.

"Terms," he begged, snow salting his hair.

Kate narrowed her eyes. "They are at our mercy, Danny. What should we do with them?"

"Feed them pie!" Danny shouted before running for the stairs. With a grateful smile, Private Waxworth followed him. The others started into the inn as well.

Will joined Kate. "I can see I'll have to watch myself this winter."

The light in his eyes, the tilt of his smile, combined to make her quite warm indeed. And she knew she was the one who would have to watch herself this winter, to keep from falling in love.

The snow sparkled in her hair. Her gaze danced with merriment. Was he mad to see something more, a longing as deep as his own?

Tomorrow, he promised himself. Tomorrow he would tell her all. But the thought of seeing that admiration fade kept him up part of a cold night in his tent.

The blanket of snow ebbed away quickly the next morning, leaving puddles glistening on the road as Will headed for the inn. Miss Pringle and Mrs. Pettijohn were already out on the veranda as he rode in.

"Where are your men, Lieutenant?" Mrs. Pettijohn said with a stern look. "One of them should help a lady onto her horse."

Will followed Miss Pringle's gaze to where Kate was coming around the inn, leading one of the riding horses. His heart gave a leap as he swung down. "That's my pleasure, ma'am."

Kate met his gaze as she stopped, then nodded, and he put his hands on her waist and lifted her into the saddle. For a moment, he stood, face uplifted, gazing at her. He probably looked like a wildflower turned to the sun. Cheeks pinking, she gathered the reins, then released the button on her skirt, sending the material cascading down the side of the horse like a waterfall.

"Oh, how fine," Miss Pringle enthused as Will went to remount. "I must get a skirt like that."

Her sister nodded. "Excellent suggestion. We'll take up riding when we return. That could lead to our next adventure."

With a smile, Kate led Will out of the yard.

The road to Old Faithful was an easy path that crossed from pine forest to chalk-and-rust-striped drainage basins before he and Kate reached the area around the Grand Prismatic Spring. Waves of steam crested the road, parting as they came through. Beyond, swallows darted over the marshes. A falcon dipped on the breeze that brought the scent of pine and sulfur.

This was the perfect time to tell her, but he couldn't seem to find the words.

"Where are my manners?" he asked instead. "I should have made the introductions days ago." He patted the mare. "This is Bess."

Kate regarded him, then the horse. "Funny. I would have thought you'd name your horse Thunder or Hurricane. Danny certainly doesn't approve of Buttercup."

"Bess was her name when the Army assigned her to me," Will explained. "I never saw the need to change it. But I can't blame Danny for his opinion. Who names a horse Buttercup?"

"His father," she confessed. "You would think someone from Boston would find more patriotic names. The others are Marigold, Aster, and Balsamroot. I had to talk him out of naming Aster here Pansy. We

322

already have one Pansy at the Geyser Gateway."

"You mentioned Boston," he said. "Are you from there too?"

"Yes," she said, guiding Aster over a bump in the road. "I thought I heard a bit of a twang when I first met you."

"You can't seem to lose it no matter how long you're away from it," he agreed. "What did your parents do?" Was he chattering? No, not really. He wanted to know everything about her.

"My father was a cobbler," she answered, gaze going off over the braided curves of the Firehole River to their right. "My mother made the most beautiful hats — all ribbons and flowers and net. The ladies of Boston loved them. Can you imagine what the bison would think if I wore one here?"

He chuckled. "I wouldn't be surprised if they didn't try grazing on the flowers."

She laughed too. "What about you?" she asked. "What did your parents do?"

"Father enlisted in the military during the war," he said. "Mother took in laundry and did fancy sewing after he was killed outside Atlanta."

"I'm so sorry," she said, face puckering. "Alberta lost her husband and son in that

323

war. That's why she came West, for a fresh start."

"I can understand that," he said. This could be his opportunity! He eased into it. "Sometimes what you do, what others do, forces you to start over."

Either he'd kept his tone more even than he'd hoped, or she hadn't noticed the tension in him.

"Yet you still went into the military," she said with a smile.

How could he not return that smile? "I was named after William Prescott, a famous soldier in the American Revolution. Given his name, I was destined to join the military."

"I didn't think I would ever leave Boston," she said with a shake of her head that sent sunlight skipping down her hair, and he could only be glad she wasn't wearing one of her mother's fancy hats. "Then Toby invested in the Geyser Gateway and brought me out to look at her, and I knew this was where I was meant to be. I don't think I could go back now."

"I couldn't," he said. "Boston always felt too confining. The cavalry took me places I never knew existed."

"Where else have you been assigned?"

Another opportunity. Every muscle tightened as if to protest his intentions. "The Pend Oreille country," he made himself say, "Fort Walla Walla, the Presidio in San Francisco, the Arizona frontier, Oregon."

Kate gazed at him. "All over the West. Even Yellowstone must seem small."

There was that admiration. How could he jeopardize it? "Yellowstone could never feel small," he told her. "Kingman was right. There's nothing like it."

She grinned. "Wait until you see Old Faithful."

He hadn't convinced himself to try again before they came out of the trees a short while later to flats striped in gray, white, and orange. Kate led him toward a mound in the distance where steam rose against the hillside of pines and aspen. People were streaming out of the tents near the trees, heading for the mound.

"Come on," Kate said, touching heels to Aster's flank. "It's almost time."

They cantered up behind the group and reined in to watch. He heard the faint hiss over the murmur of voices as steam built over the mouth of the mound. Water began bubbling, climbing, growing louder. The spray shot high, higher until it splashed down across the area. A rainbow glowed in the center. Will could only stare as people around him exclaimed.

As the spray subsided, he shook his head. "Amazing."

"You stick around," Kate said with a smile, "and you'll find yourself saying that a lot."

"Lieutenant!" A corporal was moving toward them. "Trouble?"

The visitors nearest them glanced their way.

"A jurisdictional question only," Will assured him as he came abreast. "And a chance to see this marvel."

"She's a beauty," the corporal said, thumbs in his belt loops. He squinted up at Will. "So, what's the question?"

Kate touched Will's arm. "I'll be at the hotel."

He nodded, and she rode over to the dun tents clustered at the edge of the pines. He spent the next little while working out boundaries with the corporal. Then he collected Kate to start back.

"That tent hotel isn't any better than what we saw at Norris," she told him as the horses trotted up the road. "Though the hotel they're building could be a good one. I just hope they strike the tents before winter, or the snow on all that canvas will snap the poles."

"I'll mention that in my report to Captain Harris," he promised.

Behind them came a rumble.

"Get off the road," she urged him. She guided her horse to one side, and he joined her on the grassy verge. A moment later, and Elijah's coach thundered past. He doffed his hat with his free hand.

"Guests?" Will asked, waving away the dust that traveled in the coach's wake.

"Four on their way out of the park," Kate told him. "I had hoped to be back before them, but Alberta can welcome them for me."

"No shortcuts we could take?" he asked as they eased their mounts onto the road again.

"None I'd feel comfortable taking," she said, directing her horse after the coach.

"Then I suppose we should hurry." They set the horses to a trot, covering the ground quickly. And that meant he had less time than he'd hoped to confess all. Perhaps that was to the good. No more excuses, no time to hesitate.

As they approached the bend where the road curved away from the river, he cleared his throat. "Kate, there's something I must tell you."

"What?" she asked with a frown, as if she

heard the tension in his voice at last. "Didn't they want you to protect the Grand Prismatic Spring?"

"It's not that," he said. "I . . ." He couldn't look at her. He focused on the road, then started.

Up ahead, Elijah's coach lay on its side, wheels spinning and horses struggling.

20

Kate gasped, but Will moved before she did. He spurred Bess, galloped up to the wreck, and leaped from the saddle to catch the harness of the flailing horses.

"Easy, hey now, easy," he called as Kate rode up and his Bess moved off to one side.

"Elijah!" she cried, turning Aster in a circle as the mare reacted to the other horses. "Elijah, are you hurt?"

A groan from the trees beyond the road answered her. She guided Aster around the wreckage even as a shaky voice rose from the coach.

"Hello? Help us, please!"

"A moment!" Kate called.

Elijah limped out to meet her, one hand pressed to his head and blood running down his cheek. She had never been so glad to see him.

"I'm all right," he assured her, holding up his other hand as if to keep her from dismounting. "My passengers? The horses?" He glanced around, blinking as if the sun had grown too bright.

"We'll settle them," Will promised.

"Give me a moment to check on your passengers," Kate told Elijah, "and then I'll come have a look at that gash."

He sank unsteadily onto a boulder at the side of the road.

Will unhooked the last of the harness, yanked out the long straps of the reins, and pulled the team to the trees. Kate dismounted, tied Aster to a tree, and went to see to the passengers. Riding skirt buttoned high, she had to clamber up the wheels and lay on the door panel to peer inside. The interior was a jumbled mess, bodies strewn about and on top of each other. She refused to look away.

A young woman, hat askew, gazed up at her. "Can you help us?"

Kate swallowed, hating to ask the question. "Are the others alive?"

Elijah's passenger nodded. "I think so."

Will must have returned to the wreck, for she heard his voice behind her.

"Status?" he asked.

She glanced back at him. His face was pale, his stance stiff, as if he were ready for bad news.

"Two women, two men," she told him. "Mr. and Mrs. Barksdale, their son, and his wife, I believe. Only the younger Mrs. Barksdale is sensible at the moment."

"No, no," the young woman protested. "Peter is coming around. Peter, darling, speak to me."

"What happened?" The male voice was decidedly groggy.

"If you tend to Elijah," Will said, "I'll get them out."

She slid off the door to land on the road, skirt pooling. "Thank you," she said before going to see to her driver.

It took a while, but eventually Will had the four visitors out of the damaged stagecoach and at the side of the road. Elijah, riding on the outside, had been thrown clear and taken the worst of the impact. Kate managed to bandage the gash on his forehead with her handkerchief and a ribbon the younger Mrs. Barksdale offered. He seemed to be answering sensibly when she addressed him. But she couldn't like the lump on his head under his tight curls or the swelling on his knee visible through the rip in his trousers.

"I don't understand," the older Mrs. Barksdale, a large matron, said in a trembling voice as they all sat in the shade of the

331

pines. "What happened? Did we hit a rock?"

Her husband, a gray-haired titan of industry, shook his head. "Or perhaps a buffalo?"

"We didn't hit anything," Elijah said, pressing a hand to his makeshift bandage. "Something cracked. The stage tilted. I couldn't do anything except control the horses."

Peter Barksdale, a younger version of his father, drew himself up. "I must say, I expected more of this fine park. The accommodations the last few nights were atrocious, and now this shoddy equipage nearly cost us our lives."

"My stage," Elijah said in ringing tones, "isn't shoddy. I inspected it myself last night."

As long as she'd known Elijah, he had had the same routine of checking his coach, his harness, and his team before setting out. Unfortunately, it hadn't stood him in good stead this time.

"This is a harsh environment," Kate told the young man. "Everything wears out faster than you would expect."

"That's not what happened," Elijah insisted, lowering his hand. "Nothing wore out. You look at it, Lieutenant, and you'll see."

Kate and the others turned to Will. He

went to check the wreck. Kate followed.

Of the wheels now resting on the ground, one had several spokes that looked cracked, but the damage could easily have been caused by the crash. Surely Elijah would have noticed if the wood had been splintered before he started out from the Geyser Gateway. Will crouched as if to peer closer at the leather straps and wooden strips that made up the bottom of the coach.

"It could have happened to anyone," Kate said at his elbow.

"An accident, yes," Will agreed. "But this accident, no." He pointed to the long wooden strip that ran from wheel to wheel. "It was cut partway through. You can see the marks."

Kate stared at it, then at him. "What are you saying? Was this deliberate?"

Will nodded, rising. "Someone didn't want Elijah and your guests to reach the Geyser Gateway."

Kate was still fuming when they rode into the yard late that afternoon. Her guests were perched on the coach's horses, the women with legs over one side and arms clinging to their husbands. The men hadn't looked too comfortable riding bareback either, but they had managed at a slow walk. Elijah had ridden one of the other horses, face pale and breath rapid, while Kate had led the fourth horse and Will the fifth and sixth. Alberta and Pansy immediately set about making their guests and coachman comfortable.

"I'll go to the Fire Hole," Will said, turning Bess after Caleb had taken charge of Elijah's and Kate's horses, "and send word to Old Faithful and the other guard stations about the wreck on the road. My men and I will clear it up tomorrow."

All Kate could spare was a "thank you" before hurrying inside.

The older Mr. and Mrs. Barksdale had been settled in a room at the front of the hotel, their son and daughter-in-law across the corridor. Alberta had apparently dissuaded Miss Pringle and Mrs. Pettijohn from nursing them or Elijah.

"But our things," the senior Mrs. Barksdale said from one of the beds when Kate checked in on them. "Someone will steal them."

"We have very little of that in the park," Kate assured her. "But I'll send my man Caleb with our pony cart to fetch the luggage. It should be here in a few hours."

Mrs. Barksdale collapsed against the feather pillow. "We should never have come out into the wilderness."

"Now, now," her husband said with an apologetic look to Kate. "We've seen some marvels and had a little adventure. Nothing to be concerned about."

Kate couldn't argue with the glare his wife shot him. "I'm terribly sorry this happened," she told them both. "But Alberta has dinner almost ready, and we'll do all we can to make the rest of your stay safe and comfortable."

Mrs. Barksdale nodded. Her husband looked relieved.

Kate excused herself and headed up the stairs to see Elijah.

Danny was with him in his room on the staff corridor on the top floor of the hotel. During the season, he spent four nights a week at Kate's and three in his own home with his wife, Elnora, and son, Markus. A simple iron-framed bed, side table, chair, and trunk were all that graced the room, but Elnora had sewed the red-and-blue-patterned quilt across the bed, and Kate had seen where some of the stitches spelled the word *love.*

Elijah was standing beside the bed, coat off and sleeves rolled up, examining a bruise on his arm. The purple and rose spread across his dusky skin.

Kate knocked on the open door, and he

looked up.

"How bad is it?" she asked.

He put his hand on the back of the chair as if to steady himself. "I've been better, but you're welcome to come in and join us."

"He flew one hundred feet, Ma," Danny said as she ventured into the room across the plank floor. "And landed on his head." He sounded positively awed.

"Probably the best place," Elijah said with a ghost of his usual smile. "Hardest part of me, my mother used to say."

"You're fortunate to be alive," Kate said. "Lieutenant Prescott told you what we found?"

He nodded, then winced as his head must have pained him. "Yes, ma'am."

She glanced at her son, who was watching Elijah avidly, as if expecting him to jump up and fly again. "Danny, why don't you go downstairs and see if Alberta has pie ready? I think Elijah could do with a slice."

"A big slice," Elijah corrected her.

Danny dashed out the door.

"Step outside with me," Elijah said.

She doubted anyone would question her checking on him, but she appreciated his care for her reputation. She moved out into the corridor, and Elijah joined her.

"You know why this happened," he said.

Kate shook her head. "No. Why?"

He glanced both ways as if thinking his enemy was lurking among the staff rooms. Then he leaned forward. "Someone doesn't like you."

Kate recoiled. "Me?"

"The Geyser Gateway, in any event," he clarified, straightening. "Your hotel was the last hope for the Virginia City Outfitters to gain a foothold in the park. This accident was a warning."

"But to cripple a coach?" she protested. "You could have been killed!"

He eyed her. "You really think they'd lose any sleep over killing me?"

There were still those who lamented the end of slavery and saw a man like Elijah as less than others. She was thankful only a few such people had visited her hotel over the years. "Maybe not, the cowards, but they could have hurt four visitors too, and that's not good for anyone's business."

"Better to hurt a few now than to miss out on the dozens this hotel houses every year," Elijah retorted.

Kate shook her head. "This is ridiculous. I can't believe they'd stoop so low."

"I can," Elijah said, turning for his room. "And you better decide what you intend to do about it before someone really is killed."

He reached for the door as if to shut it.

"Wait," Kate said, and he glanced back at her.

"I don't want anyone hurt because of me or this hotel. If you need to take your passengers to another hotel instead of the Geyser Gateway to keep you and your team safe, I'll understand."

His smile was grim. "I won't be going anywhere until I can repair that coach. And when it's repaired, it won't be the Geyser Gateway I'll be avoiding. Old Faithful can rely on Wakefield and Hoffman from here out."

"Are you sure you want to lose that business?" she pressed.

He shoved his hands into the pockets of his trousers. "I may not have any business next year. Captain Harris is renewing the contracts for the stages as well as the leases on the hotels. With this accident on my record, I may not be back next year."

She could hear the bitterness in his voice. He'd worked hard for his concession license. It wasn't right that this accident should force him out of the park.

The clatter of footsteps on the stairs sounded a moment before Danny arrived, holding a generous slice of huckleberry pie, juice pooling on the plate. Two forks stuck out of the pocket of his short pants. "Miss Pringle and Mrs. Pettijohn want to help Elijah too."

"I know they do," Kate assured him, mind humming with Elijah's warning. "But I know someone better. How would you like to spend the night with him?"

Danny's eyes widened. "Would I!"

Elijah looked at her askance.

"If you need anything," she explained, "you can send Danny for me or Alberta."

Danny moved into the room as if ready to report.

Elijah went so far as to salute her. "Yes, ma'am, and I hope Alberta sends up a big dinner, with more pie, for me and my helper."

Kate promised to see to it and left Danny perched on the bed and peppering Elijah with questions about the wreck.

But her coachman's accusations remained on her mind. The Virginia City Outfitters had tried to buy her out, then run her out with rumors. Would they really go so far as to harm a driver or her guests? Had they had an agent at Old Faithful? Perhaps one of the other coach drivers?

Yellowstone had seen stagecoach accidents before, but the causes had always been put down to inebriated drivers or dangerous road conditions. Elijah never drank on the job, never drank at all, that she knew, and the road to Old Faithful had been fine for her and Will, even after the snow yesterday. But if Will hadn't noticed the broken bit under the coach, she would still have wondered how the wreck could have happened.

The question was: what was she to do about it?

Kate was pacing the porch when Will and Smith rode by that evening. Will could only wonder whether she'd heard the news he was bringing. As if in apology, Smith tipped his cap to her before continuing around the geyser field. Will stopped in front of her.

"Everything all right?" he asked.

She moved to the rail as if his concern fueled her steps. "Elijah should be fine. The Barksdales too. But Will, Elijah is certain this accident was caused by the Virginia City Outfitters."

He nodded slowly as the accusation sunk in. It certainly aligned with the news he'd received from Mammoth Hot Springs. "Makes sense."

Kate threw up her hands. "None of this makes sense. This is a thirty-bed older hotel. You know what it takes just to maintain it. They could build a modern marvel with telephones. Why harass me?"

"Because you have a lease," he said. "The Yellowstone Park Association has bought up nearly everything else. And the Department of the Interior doesn't seem disposed to grant new leases. You're the only hope the Virginia City Outfitters have of gaining a place in the park."

Kate came down the stairs to him and put a hand on his saddle. "Elijah said the same thing. If you're that certain, tell Captain Harris. This accident wasn't Elijah's fault. The Virginia City Outfitters can't be allowed to get away with it. Someone might have been killed."

The need to help her was nearly overwhelming, but he knew what Captain Harris would say. He covered her hand with his. "I'll report the incident, Kate, and my suspicions of its cause. But I can't indict the Virginia City Outfitters. We have no proof. I'm sorry."

She yanked back her hand, and he felt as if she'd struck him.

"No proof?" she cried. "What about the cut board under Elijah's coach?"

"It appeared to have been cut," Will reminded her. "But we can't prove who cut it."

She bit her lower lip as if holding back words.

Will swung down from the saddle. "There's more. Give me a moment to hitch Bess, and we'll talk."

She didn't look ready to talk. Her color was high, her face set. But she climbed the steps and went to sit stiffly on the porch swing on the side of the hotel.

Will tied Bess, gave her a pat, and joined Kate.

"Please tell me no one else has been hurt," she said as he sat beside her, swing shifting.

"No one was hurt," he answered. "But there's a problem. When I telephoned Mammoth Hot Springs about the wreck, Lieutenant Tutherly told me about a fracas there. Were you expecting a load of supplies?"

She nodded. "The last of the year — canned goods, barrels of flour, salt pork, and salt — meant to last us through the winter until the first wagons make it in next spring."

That's what he'd feared. "They're being held at Mammoth Hot Springs. One of the other drivers is offering to pay the teamster double the price to divert the supplies to Virginia City."

She surged to her feet with such force the

swing rocked beneath him. "That's not fair! I paid for those supplies — half down, half on delivery."

She was right. It wasn't fair. But there was only so much Captain Harris could do. As it was, they were fortunate the teamster had requested the Army's aid in resolving the issue.

"If the freight company takes the deal, they'll no doubt reimburse you your down payment," he offered.

"That won't help," she protested. "There's no time to get more here before winter sets in. Without those supplies, we won't be able to house you and your men, Will. We may not have enough food for Danny, Alberta, and me."

He rose to face her. "Then we better fetch those supplies."

"How?" she demanded, gaze searching his. "I have a pony cart big enough for three. Elijah's stagecoach is wrecked. You and your men all together couldn't carry everything by horseback." She shook her head. "Elijah was right. The Virginia City Outfitters are out to ruin me."

Will took her hand. "We won't let them."

She sucked back a breath that sounded suspiciously like a sob. "A nice promise, but I don't see how you can keep it."

Neither did he, but that didn't matter. She'd made this hotel a home — for herself and Danny, for Alberta and Pansy and Caleb, for Elijah and her guests, for Will and his men. There had to be something he could do to keep her from losing it.

"First we have to convince the freight company to deliver those supplies," he said. "Then we have to make sure Captain Harris, the Department of the Interior, and every last guest this year knows the Geyser Gateway is the finest hotel in the park."

She cocked her head. "How do you propose we do that?"

"Pack a bag," Will said. "And bring your best dress. Tomorrow we're riding to Mammoth Hot Springs. I'll get you in to see Captain Harris, and we'll settle this."

21

Mammoth Hot Springs had changed since the last time Kate had visited. The steaming waters still ran down the travertine terraces, in streaks of orange, apricot, and cream, like a giant layer cake. Bubbles still popped in the hot water, fueling the smell of sulfur. But the view was partly blocked now by the National Hotel.

Kate reined in and stared at it. Four stories tall at its highest point, the green building with its red roof was easily four times as long as the Geyser Gateway. A wide covered porch ran along the front, and multi-paned windows gazed out at the park. She wasn't sure if the turret near the front entrance held stairs or fancy sitting rooms for the guests. Three Wakefield and Hoffman stages were disgorging visitors, while another, precariously loaded with a half dozen people on the top, was about to leave.

"Why would the Virginia City Outfitters

want to compete with this?" Kate asked Will, who had stopped beside her.

He just shook his head.

He had said little on the trip north. Perhaps he'd been awed by the views. The stands of aspen along the Madison River were turning gold with the fall. She and Will had ridden past them and up into the Norris Geyser Basin, stopping briefly to check in with Sergeant Nadler.

"I haven't given up on finding that poacher for you," he'd assured Kate. "We discovered his packs on the road below the basin, buffalo hide and all. If he left, he left empty-handed."

"Do you think we've seen the last of this Jessup?" she'd asked Will as they'd continued north.

"I don't know," he'd admitted. "But at least he understands we're on our guard against him."

Will had seemed equally on guard as they traveled through forests and stream-veined meadows dotted by asters, where antelope raised their heads to watch them ride by. His gaze roamed the way ahead, as if he expected an outlaw waiting in every pine grove. Kate had pointed out the craggy cliff with obsidian glittering among the stones, the placid waters of Swan Lake. Gradually, sagebrush had begun to replace some of the grass, and elk moved among them, browsing. She and Will had ridden up through reddish cliffs, with rocks tumbled down near the edge of the road, then out onto the planks of the Golden Gate bridge.

"Lieutenant Kingman's pride and joy," Kate had said as she caught Will peering over the rail of the trestle to the river far below. "You should have heard the noise when he used explosives. Sometimes I thought you could feel them even at the Geyser Gateway."

Will raised his head, face slightly green, as the planks creaked beneath them.

When he remained silent as they started up the final leg, she pressed the issue. "Concerned about your men?"

He seemed to gather his thoughts from a distance. "No. Most are clearing the wreckage of Elijah's stage off the road, with the help of some of the Old Faithful detachment."

"I'm just glad Elijah made it through the night without having to send Danny for aid," she told him. "He groaned as he came down the stairs for breakfast. I made him promise not to ride out to help with the work."

"He shouldn't have much to do at the inn

347

either," Will said. "I left Private Smith in charge of patrolling, with firm instructions not to spend the entire time lounging on the porch."

Kate had smiled. "You should have warned Alberta too. I think she's taken a shine to Private Smith."

He had nodded, but his lips had compressed as if he refused to say more on the matter.

Now he directed her to the old Norris blockhouse, where Captain Harris had set up his offices. The whitewashed building stood on a rise overlooking the area, with a two-story center, slanted short wings on either side, and a three-story gun turret at the rear. A private who didn't look as if he'd started shaving yet came to see to their horses and saddlebags.

"Take Mrs. Tremaine's bags to the guest quarters," Will told the pimple-faced youth.

"No," Kate said before the private could move. She nodded to the massive hotel across from them. "I want to stay there."

Will leaned closer to her and lowered his voice. "Do you think that's a good idea? I know you want to compare the competition, but I don't trust them. The Yellowstone Park Association also offered to buy you out. You could be spending the night in the lion's den."

"Then I will emerge unscathed, like Daniel," Kate promised him.

He regarded her a moment, mossy eyes as unfathomable as one of Yellowstone's hot pools. Then he nodded and straightened.

"Very well, Private," he said. "Take Mrs. Tremaine's things to the National Hotel and secure her a room."

"Sir, ma'am." He led the horses down the hill toward the stables.

Will and Kate entered the building.

Captain Harris's office was on the second floor. The poor fellow's desk was a couple of planks across sawhorses, but he had managed to cover it with maps, building plans, and lengthy lists. He rose from behind the pile at the sight of her. She'd met him on his first tour of the park when he and his troop had arrived last month. His sandy hair never seemed to muss or his uniform to lose its press, despite the challenges of Yellowstone.

"Mrs. Tremaine," he said with a nod. "A pleasure to see you again, but I believe I know the reason. I understand there's been an issue with your supplies." He waved her toward one of the two chairs on the other side of the desk.

"I'm very glad to hear you acknowledge

their ownership," Kate said, refusing to sit and thus keeping Harris on his feet as well for propriety's sake. "I paid for them. I expect them to be delivered immediately."

His look never wavered. "You would have to take that up with the freighting company. The Army cannot involve itself in civilian matters unless they directly relate to the management of the park."

Beside her, Will shifted just enough that his hand brushed hers. She glanced at him, and his head inched back and forth. Warning her. As the most senior officer in the park, and head of his troop, Captain Harris was likely unused to people arguing. And it was easier to catch flies with honey than with vinegar.

Kate offered the commanding officer a smile. "I understand. And I do appreciate your efforts. Your men have been stalwart champions in protecting the land and its resources. I commend you on your leadership."

He inclined his head. "Thank you, Mrs. Tremaine."

Will relaxed beside her, but she couldn't leave it at that. Too much was at stake.

"I assume you mean to feed your men," she said.

Captain Harris blinked, and she thought

she heard Will sigh.

"A savvy general once said an army travels on its stomach," the captain acknowledged.

"Then you intend to send additional supplies for Lieutenant Prescott and his men to overwinter."

"Certainly." He frowned at Will as if he wasn't sure why she was asking. Will kept his gaze fixed over his commanding officer's shoulder.

"I hope the supplies can withstand freezing temperatures," Kate said sweetly. "You see, without the supplies being held here, my staff and my son and I will have to close the inn and winter elsewhere. I will have to rescind my offer to house your men through the worst of the snow."

His face hardened. "I am unaccustomed to blackmail."

"And I am unaccustomed to these relentless attacks on my livelihood, my friends, and my guests." She took a step closer, gaze drilling into his. "Are you aware that before the Virginia City Outfitters stole my supplies, its representatives offered to buy my establishment with a warning not to refuse, spread vicious rumors about me and my hotel, attempted to hire away my staff, and caused an accident that injured my driver and four visitors?"

351

"I am kept apprised of all activities in Yellowstone, madam," he said, though he looked to Will, who stood taller. "But, as I said, the Army cannot interfere with civilian matters."

"Even when they involve two of your concessionaires? Mr. Freeman's stage has been crippled, his spotless reputation damaged. I won't see him punished for someone else's ill-advised actions."

Captain Harris's face was stern. "Rest assured your concerns have been noted and will be included in my assessment of the leases and contracts next spring."

He simply didn't understand. "I may not be returning next spring unless I can maintain the hotel over the winter. Is there nothing you can offer to assist?"

He spread his hands. "I have fifty men to manage nearly two million acres. Even if I was allowed to intercede in civilian affairs, I wouldn't have the staff."

Will stepped forward. "Thank you, Captain, for allowing Mrs. Tremaine to make her case. With your permission, I'll spend the night here before escorting her home tomorrow. Unless you have other duties you'd like me to attend to, I could speak to the teamster and see if anything can be done to free up her supplies."

She thought the captain would argue, set him to some more important task for the Army. But he nodded. "Very well, Lieutenant. I believe you'll find Mr. Boyne, the teamster, at the National Hotel."

Of course they would. The Virginia City Outfitters were very likely putting him up in style in the hopes he'd give in to their proposal.

"And Mrs. Tremaine," Captain Harris added, "I hope you'll join my officers and me for dinner tonight."

"We'd be delighted," Will answered for her.

Kate merely smiled, but she rounded on Will the moment they stepped outside.

"How dare you speak for me! After that interview, I have no intention of sitting down to a meal with Captain Harris or any of his men. At the moment, I'm not sure about you."

He grimaced. "Sorry, Kate. There wasn't time to explain. Trust me on this. You are your own best advocate — for the park and the Geyser Gateway. I wasn't the one who convinced Captain Harris to allow me to assist you. That was all you. It won't take much to persuade him to side with you against the Virginia City Outfitters either."

She couldn't believe that, but she had to

eat, and she wasn't opposed to making the Army pay for the meal after coming this far. "Very well. At least he allowed you to help with this teamster. Let's find him and get this over with."

It took a little effort, but they located Mr. Boyne out at one of the stables, checking on his horses. A big man, gut swelling over his dusty brown trousers, he nodded to Kate when Will introduced her.

"Ma'am. You must be here about your supplies."

Kate kept her temper with difficulty. "Yes. I've been expecting delivery any day. When are you heading to the Lower Geyser Basin?"

He tilted his head to glance out the door toward the back of the big hotel, then returned his gaze to hers. "I've been asked to send the supplies to Virginia City instead."

"So I was given to understand," Kate said. "I'm sure there's been a misunderstanding. My hotel is not part of the Virginia City Outfitters, Mr. Boyne. Your contract is with me, not them."

"My contract is with the merchant in Bozeman, ma'am," he said, broad face apologetic. "They like the idea of additional profit."

Was everyone greedy? "They stated their prices; I paid them," Kate told him. "They cannot raise their prices now."

He licked his flabby lips. "Maybe you could match what the Virginia City Outfitters are offering."

"Maybe the merchant could honor his word," Will put in.

He shifted on his feet. "It's not for me to say."

Honey, remember? Kate put a hand on his arm. "Please, Mr. Boyne. I need those supplies to feed my staff and my son through the winter. I don't have the extra money to pay more or buy more. But I can promise you, if you deliver to the Geyser Gateway, I'll give you a lovely room and the best pie west of the Mississippi."

He gazed down at her, eyes bloodshot from the dust of the road, face burned from the sun. He'd likely driven the worst roads of the West and lived to tell the tale. What were her problems to a man like that?

Suddenly, he snapped a nod. "I'll do it. I'll deliver them. I've been stuck at that hotel for three days while the merchant and the Virginia City Outfitters telegraphed each other. They don't care about my time, my horses. At least you treat me like a gentleman."

Relief left her sagging. "Thank you, Mr. Boyne. If you reach the inn before I do, tell Alberta, my cook, that I said to treat you not like a gentleman, but like a king!"

They were all predisposed to do her bidding. Will wasn't surprised. She had a way about her, a sparkle in those misty eyes, that engaging grin. And Boyne was right. Kate treated everyone with respect and admiration.

Until they wronged her.

Captain Harris was lucky. The fire in her eyes at his initial refusal could have burned down the blockhouse. As Will escorted her to the National Hotel, he was a little afraid he'd lost some of her respect. But he knew what he was doing. Kate had persuaded him to see the park in a new light. She convinced her guests the same way. She'd just encouraged Boyne to defy his employer and deliver her supplies. She'd have Captain Harris singing her praises before dinner was over.

"Dinner is usually at six," he told her as they approached the hotel porch. "I'll come for you at a quarter to."

"Is that why you suggested I bring my best dress?" she asked as they started up the steps. "To show me off to your captain?"

He darted ahead and held open the door

for her. "Not to show you off but to show up everyone else in the room. You have a presence, Kate. Use it to your advantage."

She glanced at him out of the corner of her eyes, as if she doubted that. Then she jerked to a stop on the floor and turned in a circle, gawking like the visitors she hosted.

It was an impressive place. He couldn't argue that. They had walked into a rotunda more than forty feet wide, with hallways leading off in various directions. Fine woodwork covered the pillars holding up the second story and edged the stairs and landing.

To one side, through open doors, he spotted leather-bound chairs and brass spittoons that proclaimed the gentlemen's parlor, while more dainty chairs dotted the room on the other side of the rotunda for the ladies. In between, along one wall, framed pictures and a long table displayed curiosities of the park, while straight ahead, past the clerk's station, stretched a dining room nearly as big as the first floor of the Geyser Gateway, with tables draped in white linen.

The young clerk behind his mahogany desk waved a hand at them. "You must be Mrs. Tremaine," he warbled.

Looking more than a little stunned, Kate wandered up to him. "Yes."

"A pleasure to have you with us," he assured her, green eyes bright in his square face. "I've been instructed to put you in the Presidential Suite."

She looked to Will, then back at the clerk, and her usual aplomb fell over her. "A typical room will do," she informed him.

"I'm afraid they're all full," he said, offering her the brass key with a regretful smile.

"So late in the season?" she asked with a frown.

"We're nearly always full," he said blithely. "All four hundred rooms. The price of having the best hotel in the park."

Her face darkened.

Will reached around her to accept the key. "Which way?"

"Down the north corridor, the corner rooms, with a commanding view of the terraces." A dimple popped into view beside the clerk's mouth. "I took the liberty of having her bags delivered."

Will stepped aside so Kate could head for her room.

The wide corridor was well lit with lamps suspended on brass chains from the ceiling. Kate stared up at them. "So, it's true. They have electricity."

"Only in the public areas," Will assured her, glancing at the brass plates on the doors

358

that proclaimed each room's number. Her key's number matched the one on the double doors at the end of the corridor, which gave way to a parlor as big as his would-be cabin, with a massive brass bedstead visible through the door on the left.

She sank onto the horsehair-covered sofa, shoulders slumping. "I can never compete with this."

"You don't have to," Will told her, turning from the view of the terraces out the curtained windows. "Not everyone can afford to stay in a place like this, certainly not in the Presidential Suite."

She snorted. "Presidential Suite. They make it sound as if the president himself actually stayed here. This hotel was only half finished when the previous president, President Arthur, rode through the park after I first arrived."

"That's the difference between this place and the Geyser Gateway," Will told her. "It's all flash in a pan. Your hotel is genuine."

She glanced up at him. "You really think people will favor the Geyser Gateway?"

"You're closer to the bulk of the major sights," Will reminded her. "You're reasonably priced. And you have Alberta's pie."

Her smile was soft. "True. No one's ever refused a piece of Alberta's pie."

"Then don't worry. Just be yourself around Captain Harris, and he'll approve that lease next spring, no question."

She rose, chin coming up. "I'll do it. But I don't want another one-year lease. A ten-year renewal would give me and Danny the security we need. That's what I'll push for tonight. Thank you, Will, for the opportunity."

She came to him and pressed a kiss to his cheek. He felt as if her touch reached down inside him to the honor he'd tried so hard to nurture, set it blossoming like a flower in the sun.

Would she still think so highly of him when he told her the truth? He hadn't been willing to burden her on the way north, knowing what she might face. If she returned triumphant, as he expected, he would tell her on the way back to the Geyser Gateway.

And pray she would still smile so softly at him.

22

Kate had never considered herself a woman who charmed men into doing her bidding. But then, she'd rarely been put in a position where she had to try. She hadn't had to work to attract Toby. He had never met a stranger — only friends. It wasn't appropriate for a businesswoman to charm her guests. Her approach had always been franker, but after Toby's death she'd become downright cautious. Still, if Will thought her mere presence at dinner might convince Captain Harris to recommend the Geyser Gateway for a ten-year lease, she was willing to give it all she had.

She'd brought the dress she'd worn the night they'd dined with Lieutenant Kingman. Riding for miles in a saddlebag, no matter how carefully packed, hadn't helped it or the petticoat she'd wear under it. But there was a bell pull in the hotel room, and a yank brought a helpful maid who took the items away for pressing.

Who in Yellowstone needed their clothes pressed on a regular basis? Elk didn't care what you wore; the geysers didn't judge you on the number of wrinkles. Did the visitors judge her hotel against this one?

Once more, despair threatened. If she spent every last penny of profit, she could never afford electric lights. Where would she put separate rooms for the ladies and the gentlemen to lounge without losing beds? And she'd seen some of the other amenities: a Steinway piano, not one but two billiard tables, room to host a ball.

Small wonder Captain Harris hadn't renewed her lease past the spring after seeing this palace.

She raised her head. No. This wasn't a palace. It was a luxurious hotel, but not nearly as warm and cozy as the Geyser Gateway. She'd take Pansy's steadfast care over the work of any other maid. Surely no employee was as enthusiastic about the wonders of the park as her Danny. And who could possibly rival Alberta for a welcome? The Geyser Gateway provided comfort and sustenance to all who visited. Her goal was to keep that trade for years to come. She would not give up.

She was in the lobby, waiting for Will, well

before the appointed time. Several gentlemen, guests of the hotel, wandered past, one going so far as to ogle her through his gilt-edged monocle. She ignored them to peer instead into the dining room. Cane-backed chairs? Not as good as her wooden ones, but she would be hard-pressed to match that crystal chandelier. Then again, it probably only sparkled so brightly because of its electric bulbs.

A waiter with a long white apron bearing nary a spot on it hurried up to her. "May I seat you, madam?" he asked, as if the room wasn't nearly empty.

"No, thank you," Kate said. "But I'd love a peek at your menu."

"Of course."

He returned with a pasteboard card, which Kate scanned before handing it back with a smile.

"Ice cream, what a treat," she noted.

His smile broadened. "We have it every day."

Every day! Where did they get the ice, let alone churns for so much? What, was there an employee named official ice cream cranker? Well, at least they didn't have pie. That was still Alberta's calling card.

And the room was suspiciously empty, particularly when the clerk had indicated the hotel was full. Perhaps they had to eat in shifts.

She returned to the rotunda to find that Will had arrived. He was once more in his dress uniform, and she couldn't help admiring how well it looked on him. That square-cut navy coat emphasized his shoulders. The gold stripe on his trousers followed the strong line of his legs. As his gaze met hers, he stopped, then bowed. "Mrs. Tremaine. A vision."

Cheeks feeling warm, Kate bobbed a curtsey as he straightened. "You look pretty nice yourself."

He rubbed his freshly shaven chin. "Mammoth Hot Springs has a few more amenities than our camp at the Fire Hole."

She glanced back at the dining room entrance, where two couples in fine evening wear now stood. "So I noticed."

"This place still can't hold a candle to the Geyser Gateway," he told her, offering her his arm.

At least he agreed with her. Kate put her hand on his. "Thank you. Shall we?"

He accompanied her out the door.

The night was cooling. The moon had yet to rise, and fitful clouds crossed the stars. But the lamplight from the hotel and the various buildings surrounding it lit their

364

path up to the Norris blockhouse. The bubbling of the springs and the fall of water followed them. Steam drifted on the breeze, bringing with it the familiar scents of sulfur and pine.

"You feel that nip in the air?" she asked as they crested the rise. "It won't be long now."

He reached the door and held it open for her. "I'm looking forward to it."

She laughed as she slipped past him into the building. "Let's see how you feel come spring."

He met her gaze. "My feelings won't change."

The warmth of his regard once more flushed heat into her cheeks.

"This way," he said.

The officers' mess at the back of the first floor was directly below the gun turret, so the windows were few, small, and high. A round table draped in gingham sat in the center of the whitewashed space, surrounded by mismatched chairs she assumed they had plundered from other buildings. A potbellied stove gave off a welcome heat.

Captain Harris and two lieutenants were standing on either side of it. The commanding officer came to greet her. "Mrs. Tremaine. You grace us with your presence."

"Always delighted to join such fine officers," Kate replied.

He introduced her to his staff. Lieutenant Vickers was a bright-eyed young man who tripped over his tongue in his hurry to make a good impression. Lieutenant Tutherly, Harris's adjutant, was more in command of himself, bowing over her hand. His face was distinguished by prominent ears, a large nose, and a bristling mustache that stuck out well beyond his firm lips. His conversation was more measured, as if he hesitated to state an opinion that might contradict that of his commander. Like Will, they had shaved recently, and their hair was slicked back from their faces.

Still, it didn't seem right they should outrank him. Will stood, confident, calm, answering questions put to him with nary a hesitation. There was no question in her mind which of the three would be more likely to come to her aid swiftly in an emergency. He was a geyser to their mud pots.

And what would he think to know she'd compared him to a geologic formation!

Captain Harris offered her his arm and led her to the table, seating her on his right with Lieutenant Tutherly on her right and Will beyond him. Vickers was between Will and the captain.

Kate had just draped her napkin across her gown when a private brought in a platter of sliced beef followed by a tureen of mashed potatoes and a bowl of gravy. It looked like Alberta had chosen well when she'd decided the menu for Lieutenant Kingman's dinner — it seemed to be standard Army fare. Captain Harris said grace, and they all dove in.

But this was nothing like what Alberta had served. Stringy, too salty, and what was in that lumpy gravy? Kate hid her distaste over a long drink from the overly tart lemonade before her.

"How many visitors did you have at the Geyser Gateway this season, Mrs. Tremaine?" Captain Harris asked, forking up another mouthful as if he hadn't noticed the state of the food.

Kate poked at the gray mass of mashed potatoes and couldn't make herself take a bite. "Double last season. The reports in the newspapers from those who have visited seem to have made the public more aware of Yellowstone."

He nodded, stirring the gravy into his mashed potatoes. Would that help the texture? "And you've had no troubles with vandals or poachers?"

Kate looked to Will, who quickly swallowed his food as if getting down a bitter dose of medicine.

"A few guests had to be taught the proper respect for the formations," he allowed. "We only found evidence of the one poacher."

"Jessup," Vickers growled. "The fellow's a blight."

"Slippery, though," Tutherly commented. "We still don't know where he went."

"He'll be back," Captain Harris warned them. "Men like him will continue to plague Yellowstone until we have rules and the means to enforce them."

"For everyone," Kate added. "I noticed the National Hotel had elk on the dinner menu."

Captain Harris leveled his fork at Vickers. "I thought you took care of that, Lieutenant."

Vickers colored. "I have had detailed discussions with the hotel management." He nodded to Kate. "I'm sure it was only what they had left from our last conversation, Mrs. Tremaine."

She highly doubted that. "Of course, Lieutenant. And it may have been brought in from outside the park. But I promise you the Geyser Gateway will never serve an ounce of game."

"Forgive me, Mrs. Tremaine," the commanding officer said, signaling to his private to pour more lemonade. "You are here as our guest, not to talk business. How is your son? Danny, I believe?"

And here she had been hoping to talk business. Still, considering all the people with whom he must have interacted since arriving in the park, she was impressed that he remembered her son.

"Danny is well," she told him. "He's taken to mimicking your troops, especially Lieutenant Prescott."

"Has he?" Captain Harris eyed Will, who seemed to sink in his chair.

"Indeed. And he is fascinated by baseball. Lieutenant Prescott told him about it and has been tutoring him in the sport. He happily tells anyone who will listen about the game he played last week with Lieutenant Prescott and his men and Lieutenant Kingman and the engineering crew."

"Must be nice," Lieutenant Vickers said with a look to Will. "Having nothing better to do."

Will inclined his head. "We patrol the Lower Geyser Basin a minimum of twice a day and maintain the camp. If we have a moment to reciprocate the fine hospitality shown us, it seems a good use of our time."

"Is it so much more difficult at Mammoth

Hot Springs?" Kate asked, locating a piece of meat that yielded to her fork.

"Rather challenging," Tutherly allowed.

Vickers wasn't content to leave it at that. "I'll say. The visitors, the supplies coming through, the infrastructure we must construct. And the fire didn't help."

"I can see all that would stretch you thin," Kate commiserated. "It's hard enough managing a hotel in one of the busiest visitor areas of the park. At least I don't get many complaints to deal with. Having Lieutenant Prescott and his men patrolling has only helped."

"Yes, Lieutenant Prescott is a wonder," Captain Harris said, holding the nearly empty tureen out to Kate. "May I interest you in a second helping of potatoes, Mrs. Tremaine?"

She'd gag. But he'd given her an opening. "No, thank you. I hope you didn't use your last potatoes on me. How are you fixed for winter supplies, Captain?"

"We should be fine here at Mammoth Hot Springs," he said, scooping out the gray mass for himself. "I am told it's rare a teamster cannot reach Gardiner at least. And I can send men for the supplies if we need them here, unlike other areas of the park that are more remote."

Kate made a face. "Oh, then the manager of the National Hotel hasn't offered to house you over the winter?"

His smile was crisp. "He has not."

"Pity." She smiled at the other two lieutenants. "Well, you are all welcome at the Geyser Gateway any time you'd care to visit. We fully support the Army's good work in Yellowstone."

She allowed Captain Harris to steer the conversation into other areas for the remainder of the meal, which ended with a dessert of bread pudding that wasn't too bad. But Kate made sure to bring the discussion back to hotels before she left.

"Thank you for a lovely evening," she told Captain Harris as he and Will accompanied her to the door. "I do hope we'll have an opportunity to return the favor soon."

"I'll see if I have time before winter sets in," Captain Harris replied. "But certainly when I come through on my inspection tour next spring."

"And if I could improve the Geyser Gateway in any way before then?" Kate asked. "What would you advise?"

He smiled. "From what I understand, the Geyser Gateway is a rare jewel. Just see that it retains its shine." He bowed to her. She inclined her head.

As he straightened, he looked to Will. "Report to me after you escort Mrs. Tremaine to her hotel, Lieutenant."

Will saluted. "Sir."

Kate waited only until the door had closed behind them before turning to Will. "I've gotten you into trouble, haven't I? Something I said upset him."

"It wasn't you," he said, starting back for the hotel. "You were perfect tonight, Kate, as I knew you would be. We're leaving in the morning. Captain Harris probably just wants to relay orders."

She wished she could be so sure, but she couldn't help feeling that, by praising Will, she'd somehow blundered in the captain's eyes.

How had he attracted the admiration of such a woman? Will could only marvel as he climbed the steps to the porch of the National Hotel, where lamps glowed through the windows. It wasn't fully occupied, despite what the clerk claimed. The staff hoped to impress her. So did Captain Harris and his men. Truth be told, so did he.

"I'm glad you were with me tonight, Will," she said, pausing on the porch. "It was good to have a friend in the room."

"You can always count on my support, Kate," he promised.

Still she hesitated, watching him, as if she was hoping for more from the evening. His heart started a fierce tattoo, calling him to action. Slowly, carefully, he bent and brushed his lips against hers. Once again, he was certain the earth trembled.

But this time the quake was inside him.

"Good night, Will," she murmured with a soft smile. Then she slipped into the hotel.

Will walked back to the government buildings. Good thing no one else was about, or they might have commented on the swing in his step. How could he not be optimistic when she looked at him that way, encouraged his kiss?

He was directed to his commanding officer's quarters on the south side of the blockhouse. One look at Harris's face, and all confidence fled.

"You wanted to see me, sir?" he asked, coming in and closing the door. The room was perhaps ten feet wide and a dozen long, and it had been filled with a wooden bedstead, campaign chest, washstand, and folding camp chair. Harris had removed his jacket and was giving it a good brushing, suspenders flexing with his cotton-clad shoulders.

"I wanted to talk to you about the conversation at dinner," he said, running the stiff brush down the wool.

Perhaps someone *had* misspoken. "If I said anything untoward, I apologize."

Harris gave the coat a good shake, studying it as if it had offended him. "It wasn't what you said. It was what Mrs. Tremaine said and you did not say. It is clear the lady has feelings for you."

Hope shot skyward, like a grouse flushed from the grass. It fell as quickly. "Mrs. Tremaine is grateful for the work the Army is doing in the park, sir," Will said. "Nothing more."

"She made her gratitude abundantly clear." He lowered the coat and met Will's gaze. "It is unbecoming of an officer to raise a lady's expectations when he has no intention of meeting them. I assume, therefore, that you harbor feelings for Mrs. Tremaine."

He could deny it. He should deny it. If anyone had the right to know how he felt about Kate, it was her, and before anyone else. Yet, if he denied it, Harris might reassign him elsewhere in the park, forcing him from Kate's side.

And he would make himself a liar.

"I admire Mrs. Tremaine more than I can say, sir," he answered.

Harris hung the coat on a peg against the wall with maddening calm. "Does she know about the incident in Oregon?"

He would never have called the tragedy an incident, but Will kept his head high. "I plan to tell her soon."

"Good." Harris turned to him. "That may well put an end of the matter."

The words were a bullet to his hopes. "I fear as much, sir."

Harris closed the distance between them. "If not, then consider your next steps carefully. The Army thought enough of you to give you a second chance. The gift came with the demand of loyalty. I do not expect us to stay in Yellowstone long. Kate Tremaine does not strike me as the sort to follow the drum. You will have to choose between your career and her."

23

Kate wasn't sorry to leave Mammoth Hot Springs behind. The National Hotel was beyond what she had imagined, but the long corridors seemed too empty after the bustle of the Geyser Gateway. And that dinner last night could never compare with Alberta's cooking. Kate may not have convinced Captain Harris to issue a ten-year lease, but she had achieved one of her objectives. Mr. Boyne and his wagons had headed south, fully loaded, early that morning.

Now she rode beside Will, sun rising over the plateau on their left and anointing the dusty ground with patches of gilt as the shadows from the mountains retreated. Following the winding way south, all she could smell was pine and fresh water. A hawk called overhead before diving for prey against the gold of aspen.

"With this shipment and Alberta's canning, we should have plenty for winter," she told Will as the horses walked past a white tumble of rocks that were all that remained of an ancient slide.

"Then it was worth the trip," he said. He tilted back his head and took a deep breath, as if relishing the cool air as much as she did.

"What did Captain Harris want last night?" she asked.

He dropped his head and aimed his gaze on the road. "He wanted to know my intentions toward you."

"Your intentions?" She started, and Aster balked. She urged the mare forward. "Who does he think he is, my father?"

"He was more interested in protecting the Army's reputation than yours," Will said with a shake of his head.

"And should I applaud him for that?" she demanded.

"No," he assured her. "But his point is well taken. I have no right raising your expectations, Kate."

She still wasn't sure whether to be insulted by the captain's interference. But Will's words made the air seem chillier. "So, you have been dallying with me."

"No, I . . ." Now Bess sidestepped, as if she felt her master's agitation. He patted her and eased her back along the road.

377

"I meant I have no business entertaining the notion of courting a lady unless she knows what she's getting into," he said, hand tight on the reins.

Courting. Her nerves tingled. The first kiss could have been the result of the moment. But last night? She'd stood on the porch, waiting, wondering, hoping. And her hope had not been in vain. That second kiss had made sleep difficult. Why else offer it if not with the expectation that they were courting?

But courting implied taking a chance, the willingness to make a commitment. She was a mother, a businesswoman. Did she really want to take a chance on marrying anyone again?

But it wasn't anyone, it was Will. And she knew the answer was yes.

Yes, she was willing to try. Yes, she was willing to offer her heart. Yes, she was falling in love.

"I'm coming to know you," she told him as they neared the Golden Gate. "So I'm not approaching the matter of courting blindly. I have some inkling of your character. I've seen how well you treat Danny, your men, and my staff and guests. You have an orderly disposition and a kind heart."

His brows quirked. "You might withhold

judgment until you know all."

"What more is there to know?"

They clattered onto the bridge, the world dropping away on one side. When he still didn't answer as they reached the road beyond, she glanced his way. His shoulders were hitched up, as if trying to carry a heavy load.

"Will?" she asked, stomach falling as if she'd gazed over the precipice. "What more should I know?"

"Forgive my hesitation," he said, voice rougher than usual. "It's not a pretty tale."

Had she been wrong to trust him? As with Toby, had she rushed in without sufficient consideration? Had she risked the reputation of the Geyser Gateway, the safety of her son, the depths of her heart, on a phantom? The very idea made her throat tight.

"Perhaps I should hear it," she allowed.

He nodded as if accepting his fate. "You may wish you hadn't, but very well. When I joined the Army in Boston, I was sure I was bound for glory. Worse, I was a cocky recruit: brash, undisciplined. But I managed to distinguish myself and rise in rank quickly. I'm ashamed to say I didn't pay much attention to the men under my command. Advancement and recognition were all that mattered."

She found it hard to reconcile the person he described with the man riding beside her, face guarded. "You must have mended your ways."

"Dishonor forces a man to see things differently."

"Dishonor!" She wasn't sure what to say, how to react, only that the word could have no association with this man. "How could you possibly act dishonorably?"

He shook his head, but at her disbelieving tone or his own actions, she wasn't sure. "Far too easily, I assure you. We'd been sent to Oregon to chase Bannock, who had left their reservation. A rancher wanted to thank us for our efforts. He invited me and my men to dinner. I took the offer, but I sent my men on patrol. You see, the rancher had a pretty daughter, and I didn't want her distracted from fawning over me."

"Well, that was a bit arrogant," Kate acknowledged. "But I've heard of men doing far worse."

He glanced her way, and his eyes were hollow. "It was worse than I could have imagined. My men were understandably angry about being slighted. They happened upon a band of Bannock women and children while on patrol. They slaughtered them, every last one."

Bile rose in her throat, and Aster stuttered in her step. "No!"

"Yes," he said, voice now merciless. "I carry their blood on my hands, Kate. If I had been where I should have been, if I had led my men as I should, I would have seen those families escorted to safety. But I wasn't there. Because of my selfishness, they died. I will never forgive myself."

Emotions swarmed her — revulsion, denial, disgust. He had made an error, and the consequences were too high. Nothing she could say, nothing he could do, would ever erase that.

"Those poor people, caught in the middle," she murmured. "But your men bear a greater shame. They had a clear duty, and they failed."

He guided Bess down the road toward the flats, his shadow rippling across the boulders beside them. "Easy to say when you haven't faced hostiles. My men were jittery, afraid of an ambush. Anyone who looked remotely like the enemy was to be destroyed."

"You're making excuses for them," Kate said, holding Aster steady as they descended. "The mere presence of the children should have warned them this was not a band bent on fighting. I cannot see this as anything but a tragedy, for all concerned."

His face was so tight she wondered he could speak. "The Army saw it even more harshly. My sergeant was hanged, my corporals sent to prison for three years. My men were reassigned to better leaders. And I, the cause of it all, I was demoted to corporal, stripped of the spurs every cavalryman treasures, and given a month of hard labor, as if those were just punishments for the harm I'd caused."

His lips curled, as if he tasted something bitter, but she thought the bitterness was inside him. He expected her censure, was sure he deserved it.

"I don't know much about the inner workings of the Army," she said. "But I was under the impression it wasn't easy to break through the noncommissioned officer ranks to lieutenant. That would be even harder after a disciplinary action, I would imagine. And yet here you are, and not solely on bravado, I think."

"I've done all I can to be worthy of the rank this time," he acknowledged.

And still didn't think it was enough. She couldn't help remembering his statement earlier, about not raising her expectations. "Then I suppose befriending me and Danny has just been part of your penance."

His gaze met hers. "Everything I do is in penance."

Kate smiled though her heart protested. "Thank you for telling me, Will. You're right. I could have mistaken your attentions for something more."

He reined in, and she pulled Aster to a stop as well. The horses were not breathing nearly as heavily as he was, as if he'd traveled the greater distance.

"That's not why I told you, Kate," he said. "I care about you, more than I have any right to care. Even Captain Harris noticed. And I thought you might have been coming to care for me. You deserve to know the truth."

And he thought she'd give up on him, perhaps order him away from her and Danny. How could she make herself take such a step? His awe of the wonders around them had reawakened hers, broken through some of the wall of caution she'd built around herself after Toby's death. Because of Will's kindness, she'd forgiven herself for not going out to help Toby that night.

Her kindness might not be enough to help Will. His guilt was multiplied by the number of the dead. Yet how could she throw the first stone to condemn him?

"What truth?" Kate challenged him. "That

you are sincere in your concern of the men under you now? That you take your duty to protect Yellowstone seriously? That you work every day to be the best leader, best friend, best example? I knew that already."

He frowned at her. "Did nothing I just told you change your mind about me?"

"No," she said. "I can never truly empathize with such pain. I'm not sure I would have liked the man you were then. But I see someone different now. A man who takes time away from his duty to teach a lonely seven-year-old baseball. Who cranks an ice cream churn for an hour in the heat to please two elderly women. Who holds a widow while she cries over the loss of her husband. That's the man I see. I hope you make his acquaintance one day."

He might not listen. He might not be ready to forgive himself. But there wasn't much more she could say. Leaving him to consider her words, she resolutely set Aster toward home.

He didn't know whether to hug her close in thanksgiving or argue with her. With them both on horseback, hugging was impossible. And he couldn't quite bring himself to argue. Her acceptance felt too good, like a cool breeze across the desert. He could take a deep breath for the first time in a long time. He urged Bess to catch up with her.

"Thank you," he said as he came abreast.

She glanced his way. "No need for thanks. I just hope you'll remember what I said."

"I will," he promised. "Sometimes I think I see that man you described. It's easier here."

Her gaze went out over the terrain. They had reached the Swan Lake flats, the grass and sage rising toward the Gallatin Range beyond. Four young elk trotted toward the placid waters, which reflected the vibrant blue of the sky.

"There is peace here," she said. "And a purpose."

"It's not just Yellowstone," he told her. "It's you and Danny and the Geyser Gateway. It's Alberta's pie and the way she makes room for each of us at her table. It's the camaraderie among you all. I never knew what home felt like until I came here."

Her gaze met his, sparkling silver. "Oh, Will, I'm so glad."

So was he, and never more so than this moment. "So, Kate, I have to ask. Will you allow me to court you?"

He hadn't planned to ask. Some part of him persisted in the notion that he hadn't earned the right. Yet her kindness, her sympathy, had opened a window to the sun, and he wanted to bask in the light.

She looked away, toward the pines above the lake, and he felt as if she'd slammed that window shut.

"Are you sure that's what you want?" she asked. "You told me before it wasn't so simple. Is it any simpler now?"

"Yes, now that you know the truth," Will told her.

She did not look convinced. "You're an officer in the US Cavalry. One day, you'll be assigned somewhere else. I won't leave the park."

Captain Harris had warned him as much. He knew his answer. "I wouldn't ask you to leave Yellowstone. I'd leave the Army."

Her brows shot up. "You'd do that, even after the Army gave you a second chance?"

He drew a breath as they moved into the pines along the twisting turns of Obsidian Creek. "I've devoted the last eight years of my life to removing the stain of that day. I'm ready to resign. Next fall at the latest. I expect we'll be in the park at least until spring. At worst, I would be assigned else-where for six months before I could return to you."

She didn't argue, but she didn't agree either. She faced the road ahead, as if the pines and creek held more secrets than he had shared. "And I might not have a home for you to return to. Captain Harris or the Department of the Interior may decline to renew my lease."

"You'll get that lease," he assured her. "They'd be stupid not to renew."

She snorted. "I've lived through three lackluster superintendents before Captain Harris. I've seen my share of stupid. But I suppose we won't know until spring."

Did that mean she was giving him until then to court her? He was almost afraid to ask. They traveled companionably past Obsidian Cliff and up into the hills beyond. The sage was blooming, the yellow brightening the area. She remained quiet as they neared Roaring Mountain, where the snowy white soil of the pine-dotted hill smoked and sputtered, but Will couldn't seem to get comfortable on the saddle. As they came up into the Norris Geyser Basin, he couldn't let the matter lie.

"You never answered my question," he said as they trotted past the guard station. "May I have the honor of courting you?"

She nodded to Rizzo, who was on patrol in the geyser field and had waved a hand to them. "We're going to be spending at least five months in close proximity, Will. A courtship might get messy."

Disappointment pushed down on his shoulders. "Of course."

"So, I suppose you'd better get to it before the snow flies." She put heels to Aster, and the mare broke into a canter. He spurred Bess to keep up, heart soaring.

They reached the Geyser Gateway by late afternoon and turned the horses into the corral so Caleb could give them a good rubdown and a rest. Will couldn't help admiring the swing in Kate's step as she crossed the yard to the veranda. He rather thought he was sauntering a bit himself, although he still couldn't quite believe she'd encouraged him to court her, especially after he'd shared his past. Perhaps he'd finally turned the corner.

Mr. Boyne had arrived before them, and Will was pleased to see his men helping unload the supplies under Alberta's watchful eye. Captain Harris might have protested the Army getting involved in civilian matters, but Kate wasn't the only one who'd benefit from the food. The least the cavalry could do was see it safely stored.

After hearing Lercher's report, Will went into the inn. He found Kate and Danny in the salon, where Elijah was resting on the couch with Miss Pringle and Mrs. Pettijohn watching over him from chairs at either end.

"Private Lercher tells me the Barksdales moved on," Will said after greeting the older ladies, the driver, and Danny.

Mrs. Pettijohn sniffed. "They lacked what is required to survive the wilderness."

"Now, dear," Miss Pringle reminded her sister, "anyone might have been rattled by that terrible carriage accident. Look at our valiant driver here." She beamed at Elijah.

"But all is not lost," Kate said. "Private Franklin was able to reattach the wheel and bring the stage back to the barn, I understand."

Elijah nodded. "Right side door's caved in and the paint's scraped bad, but she can be fixed."

"Praise the Lord," Miss Pringle declared, clutching the Bible that had been resting in her lap.

"And the US Cavalry," Mrs. Pettijohn added. "I see your mission was a success as well, Lieutenant."

For a moment, he thought she meant courting, and he glanced at Kate, whose cheeks were turning pink. Then he realized she must mean the supplies.

"Yes," he said. "Quite successful."

"Maybe we could play baseball later,"

Danny put in. "Ma, Alberta, Pansy, Miss Pringle, and Mrs. Pettijohn could play too."

"Ladies against gentlemen," Kate suggested, twinkle in her eyes.

"Not enough time before the rain," Mrs. Pettijohn declared. "I can see that dark cloud on the horizon from here."

Will frowned, moving toward the window. "It was a clear day when we rode in."

Danny scrambled to join him. He must have reached the same conclusion as Will did, for his eyes widened even as Will's stomach plummeted.

"That's not a cloud," Danny cried, whirling to face his mother and the others. "That's smoke. Ma, the forest's on fire!"

24

Horror pushed Kate to her feet and propelled her to Will and Danny's sides. Beyond Fountain Geyser and its little sisters, over the top of the pine-covered hill, ugly brown smoke billowed, flashes of red showing through. She could almost feel the unrelenting heat.

She whirled to face Will. "If the prevailing winds hold true, the fire will head northeast."

Out of the corner of her eyes, she saw Mrs. Pettijohn heave herself up. "That's directly at the hotel!"

"And it could cut off the road south," Kate agreed. "Will, ask Mr. Boyne to take Danny, Elijah, and our guests up to the Fire Hole. They should be safe there. If not, they can continue to the guard station at Riverside."

"This is like the Confederates all over again," Mrs. Pettijohn declared, double chin quivering in indignation. "My husband and I refused to run when they rode into town. I refuse to run from trouble now."

"Might we at least walk?" Miss Pringle suggested, rising as well.

Elijah climbed unsteadily to his feet. "I'm not leaving, Mrs. Tremaine."

"Yes, you are," she told them, striding away from the window. "You all are. I can convince you to do what's needed, but you can't convince a fire."

Will followed her, Danny right behind. Her cavalryman stopped, head up and eyes stern.

"As commander of the detachment protecting the Lower Geyser Basin, I order you to do as Mrs. Tremaine says."

Mrs. Pettijohn squared her shoulders, eyes narrowing, as if preparing herself for a fight.

"Oh, good," her sister said with a relieved sigh. "Come, dear. Let's gather what we can."

"They may listen to you," Elijah told Will as Mrs. Pettijohn gave in and followed her sister down the corridor. "But I don't have to. Everything important to my business is right here. I'm not leaving."

Will's jaw hardened, but Kate understood. She put a hand on Will's arm. "See to your men. Elijah and I will be right behind you."

Will shook his head. "I want you and Danny on that wagon with the ladies."

"Can we, Ma?" Danny's voice was small.

Kate bent to pick him up and hug him close. Oh, so heavy now! "It's all right, Danny," she said against his hair. "You go with Mr. Boyne. We'll send Alberta and Pansy too. I'll bring you home when it's safe."

"All right." He sniffed bravely.

Will held out his arms, and Kate transferred Danny to him, though something inside her begged her to hold on. Will started for the kitchen.

"I'll gather buckets and shovels from the barn," Elijah said beside her.

Kate touched his arm. "Are you sure you're up to this?"

His dark eyes glittered. "This is my home nearly as much as yours. I won't give it up so easily."

With a nod and a squeeze of his arm, Kate released him, and he made for the front door.

Even as the door banged shut, Miss Pringle hurried from the hallway, clutching a small case. Right behind her came Mrs. Pettijohn, head crowned with a black-feathered hat.

"I took the liberty of calling on Mr.

Jones," she told Kate. "He was not in his room."

Mr. Jones! Once more, Kate rushed to the window, but the only thing moving on the geyser field was the steam flowing in the breeze.

"Did he tell you where he was going today?" she asked her lady guests over her shoulder.

"He did not," Mrs. Pettijohn informed her, as if much put out by this dereliction of duty.

"Perhaps he went fishing again," Miss Pringle suggested, edging toward the kitchen. "It seemed to me he was headed toward that footbridge over the river."

If he had gone to the Firehole River to fish, he was likely out of the way of the fire or at least partly protected from it by the water. Kate could only send up a prayer for his safety as she escorted her ladies to the kitchen.

The back door was open, and Kate could see Pansy already up in Mr. Boyne's wagon. Caleb was busy helping the teamster put the horses in harness. Alberta was still in the kitchen, wrapping a pie in cloth.

"We'll need it for dinner," she protested as Kate went to shoo her toward the door. "And what about the ham?"

"You are more important than ham," Kate insisted, making sure her cook descended the back steps. She didn't have the heart to point out that there might not be a dinner, or a hotel, by the time the fire burned out. The very thought sent ice down her spine.

Lord, help us! She felt the desperation in the prayer. The National Hotel had been so impressive, but it was nothing to this little piece of Wonderland. *Don't let me lose my home!*

Every moment it seemed harder to catch her breath, as if the smoke was crowding her lungs even now. Then, Will came in the door, steps brisk, head high. Just the sight of him draped a soft blanket around her, cocooning her against her fears. She drew in a breath, focused on the task at hand.

"Smith is headed to the Fire Hole to telephone the other stations," he reported. "Lercher is taking the horses to camp. Waxworth has agreed to stay and watch the stock and chickens. If the fire gets too close, he'll set them free to escape."

Kate frowned. "What about Caleb? He's devoted to the animals."

"He's more devoted to you and the Geyser Gateway," Will assured her. "He told me he wanted to fight the fire with us."

"He actually spoke to you?"

Will shrugged. "Let's just say he made his wishes known, and I wasn't about to refuse help."

Kate nodded. "Your men fought a fire near Mammoth Hot Springs. The Army must have equipment — a water wagon, buckets."

He shook his head. "Congress in its great wisdom did not appropriate funds for firefighting equipment, even though Captain Harris requested it. Best we can do is build a firebreak between the flames and the hotel, allow the fire to burn itself out at the river. I wish you would reconsider and leave with the others."

She didn't reconsider it a moment. "Do you know the best place to build a firebreak?" she countered. "Or the safest route to the fire from here?"

"Caleb could tell us," he insisted.

Kate put a hand on his shoulder. "I'm impressed he was brave enough to speak to you and to come with us, but Caleb rarely sets foot off the hotel property. Face it, Will. You need me. Now, let's collect Elijah, your remaining men, and what tools we can and head out before the fire gets any closer."

The blaze was gobbling up the forest between the Grand Prismatic Spring and

Lower Basin Lake when Kate, Will, Elijah, Caleb, and Privates Franklin and O'Reilly climbed the hill to the southwest of the hotel a short while later. Will had her ax, Elijah held a hatchet, and Caleb clutched a hoe. The privates carried shovels, and Kate held the handle of a bucket in each fist. As far as firefighting equipment went, it wasn't much, but it was the best they could do.

The flames had already crested the hill on the other side of White Creek below them. Fanned by a fitful breeze, the fire jumped from tree to tree, soared up the pines, and raced across the needle-covered ground. It thundered with a voice that demanded more, always more.

Not her hotel.

"There," Kate said, pointing to the thin ribbon of the creek in the draw between the two hills. "If we cut the brush back on either side, we might create enough of a break to stop the fire. Once it reaches this hill, the heat will push it up and over. We must prevent that."

"Agreed." Will shifted the ax to his shoulder. "Franklin and O'Reilly, cross the creek and clear that side. Elijah and Caleb, with me on this side. Kate, stay high where you can watch the fire's movement. Keep us apprised of any changes."

She didn't like sending them any closer to the inferno, but he was right. The five of them stood a better chance of clearing the area than she did. Her riding skirt — truth be told, any of her dresses — made it nearly impossible to do the work they were about to do. She had to trust in him, in Elijah and Caleb, in Franklin and O'Reilly, to see this through. Once more her chest felt tight.

"Be careful," she said, and he nodded before heading down the hill. Franklin and O'Reilly each took one of her buckets and followed.

It was humbling. Never before had her fate seemed so out of her hands. Fear had held her prisoner the night Toby had been killed, and she'd found a dozen ways to make herself feel more in control since then. This? These flames, this heat, the roar and the crackle — she could do nothing against them.

Except watch and pray.

So, she did both. Words trembling on her lips, she alternated between watching the flames speed closer and watching Will working. While Caleb pulled fallen timber away from the water's edge, Will and Elijah cut down and removed a few pine saplings that had sprung up. Franklin and O'Reilly used their shovels to dig up saplings on the opposite bank. Slowly, a ten-foot swath grew along the creek even as the flames showed brighter behind Will and the others. The proximity to the warm water had kept the grass green even into autumn. Would it withstand the heat of the fire?

On the far side, a pine fell, a blazing torch flashing through the smoke. Kate stiffened. Before she could cry out, Franklin and O'Reilly splashed through the creek to safety. But a billow of smoke veered toward her. She coughed as the acrid air surrounded her, then brought up her arm to cover her nose and mouth, waving the darkness away with her free hand.

Through a break in the smoke, she sighted Will below her, hacking through the tree to prevent the fire from reaching his side of the break. Caleb tugged on the limbs as if he could drag it himself. Will's men dumped buckets from the creek onto the pine, the bark hissing as if in protest.

Batting away the rest of the smoke, Kate forced herself to focus on the fire. She followed its track along the creek in both directions. It swallowed downed limbs, the sunbleached timber blazing up. The flames danced to their own breeze, waving arms of red-orange. But the firebreak seemed to be holding to the east. And toward the west . . .

One last fallen log breeched the creek. The fire hopped up onto it, skipped along it, and jumped down to the grass.

Cutting off Will, Elijah, and Caleb from the others.

"Will!" she shouted in warning, but her cry was lost to the crash of another pine falling. The smoke swarmed up, hiding them all from view.

Will's arms protested, but he kept swinging Kate's ax. Beside him, Elijah grunted as his hatchet bit into the trunk. Sweat beaded on Caleb's forehead as he came in to yank back a limb. A few more yards, and they'd have flanked the fire. A crash on the other side told of another pine falling. Smoke swirled around him, clogging the air, clogging his lungs.

He stopped swinging, so blind he was afraid he might hit Elijah or Caleb. He couldn't hear anything other than the crackle of the fire. The heat pressed against him like a wall, shoving him away. He wiped his face with the back of his hand, smothering a cough.

"Lieutenant!"

At Elijah's cry, he turned to find the fire behind them. At the moment, it struggled for purchase on the cleared area, but already it trickled toward the hill. And Kate.

"Beat it out!" Will shouted, shoving the ax blade under the grass and tipping up the sod to smother the flame. Caleb hurried to help.

Franklin and O'Reilly must have seen their predicament, for they materialized out of the smoke. First they toppled the fallen tree into the water of the creek, setting the fire to hissing as it went out. Then they took their buckets to the flames.

But the trickle of red had reached the drier grass at the base of the hill, devouring it greedily. In a moment, they were cut off, fire on all sides and smoke reaching fingers toward them. Still he kept beating at the blaze, determination and desperation building.

"Will!"

The smoke parted to reveal Kate, hands outstretched. "It's out. This way!"

He and the others hurried to her side.

One arm over her nose, she pointed with her free hand. "Up the draw. We can get away along the Firehole."

"Go!" Will urged her, and he led the men after her.

The creek came out from among the pines at a wide plain before joining the Firehole River. Will glanced back the way they had come. The ground was blackened and smoking on the northern side, the creek beginning to bleed ash.

"It's holding!" Franklin pointed toward the hill.

Except for the one place the fire had jumped the creek and they had beaten it out, the blaze remained on the south side. Already, the flames were shrinking, their sound softening, as the fire ran out of fuel.

Will put an arm about Kate's shoulders. "We did it."

She leaned against him. "Thank the good Lord."

"Amen," O'Reilly said, and for once he didn't accompany the statement by spitting.

As Caleb wrapped his arms around his waist and shivered, Franklin eyed the forest.

"Strange place for a fire to start," he mused, as if seeing the area with his engineer's eye. "There aren't any campsites in the area. People usually continue down to Old Faithful. And we haven't had any lightning strikes."

"Jessup again?" O'Reilly guessed, and this time he did spit.

"That poacher?" Elijah asked. "He must be long gone by now."

Caleb nodded.

"And why would he start a fire here, even

402

if he was in the area?" Kate put in. "There's nothing in direct line of this fire — no major herds, no Army station."

"Just the Geyser Gateway," Franklin pointed out.

Kate shook her head. "He would gain nothing from burning me out." Suddenly, she stilled. "But someone might." Her gaze darted to Will's. "You don't think the Virginia City Outfitters would stoop this low?"

"They gain little either," Will told her. "They wanted your building and lease, not a burned-out shell. We may never know how this started, but however it started, it was too close for comfort. O'Reilly, Franklin, sweep the area and report back to the hotel. When we know it's clear, I'll ride for the Fire Hole and send everyone home."

"Sir!" The two saluted and headed back down the creek.

As Caleb shifted on his feet, Elijah watched them go, eyes narrowed as if he could see the path of the arsonist even now.

Will looked to Kate. "You saved my life."

"You might say I was doing my duty," she said, but that grin he so appreciated flashed into view in a face streaked by smoke. "Besides, it would have been hard to finish our courtship with you burned to a crisp."

Caleb dropped his arms and beamed.

Elijah looked just as pleased. "Courtship, huh? Well, how about Caleb and I head back to the hotel, and you two take your time?"

Caleb bobbed his head. "Congratulations, Mrs. Tremaine, Lieutenant."

He hurried to follow Elijah as the driver started up the banks of the Firehole.

As soon as they rounded the bend, Will pulled Kate closer and kissed her.

Thanksgiving and joy made a powerful combination. He wanted to drink her in like water, breathe her in like a spring breeze. She clung to him, body trembling, giving him her kiss, her heart. He couldn't seem to let go.

Then she pulled back and rested her head against his chest.

"If anything had happened to you . . ."

"I felt the same," he murmured, allowing himself to stroke her thick hair. "You warned us when you took us around the first time. There are too many ways to die in Yellowstone."

"But only one way to live," she argued. "You're helping me see the wonder here again, Will. I don't want to lose that. I don't want to lose you."

"You won't," he promised, hugging her

close. And he could only hope that he would be able to keep that promise.

close. And he could only hope that he would
be able to keep that promise.

25

The fire burnt itself out completely two days
later. Will's men kept patrolling the area
from dawn until dusk to make sure. Kate
insisted that everyone but her, Elijah, and
Caleb stay at the Fire Hole for safety's sake.
Will tried once again to send her north as
well, but she refused. It was her responsibility to see to the hotel. The blaze left behind
acres of charred forest and blackened
ground. She could only be thankful that the
Geyser Gateway had been spared, and even
more grateful that Will, his men, and Elijah
and Caleb hadn't been hurt.

Thank you, Lord!

Elijah moved out to the barn to sleep. He
said it was to help Caleb keep an eye on his
horses and the stock, but she thought it was
as much to safeguard her reputation. The
hotel felt empty without Danny, Alberta,
and Elijah. Her steps echoed on the hard-
wood floors. She couldn't make herself start

a fire in the hearth, even though the nights were cool. And she missed her son more than words could say.

Still, she had enough to do to keep her mind occupied and hands busy, even though the Wakefield and Hoffman stages didn't stop as they thundered past on their way south to Old Faithful and north toward the Norris Geyser Basin or out of the park. She helped Elijah and Caleb feed, water, and calm the animals. She also cooked for them and Will and his men.

"It's the least I can do after you saved the Geyser Gateway," she assured them when Will protested. "Although I haven't Alberta's skills."

"Neither does Waxworth or Smith," Franklin assured her.

Will managed a tired smile.

The only fly in the ointment was the disappearance of Mr. Jones. He didn't return to the hotel the night of the fire, and Will and his men hadn't seen any sign of him as they patrolled the area.

"Although if he's up at the Fire Hole or down at Old Faithful, we won't know until we settle back into our usual routine," Will told her. "We're too busy making sure this fire doesn't flare up again."

Alberta eased her mind when she and

Danny and the others returned Saturday morning. Kate heard the sound of a stage and rushed to the veranda in time to see the Wakefield and Hoffman driver pull into the yard. He must have made a special trip just to deliver her people. The coach had barely come to a stop before Danny leaped out and ran for her. Kate flew down the steps and caught him up in her arms. Eyes closed in thanks, she held him tight.

"The hotel looks good," he said, sounding a little disappointed, as if he had been hoping to see some evidence of the fire that had kept them apart.

Kate released him as the driver began handing down Alberta, Pansy, Miss Pringle, and Mrs. Pettijohn.

"The hotel is fine," Kate assured them all as they gathered around her. "And I'm so glad you are too."

"Even Mr. Jones," Alberta reported. "We found him at the Fire Hole."

"Enjoying their unsavory accommodations," Mrs. Pettijohn added with a sniff.

Miss Pringle heaved a happy sigh. "The Geyser Gateway is ever so much nicer, Mrs. Tremaine. I'm sure he'll see the wisdom of returning."

He must have, for their lodger reappeared Saturday afternoon and took up residence in his room as if he had never left them. Kate decided not to question him. He had a right to go where he willed, and another night paid was all to the good as the season neared its end.

"Tell me about the fire again," Danny begged when Will and Private Smith stopped by on their final patrol of the day Saturday. "Was it scary? How hot was it? Can I go see?"

"I'll tell you all about it tomorrow," Will promised, face lined and boots dusty.

"When you come for services," Kate suggested.

He regarded her a moment before nodding. Then he and Private Smith headed north for their camp.

Kate almost called him back but shook her head. He was in no danger, and neither was she. All she knew was that she felt safer, happier, when Will was near. That boded well for their courtship.

A courtship. Hers and Toby's had been short, but that had been a simpler time, and she'd been less experienced with life. Still, she remembered courting — learning about the other person, doing things to please each other. What would please Will? She wasn't tremendously good at baseball, and he had Alberta to bake for him now. She needn't sew him something — the Army saw to his clothing. And she wasn't the sort to sing or recite poetry.

What about a love letter?

That was it! She could write what she admired about him. Perhaps enclose a lock of her hair. That way, he could read the words when doubts about the past assailed him. The deaths of innocents would likely always haunt him, but he could remember how he had dedicated his life to helping others. She took a moment to write as the others settled in for the evening.

For dinner, everyone except Mr. Jones gathered around one of the dining tables. Elijah was only too happy to tell Danny and the ladies about the fire.

"How brave you all were," Miss Pringle gushed over the pie Alberta had saved.

"How valiant," Mrs. Pettijohn agreed. "I must write to the Department of the Interior and commend Lieutenant Prescott and his men."

"Handy fellows to have around," Elijah agreed. He winked at Kate. "And I understand they might be around more often, especially Lieutenant Prescott."

"Oh, did you manage to bring him up to scratch, dear?" Miss Pringle asked Kate.

"What's up to scratch?" Danny asked,

glancing between them.

Kate's cheeks felt hot. "Lieutenant Prescott is a good friend. We'll see if he's anything more."

Danny frowned. "What's better than a good friend?"

"Two of them," Elijah said, giving him a nudge. "Now, why don't you tell me about that baseball game of yours again? I hear it was something."

Danny's eyes brightened, and he launched into his tale of triumph.

Kate only half-listened and not because she'd heard it so many times before. She had agreed to a courtship, possibly a marriage. She didn't doubt that Danny and Will would get on well together. They had been a team from nearly the first moment Kate had discovered Will on the geyser field. Danny clearly admired him. What would he do if this courtship didn't end the way she hoped? He'd already lost one father. How much worse to lose two.

She didn't have a chance to talk to Will about the matter or give him the letter she'd written, until he arrived just after breakfast Sunday. Mr. Jones had headed out right before. Mr. Yates was expected at any time. Danny, Elijah, Alberta, Caleb, Pansy, Mrs. Pettijohn, and Miss Pringle were already out in the salon waiting, while Kate finished the last of the dishes. As was his habit on Sundays, Will came in through the kitchen.

Kate set down the dish she had been drying. "Are you ready to be a father?"

He froze in midstride toward her. "Today?"

"Today, tomorrow, for the rest of your life. You asked to court me, Will, but we have to remember Danny. If you marry me, you make yourself an instant father."

He nodded, limbs slowly relaxing. "I know. When I first arrived in Yellowstone, I wasn't sure how to react to Danny. All that movement. All those questions."

Kate smiled. "All those questions. Everything he needs to learn to grow up to be a man. It's a big responsibility."

"I can see that." He took a step closer. "Am I the sort of man you want as an example to him?"

Kate closed the distance and pressed a kiss against his cheek. "A man who learns from his mistakes? Who tries every day to be the best he can be? I can't think of a better example."

He rested his forehead against hers. "I will never deserve you."

"You deserve love," Kate said. "Everyone does." She slipped her hand into the pocket on her gown and drew out the letter. "When you doubt that, read this."

He accepted it with a quizzical frown.

From the salon came the sound of voices. Kate pulled back and caught his hand. "Mr. Yates must be here. Join us for worship."

He didn't budge at her tug. "Are you sure that's wise? I haven't been in a very long time."

Likely since that horrible tragedy in Oregon. "Yes," she insisted. "I'm learning that God wants to hear from us. He wants to hear from you too. Now, come on. Danny is expecting you."

A husband, a father. It was a dream he'd never thought to reach. Would God really allow him such joy after what he'd done?

He felt like the shadow to Kate's light as she led him into the salon. The dining chairs were lined up before the hearth, sofas pushed back to the walls, to give the traveling minister space to conduct the service. Kate moved into the last row with Danny, leaving a chair open beside her. Will couldn't make himself take it. He stood behind her instead, back against the wall and feeling as if he faced the enemy across a battlefield.

Mr. Yates offered them all a smile before beginning in prayer. The words washed over

413

Will: praise for such beautiful surroundings, thanksgiving to have been spared from the fire. Then the minister started a song. Will had heard it before, but he couldn't find his voice to join in. The room seemed to be darkening, but he feared the darkness was inside him.

Mrs. Pettijohn's voice boomed out over the others as they launched into the third verse.

Oh to grace how great a debtor
Daily I'm constrained to be.
Let Thy goodness like a fetter
Bind my wandering heart to Thee.

The words shoved themselves past his lips, lending his baritone to the ladies' higher voices and Kate's alto.

Prone to wander, Lord, I feel it,
Prone to leave the God I love.
Here's my heart, O take and seal it
Seal it for Thy courts above.

Humility flowed over him, an awe as deep as when he'd seen his first geyser, watched the bison roam their grounds, and felt Kate's acceptance. As if she understood, she reached over her shoulder with one hand and caught his.

It seemed God still wanted his heart.

Joy bubbled up inside him like mud from a paint pot. He'd nearly forgotten the words of the hymn until Mrs. Pettijohn's voice had broken through, but the promise called to him, urged him closer.

How great a debtor to grace.

Grace that could cover even his sin.

He clung to Kate's hand, to the hope the song offered. He dropped his gaze to her raven hair, which seemed to be shimmering. Perhaps it was because of the tears pressing against his eyes. He closed his lashes against them.

Lord, thank you for reminding me how much you love us. I didn't deserve a second chance from the Army. I certainly don't deserve a second chance from you, but I'm so grateful you offer one. Now I have an opportunity to share that sort of love, with Kate and Danny. I don't know whether I have it in me, but I aim to try. Please, help me. Protect them, bless them, keep them. That's all I ask. Amen.

When he opened his eyes, the room seemed brighter, his heart lighter. He drew in a breath, raised his head, and listened as Mr. Yates spoke of devotion, dedication, and determination. All Will could think about was the future. Kate didn't release his hand until the minister had finished speaking and

415

closed the service.

"Thank you," she said as she rose and smiled at him.

Will shook his head. "I should be thanking you. That was good."

Her smile widened. "I agree. Come meet Mr. Yates."

Once he would have balked. Now, as Danny ran to see Private Smith on the geyser field, Will accompanied Kate up to the minister. The fellow's eyes crinkled behind his spectacles as Kate introduced Will.

"So, this is the famous Lieutenant Prescott I keep hearing so much about," he said, shaking Will's hand.

"And you're the famous Mr. Yates," Will countered.

The minister laughed, releasing him. "I don't know about famous. At least I'm not infamous." He turned to Kate, face sobering. "And I don't generally pass along gossip, but I thought you should know what I heard at the Fire Hole Hotel, Mrs. Tremaine."

Kate frowned. "More rumors about the Geyser Gateway?"

"No, indeed," he assured her. "I don't generally stop there, but I saw more coaches than usual, so I thought I'd see if anyone

416

required my services." He tugged down on his waistcoat. "They did not. A rough bunch there at the moment."

"We keep an eye on them," Will told him. "At least, we did until this fire commandeered our time."

"Now that the fire's out, you might want to stop by this afternoon," the minister replied. "I understand Roy Jessup was recently seen in the vicinity."

Kate stiffened. So did Will.

"They told you that?" he asked.

The minister glanced between them. "I heard his name mentioned and went so far as to inquire. He was swapping stories in the gentlemen's room there only yesterday."

A blaze built inside him, hotter than the inferno they'd fought. "I'll ride up this afternoon."

"Do you think he could have anything to do with our fire after all?" Kate asked, face tight.

"I should hope not," Mr. Yates said. "But I know he's been associated with arson in the past. I just thought you should be warned."

Kate thanked him for his trouble, but Will's mind raced. Sergeant Nadler and Elijah had been sure the poacher was out of the park by now. But if he had been as close

417

to the Geyser Gateway as the Fire Hole Hotel, he could have started the fire that threatened the area.

As the minister turned to speak to Mrs. Pettijohn, Will stepped aside with Kate.

"I don't like it," she said. "Jessup, at the Fire Hole? What's he doing? You could ride by at any time."

"Once the denizens of the Geyser Gateway arrived with news of the fire, he had to realize it was keeping us busy," Will pointed out.

"But did he need to learn about the fire from Alberta and the others?" she asked, eyes narrowing. "Or could he have set it after all, to flush game?"

"I wondered the same thing, but you said it yourself: there were no major herds in the area."

Her eyes widened, and she clutched his arm. "That's it, Will! He located that one bison north of here. He must believe there are others nearby. He was trying to scare them into moving and revealing themselves."

Will nodded. "The season's nearly over. Nadler found his pack and the buffalo hide and pieces. Jessup must have nothing to show for his efforts. He's getting desperate."

418

And desperate men did desperate things, which meant Kate, Danny, and her beloved buffalo were in danger.

26

Jessup, in her own backyard? Kate's hands bunched at her sides. The need to run to their special spot, count every shaggy head, nearly pushed her out the door. But Will had the right of it. Better to track this rumor to its source.

Still, she was on pins and needles for the rest of the afternoon, until he returned from the guard station.

"No sign of him," he reported, hitching Bess to the post as Kate leaned out over the veranda railing. "No one noticed which way he went when he left. No one knew where he'd been holed up before reaching the hotel. But we're alerted to his presence now, Kate. If he's still in Yellowstone, we'll find him."

She wished she could believe that. Will and his commander had thought Jessup gone twice before. He could have headed anywhere in the millions of acres that composed Yellowstone. The cavalry could only cover so much ground.

So could Will. He pulled off his gauntlet. "I'll walk the geyser field. Care to join me?" He held out his hand.

Miss Pringle and Mrs. Pettijohn were inside packing. Mr. Jones remained closeted in his room. No other visitors from the Fire Hole were on the field. There was no reason to patrol, but she recognized the gesture. A gentleman courting a lady might ask her to walk through the park on a Sunday afternoon. Here the park was all around.

Kate came down the steps and took his hand. "I'd be delighted."

How many times had she strolled this path over the years? It had never felt so comfortable, so companionable.

"Which one's your favorite?" he asked as if they were discussing dresses instead of mighty geysers.

"Jelly," she admitted with a nod toward the southwest. "The color reminds me of huckleberries. What about you?"

"I like something with a little more height," he said as they rounded the mud pots. He raised his voice over the plop-plop. "Fountain reaches for the sky."

"We'll have to go back to the Norris Geyser Basin," she said as they turned for

Silex Spring, the scent of sulfur hovering like a dandy's perfume. "Steamboat Geyser can reach three hundred feet. It's the largest in the park."

He tucked her arm closer. "If we go back to Norris, it will be after I leave the Army. I'm not sharing you with Nadler and his men again."

Kate glanced at him in surprise. "Why, Will, were you jealous?"

His gaze went out over the geysers to the west of them, where Clepsydra was spouting off with puffs of steam. "More than I should have been, I suppose. Seems I still want my share of the attention."

She squeezed his arm, and he returned his gaze to hers. "You don't have to worry," she promised him. "To me, you're as magnificent as Fountain Geyser. I realized when we were at Mammoth Hot Springs that the other cavalrymen are just mud pots."

"That's mighty high praise, ma'am," he said, but his moss-colored eyes danced with laughter. "At least you didn't call me Old Faithful. I'd hate to think I was that predictable."

"There's a great deal to be said for predictability," she assured him, leading him toward the Celestine Pool and out of a plume of sulfur. "I admit that's one thing I like about you, Will. I can count on you."

He brought her hand to his lips and kissed the back. "Always and forever."

Always and forever. She could get used to that.

They said goodbye to Pansy, Caleb, Miss Pringle, and Mrs. Pettijohn the next morning. Because Elijah's stagecoach wouldn't be repaired for some time, Kate's guests had arranged for a Wakefield and Hoffman stage to carry them and Kate's staff north. Pansy hugged Danny and Kate, tears shining in her eyes.

"You will be careful, now?" she begged.

"We will," Kate promised.

Caleb ducked his head respectfully, but his gaze, when he looked at Kate, held more confidence than she'd ever seen. "I'm going home to my ma and pa's ranch, Mrs. Tremaine, but I hope to come back next spring."

"We'll be glad to have you," Kate told him.

With a shy smile, he boarded the coach.

"At least we didn't have to travel in Mr. Boyne's wagon again," Miss Pringle said as Will and Private Smith helped load her things onto the coach. "I felt like a sack of bone meal."

"More like a cask of fine wine," her sister

corrected her, adjusting her feathered hat.

"Thank you for staying with us at the Geyser Gateway," Kate told them, the familiar farewell even more heartfelt this time. "I hope you'll come again."

"At our age, it isn't wise to make promises, dear," Miss Pringle said with a sigh.

"Nonsense," Mrs. Pettijohn declared. "We will see you next season, Mrs. Tremaine." She leveled her gaze on Will. "And I expect you to have made considerable progress before then, Lieutenant. Faint heart never won fair lady."

Will saluted her. "Ma'am. I will do my utmost."

Miss Pringle nodded. "I would expect no less from the US Cavalry."

Private Smith retreated to the porch, but Danny ran beside the coach until it passed the geyser field, and Kate waved until the vehicle disappeared beyond the curve of the road.

"Some guests become more than visitors," she explained when Will glanced her way.

"That's my hope," he said.

Kate smiled as Danny ran back to them. "You don't need to hope, Will. You graduated from visitor to family days ago."

Danny gave a little skip as he came up to them. "And you're going to stay with us always."

Will took Kate's hand. "How long is always?"

Danny spread his arms as wide as they could go. "This long."

"That's a long time," Will acknowledged. "You sure you want me here always?"

"Sure!" Danny dropped his arms. "We like you."

"You promised Elijah you would help him this morning with his coach," Kate reminded him. "You better get going."

"Yes, ma'am." He ran for the barn.

Kate turned to Will. "Join us for dinner?"

He touched his hat. "I'd be honored."

"No honor involved. You heard Danny. We like you."

He raised a brow. "We?"

"Danny, Alberta, Elijah."

"But not Kate?"

She laughed. "Oh, most especially Kate. I thought I'd made that clear."

"Fairly clear," he said, taking a step closer. "But I wouldn't mind another demonstration."

His eyes looked soft, his lips even softer. Though she knew Private Smith was watching, Kate stood up on her toes and pressed a kiss to Will's cheek. He was grinning as she stepped back.

"Smith," he called, and his private came down the steps to remount with a sigh.

She smiled as they headed south toward the Grand Prismatic Spring. She was still smiling an hour later when two riders reined in at the front of the hotel.

Brush in her hands, she paused in painting the southwest wall. Only one saddlebag — they weren't touring. And those tooled leather boots were a little too fancy for men looking for work.

"Welcome to the Geyser Gateway," she called as they hitched their horses. "How can I help you?"

The taller of the two adjusted his wide-brimmed tan hat. "We're looking for Mrs. Tremaine."

"You've found her." Kate put the brush in the paint can and headed down the veranda.

They came up the steps, long coats back over the holsters on their hips. Six guns, in the park? Though they were both taller than she was, she refused to back away.

The one who had spoken held out a piece of paper, while his stockier companion glanced around.

"This is from the Virginia City Outfitters," the taller man said.

Kate accepted the paper with a frown.

"We have mail. No need for special delivery."

"It was important that you receive it," he said. "We're here to take back your answer."

Kate opened the note, scanned the words, then shook her head. "This offer is less than the last one they made. I refused it. I refuse this."

He cocked his head, sending lank brown hair along one cheek. His face had been weathered into hard lines, or maybe it was the steely gray of his eyes that made him seem as immovable as granite.

"You sure about that?" he asked. "It can't be safe for a widow out here all alone."

She should have brought her paintbrush with her. Let him look so smug with a stripe of yellow down his chest.

"I do all right," she told him. "Tell your employer the answer is no."

He straightened. "That's a real shame. I wouldn't want anything to happen to your little boy."

Cold doused her. "You leave Danny out of this!"

He lowered his head to meet her gaze. "I'm not the one putting him in danger. You are. If you're smart, you'll take the money and go."

She could hardly breathe. "Get off my land."

He straightened with a smirk. "It's not your land, is it? This is government property. You have a lease, and a short one at that. How much money do you think this place will be worth when the Department of the Interior refuses to renew?"

"Alberta!" Kate shouted. "Bring me my rifle!"

"Is there a problem, Mrs. Tremaine?"

Will's rough voice had never sounded dearer. The men in front of her turned, hands on their guns, and she saw him on Bess, rifle in his arms. Private Smith rode beside him.

The taller man held up both hands. "No problem, Lieutenant. We were just leaving." He glanced back at Kate. "I hope you take my advice, Mrs. Tremaine."

"Never," Kate spat out.

With a grim smile, he and his companion descended the steps to unhitch their horses under Will's sharp gaze.

"I'll see you up the road," he told them. "The terrain is trickier than it looks. We wouldn't want you getting lost on your way out of the park. Smith, stay with Mrs. Tremaine."

Rifle in his grip, he directed Bess with his

knees and followed them from the yard.

"Are you all right, Mrs. Tremaine?" Private Smith asked solicitously. "Perhaps a piece of Alberta's excellent pie is called for."

That made her smile. "Yes, Private. By all means, ask Alberta for pie. I'll be here, keeping an eye out for Will."

Hired guns, in the park. Who would have thought it possible? All Will knew was that he never wanted to see such a look on Kate's face again — half defiance, half terror.

"Just what did you advise Mrs. Tremaine?" he asked as he herded the two men north toward the Fire Hole area, rifle at the ready.

"The Virginia City Outfitters made her a fair offer to buy her lease," the taller tossed back over his shoulder. "Not our fault she refused to listen to reason."

Will spurred Bess and passed them, then wheeled his horse to confront them, forcing them to rein in. "You tell your employer that Mrs. Tremaine has the trust and admiration of the US Cavalry. You threaten her at your peril."

It was a bluff. He had no authority to bring in the cavalry, even though each of his men would likely have stood by Kate.

The taller man knocked one finger to the

brim of his hat. "Appreciate the warning, Lieutenant. You might carry a similar one to the lady. The Virginia City Outfitters don't take kindly to refusal. She'd be wiser to leave while she can."

"So would you," Will said. "If I see you around these parts again, I'll arrest you for squatting. Ride north, and don't look back."

"Lieutenant."

Will directed Bess out of their way and watched until they disappeared among the pines. Then he stayed where he was for another quarter hour to make sure they didn't double back.

He found Kate, Alberta, and Smith on the porch when he returned. An empty plate and fork in his lap, Smith had his pistol drawn, Kate had her rifle in her arms, and Alberta cradled a cast iron fry pan as if she knew how to use it for other than cooking.

"Are they gone?" Kate demanded.

"For now." Will swung down and hitched Bess. "Is it true? The Virginia City Outfitters made you another offer?"

She leaned back as if to distance herself from the very idea. "A ridiculous offer. I refused it like I refused the others."

"Bullies and louts," Alberta pronounced, gripping her pan tighter.

"I'll send word to Captain Harris," Will

said, climbing the steps. "He needs to know there may be hired guns in the park."

"Thank you." Kate drew a deep breath. "And thank you, Alberta and Private Smith, for keeping watch with me. I should let you get back to your duties."

"I have more pies to bake," Alberta said, rising. She nodded to Will and Smith, who stood as well. "I expect you both for a piece later."

Will joined his private in saluting her. "Ma'am."

Kate climbed to her feet as Alberta headed into the inn. "I should check on Elijah and Danny."

"Give me a moment, then I'll join you," Will said. She nodded and headed for the barn.

Will turned to Smith.

"Mrs. Tremaine was threatened, and you sit eating pie."

Smith patted the holster at his side. "With pistol at the ready."

Will drew in a breath. "Smith, you try my patience."

"The feeling is mutual," his private said with a sorrowful sigh.

He would not allow the fellow to make him lose his temper. "Walk the geyser field."

"With all due respect, Lieutenant, there's

431

no need. The last of the guests left. Might I suggest I could be put to better use?"

"Doing what?" Will asked, eyes narrowing.

"Surveying the hotel interior," Smith said. "Developing a plan for our winter accommodations."

"Making sure you get the best bed," Will guessed.

"See how well you know me?" Smith asked with a smile.

"But I don't know you," Will told him. "You served on a riverboat, you know something about fine manners, and you have trouble with cards."

"Oh, I have no trouble with cards," Smith corrected him. "It's the people holding the cards who trouble me." He tilted to one side and peered around Will toward the barn as if making sure no one else was in hearing distance. Then he straightened and met Will's gaze.

"I'm the last of a long line of gamblers, Lieutenant. I plied my trade between New Orleans and Memphis. I wore fine suits, smoked the best cigars. I never seemed to lose, even when it was in my best interest. I played against the owner of a riverboat and won, but he wasn't inclined to give me the boat he'd bet."

"Imagine that," Will drawled.

"Not a gentleman," Smith agreed. "Worse, he offered five hundred dollars to anyone who would bring him my head, not necessarily attached to my body. He seemed to think I'd cheated."

Will eyed him. "Did you?"

Smith smiled. "I didn't need to cheat. But that didn't matter. I soon learned I was safest among well-armed men. So, I joined the military and ended up in the cavalry."

"I'm guessing that means Smith isn't your real name."

He shuddered. "Certainly not. But it serves its purpose. So, you see, Lieutenant, I know how it feels to run from your past."

"You should also know that I've told Mrs. Tremaine about mine."

Smith pressed his fingertips together. "Oh, happy day. That only leaves the rest of the detachment."

Will shook his head. "Tell, then, if it suits you. I will work the rest of my life to atone for that day. If Lercher, Waxworth, and the others want to be reassigned, I'll understand."

Smith clucked his tongue. "How noble. And shortsighted. I just gave you everything you need to blackmail me in return, Lieutenant. Consider it my wedding gift."

Will stared at him. "Why would you do that?"

Smith leaned closer. "Because you actually are the better man, whether you want to believe it or not." He straightened. "And here comes the lovely Mrs. Tremaine, apparently still concerned."

Will turned. Kate hurried toward them, face tight and pale. He felt as if someone had struck his spine with a hammer, her fear ricocheting up him.

"Will," she said breathlessly as she reached his side, "Elijah said Danny went for lemonade, but he wasn't in the kitchen, and he didn't answer my call. Something terrible has happened. I know it."

27

Kate's heart raced with her thoughts. Where could Danny be that he didn't answer her? He knew not to stray far from the inn. Could those riders have returned, kidnapped him?

Will took her in his arms. For once, his strength brought little comfort.

"It's all right, Kate," he said against her hair. "We'll find him. Go get Alberta and Mr. Jones." He pulled back and nodded to his man. "Smith, fetch Elijah."

The private dashed for the barn. It dawned on Kate that it was the first time she'd ever seen him run.

She managed a breath, then made herself return to the hotel. Once again, the place felt empty, and she knew it was because of the lack of a little boy. Fear tiptoed closer, reached for her. She shoved through the door to the kitchen and Alberta's warmth.

Moments later, only five of them regrouped on the porch.

"I rapped on Mr. Jones's door," Kate told Will. "And peeked inside. He wasn't there."

"He left a while ago," Alberta supplied, shifting on her feet so that her skirts swept the porch. "Asked me to pack him a big lunch. Should I have told you?"

"No," Kate said. "It doesn't matter now. The important thing is to find Danny."

Alberta nodded, face pinched and hands wrapped in her apron.

Will stepped forward. "Elijah, Alberta, search the inn, the barn, and the outbuildings, especially any place Danny might hole up. He could have fallen asleep somewhere and just isn't hearing our calls."

Elijah nodded. Alberta pulled her hands free to give one of Kate's a squeeze. "We'll find him," she promised. She and Elijah went back inside.

Another time, Kate might have taken umbrage that Will thought he must lead them all, but right now she was grateful for his command. The fear had reached her side, was wrapping steel-cold arms around her, and she felt no more useful than the night Toby had been killed.

Don't let me panic, heavenly Father. Help me be strong for my son.

Will turned to his private. "Smith, go to

the station and bring back the rest of the men."

Smith didn't argue. He went for his horse.

Kate touched Will's arm. "What about us? If you ask me to sit here on the veranda, I'll go mad with worry."

"I would never ask you to sit and wait," he said, covering her hand with his. "There's one place Danny might prefer. We should check our special spot."

Their special spot. Relief was swift, but fear immediately regrouped, dug its fingers into her heart. To go so far, alone? What if Danny met a cougar, a bear? And the bison! Her son knew how to behave around the great beasts, but would Big Bertha take exception to his presence? Kate broke away from Will, lifted her skirts, and ran down the steps. Will was right beside her.

They sped past the edge of the geyser field, steam parting before them, and thudded across the footbridge so quickly the planks shook under her feet. Will took her elbow to help her over the rougher parts of the trail, but their rush still felt agonizingly slow. Every moment counted.

As they approached the first meadow, she wanted to shout Danny's name, but she pressed her lips against her teeth to keep them closed. If he was out among the bison, she could cause a stampede by any sudden movement or sound. She slowed her steps, trying not to think about those heavy hooves, sharp horns, and massive bodies colliding with her son.

Will caught her arm as they reached the meadow, keeping her in the shade of the pines. She stared out across the rippling grass and slumped.

"They aren't here."

Will nodded. "And neither is Danny. Quickly. We'll check the upper meadow."

But it was the same there. Even the bison had disappeared, as if fleeing an unknown enemy.

Her breath hitched. "Oh, Will, where can he be?"

Will cupped his hands around his mouth. "Danny Tremaine!" he bellowed, sound no longer important. "General Tremaine! Report for duty! Now!"

The words echoed against the hillsides, but no voice piped up to answer, and no little boy came running out of the trees.

But something moved on the far edge of the meadow, with a back as humped as a bison's. The grizzly stopped, head swinging in their direction. A low, guttural growl rumbled out.

Kate couldn't breathe, couldn't think. She

hung on to one thing.

Please, Lord, not my son. Protect him as only you can. Keep him safe.

Will stepped between the bear and her. "Don't run, Kate."

"Not this time," she said. "That thing is not going to stop me from finding my son."

He glanced back at her, and she knew he wasn't the only one to look surprised by the strength in her voice. She felt it — bright and clean and sure. The fear was gone, replaced by a calm and a peace she wouldn't have thought possible. That sort of peace came only from one place.

Thank you, Lord!

"Well done," Will said. He edged back and took her hand, drawing her farther into the trees. As if assured they would be no threat, the grizzly lowered its head and continued on its way.

Kate took two steps and stumbled. Will's hand was there to steady her. She shot him a grateful smile, straightened her shoulders, and headed back toward the hotel, clinging to him and her faith.

"Could Danny have been taken by those men from the Virginia City Outfitters?" she asked, voicing her second greatest concern as they neared the footbridge. "One of them threatened him."

"We would have seen them ride back," Will said, his presence a rock she could lean on. "And it's open enough around the hotel. Alberta, Elijah, or Smith would have noticed a stranger."

There was that. Yet why else would Danny be missing?

Private Smith was waiting on the veranda when they returned. Out on the geyser field, O'Reilly was calling, his figure partially hidden by the spray of a geyser. Danny's name drifted back to her over the sizzle and pop of the mud pots. The call echoed from behind the inn in Lercher's accented voice.

Smith straightened away from the railing as they drew closer.

"Waxworth rode south to check the road," he reported in his drawl. "O'Reilly, Franklin, and Lercher are helping Elijah and Alberta search the property."

"And what are you doing?" Will asked suspiciously, wiping sweat from his brow.

"Solving a mystery, I believe." He handed Will a piece of rolled cloth. "A batch of these was delivered earlier from Captain Harris. He'd like them affixed to trees along the road and posted in public places."

The printed muslin wrinkled in Will's grip. "Later. Right now, our focus must be on Danny."

Smith nodded to his hand. "If you look at it, it might tell you who took Danny and why."

Kate's head jerked up. "Took Danny? So, I was right? He was kidnapped."

Smith spread his hands. "It's a distinct possibility."

Will unrolled the cloth, and Kate crowded closer.

Wanted, it read, *for arson and poaching: Roy Jessup.* The picture showed an older man with grizzled hair and crooked teeth.

"Jessup?" Will asked. "We've seen no sign of him near the Geyser Gateway."

"I have," Kate said, body starting to tremble. "That's the man I know as Mr. Jones."

Will stared at her. "Jones? Your elusive boarder?"

She nodded as he lowered the wanted poster. "Yes. But Alberta said he rode out earlier."

"After offering to take Danny with him, I warrant," Smith said.

Will rounded on him. "You knew."

Smith held up his hands again, but this time in a gesture of surrender. "I met Jones while on patrol a while ago. We chatted. But I'd never encountered Jessup, so I didn't make the connection. As soon as I saw that sketch, I knew. A shame, or I might have warned Danny." He bowed toward Kate. "And you, Mrs. Tremaine."

"But why?" Kate asked, glancing between them. "What could he want with Danny?"

"Can you think of a more willing guide to the area?" Smith asked.

Will couldn't. Danny always wanted to share his special spot with people he considered friends, and he considered most people friends. Besides Kate, no one likely knew more about the Lower Geyser Basin than Danny. But Jessup had to realize they would come after him.

"Has Jessup ever shown interest in Danny?" Will asked her.

"Danny and the bison," she acknowledged, shivering as if the day had cooled. "And me, for that matter, though I thought he was only trying to set up a dalliance."

Something hot shot through him.

"Trying to set up a guide, more likely," Smith said before Will could respond. "It was well known you were helping us, Mrs. Tremaine. He likely thought you and young Danny knew the best places to look."

Will shook his head. "So, Jessup sneaks in under our noses, makes friends with Danny, tries to get him to tell him where to find the bison, and, when Danny resists, kidnaps him."

"Will." Kate's voice was sharp. "What will he do? Will he hurt Danny to make him talk?"

It was possible. If Jessup hadn't hesitated to start fires that could have caused a dozen deaths — near Mammoth Hot Springs and in the Lower Geyser Basin — he likely wouldn't balk at harming a child. But Will refused to worry Kate with what might be.

"We need to find them," he said. "We know Danny hadn't told him the truth yet."

Kate nodded, though Smith glanced between them as if wondering what Will meant.

"So, they must be somewhere else," Will continued. "Where would Danny lead him?"

Kate started, eyes widening. "As far away from the bison as possible. The opposite direction."

"Fairy Falls," Will realized. "He hid from us there. He might hope to do the same with Jessup." He whirled to face Smith. "Get Elijah, Lercher, and Franklin. I'll call in O'Reilly. We'll gather weapons and march in five."

"I'm coming with you," Kate said, head up and eyes flashing as brightly as the first day he'd met her. He'd pitied Ponsonby then for incurring her wrath. He wouldn't want to be Jessup when she caught up to him.

"I was counting on you joining us," he told her. "Fetch your rifle. We have a long walk ahead."

Will was right. The walk to the falls seemed interminable. Though the sun remained high and the day warm, cold surrounded Kate as she gripped her rifle. Jessup had started fires, returned to the park when he had been warned to stay away, killed animals for profit. Would he stop at harming a little boy who stood in the way of his plans?

Trust, Kate. Remember, you don't have to do this alone.

Alberta and Private Franklin had stayed at the hotel in case Jessup returned, but Will was a steady presence in front of her on the trail. His head turned from side to side as he scanned the area. Elijah and Privates O'Reilly, Lercher, and Smith walked behind her ready to help. She had allies, and so did Danny.

Thank you, Lord. I've taken on so much on my own, but I see now you send help just when I need it.

Ahead, she heard the splash of the falls. And a voice, strident and demanding.

"Where are you, boy? Get out here, now!"

Her spirits leaped with her steps, and she shifted her rifle to grab Will's shoulder with one hand. "He escaped!"

Will stopped and turned, finger to his lips. Then he motioned Elijah and Private O'Reilly to the right and Lercher and Smith to the left. With a nod to Kate, he crept forward, his own rifle at the ready.

She had to force her feet to slow when all she wanted was to dash down the path to Danny. Instead, she followed Will into the dip around the falls.

The man she had known as Mr. Jones was standing at the edge of the pool, rifle cradled in his arms, one foot up on a boulder as mist swirled around him. But she nearly cried out in thanks when she realized Danny was nowhere in sight.

"That's enough, Jessup!" Will shouted over the tumble of the falls. "Drop the gun."

The poacher turned. His face was hard, eyes narrowed. The buckskins stretched across shoulders strong enough to carry a bison's head. How could she have ever taken him for infirm?

He leveled the rifle on them even as Will's gun came up. "Looks like we're at a draw, Lieutenant."

Kate aimed her rifle as well. "Not even close."

From the northeast, Smith and Lercher stepped out of the trees. From the northwest, Elijah and Private O'Reilly raised their guns. O'Reilly spit.

Jessup shook his head and lowered the gun.

"Set it down and raise your hands," Will ordered.

Left with no other choice, the poacher complied.

"Where's Danny?" Kate demanded as Elijah and Private O'Reilly moved in to take him into custody.

"I have no idea," Jessup said, jerking as O'Reilly tied his hands behind him. "He's a clever young man, your son. Led me up a creek and disappeared."

28

No! Danny had to be here. Once more, Kate glanced around, searching for an ever-moving body, so precious, so dear.

"He's hiding," Will said beside her. "Call to him."

"Danny!" She raised her voice as loud as she could, each word a prayer. "Daniel Tobias Tremaine! Come out! It's safe."

Something shifted in the shadows behind the falls, and the spray parted as Danny darted through. Kate dropped her gun and ran to meet him as he waded through the shallows.

She hugged his trembling wet body close, thanksgiving as swift as the falling water. A moment more, and two strong arms wrapped around them both. She leaned against Will, warm, safe.

"I knew you'd come," Danny said, teeth chattering. "I knew you could find me."

"You were very brave and very clever,"

Kate assured him, refusing to let him go.

"I just had to wait," Danny said. "I knew Lieutenant Prescott would come, because he protects people and animals, and he's going to be my pa. Right, Lieutenant?"

Kate turned to meet Will's gaze over Danny's head. His surprise at the statement quickly melted into something more.

"Right, Danny," he said, though his gaze held hers. "If your mother wants me."

Danny squirmed to look at her. "Please, Ma? I think he'd make a real good pa."

"So do I," Kate said, heart full.

Will bent and kissed her softly, a promise, a pledge she held to her heart. Then he straightened. "And I know what a good pa would say now. Let's get you warm and dry."

While Elijah and Private O'Reilly stood guard over Jessup, Private Smith and Will took off their cavalry coats and bundled Danny in them. Kate couldn't seem to stop hovering. Though she knew Danny could walk, she picked him up and carried him away from the waterfall, until Will took the burden from her.

Like so many of my burdens, Lord. You knew what I needed, even when I never thought to ask.

She stood for a moment, watching her son and the man she loved walk down the path.

Danny's hands were laced behind Will's neck, and he grinned at her over Will's shoulder. She could trust Will, with her heart and with Danny's. She had never thought such a thing possible.

With an awe as great as any she'd felt in this wondrous park, she followed them back to the inn.

Jessup didn't speak until they came out into the yard.

"You can escort me out of the park again, but you know I'll be back," he warned.

As Kate drew level with Will, Danny looked to her, eyes wide. She put her hand on his leg.

Will lifted him closer too. "Not this time, Jessup. Kidnapping a child is against the law in any state. We'll deliver you to the authorities in Evanston."

Private Smith smiled at the poacher. "And if they are inclined to allow you to go free, you won't get far. We'll have your likeness posted at every stop. Each cavalryman, hotelier, and visitor in the park will know who you are."

Danny sagged against Will in obvious relief.

Kate took charge of her son on the hotel veranda as Alberta rushed out to hug them and Private Franklin went to join his detachment.

"He'll be all right?" Will murmured, hand on Danny's shoulder.

"He'll be fine," Kate promised.

"I need to alert Mammoth Hot Springs and see about a detail to take Jessup north. When I get back, we must talk."

"About a great many things," Kate agreed.

He bent closer. "About only one thing. I love you, Kate, and I want to spend the rest of my life making you and Danny happy."

"Now that," Kate said, "is a duty I'd be proud to share, Lieutenant."

He kissed her, quick and sure, then headed for Bess. And Kate walked into her inn, an engaged woman.

An engaged woman!

She nearly staggered with the joy of it. Her wonder must have been showing on her face, for Alberta and Danny were staring at her.

"Mrs. Tremaine?" Alberta asked. "What's happened?"

"I'm going to marry Lieutenant Prescott," she said, the words seeming to glow in the very air.

Alberta clasped her hands together. "Oh, marvelous! Just marvelous! Our family is growing!"

"And he's going to be with us forever," Danny said, starting to jump up and down.

Forever. 'Til death do them part. She'd made that pledge once before. She'd feared to make it again. But Will was strong, sure, clever, and capable. Whatever the future held, she could count on him.

He'd planned to woo Kate with flowers and romantic gestures, but Will couldn't be sorry Danny had forced his hand. The decision felt right. He was on a good path at last, with the best possible guides: Kate and Danny. He was going to be a husband and father, and he had his heavenly Father's blessing. He felt lighter, cleaner, than he ever had.

Thank you, Lord!

The praise kept repeating itself in his mind as they made sure of Jessup. Waxworth met them coming out of the Geyser Gateway yard. He joined with Lercher and O'Reilly in volunteering to take the poacher north. Some of the fire had gone out of Jessup. His head was bowed as he rode off that afternoon. As soon as they were on their way, Will went to the Fire Hole Hotel to telephone Mammoth Hot Springs. He discovered a message waiting for him.

"I was about to send someone to deliver

451

it," the manager of the Fire Hole Hotel confirmed as he handed it to Will. "Your commanding officer has decided to tour the park before winter sets in. I promise you, we will be ready."

So would the Geyser Gateway. Will would make sure of it.

Kate sprang into action as soon as he told her that evening. He and Smith had come through on their final sweep to find all the current denizens of the hotel on the veranda. Kate was at the rail, Alberta and Danny sat on the bench, and Elijah was on one of the dining chairs, polishing the brass of a stagecoach door handle.

"Three days!" she exclaimed when he told her the news. She turned to Alberta, who rose from the bench. "Huckleberry pie and whipped cream."

"So he sees the virtue of keeping a cow," the cook agreed with a nod.

"We'll have to bleach and press the tablecloths and polish the chairs and banister. Oh, what a shame Pansy's gone for the year."

"I'll help, Ma," Danny offered.

Kate's gaze was off in the middle distance. "Is there time to put in another porch swing?"

"Kate," Will said, climbing the steps and

reaching for her hands.

They fluttered away like startled birds. "And your stagecoach, Elijah! I don't want Captain Harris to think we lack transportation."

"I'll have it ready, Mrs. Tremaine," Elijah promised. "I'd like to stay in his good graces too."

"Kate," Will tried again.

She started pacing, skirts flapping. "I'll need to repaint the trail markers, air all the beds, sweep the porch, clean the chicken yard . . ."

"Kate!" He managed to catch her hands as she passed. "Make a list. Delegate. My men and I stand ready to help. It's the least we can do after all you've done for us. But even if you sat on your hands for the next three days, the Geyser Gateway would still be the finest hotel in the park."

"Three days." Her eyes gleamed. "Three days is a very short time. We should start now."

And they did.

Will had had difficult details before — escorting peaceful tribes through hostile territory, chasing outlaws through rugged canyons — but nothing prepared him for Kate's campaign. She was already working when he and his men rode in just after dawn each morning, and he feared she kept working when they left as dusk was falling. And always she complimented them on their efforts.

"Not a squeak from the third step now," she told Franklin, passing him with a rug she had just beaten. "Well done."

"Such elegant lettering," she marveled to Smith, who was repainting the trail markers. "Our visitors will be impressed."

"So shiny," she commented to Elijah when she came to see the progress he and Will were making in fixing the stagecoach. "I can almost see myself in that yellow varnish."

She was everywhere, doing everything. His most important job was to make sure she had enough rest. He thought she might fight him on that, but she seemed to sense that she needed more than work. They played baseball one evening on the field across from the hotel, with Elijah and Alberta taking positions. They laughed together as they finished the map she had first promised Will, and he was pleased to see how many of the places he could remember now that he knew the park better. And she took him and Danny up to the bison's home to confirm they were all there and safe.

"They know how to hide too," Danny said.

Kate met Will's gaze over her son's head.

"And when to show themselves for who they are."

And Will could only marvel once again that this woman cared for him.

The letter he finally had a chance to read one night proved as much. Indeed, her words humbled him.

Dearest Will, she'd written. *Thank you for telling me what happened years ago in Oregon. I grieve for those who were so cruelly slain. I grieve for the anguish their deaths caused those who loved them. And I grieve for your broken heart.*

It is that broken heart which proves you are a better man than you know. Who else would encourage Private Smith despite his insolence? Give Private Franklin a chance to show his skills? Who else helps everyone around with no thought of recompense?

You are a good friend, a guide, a warm light in the darkness. I will be forever grateful you came into my life. I can't wait to see what the future holds, together. Kate.

He let a tear fall, unashamed. The mirror she held up showed a man he had hoped one day to become. Because of her, and for her, he would always be that man.

Unfortunately, the talk he had been hoping to have would have to wait until this inspection was over. But she had accepted his impromptu proposal, allowed his help in everything from shining silver to making beds, written him of her admiration. That had to count for something.

Captain Harris would start his inspection at the guard station, so Will and his remaining men were in camp, in their dress uniforms, when their commanding officer and his aide arrived three days later. Franklin had finished the roof on the cabin, and they'd been using the space to store their gear. Harris walked around the outside, stepped inside, glanced around, and stepped out with a shake of his head.

"We calculated the amount of wood needed, but this is spartan, even by Army standards," he told Will, who was waiting with Franklin and Smith. "And inadequate for six men through the winter months. I begin to see why you approached Mrs. Tremaine."

He was even less impressed with the Fire Hole Hotel and its cottages. "Limited capacity and rude construction," he informed Will as they rode away from the place. "I will encourage the Yellowstone Park Association to improve the buildings before next season."

The next stop on the tour was the Geyser Gateway, and Will's saddle felt unaccountably stiff, Bess's gait stiffer, as they approached the geyser field from the north. By the way Franklin was shifting on his horse, as if the leather had grown hot, he felt the same way. Even the normally unflappable Smith kept darting glances at their captain as they reined in at the front of the hotel.

Kate, Danny, and Alberta were standing on the porch as if they'd known Captain Harris and the others would arrive at exactly that moment. Kate's black hair gleamed in the sunlight as she stepped out of the shade, navy skirts settling around her trim figure.

"Captain Harris, Lieutenant Tutherly, gentlemen, welcome to the Geyser Gateway."

Captain Harris swung down, and Tutherly took his horse and the captain's to the corral. "Mrs. Tremaine, a pleasure to see you again. And this must be Daniel the lionhearted."

Danny, who had come to her side, hair slicked back and shirt tucked into his short trousers, stared up at him. "Why did you call me that?"

He bent to put his head on a level with the boy's. "Because it would take a man with the heart as brave as a lion's to stand up to Roy Jessup. Well done, Soldier."

Danny stuck out his chest. "Lieutenant Prescott says I'm a general."

Will's cheeks felt warm as the captain straightened and glanced his way. "I should have realized I was outranked." He turned to Danny. "What are your orders, sir?"

Danny glanced from Kate to Will and then to Captain Harris. "Tell my ma how nice her hotel looks. She worked real hard so you'll like it."

Now Kate was blushing. "That's enough, Danny."

Captain Harris chuckled. "Listen to your commanding officer, son. And show me around this fine hotel of yours."

"This way," Kate said, stepping aside, and Alberta hurried to open the door for them.

It took nearly two hours for Harris to inspect the hotel, the grounds and outbuildings, and Elijah's stagecoach.

"I understand you had some trouble," he told the wiry driver as they all stood in the cool shadows of the barn.

Elijah smiled at him. "Nothing I can't handle, Captain."

Harris nodded. "Then we will hope to see you again next spring. Wakefield and Hoffman could use the competition. From what I can see by the way you've recovered from this incident, you'll keep them on their toes."

Elijah saluted. "I'll do my best, sir." As the commanding officer headed for the wide doors, he grinned at Kate. "Looks like you'll be seeing me again soon, Mrs. Tremaine."

"I wouldn't have it any other way," Kate assured him.

With a nod of respect to Elijah, Will directed her out the door for the geyser field beyond.

Throughout the tour, Will had kept pace, answered questions posed to him, listened as Kate answered others. Harris's face remained calm, thoughtful, while Kate's began to grow paler. Will couldn't have said which way the wind blew. He wanted to step between his commanding officer and her, shelter her from whatever might come. The best he could do was squeeze her hand from time to time behind the captain's back.

"Is there anything else?" Kate asked as they headed back toward the hotel.

"Perhaps a slice of that marvelous huckleberry pie I've heard so much about," Harris said.

"Of course. We were hoping you might stay to dinner. I promised to reciprocate your hospitality at Mammoth Hot Springs."

He smiled. "You have already reciprocated

459

it a dozen times over by hosting visitors in such an excellent establishment." He turned to his adjutant. "Lieutenant Tutherly, a piece of pie for you as well?"

He nodded to Kate. "I'd be delighted, ma'am."

"I'll have it ready in a moment," Kate promised. She smiled at Will. "And of course our valiant cavalry detachment must join us."

"Ma'am," Franklin said eagerly while Smith swept her a bow.

She lifted her skirts to climb the steps for the door.

Captain Harris remained on the ground. "Lieutenant Prescott, a moment."

Tutherly glanced at Will before moving around the hotel. Will supposed he was checking on their horses in the corral. Smith and Franklin remained respectfully behind them.

"Sir?" Will asked.

Harris eyed him. "How much assistance have you given Mrs. Tremaine since arriving?"

He had to go carefully. He knew how Harris felt about the proper division between Army and civilian duties.

"I needed a guide. Mrs. Tremaine agreed to serve in exchange for some minor help

— repairing stairs, clearing chimneys, that sort of thing. Any other assistance rendered came solely under our duties to protect the park and ensure the well-being of its visitors."

Harris's brow quirked. "I see. You might tell Smith the word geyser does not have an *A* in it."

"It does in Louisiana," Smith drawled.

Will shot him a look before meeting his commanding officer's gaze and standing straighter. "Sir."

"At ease, Lieutenant," Harris said. "You've done a fine job here. I just want to be certain Mrs. Tremaine can continue to maintain this establishment after the Army moves on."

"Mrs. Tremaine managed this hotel for a year on her own before the Army arrived," Will reminded him. "Anything we've done only gilds the lily."

Harris nodded. "Very good. And I trust you heeded my advice about the lady?"

Will thought he heard Franklin cough.

"I have," Will told the captain. "Mrs. Tremaine is fully cognizant about my past."

"And still willing to befriend you," the captain mused. "An amazing woman."

Will smiled. "Yes, sir."

The front door banged, and Danny skid-

461

ded out onto the porch. "Hurry, Captain Harris. The pie's waiting."

Harris saluted him. "Coming right up, General Tremaine."

They all gathered in the dining room with Elijah, where Alberta and Kate served warm pie with a generous dollop of whipped cream.

"Excellent," Captain Harris declared after the first bite. "What's your secret?"

Alberta beamed. "A few drops of lemon, Captain. It brings out the flavor of the berries."

"That it does." He continued eating. Kate met Will's gaze and squeezed her shoulders up, gray eyes sparkling. Will could only hope Alberta's pie had done the trick.

At length, the captain and his adjutant finished, and Franklin and Smith swallowed their last bites. Kate walked Harris and Tutherly out to the porch. Will and his men, Elijah, Alberta, and Danny followed.

"There is one more thing I meant to accomplish on this tour," Captain Harris said. He nodded to Tutherly, who went for a saddlebag draped over the porch rail. Will realized the adjutant must have fetched it from the corral. Now, he brought back a cloth bag that clinked as he handed it to the captain.

"Lieutenant Prescott," Captain Harris said in a tone that demanded Will stand at full attention. "It has come to my notice that your behavior and accomplishments while on this detachment have exemplified the high standards we have of a cavalry officer." He opened the bag and drew out a pair of spurs, the silver gleaming in the sunlight. "I therefore present you with the spurs worn by men of honor, valor, and courage, the men of the US Cavalry."

Will kept his arm stiff to salute lest the captain see that he was shaking. "Sir."

Captain Harris nodded to Tutherly again. The first lieutenant took the spurs from the captain, then crouched and fastened them around Will's boots. Rising, he offered Will a salute. So did Captain Harris, Smith, and Franklin. Alberta clapped her hands together, Elijah nodded, and Kate beamed.

"Can I have some like that?" Danny asked, gazing down at the shining spurs Will had never thought to wear again.

Captain Harris ruffled his hair. "When you earn them, young man."

Danny saluted.

Kate came to take Will's arm. "Congratulations, Lieutenant."

He nodded, words failing him. Everything he'd ever wanted was in his grasp: honor, friendship, love, as shiny as the spurs on his heels. He would strive to live in a way that did them proud.

29

She could see what this honor meant to Will. Those spurs — it was as if Captain Harris had given him back his dignity, his worth. Only she knew how hard he had worked to regain them.

Captain Harris turned to her. "Mrs. Tremaine, allow me to extend my congratulations to you as well. The Geyser Gateway is everything our nation should expect from hospitality at Yellowstone — warm, welcoming, and wondrous. Good food, comfortable surroundings, and a respect for what nature has bestowed."

Kate inclined her head. "Thank you, Captain. We do everything we can to achieve those goals."

"That is abundantly clear," he told her as she straightened, "which is why I will be recommending that the Department of the Interior renew your lease, for ten years."

She stared at him. "Ten years?"

He arched a brow. "Unless there's a reason to shorten that time."

"No, no," she hurried to assure him, feeling as if the veranda quaked below her. "Ten years is marvelous. Perfect." She managed a breath. "Thank you for trusting us with Yellowstone. We won't let you down."

"I believe it." He leaned closer. "You should know that the Virginia City Outfitters are struggling financially. I understand their holdings will shortly be purchased by the Yellowstone Park Association. You should not be troubled by them again."

Truly, it was more than she'd dreamed possible. She looked to Will, who was smiling so widely his whole face broadened.

"We did it," she said as they sat on the porch swing together after Captain Harris and Lieutenant Tutherly had ridden south for Old Faithful and Will's men were getting the horses ready to return to camp. Alberta, Elijah, and Danny were inside, helping themselves to a second piece of pie in celebration.

Will took her hand, brought it to his lips for a kiss. "You did it. No one has worked harder for this than you, Kate."

She had worked hard, for Danny, for this hotel, for stability. And she wanted only to share it with this man who had come into her life so unexpectedly. Loving Will was like discovering the wintering grounds of the bison, like watching a geyser touch the sky. It gave her hope for the future.

"The Geyser Gateway has always been more than a hotel," she told him. "It's a home. Our home, Will. Mine, Danny's, yours."

"A home where the buffalo roam," he said with a smile. "And the deer and the antelope play. I don't care what that song says. It's not the animals or the scenic wonders. You make it a home, Kate."

"Then let's set a date," she said. "I love you, Will, and I want you here, always. Let's marry first thing in the spring, when the wildflowers start to bloom."

He laughed, cuddling her closer. "Let's marry October fifteenth, before the snow falls in earnest. I've heard too much about a Yellowstone winter to want to wait it out to marry you."

Married before winter. Safe together. Nothing sounded better.

"Perfect," Kate said. "I'll send word to Mr. Yates so he'll be sure to come out that late. I want our wedding to be the best in Yellowstone."

"I already have the best in Yellowstone," he said. "I'm marrying you. Together, life will be nothing short of wondrous from here on out."

And it was.

Dear Reader,

Thank you for choosing Kate and Will's story. When I learned the US Cavalry rode to the rescue to manage our nation's first national park, I knew I had to write about it.

Fortunately, we have many rich resources on the early years of the park, from the archives of the Heritage and Research Center in Gardiner, Montana, to websites, books, and reports, including the first report Moses Harris wrote to Congress. It was from that report that I learned about the snowstorm in September. Harris was a real captain in the cavalry; he led Troop M to manage the park. His adjutant, Lieutenant Tutherly, and Lieutenant Kingman of the US Army Corps of Engineers are also historical figures who served the same roles then as they do in the book, though I have taken the liberty of interpreting their characters and words. My thanks to Alicia Murphy, National Park Service historian, for her help deciphering the wealth of sometimes confusing information. Any mistakes in interpretation are my own.

The location and descriptions of the guard stations and other facilities at Mammoth Hot Springs, the Norris Geyser

Basin, and Old Faithful are also as realistic as I could make them, as are the descriptions of the wonders of the park. The Yellowstone Park Association did own most of the hotels in the park in 1886, but the Virginia City Outfitters are my own creation. And while we know today that the amazing colors of the hot pools are associated with heat-loving bacteria, it was widely held in Kate and Will's time that minerals caused the coloration.

The story of the bison is nearly heartbreaking. At the time the Army rode into Yellowstone, historians estimate fewer than thirty of the beasts remained in the entire park. Small wonder Kate tried so hard to protect them.

I have changed a few things from history. There was no hotel where the Geyser Gateway is located, although the Fire Hole Hotel did exist to the north. Though Captain Harris did plan to have his men overwinter in the field, the snow and cold proved formidable enemies, and all cavalrymen were recalled to Mammoth Hot Springs. And though everyone at the time expected the Army's tenure to be short-lived, soldiers guarded the park for more than thirty years. In addition, the Fountain paint pots described in the book are more colorful than what you might see today. Geologists believe an earthquake in the twentieth century changed their physiology, because reports from the 1800s describe them more vividly.

Of course, no national park is more vivid to me than Mount Rainier, which I can see from my own backyard.

ABOUT THE AUTHOR

Regina Scott started writing novels in the third grade. Thankfully for literature as we know it, she didn't sell her first novel until she learned a bit more about writing. Since her first book was published, her stories have traveled the globe, with translations in many languages including Dutch, German, Italian, and Portuguese. She now has fifty published works of warm, witty romance.

She credits her late father with instilling in her a love for the wilderness and our national parks. She has toured the Grand Canyon, Yellowstone, Crater Lake, Yosemite, the Olympics, and the Redwoods and currently lives forty-five minutes from the gates of Mount Rainier with her husband of thirty years.

Regina Scott has dressed as a Regency dandy, driven four-in-hand, learned to fence, and sailed on a tall ship, all in the name of research, of course. Learn more about her at her website at www.regina scott.com.